The green eyes stared into his for another moment, and then the image faded. Lian was shivering, chilled hands gripping each other. His future had been rescaled. He had not merely to leave a message in the Archives, he had, tomorrow, to board the ship for Burdania. He had focused on one so as not to think of the other. Sixty-six years and five generations ago, the Explorers had activated an untried stardrive too close to their homeworld. Their descendants would only now learn the consequences. *He* would learn the consequences.

Alison Sinclair has spent much of her life living alternately in Scotland and Canada. She entered university at sixteen, gained a B.Sc in Chemistry and Physics, and then a Ph.D in Biochemistry. Structural Molecular Biology subsequently became her discipline, with a side interest in neuroscience, and today she is a research fellow at the University of Leeds. Her interests are legion: she has fenced competitively and won a number of writing competitions, practises Aikido and archery when she has time, sings with the Leeds Philharmonic Chorus – and she 'reads anything that holds still, oh, and the advertisements on the sides of buses which don't'. Alison Sinclair has been writing since she was a teenager and is currently working on her second novel.

LEGACIES

ALISON
SINCLAIR

To Rebecca,

With best wishes.
(May yours make the
bestseller list.)

Alison Sinclair
Calgary, August 9
1996

MILLENNIUM

First published in Great Britain in 1995 by
Millennium
The Orion Publishing Group
5 Upper St Martin's Lane
London WC2H 9EA

ISBN: 1 85798 401 3

Typeset by Deltatype Ltd, Ellesmere Port, Wirral
Printed and bound in Great Britain by
Clays Ltd, St Ives plc.

Thanks to:

Lynda Jane Williams, without whom the Burdanians might never have made it through UVic.

Deborah Beale and Charon Wood, for glimpsing a story in the undergrowth and instructions on the use of the (editorial) machete; and Caroline Oakley, for guiding the manuscript (and the writer) through the brave new world of copy editing, typesetting, and beyond.

Daniel and Isabel Sinclair, my parents: this is what comes of all those readings of *The Little Red Engine*.

Kathryn, my sister and fellow traveller on many early imaginative voyages.

PROLOGUE

TARIDWYN

During his last night on his birthworld, Lian D'Halldt went to leave a message for the future, and, instead, received a plea from the past.

The message he was to leave was one tradition demanded of departing spacefarers, formerly on their homeworld of Burdania, and now on this colony of exiles. His image would join those of the many dead, and the eight living, his fellow travellers, in the Explorers' shrine. Lian would have avoided the obligation if he could. He did not want to become one of the colony's ghosts. There were already too many.

But if he avoided it, he would upset the other eight, who knew he would not resist tradition lightly, who would imagine reasons unintended. It was kinder to all to yield than to explain.

Nevertheless, he went by night, wanting no witnesses. Above the colony buildings, the dim planetary sun stood near its zenith, but for the five generations since its founding, the colony had held fast to the climate, seasons and cycles of the homeworld, Burdania. Within its windowless rooms and above the miniature seas, steppes and mountains of the habitats, it was night. Wakefulness was a small treason to Burdania; Lian expected, and hoped, to meet no one.

That was, in part, because he was wearing the stone-coloured robes and caul of the *kinder'el'ein*, the ancient race native to this world. The choice was deliberate, something else he would not wish to explain. He knew, even if Burdanians would not acknowledge it, what they owed the *kinder'el'ein*. If he were not to return, if nothing were to change, he wanted his

1

robe-clad image to show new generations an alternative, and to make them ask *why*.

He slipped a finger beneath the caul, touching a fine scar on the back of his head, and hoped they would ask more cautiously than he had. His childish inquisitiveness had earned him a lifetime's rebuke, one reissued with every halting word he spoke.

By habit he went from his room to the first exit, choosing the outside route over the corridors. The noonday air was heavy and humid, the sun a dull orange the size of his fist. He could have obscured Burdania's fierce blue-white sun with a finger-tip. Beyond the boundary wall, sun-fed jungle towered, bolstered by undergrowth and cabled with vines. It dwarfed the colony's tallest structure, the golden dome of the debating hall and Archives. Lian let his eyes travel up the curve. He remembered warm light welling between his spread fingers as he knelt on golden translucency, peering down at the speakers below. He was deemed too young to enter the chamber while his elders debated return to Burdania. He entered nonetheless, catastrophically. Half a lifetime later he still dreamed of an endless plunge into brightness.

Which was his final, maybe strongest, impetus for going by night. He wanted privacy to create the message as he wanted it. Let records elsewhere show the legacy of his fall, his enduring struggle with words. This one would not.

Beside the debating hall were the Archives, repository of all the knowledge they had brought from Burdania and everything they had learned since. The system sensed his entry and brought up the lights. Interaction booths lined both walls, interspersed with curved cylindrical microhabitats. Within one of those Lian glimpsed the dusty flurry of some small, panicked creature. He said quickly, 'Lights – dim.' They did. 'I – am Lian D'Halldt. I – leave for Burdania – tomorrow. I – must leave – a message. For the – shrine.'

Silence answered him. He touched open the door of the nearest booth. As the door slid open, the light within came on, showing a booth with chair, screen, touch plate. A silver web shimmered on the touch plate. He went closer, curious, and recognized the web as the Archival information structure. He

2

drew breath, to ask for a simplified version, such as children used, and held the breath. The display was active, a spark flickering along strands, marking locations as the Archives searched. It fixed, steadied; the web swelled off the edges of the plate as the program converged on its target. And from behind Lian, a voice spoke,

'You are going back.'

Lian stiffened, suddenly chilled. He knew that voice. He had never expected to hear it uninvited. He whispered, 'I did – not ask.' But no one answered; there was no one to answer.

He could have left. The computer would have sensed his absence and snuffed the image. But his message would go unrecorded. Bracing himself, he turned, slowly, to confront the image forming in the centre of the booth.

He had been young when he first appeared to Lian. Now he was old, seated. His hair, once brilliant titian, had faded to dull gold. His face seemed little changed, but his eyes, once vividly haunted, were merely tired and bleak. Lian eased out of their line of sight, but the image turned as he moved, and when it spoke, it was directly to him:

'I am Islain Nors, last surviving commander of the three ships which left Burdania. I record this last message for whomever of my direct descendants is first to return to Burdania. Forgive me this intrusion. I do not know whether you would hear me willingly. I do not know who you are, or how much time has passed. I will not insert templates into this message to give the illusion I do. You may have seen my confession—' A quirk of expression, which may have been humour. 'I was much younger then. Confessions are for the young, who still believe in some exonerating power. I am old. I know there is no exoneration; an eternity of oblivion will finally be welcome.'

He leaned forward slightly, thin hands gripping the arms of his chair. 'I know you have courage. I hope you have compassion, and can forgive us both what we may have done, and what we could not do. I hope, for your sake, and for ours, that what you find is less terrible than what we have imagined. We did not intend what we did, but intentions never last as deeds do. Our leaving may have destroyed our homeworld. We

3

can cry to eternity that it was never meant, that it was a great carelessness, but it happened. We can only beg of the future, of our descendants, of you, to do what you can to set right our wrong.'

The green eyes stared into his for another moment, and then the image faded. Lian was shivering, chilled hands gripping each other. His future had been rescaled. He had not merely to leave a message in the Archives, he had, tomorrow, to board the ship for Burdania. He had focused on one so as not to think of the other. Sixty-six years and five generations ago, the Explorers had activated an untried stardrive too close to their homeworld. Their descendants would only now learn the consequences. *He* would learn the consequences.

Lian walked forward to where the image had been and said, huskily, 'Record – me.'

Around him, sources and detectors kindled. Blue light sparkled briefly on his hands. Blue lines flickered across his clothing, sampling contour and spectrum. Lian drew a shuddering breath and composed his hands by his sides. 'I am Lian D'Halldt. I am the – last member of the mission from – this colony to Burdania.' Blue light brushed his eye. He discarded all the other sentences he had so painstakingly assembled. He said only, with all the authority he could summon, 'I go in – hope.'

ONE

BURDANIA

Sixty-six years (Burdanian)
after departure from Burdania

The sun was a blue-white point in blackness. The planet an arc of softer white. Both were illusionary, a recasting of data from the ship's skin to suit the Burdanian eye. This illusion, Lian did not mind. Here was an illusion to banish a horror.

The colony's record of Burdania ended with the last incoherent scans through distorted space. No planet, no *thing* had ever been caught in a drive interaction. The scan results, like the physics, had to be recast into metaphor. For sixty-six years the colonists' image of Burdania had been of a sphere drawn long, and blazing. No more.

Burdania had survived, with integrity. Its gross measurements tallied with record; its axial cant was no more, no less than before. Its atmosphere remained unchanged, implying a biosphere. The reflectances were those of cloud, land, ocean; the temperatures much as those in the corridors and habitats of the colony.

Whatever else they found, they need never again accept the apocalyptic scenarios of their simulations. They need never peer through blue and yellow fire to catch their last glimpse of their homeworld.

But the rest was silence. After sustained discussion they sent messages before them, which went unanswered. They intercepted no transmissions, scattered or directed. No communications with satellites or addresses to the stars. They detected no magnetic or electric fluxes other than those natural to the planet's core. No illumination from the nightside.

Thovalt's right hand danced on the arm of the pilot's chair.

The hand was all Lian could see, the hand and a crescent of charcoal-grey sleeve. Thovalt's fingers were long and un-commonly supple, nearly grotesque. Isolated, under the harsh light of the forecabin, the hand brought to mind something from the jungles of his birthworld: an insect, sprayed with a predator's venom, dancing to death. Lian owned to himself, if to no one else, that he was a little frightened to have Thovalt at the helm. He had earned his place there, brilliantly, but his moods were an unstable chiaroscuro, and he enacted his impulses.

The forecabin was compact, accommodating six people. The ship's present complement was five, the others remaining aboard the parentship. The ship was tripartite: the stardrive and its controllers were left at system's edge; the intrasystem drive would be left in orbit; a small shuttle, of which this forecabin was part, would make landfall. The pilot's station was fore and below, in the snubbed snout of the craft, sunk by half a bodyheight. The front screen swept back and up above the pilot's head; sitting at the station, one seemed to be sitting in space. Lian, who was prone to vertigo, found it profoundly disorientating. The interface between pilot and craft was through the helmet and gloves mounted on his chair, which were just now in inactive mode, clinging like relict exoskeletons to the side. Two auxiliary stations flanked the pilot's, recessed beneath the main deck, one ancillary to pilot and navigation, the other for medical monitoring. All members of the mission had a reporting implant. On the deck above and behind the pilot's station was the main scan station and computer interface, and to the rear of that, the two chairs which accommodated additional personnel, Lian being one, and the mission's medic, Lors, the other.

Thovalt's hand suddenly clenched on the arm. He pulled himself forward against the inertia harness, to peer past the mounted glove. 'Get me an enhancement!' he flung at Alystra, who was monitoring the scans. It was more than an order; it was an ultimatum.

Alystra turned her head barely enough to see him out of the corner of one eye. Before the long confinement of the voyage they had merely been markedly unlike. Now each worked to be the antithesis of the other. Their single common trait was that they were aware of their audience. Otherwise they were opposites. Where Thovalt was volatile and sometimes disordered in thought, Alystra was fastidious, emotionally and mentally. Where Thovalt was flamboyant, Alystra was mannered, precise.

'Andra,' Thovalt said. 'Do it.'

Alystra's hands went still, poised clear of the touch-sensitive counter. Beyond the metallic tendons of the glove, Thovalt's visible eye glittered dangerously. There was a silence. From below the deck, at the auxiliary station, Andra D'Lynnan's voice said, 'I'll take it, Alys. We're past Balath's orbit, and there is something I have been wanting to try.' As a senior Archivist, accustomed to reviewing vast quantities of material, she was the best suited to monitor the complex parameters of insystem flight. She was also Thovalt's birthmother, as long-boned, long-handed, and bright-eyed as he. She had long denied any understanding of him.

Alystra said, dispassionately, 'Exchanging inputs, now.' As one, her banked screens flickered and changed, exchanging the long planetary view for the short view. Alystra studied them for a moment, and then immobilized the display on three of the twelve screens, scaling down her task. She was not an Archivist; she was the colony observer and recordkeeper. Thovalt said, teasingly, 'Look sharp, now.'

Lors, irked beyond wisdom said, 'Just fly, Thovalt.'

Thovalt drew breath to answer, but neither Lors nor Alystra was looking at him. The screen had changed.

'Oh, sweet reason,' Lors breathed.

Andra said from below, 'If I do a differential overlay of current with historic records, I can resolve three regions of gross anomaly— Taking albedo without cloud cover—' Mid latitude they saw a bruised area like a thumbprint on a fruit. The image flickered, turning through half a day. Now there were two bruises, a large and a small. 'Ignore the arcs at high latitude; they indicate movements of the icecap. If one examines ground contour—' The planet enlarged, became multicoloured. 'Over sixty-six years there will have been some natural shifts due to geological activity – there are several new

7

islands in the southern ocean. But if I set the filters high enough—' The planet greyed. Except in those three areas, which were still stippled and ribboned with green and yellows. 'If the reflectance is analysed—' White poles, pale seas, yellow-white steppes, blue forests, and three areas – one outlined with a peninsula, one on the mainland, one on a large island continent – of grey black.

'You know where these are,' Alystra said. She slid fingers over the touch controls, and a silver net dropped from space to enwrap the planet. Lines and lettering shimmered against the grey black. 'This,' Alystra said, 'indicates settlement. The changes coincide with the most densely settled areas. Lltharran plain; the Sor plain; D'Alna island – a minor subcontinent in itself.'

Lors stared at the overlaid map as though at a diagnostic chart. In those bruised areas he diagnosed grave affliction.

'Also,' Andra said from below, 'the three main nexi for the planetary archives—'

'That's – not it,' Lors said. Only Lian heard him.

Thovalt said, 'What's happened there?'

'Considerable environmental alteration; at a guess, denudation, perhaps desertification—'

'The drives,' Lors said, finding his voice. 'Those three areas. The ships were built there. They orbited – above there. The drives were fired—'

Thovalt's hand came up, caught the glove, jerked it down into engaged position. The poisoned insect scrambled into shelter. Alystra's screens lit up with input from the symbiotic navigational interface. An alert chimed from the vacant medic's station. Alys said, 'Thovalt, what are you doing?' The ship answered her; they felt the acceleration as it responded to the movement of Thovalt's fingers. Before Alystra's face, space fanned in coloured slices, displaying past, present, possible trajectories. 'Transferring input to auxiliary station,' said Andra from below, and on Alystra's screens Burdania reappeared. Andra said, 'Thovalt, put us back on course, *now.*'

'But it is already too late,' Lors said, half to himself. 'He knows that better than I.' To Lian he said, 'At this velocity we cannot possibly alter trajectory enough to avoid—' He stopped.

Thovalt withdrew his hand from the glove. Pushed up the helmet.

The screen flickered slightly and refreshed itself. Blue-white star. Planet like a broken shell, worn translucent by the sea. Neither had shifted. Neither would. Thovalt's protest spent itself in silence. The computer righted their course; they continued their descent.

White sunlight woke Lian. A ribbon of light straggled from the part-open door to the forecabin. Lian heard movement and rolled slightly to see a smudge of white hair in the shadows beside the storage lockers.

'Ach.' The whisper, like the white hair, was Lors'. He was on daytime scanwatch. 'I was looking for— Never mind.' He scuttled back to squat beside Lian's bunk. 'Go back to sleep. Sun's not set.'

'Setting,' Lian whispered. He listened a moment, heard no stirring from any of the three other bunks. He made a decision. 'I'll – join you.'

He slipped into the forecabin, braking the door with a hand as it closed to mute the sound. He stopped, amazed. The ship's plating had been opened, the projection screens retracted, leaving only a simple window. But that was not what surprised him. Even, to his dismay, shocked him a little. 'You've – no camouflage.'

Lors glanced up from the scanners. 'Have to conserve power,' he said.

Lian climbed down into the pilot's bubble and looked up. He was still astonished by the hue of Burdania's sky. No habitat, no holoillusion, had that depth of violet.

'Watch your eyes,' Lors said. 'I've no filters on.' He said, rather wryly, 'I've been trying to adapt.'

The voyage had alternated hope and despair. First the pure joy of the sight of Burdania's blue sun, and the small, white planet. Then growing despair, as they travelled inward through silence. Hope again at the suggestion of a healthy biosphere. Followed by the discovery of the planet's scars. That had been the worst time. When their shuttle had undocked from the driveship outside Burdania's system they had abandoned any

9

swift escape. They passed beyond the point of no return, committed to confirm the life or death of their people. For the three last days of inward flight Thovalt and Alystra had remained at their stations, unsleeping; Andra had simply slept until shaken awake for course alterations; Lian and Lors preserved rituals of normality, eating, sleeping, making leaden conversation. Under computer guidance, oblivious to its passengers' misery, the ship slid into high orbit. From that orbit they at last detected tiny settlements, flecks of cultivated land, signs of life.

And little else. In the days since they made first landfall, they had heard no murmur of telecommunication, nor detected a single electrical impulse. With one exception, which had brought them here, where they would not, otherwise, willingly have come. This had been Lltharran, a centre of knowledge, culture and government. Built on the tamed meanders of a dotard river, it was an old, refined city, renowned for its white buildings and for its gardens. It had also been home to an enclave of Explorers. Within that enclave they had built one of the three prototype stardrives for installation in one of their returned ships. Though they did it in secret, with hoarded wealth, they intended no evil. Nor did their opponents in the debating chambers which governed Burdania. Both wished the best for their people. So the Explorers built their drives in secret, and their opponents, learning of this, tried to impound them . . . and the ships took premature flight.

Theoretical physics was beyond Lian, intellectually. Chaos physics was alien to him, philosophically. He was, at essence, a naturalist, a believer in life. Which, he thought, was why he had never believed what the drives might have done until he looked out at Lltharran plain. The river remained, a tangled wire between the yellow foothills and violet sea. The land remained, just emerging from the long winter. Great stretches were patched and banded with black, grey and brown. In places the topsoil had fused to a black slate. In others the soil had been left impregnated with heavy metals. A few regions were dangerously radioactive. In between were stretches and islands of fertility, where fragments of normal vegetation survived: hardy grasses, durable shrubs, the occasional copse or even small

10

forest. To Lian's naturalist's eye, the ecosystem was pathetic-ally diminished. The old city was not at the centre of the devastation – which was further south – but the fair white city lay in ruin, its foundations reduced to a half-buried latticework along both sides of the river.

There was life in it still. Half a mile downstream the river kinked around a knoll, and below the knoll, on both sides of the river, rough grey and white buildings had been raised upon the white foundations. By their best accounting, well over a thousand people lived here. That in itself would not have brought them here, but on the knoll was a building, and that building was warm to their scans. It had been a space science centre, built with the technology which had constructed starships. The solar panels on roof and upper walls remained functional, and functioning; electrical fluxes moved within its walls and artificial lights shone from its windows. After wasteland and ruin it seemed a miracle, but . . . *Why it alone?*

Lian realized he was letting pass the chance of speaking to Lors uninterrupted. He climbed out of the bubble and settled on his heels beside Lors' chair. Only four of the screens were alight. One, Lian recognized as medical data, the traces of the sleepers as they slept, and of himself and Lors.

Lors sighed, and leaned back. 'We will have to move on. Even if we could support continuous holo and scan, there is the river. It's going to flood. You've seen the scans of the upper floodplain. We're too low here.'

They had landed the shuttle, by night, five days ago, on the edge of the ruins, hidden from the new settlement by a long ridge. The shuttle was small enough, and Thovalt skilled enough, to fit it inside one of the largest basements. By day they kept it under a holographic camouflage, in case anyone from the settlement downriver should happen by. In their nocturnal explorations, they had found excavation sites, ruins opened, pegged and covered with boards or canvas. But nobody had come; they were occupied by preparations against the river. From behind Lors' station, Lian could see over the ruined walls to the river itself. The water was brown and ropy, thrusting at its banks. Outside their windows, the walls were striped with floodmarks.

11

Two days ago they had mounted cameras on the ridge, overlooking the dykes around the settlement. Small, drably clad figures laboured over them, building them up stone by stone, from dawn to dusk, and for the last two nights, by firelight. They had carts to drag the stones from ruin to dyke, but only their muscles, and primitive pulleys, to lift them.

'What about – the people?'

Lors said, 'They have managed for sixty-six years without us.'

'How long – will we hide?'

Lors did not answer.

Lian ran a hand through his hair, shaking a few black strands free. He said, 'I thought – my hair – would get thicker.'

'That will take a while yet.'

'My skin – is brighter.' He held out a narrow hand, showing off its lustre, waxy secretions evolved as protection against the intense Burdanian sunlight. 'Though I – haven't been out – much in – daytime.'

'You have something on your mind,' Lors said, to the screens.

Lian said, 'I am afraid for them. The people – in the settlement. We saw the flood upstream. There is nothing to – stop it coming. The people have no machinery. Mud and – gravel to stop the dykes. And afterwards— Bad-flooding could reach those – badlands. Wash poisons. Radiation. They drink from it. They water their plantings. They may not be able – to tell.'

'We do not know that, Li. That building on the knoll – it was a science centre, once. There is a great deal of knowledge, analytical and computing power, stored up there, if they can use it.'

'We came – to *help* them. But we – hide from them. Land by night. Stay-away from them. Watch. Behind screens. This is *wrong.*'

'I agree with you, yes, but I also agree with the others.' Lian lifted his head, and blinked as sunlight spat into the corner of his eye. Catching that, Lors said, 'You want me to talk for you, again, don't you?'

Caught, Lian said nothing.

12

'You are quite capable of putting your own viewpoint—'

'Don't – lecture me, Lors.'

'Then do not try and manipulate me into speaking for you.'

Rebuked, frustrated, Lian said nothing. Lors leaned back in his chair, watching the patterns on the screens. The shadow of the windowsill was moving slowly up his shoulder; only his face and head were illuminated, and Lian's were in cool darkness.

Lian thought of individual faces Andra had isolated from the images. Young faces, in the main, exhausted, unwashed, grim. Some of them were nearly familiar: a dark, austere man who reminded him of his father. A small woman, shoulder-high to most of her fellows, with an imposing manner and eyes the colour of a late afternoon sky; she seemed to be responsible for much of the organization and coordination. A woman and a young girl with the same bright orange hair. The woman seemed to be a medic or first-aider: Lors had blanched, watching her splint a man's wrist.

Lian summoned his resolve. 'I – know there may be – more ruins than there should be. All the buildings broken, but one. But when the ships launched – the Archives would have been – changed. Knowledge lost. There is nothing – sinister in ignorance. We – cannot know how it was for them. To be patient is one – thing. To fear and – disdain, another.'

'You mustn't think—' Lors started, and then he took in what Lian had been saying and turned to stare at him. For a moment Lian thought he had gone too far. Lors released a slow breath. 'Sweet reason, Lian. "Fear and disdain"— Why?'

For the same reason, Lian thought, as you recognized it when I said it. He refused to believe that his intuition was as uncanny as some claimed. He was the better observer, that was all.

'Fear and disdain,' Lors muttered, eyeing the scans with unusual moodiness. 'Who?' Looked round at Lian with a defensive flash of eyes yellow in the light. 'Me?'

Lying would be pointless. 'A little.'

'But not you?' There was a sting to Lors' voice.

Lian said quietly, specifying his own emotion without stating its object: 'I *am* worried.'

'You should be. Five generations ago this world was

13

launching starships.' There was a brief silence, then Lors abruptly conceded. 'Very well, I admit to part of your charge. Fear, yes. These people are not as I hoped to find them. I do not know what has happened to them. They seem to have gone very far down: lost technology, electricity, machinery. That seems – impossible to me. And if it is because of the driveshock, as it may well be, I do not know how they will react to us. Remember, Lian, I am medically responsible for all of you. I have only the supplies, skills and resources I brought with me. I am not going to advocate any action that will put you at risk. But disdain, no, that I do deny. They are still alive, even under these terrible conditions. They live in community, seem cooperative. Does that sound condescending?' But whether his challenging tone was an anticipation of Lian's reaction, or in response to his own doubts, Lian could not tell. 'I do not disdain that,' Lors finished strongly.

There was a silence.

'I – cannot say there is nothing – *to* fear. But we – cannot know them this way. Observing. From a distance.'

'You don't think I haven't realized that our robotics could build and seal a better dyke than any they have. Never mind those shacks they live in. Never mind the state they will be in medically – though the ones I've seen look strong enough.' Lors winced, remembering that broken wrist. 'I do not need to be reminded. *Most* of these ruins date from the time of leaving, sixty-six years ago,' he said. 'Most of them have the scan signature from the driveshock – but some, Lian, do not. Some of them should have survived – the one we are in, for instance. This area survived the driveshock. It was destroyed *afterwards*.'

'But – years ago,' Lian said.

Lors suddenly leaned forward, resting his head on his hands. 'If I keep talking to you, I will talk myself right around to your position, if I am not there already. I agree with everything you have said and tried to get me to say. In principle. But in practice—' He lifted his head, and gave Lian a weary, squinting look. 'In practice we must be cautious.'

'What – would you want – to know about them? Before you would go to them?'

14

'Lian, Lian.' He sighed, said reluctantly, 'That they will do us no harm. That we will do them no . . . further harm.'

'How – will you know that?'

When Lors did not answer, Lian quietly excused himself, and went outside. He felt he had accomplished something; to have demanded more would have been cruel. And sunset fascinated him. On the planet of his birth he knew sunset as a red veil over all but the bare sun itself. Burdanian eyes were blue-acute, red-blind, evolved for *this* blue-white sun. This light offered him all the changing hues of light and landscape.

He climbed carefully on to the rubble beneath the southern wall, and looked out at the gilded, devastated land. The ruins before him sloped down towards the river, their walls a shining maze in the last of the sunlight. The spaces between them were dense with grass and shadow. The river roiled past, heavy with flood. Ripples and eddies flexed like muscles beneath a brown skin. He could see in the distance its downstream course, as, having looped the settlement, it meandered southwards into an indigo haze. On the plain, mauve gloom welled up from the dips and the valleys. In the sky, the first brilliant stars were already kindling.

To the right was the ridge which shielded them from the settlement. The rebuilding had taken in a crescent of three low hills on this northerly bank, and the knoll and rise within the river loop. The knoll and the three low hills might be secure against the river, but the rise was very slight; the dykebuilding was concentrated around it. This settlement was one of the largest they had scanned, and the only one to lie within a major area of devastation. It was an anomaly. It could not support itself. The weather was harsh, the river a menace. Yet here they stayed and prepared their defence.

Lian rested his chin into his folded hands. There was another high, well-preserved wall to his right. There was a mural on it, still recognizable as an undersea scene, now much cracked, faded and stained. He carried in his pocket a smooth stone with painted orange scales. He could not tell where it had come from. No orange remained on the standing mural.

15

The wind shifted, swirling amongst the ruins, and brought with it voices. Lian lifted his head, alert. An instant later an eddy sucked them back.

Lian thought: Lors would surely warn me if . . .

The wind died. In the stillness he heard the voices again, disembodied and unfamiliar. Something had changed beyond the wall. Dark bands rippled along the ridges, and for an instant he stared in horror until perspective reasserted itself, and he perceived shadows, cast by someone moving behind the wall.

Within his pocket his transceiver said, 'Lian!' He swung round so swiftly that vertigo turned the incomplete holoillusion into hallucination.

'What was that?'

He had started down from the heap of rubble; at the strange voice he wrenched himself back, fingers digging into crumbling stone. The long bands of black behind the wall were still. He felt them listening.

The shuttle's grey panels crumpled, its straight lines wavered into rubble, mulch and mud. He thought: *I had no idea the power was so low.*

'I don't know.' He heard stones crunch on the other side of the relict mural. They would surely hear him as he dashed for the shuttle door. They might see the shuttle itself if the illusion did not settle in time.

But he understood their words, their speech. He understood what they were saying.

Lian wedged a booted toe into a cleft and boosted himself up, hooking the other heel behind a jutting stone and folding himself over the wall gracelessly.

His transceiver squawked again. He hissed, 'Hush!'

There was a wind-filled, pulse-metered interval. The last rays of sunshine lifted off the earth. He stood up, exposed in a clear, cold afterlight.

A figure appeared through the doorway at the far end of the wall. Then a second. They came forward slowly, but with the bleached sky behind their heads he could not see their faces. He was breathing hard; the frigid air petrified his throat. He crossed to the mural and put a bracing hand on a web of painted seaweed. His transceiver had not made so much as a crackle; perhaps now the others understood what he had done. Perhaps they thought he had simply gone mad.

The strangers stopped before him, the woman standing squarely in his path, feet set very wide apart and turned outwards, the man half a step behind and at her shoulder, though he could have looked directly over her head with ease.

Both were younger than himself. The woman's green-flecked eyes flicked up and down, assessing him with the swiftness of the capable young. Her face was sharp-featured and alert beneath a cropped cap of hair. The man reminded him at once of Thovalt, in a way that he could not define, because in every particular they differed: his colouring was softer, dun and grey to Thovalt's black and hazel; he stood as tall, but broader; his eyes were gentler, steadier.

His next impression was of colour. From a distance, the natives had seemed a drab people. He saw now the high colour and lustre of their hands and faces, the two-tone streaking in the woman's hair, the shading of the thread of their heavy, coarse-woven outer garments, half jacket, half cloak. The woman's was mossy green, the man's dark grey with a purple tint. She was bareheaded, while he had adapted a length of the fabric as a hood. They were shod, but in what Lian could not tell, for their lower legs were wrapped in muddy rags, lashed on with cords, and sagging over the boots.

The woman said: 'Lara D'Alna.'

The man: 'Rathla Zharlinn.'

Names, Lian thought, with a joyous shock. They were giving him their names.

'Lian,' Lian said. 'Lian D'Halldt.'

'Islander!' the woman said. From her inflection the word could have been 'Brother!' She nudged the man, Rathla Zharlinn, jarringly. 'That's an Islander name.' She swung back to Lian, bright-faced. 'Where from? What ship? Have you just arrived? You must have barely made it, you realize? I haven't seen you in Lltharran. Did you come with—'

17

Rathla Zharlinn interrupted. 'Are you wanting answers, or not?'

She opened her mouth to resort, closed it. 'Where are you from?' she said, primly.

Had either of them shown him the least distrust he would not have dared do as he did. Her tone was commonplace; she asked a simple question of a stranger. Neither had reacted to his accent, his pallor, his clothing, or to any of the other marks of his otherworldly origin. He was not dressed as they were, but his jacket and trousers were heavy, dark and plain for warmth and night-work, and his boots, perhaps more revealing, were scraped and clarted with mud. Could they truly mistake him for one of themselves?

Lara said, 'You are Islander, aren't you?' Even then there was nothing in her manner but her youthful impatience.

He said, 'I am from—' He committed himself, using the Archival name for the most remote of the southern islands, 'the C'Rynn reach.'

'You don't sound very convinced,' she said. For an instant he thought he heard 'convincing' and his breath froze in his throat. Then his wits caught up with him, and he said shakily, 'Home seems – far away. Do you – live here?'

'At present. I'm from the Sor and Lara's from Lesser D'Alna. We're Restorers' Guild.' He paused, anticipating a reaction. Lian had none to offer. Lara said, 'You've never heard of us.'

Zharlinn panned with a hand, giving Lian the chance to glance over his shoulder and assure himself that the shuttle's camouflage had coalesced. 'We're trying to restore the old technology. We dig bits and pieces out of these ruins, and people bring us relics from other parts of Burdania. We try to get them working again.'

'What – kind of bits and – pieces?'

'Anything we find. Lamps. Voice-projection apparatus, allows us to speak over long distances. Record-keepers which preserve voices and pictures, without handwriting.' His tone was tight, a little defensive.

'They used these things,' Lara said, more easily. 'Seventy, eighty years ago. The ruins are full of them. If we can get them

18

working, understand how they work, we can learn how to make our own.'

'Get them accepted,' Rathla Zharlinn said.

'Are they – unacceptable?' Lian said.

'We have the *isk'dar*'s support.'

Lian did not understand how that answered his question. 'The *isk'dar*?'

Zharlinn looked at him oddly. Lara laughed. 'Aye, things have changed around Lltharran. She's no Linn Travassa, I assure you.'

Lian drew a breath. His ribs twinged with tension. 'I am – beginning to realise – how isolated we – have been,' he said, truthfully. 'I know – nothing of the *isk'dar*.'

'She'll be wanting to meet you. We thought your name had died out. She'll be pleased it has not.'

'Why – should she want – to meet me?'

Lara glanced at Zharlinn. Zharlinn at Lara. 'We should let her explain,' Lara said.

Zharlinn said, 'Have you a place for the night, or will you come with us?'

Lian's mind blanked. Zharlinn continued, marvellously oblivious: 'We're a small household. We're always glad to have passers through, and hear the news. And since the light's going, we should do likewise. These ruins can be dangerous in the dark. Unless you do have elsewhere to stay.'

'No,—' Lian collected himself. 'No, I accept. I do – accept.'

'Then bring your pack and—'

Pack! To have travelled any distance he would have needed supplies. 'I – I left – my pack—' he said, in blind excuse. Then, hearing himself, inspiration came. He waved a hand vaguely westwards. 'I wanted to – explore. I – was not paying attention to time. If I might— If I might borrow what I need, I will – return for it – later.'

'You'll not be the first to come empty-handed,' Lara said, with a sideways glance at Zharlinn.

Lian said, carefully, thinking of the shuttle, 'I – had not seen anyone here – before. Why – are you here if the ruins – are dangerous?'

19

'Checking our diggings,' Zharlinn said. 'The river's about to break its banks. We had to seal those we could.'

'But – the floods—'

Lara D'Alna laughed. 'So nobody told you what Lltharran was like in the spring.'

TWO

TARIDWYN

Fifty-nine years (Burdanian) after departure from Burdania

Thovalt Aslinn arrived unannounced at the *kinder'vos* on the seventh day before *en'vos'neen'el*.

Lian was kneeling in a vegetable patch picking out dead leaves and ungerminated seeds. When he raised his eyes he looked directly at a sunken wall, moss-upholstered, corded with marbled vines and acreep with insects. When he raised his head he could see the ragged rising edge of the jungle. The garden was littered with its burgeoning. He had to look straight up to see the green evening sky. At his back, the huge red sun slid towards the sea-horizon. His shadow was already diffuse at the edges. Real hand and shadow hand clasped over a spiked seed.

Further along, his parents, Sara and Thaorinn, and Jahde, in all respects that mattered Lian's fifth grandparent, were rebuilding part of the wall. The *kinder'vos* was built of stone, stone cells along stone paths, stone walls against the jungle's perpetual encroachment. Its origin had passed beyond living memory; they might be rebuilding the wall for the thousandth or ten thousandth time. Cradling the seed on his lap, he turned to watch them. Sara was resting on a mound of stones, emerald-green robes spread around her. Thaorinn matched pace and motion with Jahde, to the smallest detail he could master. Jahde towered over him – Thaorinn's ear would have just come above the jutting crest of Jahde's ribs – a ponderous, slow-moving pillar of stone-coloured cloth and caul. Jahde was *kinder'el'ein*, native to this planet and very old: as the *kinder'el'ein* measured years, almost one hundred and eighty:

21

as the Burdanians reckoned, sixty-five. Old enough to have seen the Burdanian ships make landfall, five generations ago.

Jahde suddenly met his eyes with *kin* great, whiteless ones. He flushed, wondering what *kin* might have sensed in him. He turned quickly back to his task, one which was essential, and, for him, an honour. The *kinder'el'ein* disliked the way Burdanians handled living things. Lian had expected to be relegated to building the wall alongside Sara and Thaorinn.

It would not have occurred to the *kinder'el'ein* to reject the Burdanian presence in their world. They were an ancient, gracious, peaceable people. If they were past their early curiosity about other species, they understood it in the Burdanians. But the Burdanians were not easy guests. All *kinder'el'ein* shared *vos'neen*, the commonality of living things. Strong feeling dispersed like ripples in an ocean. Burdanians did not share *vos'neen*; they were volatile, intense individuals, shocking to sense. When they cleared living jungle to build their own colony, it had been an outrage to *vos'neen*. Most *kinder'el'ein* had forgiven them their insensitivity; some had not. The colony, with its metals and its electrical fields, was an enduring irritant to the awareness of sensitive *kinder'el'ein*. The two peoples seldom mingled. Burdanians found the environment too warm, too humid, the sun too dim, the air heavy with greenhouse gases. They withdrew behind their colony walls, into their cool, brightly lit corridors and artificial habitats, microcosms of the Burdania they had left. Thaorinn D'Halldt was an exception: he had lived in the open jungle and in *kinder'el'ein* settlements for four years before coming to rest here, in this *kinder'vos*, long before Lian's birth.

A *kinder'vos* was an unusual place for a Burdanian. It was a retreat for the elders of the *kinder'el'ein* third sex, the *kindereen*. In addition to *vos'neen*, the *kindereen* had the most powerful sense of *en'neen*, the commonality of the dead. They were also the longest lived. After their mates were dead and their children well mated, *kindereen* withdrew to nurture and commune with *en'neen*. In the great ceremony of *en'vos'neen'el*, which was impending, the *kindereen* united to draw together the living and the dead.

Thaorinn had rejected, utterly, his heritage, and dedicated

himself to understanding the *kinder'el'ein*, to *becoming kinder'el'ein*, with an intensity which was purely Burdanian. He refused still to acknowledge the limits of his Burdanian constitution, and the long years in the jungle had undermined his health. He was a plain, sallow, silent man, who would have been gaunt but for his long, flat bones. But to him his body was merely a vessel for his mind.

Sara was as complete a contrast to the father of her son as could be. She knew the jungle as well as he, but judged her own relationship to it more wisely. She was vibrant, and considered lovely, knew that, and had taken care to preserve it. Like the *kinder'el'ein* and Thaorinn, she wore full robes and headdress in the traditional style, but hers were of light, colourful synthetic. She had a heart-shaped face, delicate features, faded grey eyes, one of which was slightly tilted. She glanced over at Lian frequently and with fond curiosity, as although she could not decide what he was, but found him appealing. To her son she had bequeathed only her transparent skin. In Lian, as in Sara, blood and emotion showed in his skin. Otherwise, Lian was his father's child. It was Thaorinn's face that Lian now saw reflected in the stone pools in the heart of the *kinder'vos*, that of a plain and frail-looking youth. A disconcerting sight, for Thaorinn's face had come on him unawares, during the last year. A year which had been largely lost to accident and recovery.

Sara had come to the *kinder'vos* to be with Thaorinn. When Lian was born he was given into the care of Telien, Jahde's *kindereen* child, and *kin* mates. They lived in a jungle settlement adjacent to the Burdanian colony. From birth, Lian had been raised amongst *kinder'el'ein*; it was only in late childhood he had spent any length of time in the colony. Thaorinn was an exception; Lian was quite unique.

He set the spiked seed in a pouch divided for that purpose, and turned his attention to the next. Even this simple task took concentration, for it was an offence to *vos'neen* to move a newly rooted seed. Naturalist's observation had to take the place of *vos'neen*, and he could no longer rely upon his memory. A year ago he had suffered a fall which had left him with a chaotic, incomplete amnesia, and a painful aphasia. Jahde would not

23

mind if he disturbed the occasional nascent root. Thaorinn would, and Sara would, because Thaorinn minded. Lian stroked soil gently away from a flattened mahogany disc, and rested his cheek on the earth, to peer beneath it. As he did, something sparked in his peripheral vision. He sat upright, blinking. High in the green sky above the jungle was a shining mote. The leaves and seeds spilled from his robe as he climbed to his feet.

Sara said, 'What do you see, Lian?' looking at him rather than upwards. But Thaorinn offered him no such indulgences; he looked himself. His sallow profile sharpened, and Lian saw the nictating third membrane flicker white in the inner corner of Jahde's eyes, as the *kindereen* reacted to his emotion. Sara watched Lian with an open, hopeful expression, perfectly sustained. When he did not answer she let it slip from her face as though it had hardly mattered and looked up. The mote was falling fast, gaining shape and definition. It was barbed and elongated, like the seeds which spun over the wall, but it glinted glass and metal.

'Ah,' was all she said.

The *kinder'vos* lay on a folded triangle of headland between river delta and sea. Most *kinder'el'ein* settlements did; water linked them through dense tropical jungle and northern forest. Only Burdanians took to the air. The *kinder'vos* garden sloped seawards, and over the lower boundary walls, Lian could see the hard grassy flats of the delta, created as the river unravelled. The small, spiky craft unfolded thin legs.

'I'll go down and pick up the bits,' Sara said, carelessly.

Thaorinn turned his head towards her, his eyes sombre and judgemental.

Sara laid a hand over his heart, and said, 'Since I do not think as you do, I see no point in indulging you with pretence when my indulgence would be better applied to doing what you would rather not. I shall not be long.' She slid past him, catching up her robes in both hands, and ran towards the listing stone arch out of the *kinder'vos*. The other *kindereen* working in the garden took little seeming notice.

Thaorinn said, not looking at his son, 'Lian, go to your cell.'

Lian did not move. There had been a time when his father

24

would have repeated himself, when he cared where Lian's understanding stood in relation to his own. Not so much that Lian obey, but that Lian understand what was asked of him and be able to explain his mind. Lian had damaged the thing in him which Thaorinn most valued: his ability to communicate. Thaorinn could not blame Lian; nor could he forgive him. Thaorinn spared Lian a bare glance as he passed him and disappeared into the gauzy shadows between the cells.

Together, Lian and Jahde watched the craft fall past the horizon and disappear into a great burst of mist. Its noise trailed after, a growling purr. The grasses thrashed and flattened, and the green rolling waves churned and broke apart in confusion. Then there was silence, but for the jungle.

'I know – it—' Lian said suddenly at Jahde. When *kin* did not respond, he plunged at the admission: 'From the – colony. Why?'

I do not know, Jahde handsigned. *Kindereen* turned mute as they matured; empathy, amplified by handsign, more than substituted for speech. Burdanian medics with a special interest in *kindereen* had devised a restorative operation, and a few *kindereen* with a special interest in Burdanians had undergone it. Jahde was one of those. But Lian had learned handsign before had learned Burdanian. His emotional acuity and deep familiarity with the *kinder'el'ein* compensated for his lack of empathy, and handsign was simple and grammatically forgiving. He lifted his hands gladly. *Can you sense the pilot?*

No, Jahde signed. *There is too much metal.*

I'm sorry, Jahde. I forgot myself.

Jahde inclined *kin* head, undistressed. *Kinder'el'ein* features had been planed almost to extinction by time, except for the wide-set eyes with their fat, vertical pupil. Expressive musculature was almost absent. *Kinder'el'ein* revealed distress or imposition by the closure of the white third eyelid, or the drawing in of the empathic receptors. Lian could see the edge of one of Jahde's receptors beneath the wing of *kin* caul, a puckered pit in the temple, quite relaxed.

So he was not prepared for what Jahde signed next:
Your father did suggest that you go in.

Lian looked away. *I'd rather be bad than damaged*, he signed.

25

Jahde's huge hand suddenly came down over his. 'Foolish,' *kin* said, in a desiccated voice.

Lian freed himself gently after a moment. *I'd rather* choose *what I am.*

Jahde did not respond, but he sensed he was the centre of *kin* attention. The *kinder'el'ein* had a gift for giving attention. Burdanians were too impatient, too often thinking of something else.

He signed: *Suppose one of you was hurt, and lost the empathies – what would you think about that person?*

I would grieve, for en *would die.*

Lian neither wanted nor expected that answer. Jahde, like all *kin* kind, was usually gentle with his sensibilities. A self-protective habit, but real. The mention of death, however, distressed him less than the pronoun used: the neuter-immature, as though the loss of the empathies meant the loss of sex and years.

He almost missed Jahde's next comment. *You will live.*

Lian's hands flashed: *And what* do? *I'm* crippled, he signed, in an outrage of self-pity.

If you wish, Jahde signed, firmly.

Lian looked back at the sea. What he wished and what he was were completely different things. *Kinder'el'ein* expected him to wish, Sara and Thaorinn expected him to learn and neither would acknowledge that neither wish nor learning could influence the imperfections of his brain. He knew his lacks: memory, language, incisiveness of intellect, coordination. He had so little self left that he kept losing it in the sun on the sea or in the movement of leaves.

Sara is bringing him, Jahde sighed.

'What?' Lian said, startled into speech.

A moment later, Sara came through the arch, robes held before her so as not to snag on the tufted grass, wearing a smile hidden from the man behind her. He barely accommodated his longer, free stride to her height and binding robes. Sara led him through the narrow tracks between seedbeds, and stopped before them, the Burdanian looking over her cauled head. 'Jahde, this is Thovalt Aslinn. Thovalt, Jahde *eith* Shereen a'Ylade aur Verren, and, of course, Lian.'

Lian peered around Jahde's robe, and found the Burdanian's eyes on him. Hazel eyes, with a disconcerting amusement in them. For a Burdanian he was tall, and looked faintly disproportioned, with long limbs, very long hands and large feet. His facial bones seemed overlong and over-pronounced, in comparison with the *kinder'el'ein*, and his black hair was bound back so firmly it looked enamelled on to his skull. He wore a shiny suit of leaden hue, slightly short in the cuffs, and a binary star pin beneath his left shoulder. Lian had seen that emblem before.

'You look better than when I last saw you, Lian,' the Burdanian said, startling him.

'I am – better,' Lian managed, knowing that his every effort at their ancestral tongue would reveal that he was not better and likely never would be. Thovalt continued to regard him as though he found him diverting. Lian eased back into the shelter of Jahde's thick body.

'Thaorinn has gone inside,' he heard Sara say.

'Ah,' the Burdanian said. 'Am I expected to follow?'

'You can if you wish. I do not presume to speak for Thaorinn in this.'

'And what would you say, Sara?'

'I?' Then Sara laughed, a blithe sound, one to be distrusted, for Sara cultivated her disrespect for serious things.

The Burdanian looked around with fascination at the black-faced *kindereen* with their heavy robes bending low to the earth. Lian kept a furtive watch on him, trying to become accustomed to the Burdanian face. He had seen this man before. He had seen the emblem.

The *kinder'vos* was laid out like a young fern, with arc upon arc of paved alleys open to the sky and lined with hemispherical stone cells. They had just entered the main vein when Thaorinn stepped out of a side alley. His clasped hands were hidden in their sleeves; his eyes shadowed and intense beneath his caul. Sara laughed. 'I have brought him to you, as he asked, as you did not – forbid,' her tone teased, but Lian had the sense that something grave was occurring, a sense confirmed when Sara said, very softly, 'Talk to him, my heart.'

Thaorinn's hands bunched inside their sleeves. He made a

visible effort to relax them, but this signing was stiff. To Jahde he signed, *Forgive us*. 'I doubt this will take long, Thovalt Aslinn,' he said aloud. Lian ducked back behind Jahde's robes as Thovalt caught his eye. Thovalt said, 'I do not remember so timid a Lian. What have you done to him, Sara?'

Sara's voice was cool. 'Go with Thaorinn.'

Thaorinn leading, Thovalt following, they turned into the alley of long-unoccupied cells. Sara set her shoulder against the wall, and gave Lian a thin smile. 'I expect you think that I am cruel to Thaorinn,' she said. 'All he need to say is "no".' She continued, using the simplest of constructions. 'He has ten years' practice. I doubt Thovalt Aslinn is prepared for that. He seemed eager to match his powers with Thaorinn D'Halldt's. The past never fades in the Archives of Burdania, and people as young as Thovalt do not see—' She said something about time's changes, which Lian did not understand. Sara saw his incomprehension, and his effort to hide it, and lifted her hands with an air of concession. *It's not about you*, she signed. *It is about something in the past. Thaorinn's past.* She pushed herself off the wall, and extended both hands to him, and he gave her hers; their hands were a match in size, and they stood nearly eye to eye. He wished he need not dread her speaking to him, but she always insisted on beginning with Burdanian. She was always nudging him forward, in her playful fashion, which confused him as Thaorinn's grim manner did not. Did it matter or did it not, to Sara? He could not ask, any more than he could have asked her not to speak Burdanian at him.

'The – star,' he said.

There was a silence. Sara said, 'Yes, that is the essence of it. The binary star was the symbol of the Explorers who made landfall here. What it means worn now is—' The grey eyes searched his face, and he perceived she was choosing her words with great care, 'that the wearer advocates return to Burdania.'

'Ships—' His throat closed on his words. His fragmented memories shifted perilously, as though something was trying to break through. Since he had come back to the *kinder'vos* Burdania had gone unmentioned. Sara stroked his face with her cool hand. 'Shh,' she said. 'Shh. We will not talk about that now.'

28

'Three ships,' said Lian. 'Landed.'

'Three ships made landfall, fifty-nine years ago. They founded the colony, west of us. If you want to talk about this, talk to me, not your father. Thaorinn prefers not to remember he is Burdanian. I . . .' she said, with a sweet, wry, smile, 'collude.'

'Thaorinn's – past.'

'Thaorinn's past,' Sara said, with a sigh, 'his shocking past, is that he was the premier orator of his generation. And as such, he once, long ago, addressed the question of whether the colony . . . we exiled Burdanians . . . should go back to Burdania. Thovalt is shortly to do likewise, and he wishes your father's help. A pity that wisdom was not matched by his manner of coming. *Flying* to a *kinder'vos*, indeed. Even I had better sense.'

'The – dome—' Lian whispered. The debates which settled matters of contention within the colony were conducted within the hall beneath the golden dome. He had a visual impression of gold against the jungle so acute as to cause him pain.

'Lian,' said Sara, warningly. Lian had seen Jahde's eyes flash bone white, and thought, as she did, that it was his doing. Then all three heard Thaorinn's shout: 'You need not count on Lian ever being competent to vote in your favour!'

Fury stained Sara's delicate skin. She dropped Lian's hand and stepped deliberately between him and the mouth of the alley as a shadow sprawled across the mossy wall. Thovalt came round the bend with a gliding stride, and an expression on his face which was not quite triumph. He was breathing quickly as he stopped before Sara. Lian was not fast enough to avoid the glance of those glinting hazel eyes.

Sara moved. There was a sound like a hand striking water, and Thovalt's head jerked aside. Then she gathered her robes so that not even a hem would brush him as she passed by, and went up the sunlit, moss-walled alley to Thaorinn.

Lian was left, staring at the Burdanian. The Burdanian stared back. His eyes were dark hazel, striated with blond and grey. The muscles around them were never quite still; the changing exposure made them glitter. A striped flush was rising where Sara's hand had connected. Seeing Lian's eye on it, Thovalt probed it with long, oversupple fingers.

29

'Your mother hits hard.'

'Sara,' Lian said. The blow came from Thaorinn's Sara, not Lian's mother. She had struck him because he had driven Thaorinn to say what he had, not because Lian had heard it. Lian had understood very young that, for Sara, Thaorinn came first. Thovalt, of course, would not understand.

Jahde caught his eye with a gesture. *Kin* signed, *Will you show courtesy to our visitor?* Lian caught his breath. *Vos'neen* would be reverberating with Sara's and Thaorinn's anger, and the proximity of the metal airship. Along with courtesy, Jahde had laid on him the responsibility of ensuring no further offences.

Lian took Thovalt to his cell. It was improper: cells were for the exclusive use of their single resident, but it was the only place he could think where he could isolate the Burdanian. He was not sure it would help, for Thovalt was visibly repelled by the moss and slime on the paths, by the lichen, fungi and moss coating the walls, by the detritus piled years deep in unused alleys. But better that than take him into the jungle, or to the sea, and possibly have him come to harm, or offend *vos'neen* further.

The Burdanians had cleared an isolated alley for their own use, away from most of the occupied cells. Thaorinn's, Sara's and Lian's cells were three in a row at the end of the alley, around a small, clear stone pool. Thovalt stared at the moss-covered stone dome. Lian held aside the heavy curtain for him to enter, which he did, stooping very low rather than brush hanging moss. Inside he would not stand still. He blundered in the darkness, banged his head on the curved wall, cursed. Lian said tightly, 'Be – still. I – feed the lamp.'

In the dark, by touch, Lian found the lamp in its niche in the wall, and beside it, the packet of nutrient substrate. He unscrewed the twist of fabric and sprinkled it into the lamp, restoppered the arm and inverted it to mix. The green glow kindled, swirled and spread throughout the clear, bowed arms. Lian replaced the lamp in its niche and turned to face Thovalt.

'That's beautiful,' the Burdanian said, unexpectedly. 'Micro-organisms – I understood the *kinder'el'ein* were bio-engineers.'

'Before *en'neen*. And *vos'neen*.'

'And now?' The muted light caught the glitter in Thovalt's eye. He looked around the cell, at the padded sleeping platform, the garments and oddments in stone cubby holes, the cleft privy to the rear. 'That's an insult,' Thovalt said. 'Burdanians despise stagnation.'

'*Kinder'el'ein* – are – not Burdanians.' Lian said. He drew a deep breath, scraping together words. 'This is – *kinder'vos*. You must not – give offence. More offence. You come in airship. *Metal* airship. You anger Thaorinn. You do not – respect – *vos'neen*. You come – here – thinking Burdanian – things. Not caring about – anything but – Burdanian things. You must – give attention.'

Thovalt was watching him, intently, as he spoke; he had the sense the Burdanian was willing him on without really listening to what he was saying. When Lian finished he looked down, turning his face away from the lamp's green glow.

He said in a low voice, 'You used to care about Burdanian things.'

Suddenly, unbidden, a fragment of memory turned up an enamelled young Thovalt. Lian knew Thovalt; he had known him very well. Thovalt was the only child of Thaorinn's brother, now dead. Such closeness was so usual in colony bloodlines as to pass unremarked, but Thovalt had befriended Lian during his spells of residence in the colony, though he was several years the elder. He had been attracted to, and challenged by, Lian's uniqueness. Lian admired Thovalt, as a child will a youth, but he was also well able to see that his pride mattered less to him than Thovalt's did to Thovalt. The friendship was eased by Lian's willing submission.

Thovalt said suddenly, 'Do you hate me, Lian?'

The question, and its white, pleading tone, took Lian by surprise. Had he sounded furious, or was Thovalt so fragile? From what he remembered, it might be so. He said, 'You – are Thovalt. My – friend.'

Thovalt closed his eyes. 'You're . . . improbable.'

'What – did you ask – Thaorinn?' There was a silence. Lian said, feeling pressured, 'I do not – remember – much.' Thovalt's eyes locked, urgently, with his. The stare made him hesitate. Then Thovalt came to himself and looked away. Lian continued, 'Something – happened. Ships – and leaving – and,' the fragments of memory shifted, showing an edge of something ominous, '*fire*—'

Thovalt crossed the cell in two strides, crowding him up against the shelf. 'Fantasy!' he said, insisted, catching Lian's arms. 'An *impression* of the input from the ship's skin. *We do not know what happened to Burdania*,' He shook Lian lightly. 'Have they made you forget, mewed up here in your stone hovel? How could Thaorinn do that? He of all people.'

The shaking had left Lian dizzy. He sought stability behind him, from stone shelves. Thovalt released him suddenly. He stalked back across the cell, disordering the swept, sandy floor, and just remembered to jerk his head aside before it struck the down-curving wall. He swung around. 'I believe I need to give you a history lesson,' he said, in a high, challenging voice. Lian cringed, thinking of *vos'neen*.

Thovalt set his feet, made a frame of his supple hands. 'Picture Burdania,' he said, 'sixty-eight years ago. Small, cold planet; blue-white sun. Fast days, slow years. A single continent caps its north and chains,' he swept loops with long fingers, 'and chains of islands, little islands,' pinched between fingertips, 'and big islands,' cupped between his hands, 'adorning the southern seas. Picture our tiny colony unfolded and spread across plains and islands. Picture eighty million people, much as we are, contentious, argumentative. The argument is about space exploration. For two hundred years we have probed and explored. We have founded colonies; they have dwindled away,' illustrated with a fluttering sinking of his hands, 'and gone to dust in three generations, or ten. We do not root in strange soil. We do not know why. So it is said, and said forcibly, that if we cannot colonize, why continue, why risk life, waste precious resources? But there are amongst us twenty generations, Lian,' Thovalt said, absorbed in his performance, 'who view even the simplicities of biological existence,' he held up his hands, examining them, 'with a fractured lens, knowing the many solutions beyond the one. Who have been launched from their planet-bound existence, never to return; who are, in essence, alien to their own kind. *They* are not going to stop voyaging.' He stopped, breathless. Composed mind, body, and hands, holding Lian's attention on his fingertips. Though his was not handsign, his mime was so vivid that Lian had a sense of understanding beyond understanding. 'Two physicists conceived a means of breaking free of physical space. They designed a ship which could travel farther and faster than any ship before. The Explorers built three such ships, in secret, one in Lltharran, one in the Sor, one on D'Alna island. When their opponents learned of the ships, they condemned them, and sought to forcibly impound them. The three ships, with such crews as they had, launched, and fired,' Thovalt said, very softly, 'the stardrive, while still in Burdania's orbit. And three drives *interacted*, and flung the three ships not merely clear of Burdania's system, but beyond the furthest point of exploration. With a lingering, incoherent image of Burdania behind them, disintegrating.

'Were we meant to live?' Thovalt asked softly, looking down into his cupped hand as though he held the question therein. 'We could so easily have died. We could not have used the drive again, not knowing what had happened, not knowing where we were. The physicists applied themselves to the equations. The navigators applied themselves to the starmaps. Soon enough we knew why and where. We knew then how to return, but we did not dare. The drive, we said. The reality was fear. We thought about death, but the habit of living was too strong, and space should do for us in the end. So we go on, into the void, by a slow backup drive. Space should do for us in the end. Except for a red star, with planets, one in particular, habitable, barely. We are Explorers, and we need distraction from our own creeping madness. So we make landfall, and we are *greeted*. The irony of it. And we talk about going on, as we talked about death, but in the end, we stay. We build a colony from the salvage of our ships, except for one. The one we keep . . . for what? Our own particularity will do for us. This world is too strange, too hot, too humid, the minerals in soil and water too variant . . . Nine hundred and fifty men and women have four hundred and thirty sons and daughters, who have in their orderly turn one hundred and ninety-eight grandsons and granddaughters. Nature indeed is merciful.' He paused, and again softly, said, 'But the one hundred and ninety-eight have

33

issue numbering two hundred and seventy-four. And the two hundred and seventy-four give birth to three hundred and forty-six, and we are *condemned* to live.

'And so, what of Burdania, left disintegrating behind us? The founding generation debates return, once, twice; the second generation not at all; the third, at a little remove, debates it four times, bitterly setting the fearful old against the bitter young, who see themselves dying out on an alien world. Then children are born to the third, and go on being born, and suddenly the third must believe that they are survivors. They immerse themselves in their world, in their children; they study the jungle, the conjunctions of three moons, the *kinder'el'ein* . . . anything but Burdania. Until their children begin to ask . . . and ask again, seven times, and the fifth the closest yet, with Thaorinn D'Halldt doing the asking, before he vanishes into the jungle. Now it is our generation's turn. And *I* will be the first.'

He suddenly crossed to Lian, crowding him up against the stone shelf. Lian's own shadow divided Thovalt's face into lit and shadowed. His lit eye quivered as he looked down at him.

'Do you not want to be there when it happens? After all this you *deserve* to be. Thaorinn might want you to be *kinder'el'ein*, but you are,' he reached up and pushed Lian's hood off his head, 'Burdanian!'

The gesture frightened Lian. He had not expected Thovalt to understand *kinder'el'ein* custom well enough to offend it. He eased sideways, away from Thovalt, pulled the hood up.

'Why—' Lian realized his futility. For Thovalt to have come to Proponent status so young, he must be highly gifted. He, Lian, was not. But he had his choice. He released held breath at the realization. Whatever Thovalt said, he, Lian, could still act on what he could not articulate.

'Why,' he said, 'do I. Deserve to be? Because I hurt – was hurt. In the dome.'

The glitter in Thovalt's eyes was still. He did not answer at once. Then he said, 'Burdania used to matter to you. You told us we *had* to go back because we owed it to the people who might have survived.' He spoke more quickly, energy rising. 'You said it did not matter what *had* happened, what our

34

forebears had done; what mattered was what was happening now, what *we* did. You were luminous in your conviction; you were *beautiful*, Lian.'

Lian watched him, from an island of calm. He would like to think that he had had conviction, been beautiful, but he did not remember being so. He had learned the hollowness of the argument that if he had truly cared, he would have remembered. Caring was ephemeral before gravity and neuronal mortality. Thovalt, he suspected, would choose not to hear that. He viewed his friend with *kinder'el'ein* eyes, and saw something desperate in his brilliance. And there was that 'Do you hate me, Lian?'

'Why—' he said again, '—want me? I cannot – speak now. Nor vote.'

Thovalt pinned Lian's raised hands between his own. They were hard, cold. 'You cannot know that,' he said urgently. 'The medics had not done with you before Sara and Thaorinn took you away. Your rehabilitation was hardly begun. Sara and Thaorinn insisted they could re-educate you themselves, and perhaps they have done so, but to *their* purpose, not yours. Have they ever told you about Burdania? Have they ever mentioned me. . . ?' He saw the answer in Lian's face. It gladdened and emboldened him. He caught Lian's shoulders. 'I will not let them silence you, as I will not let them silence me. Come back with me, Lian. Tonight!'

THREE

BURDANIA

Lara and Zharlinn's household was on the far side of the river, on the low ridge between the dykes.

Dusk gathered as they walked towards the settlement. To their right, the river moved with a massive grinding inexorability. Great pleats and darts appeared in its skin, as currents merged and dragged at outcroppings. From the bank to that skin was a very shallow step, and in places it had already overflowed, and collected in still, staring pools, lined with drowning grass.

On the far side of the ridge the dyking began, a single long wall of black stone along the riverbank. No buildings here were low to the river, but the sheltered flat between dyke and hillslope had been planted in narrow tentative strips. Even so late in the spring the crop was still spindly, shivering in the wind. The dyke itself was higher than Lian's reach, a wedge of piled stone, sealed with stone, earth, wild grass and weeds. A fringe of grass shimmered against the lighter sky. Nobody was working on it, but two people passed, carrying lanterns, which they held low to inspect each niche and crevice, and each muddy stretch underfoot.

There had been two bridges across the river. The far one had collapsed, leaving spars jutting from each bank, and pillars midstream. The near one described a high arc against the indigo sky. It was gaunt and pitted with corrosion, and buckled slightly in its midsection as the river had undercut its supports. But were it in its prime, Lian would never have set willing foot upon it. He dealt with the vertigo by finding something high and motionless to focus on. That was the straight-edged silhouette atop the knoll, the luring enigma.

A side glimpse of fire broke his concentration, and he looked down. A bonfire burned in the lee of the dykes. Tongues of flame peeled away, to expire in midair, while the weightless sparks burned against the sky. Figures slid through the smoke and crazed light, clustering and separating, meeting and parting, passing stones and words. Living shadows spattered dyke, earth and grass.

Fires and lanterns marked out the dykes' limits. They followed the river for perhaps eight hundred metres, and then curved inland. He could just see the light from the far side of the ridge. The outer dyke was as grass-bound as the one on the far bank, but the inner one was very new, raw black in the firelight, its stones unsettled. And already the base of the outer dyke was under water.

The end of the bridge abutted the double dykes and the rising slope of the knoll. They left the bridge on a broken grey path which forked at the base of the knoll, one fork climbing, the other descending behind the dykes. The bulk of the inner dyke was more oppressive than comforting, it emphasized how low they stood, how vulnerable the low buildings in its rear. Lara and Zharlinn exchanged greetings with the fire-feeders, made promises, followed them quickly with excuses, and led him uphill. Away from the firelight, amongst buildings, he could scarcely see in Burdania's meagre starlight. He stumbled often, and hardly heeded Lara's explanation of why their household, *caur'ynani*, was a house of the Islands rather than a traditional Guildhouse.

The *caur'ynani* was a squat bulk near the crest of the ridge. They stopped before a solid door, Lara's hands fumbled around a lit slot, and light washed over them, dazzling Lian. A glaring, faceted lamp dangled in a net bag, swaying with the draughts.

'One of our bits and pieces,' Zharlinn said from his side. 'A sun-powered lamp.'

The afterimage of the lamp blotted out Zharlinn's face. 'Yes?'

'When it goes out we only need to put it in the sun. They're

37

fairly common, and they've lasted well. Most of them work, once recharged.'

Lara closed the door behind them. The door was of sea-stained wood, curved slightly outwards like the flank of a ship. The lintel was carved with tiny islands in relief, each labelled with its name. Between them the wood was embossed with ripples. Lian ran his eyes down all the names he should know.

The vestibule was higher than it was wide, there being a wooden balcony on the three inner sides, just out of reach. A narrow ladder on his right led up. There was a skylight: the light lit struts and shone up into nocturnal indigo. The walls were stone, lightly plastered, and a collection of bulky cloaks hung from hooks before the ladder.

Lara and Zharlinn had pulled off their cloaks, unwrapped their muddy leggings and were unstrapping their boots. Both were wearing sweaters over trousers and tunics. Zharlinn's sleeves were rolled up, showing skin slick with wax and firmly moulded over muscle. Bruises and scratches marked his forearms.

A voice hailed them, indistinctly, from further within.

'Zhar and me,' Lara answered, craning her neck. 'And a visitor.'

Zharlinn shook down his cuffs and looked at Lian, who became aware he was staring. He bent and began to work off his own boots, leaning against the wall for balance. The plaster was coarse against his flank, and he felt the mud transparent under the relic lamp. Surely they must notice the difference between his boots and theirs when set side by side.

They did not; they gave the boots scarcely a glance. He started to unfasten his jacket, then reconsidered. The jacket seemed to have passed. The insulating jersey he wore beneath might not. And even inside it was cold.

Zharlinn said, 'Come and meet the others.'

He feared for a moment that they were headed up the ladder, but they led him into a short corridor to the rear. The ceiling felt close, and he had to make an effort to walk upright, as though accustomed to that scale. At the end they shouldered through a rust-coloured curtain into a larger room, warmer than vestibule or corridor. The light had the gentle blush of lamplight. After the sterile outdoors, the air seemed as odorous as the jungle. Some were familiar: vegetable, compost, a taint of healthy rot; and others utterly unfamiliar: spices, dye and a trace of bitter seawater. Lian was stricken with sudden, intense homesickness.

'—found him in the ruins,' Lara was saying to a small, white-haired man who sat cross-legged on the bare floor-boards, a green cloth spread across his legs. He fixed her with an aged, but bright blue-green eye. 'And you wouldn't have been interested, otherwise?' he said.

'He's Islander! From C'Rynn reach!'

'C'Rynn,' said the man thoughtfully. 'You are far from home. You are. . . ?'

'Lian – D'Halldt.'

'D'Halldt? That's a name I haven't heard for a while,' the white-haired man said factually. 'Those are hard seas in the upper latitudes . . . Ach. Where are my manners? I am Vylan D'Caul, late of the west D'Alna reach.'

'Valancy Nors,' said a stifled voice. Lian had had little chance to take in the surroundings, beyond an impression of rough furniture ornamented by coloured drapery. He had thought Vylan alone. The voice came from a couch facing the opposite wall. The wood creaked, a hand appeared, and then a braid-crowned head as the occupant heaved herself upright. Lian now saw the shadow of someone else on the floor on the opposite side. Lara skirted the end of the couch. 'Still,' she said, hands on hips. 'Thought this morning something had to happen.'

The woman looked up at her, a mature profile amused and weary. 'So did I.'

'We'll take you down to the dykes with us, shall we?'

'You'll do no such thing,' and a man got to his feet from the floor behind the couch. He topped Lara by a head. She returned his glare with impudence. 'I don't think he trusts us, 'Lance.'

'Let him be.' She started to rise, and the man put an arm round her, helping her to her feet. She was far advanced in pregnancy. He kept a hand around her as she turned. Possessiveness, Lian read, with all its insecurity. She tolerated

39

it, that was clear, but she also reached across to cover his hand with her own. Lian was curious, aware of stories he did not know. 'Valancy Nors,' she said. 'Of *tayn* Nors.'

'Tor,' said the young man, starkly. 'Of Lltharran.'

There was a silence. Lian did not know how to interpret it.

Valancy Nors eased them out of it, saying to Tor, 'I think I'll go to bed.'

He held the curtain aside for her; their voices murmured as they passed down the corridor.

'That I still don't understand,' Lara observed.

'Custom,' Zharlinn said shortly. 'She conceived; custom dictates a year's pairing.' He spoke with a bitterness which made the others look curiously at him.

'Let be,' said Vylan. 'Lian, would you like some stew?'

'Yes,' Lian said. 'Please.'

'Go and get him some, one of you?' Zharlinn went as bid.

Vylan shifted his legs beneath the cloth. Little oblongs glinted against the coarse weave. 'You'll forgive me if I keep at this?'

'What are – you doing?' Lian said, letting himself down on the floorboards, which were smoother and warmer than he expected. Belatedly, he realized that he should have first asked what they were.

To his relief, Vylan did not notice the unasked question. 'I'm sorting them. They're components of the inner workings of many of the relics. Many different types. They used to be labelled, but the labelling has worn off, so it falls to me to sort them according to what I can see.' He offered one to Lian. 'Hold it by the corners. See the rainbow on the face? The patterns are common to a type.'

Lian knew what he would see, and so he merely held the optical circuit, as prescribed. The flame in the lamp fluttered and its light glinted on one facet, spreading in coloured rings.

'What does it do?'

Vylan took it back. Turned it in his fingers. 'Transmits light as signals, I *think*. Like flashing a lantern from ship to shore. When we get a relic, we remove all the movable components, type them, and replace them one by one. If we're lucky, that's enough to get it working, and if we can get enough different

40

kinds of relic working, then we can start making guesses about what the individual bits do. These, for instance,' he passed his fingers over a small cluster, 'are switches. You touch one side, and there . . . you can see it has gone darker. Heat and pressure change their properties. Our main success has been with lamps and heaters. They're straightforward, the main puzzle is their skin-surfaces, which have to take up sunlight and re-emit as light or heat. It's not a simple fluorescence or . . . Am I getting too technical?'

'No,' Lian said, softly.

'Oh, good. The lights in *caur'isk'dari* are made of the same kind of material, and we've found fragments of it in the ruins; apparently it was in common use.'

'What is – *caur'isk'dari*?'

'Ah, that's the building up the hill. The grey one. It's the best preserved of any of the old buildings. Some of the doors still open and close when you touch them, and the lights follow you when you walk down the corridors. Disconcerting at first. We're sure there was some kind of information storage there, too, but that seems to have broken down. But we've been able to learn a great deal from what does work. The *isk'dar* has a infinite tolerance for us dismantling her walls.'

He knew the building: it was the one which lit up on scan, the one which had lured them here, the anomaly which deepened the enigma.

'I'll take you up there tomorrow,' Vylan said. 'The *isk'dar* will want to meet you. She'll be glad your *tayn* has not died out. Or croft, if you are but one family. Forgive me, I did not ask: have you come alone?'

'Quite – alone.'

'Even so, the *isk'dar* will be glad to see you. I do not know how much you have heard in C'Rynn, about the *isk'dar* . . .'

Lian took the chance. 'Nothing,' he said. 'I know – nothing. I do – not even know what the *isk'dar* – is.'

Behind him, he heard Lara's indrawn breath. Vylan gave him a rueful glance, and sighed. Then all three were distracted by Zharlinn returning with a bowl and spoon, which he offered to Lian. Both bowl and spoon were made of

41

clay, moulded, fired and glazed brown and dark green. Zharlinn went to sit down, and then paused, 'I assume you take fish.'

Spoon poised, Lian froze. Burdanians had become vegetarian long before the Exploration years. How could they have reverted? Yes, they lacked hydroponics and synthesis plants, and yes, their lives were more demanding and energetic, but the disaster had been shared by Burdanian and animal alike . . .

If he were to pretend to be one of them, he would have to eat as one. He dipped the spoon again and raised a little to his lips. It smelled of herbs and heavy oils; it tasted scalding, salt and oily. He knew, suddenly, with apprehension not unmixed with relief, that nothing would induce him to eat it, no matter what the consequences.

Zharlinn reached over and took the bowl out of his hands. 'You should have said,' he reproached him.

Lian started and stared up at him. 'I am right, am I not?' Zharlinn said. 'You'd eat it out of courtesy, but you *don't* take fish.'

'No,' Lian said, and stopped to wipe his mouth. 'But I—No,' he finished, more decisively. 'No, I don't.'

Zharlinn carried the bowl away through the russet curtain. Lian wiped his mouth again, swallowing oil. Disaster had glanced at him and turned away.

'What the *isk'dar* is . . .' Vylan mused, balancing a component on his fingertips. 'To me she is much like a shipmaster. Which is not so far-fetched, since Lltharran plain is not unlike a hostile sea. She has a shipmaster's expertise, a shipmaster's responsibility, and,' there was a slight warning in his voice, 'a shipmaster's final authority. Which in Lltharran extends beyond the needs of survival.'

'You – obey her?' Lian said. He felt as though with every question he was sliding further and further out on a thin branch.

'If you settle here, you will agree with her on certain issues. People who do not agree, do not settle. I think,' he said, in an effort to lighten the tone, 'from what I have seen of you, you will do well here.'

'What – things?' Lian persisted, feeling the branch shudder. 'I would not like to – make mistakes.'

'Restoration, for one. Re-establishing fast communication with the rest of Burdania, and extending her influence. And, the river. She will not let us yield a rope's-width of land to the river.'

'The river – looks frightening.'

'We're for it this year,' Lara said, cheerfully. She was crouching behind Lian and Vylan, balancing herself with a casual hand on Lian's shoulder. She intrigued Lian. Her self-confidence seemed mismatched with her years. In the Colony she would have still been a student, probably under examination for the privilege to speak in the debating chamber. Here she had already been tested and proven. Her voice was heard. She knew her worth. 'Heavy snow in the mountains. Spring's late and sudden. The old people say there hasn't been flooding like this for ten years. This will challenge our dyking.'

'Why – stay here? In danger?'

'We stay,' Vylan said, 'because of the *isk'dar*. And because of *caur'isk'dari*. There is nowhere else quite like it. It is essential to our restoration. Lltharran has become a centre of the effort, on account of the *isk'dar* . . .'

'Here,' said Rathla Zharlinn, returning with another steaming bowl, and Tor a step behind. 'I can't stomach *vatchin* myself.' He set down a roll of coarse bread. 'It's winter grain. Be months before the summer harvest reaches us.'

Tor stopped beside Lian, staring down at Vylan's cloth and hands until Vylan looked up at him. Tor said, 'Do you think it could come tonight?'

''Lance would be the one to say.'

Tor greeted that with a fretful silence. Lian stirred his stew, identifying constituents: strands of the yellow seaweed, *s'din*, *culli* rind, chunks of *assant* tuber. Other vegetables he had not encountered in the colony. The taste was sourer and more spicy than he was used to. The bread was gritty, just palatable if he soaked it in the soup. Nobody objected to his doing so.

While he ate, Lian looked around the room. For five people, gathered together, it was spacious; twenty would be a crowd. It traversed the building, with heavily curtained windows on both

43

end walls. The ceiling was low, with transverse beams supporting planks. The walls were thinly plastered over the stone; the plaster followed its contours.

The furniture was wood, sanded very smooth, draped with bright throws and studded with cushions. A purple blanket had been slung over the back of Valancy's couch, and another, yellow and green, lay in a tumble on the floor. A cushion covered in white-hearted sunbursts perched on the chair behind Vylan. Both inner corners of the room were filled by a webbing of coloured cords, stretched between pegs on the walls, intricately knotted, and with worked-in floats, sticks, fishbones . . . Fishers' art, perhaps. He dared not examine it more closely. He could plead frailty to cover his ignorance of fishing, but he could not be ignorant of fishers' recreation.

Three rough tables formed an uneven bench along the rearmost wall. Two plain stools were pushed beneath it, and a quenched lamp sat in a bracket above. There were three such brackets, along the wall, but only one lamp. The bench was spread with a clutter of dented, tarnished and dismantled small equipment.

Lara said, to Tor, 'Lian is asking what the *isk'dar* is like.'

'Travassan,' Tor said. He sat on the floor, leaning back against the side of the couch. 'Half mad like the rest of them.'

'I think he's in love,' Lara said, impishly.

Tor's dark glance was irritated. 'She's dangerous. Unlike the rest of you, I do not wonder how Linn Travassa came to be *isk'dar*, and how he managed to impose his will on Lltharran and Burdania. I know. *She* could do as Linn did, and you would follow her.'

Zharlinn and Lara bridled. Tor anticipated them. 'The North and the Islands broke with the Travassan *isk'dar* two generations ago. Now she's drawing them back in, and she's using you to do it. You, the Medics' Guild, the Shipbuilders . . . she has the loyalty of the most productive innovators. She uses knowledge as Linn used knowledge, to her own ends.'

'How – should she – use knowledge?' Lian said, watching him intently; his tone, his body-language, suggested an inner argument.

Tor met his direct gaze, flinched and looked down. 'I don't

44

know,' the young man said bitterly. 'If I knew of another way, I might not be here.'

Rathla Zharlinn rolled on his stomach, facing Tor, and said, 'Why not?' Vylan sent a warning glance at the back of his head, but said nothing.

'Because the edifice is corrupt and the foundation is rotten,' Tor said, precisely. 'Firstly, you rely upon the *isk'dar* . . .'

'Since,' Rathla Zharlinn said, with obvious effort at moderation, 'we are trying to reverse four generations of neglect and outright sabotage, I would say we should use all the influence we have.'

'And secondly, you are not learning for yourselves. If we are going to begin again, *we* should *begin* again, and not pick at their scraps and leavings. I am with you because I believe that we must try and solve the problems of our own existence, but I cannot, and I can never, agree with you to do it this way.'

'But the knowledge is *there*!' Lara said. 'We cannot not use it.'

'Cannot?' said black-eyed Tor. 'What kind of "cannot" is that? Theirs, I think. *We* must think our cannots and our musts, if we are not to travel their road again.'

'And in the meantime, what happens. Suffering and need-less death. Ships wrecked, diseases that we could cure, your own mother . . .'

'Peace!' cried Vylan suddenly. '*All* of you!' To Tor he said, 'Would you truly discard knowledge that could have practical good because of some historical taint? And you,' he said to Lara, 'might you recognize evil amongst the good?' He flicked turquoise eyes from one to the other. 'Recognizing that there can be risk and evil does not void what we are trying to do, it only means that we must do it with the greatest of care and the greatest of integrity, and we cannot afford to deceive ourselves! Now, will you let me work, and let 'Lance, who needs rest and peace just now, *have* some.'

'Too late, I think,' Zharlinn murmured, rolling to his feet. He crossed to meet Valancy, who had just pushed aside the russet hanging. She was wearing an ankle-length shift, and was barefoot. 'You sounded as though you were having an interesting discussion.'

45

There was an awkward silence. Valancy eased her braid over her shoulder. 'Oh,' she said. 'Shall I just go back to listening through the walls?'

'No,' Vylan said. 'Come in and sit down.'

Zharlinn settled her into the chair behind Vylan. She declined offers of a blanket and food, the latter with a queasy grimace that Vylan, at least, noted. Tor moved round to sit at her feet, leaning against the leg of her chair and her flank. Lian saw the thought with which she slid her hand down his hair to rest on his shoulder. Zharlinn was wrong. She had not sought comfort, she had sought to give it to a bitter and alienated man. Lian studied her weary, durable face, hoping that there was someone who could give her comfort when she needed it.

'We started by trying to describe the *isk'dar* for Lian,' Zharlinn said.

Valancy was not deceived. She sighed, and shifted uncomfortably, constrained by Tor's proximity. 'I have always found her kind. Impatient, but kind.'

The description startled Lara and Zharlinn, but Vylan accepted it. 'You see the difficulty,' he said, mildly, to Lian. 'To me she is a skilled shipmaster; to Tor, a danger; to Valancy, impatient but kind.'

'Rathla said – "neglect and outright – sabotage"—' Lian said, appealing to Vylan as mediator.

'Aye, Linn started it.' Vylan gave Lian an amused, resigned glance. 'He was opposed to preservation and restoration of the relics. He had them destroyed, and he stopped anyone who knew about them from passing that on. He was the first *isk'dar*; he had an imposing personality; and he could be ruthless.'

'Not could be,' Zharlinn said. 'He *was* . . .' He pressed a fisted hand to his upper lip. Then dropped it on to his thigh. 'He hasn't finished us. I *know* we can restore distance communications, maybe even within three or four years. No more needing signals, ships, and runners; we'll be able to speak to any *tayn*, anywhere. That will make finding relics and passing on knowledge so much easier. And if we can find the old way of keeping chronicles . . . I don't think there's any hope in Lltharran, but somewhere on the Islands, or in the North, away from Linn and his agents, *something* has to have survived. If we can find those records, *they'll* contain what we need to know. *That's* what we're trying to do.' And that, Lian thought peripherally, was why Zharlinn made him think of Thovalt. He had the same restlessness, the same dissatisfaction with present and place.

The greater part of his attention was preoccupied with what Vylan said, about Linn Travassa's purge of artefacts and knowledge. The evidence was there, in Lltharran's total ruin, had he wished to see it. No chaos drive could be as thorough as malign intent.

'Lian,' Valancy said, 'are you well?'

He looked up, disconcerted. She said, shyly, 'I cannot help but notice the way you speak. We have good medics here in Lltharran . . .'

'I – am fine,' Lian said. His speech was the last thing he had expected anyone to remark upon. Everyone knew him, and it. 'It is not – not – *new*.' He was stricken with disorientation, with an awareness of being amongst strangers, with the enormity of his masquerade. He made himself put words together. 'I – fell. Injured my – head. I have never spoken – well since.'

'And I have embarrassed you,' Valancy said.

Looking at her pleasant, tired face, he felt the disorientation abate, and recognized that it was less due to her observation than to the realization that the Burdanians themselves had rejected their past. He gathered himself, and said, 'But you – do not think – as Linn Travassa did?'

'Sweet reason, no!' Lara said.

'Not – even the – *isk'dar*?'

'Especially not she,' Zharlinn said, with passion.

Lian thought longingly of the shuttle, of warmth, safety, familiar voices. He was suddenly exhausted. What had he done by impulsively climbing that wall; and how quickly could he undo it? He pressed his hand against the communicator in his inner breast pocket. He said, diffidently, 'Forgive me, but I – am very tired. Might I – will you – show me where – I might sleep. A – quiet room?'

47

The room was upstairs, on the far side of the vestibule from the common room. It was narrow and wood-panelled, furnished with a bed, a rough chair, and a carved table. A canvas blind was lashed to wooden pins around the window. The window was unglazed and the canvas rattled with the wind and spilled little spurts of cold air over the floor. Above the table was a sheet of metal, polished to a reflective gleam, and on it a basin and jug.

The mattress smelled sharply of dry grasses and creaked as he lay down. He was amused to find the blankets had thongs along the sides, and the bed, toggles. Islanders, accustomed to ships, wanted everything secured.

He listened to place the voices below, and then slipped his transceiver from his inner pocket.

'Lian!' 'Of all the irrespons—' 'Why didn't you contact . . .' '. . . where are you?'

'I am,' he murmured, 'in one of the houses – across the river. I must—' He muffled their protests with his palm, '—keep my voice down.'

There was a guilty silence, and then Thovalt said, 'When can you get away?'

'I am – their guest. I thought you could – hear.'

'Had you set your transmitter properly, yes,' Thovalt said, archly. 'You have it on near pickup. We could only hear you, and not well.'

'We were anxious,' Lors added.

'What did you *tell* them?' Thovalt said.

'I – said I came from C'Rynn reaches – the one that scanned as – not well populated.'

Thovalt yelped with glee. 'They *believed* that. Brilliant!'

'Unethical,' Alystra said.

Lian flinched at the coolness in her voice.

'What would you have had him do?' Thovalt returned. 'We were about to be discovered—'

'We might have let events take their course.'

'Let events take—!'

'Thovalt,' Lors said, voice thin and sharp through the speaker. 'Alystra. Our first concern is Lian, and how he gets back.'

48

'Wait,' Alystra said. 'We should find out what Lian has learned about these people.'

'Exploit his ill-gotten gains?' Thovalt said. 'Is *that* ethical?'

Lors grumbled in the background. Alystra pitched her voice to dominate. 'You took me by surprise, given how consistently you objected to our keeping out of sight. I would be interested to know what precipitated this.'

Lian stared at the close rafters, glad that none of them could see his face. He had been so caught up in the dance of wits that he had not thought about consequences.

Alystra said, 'Do not forget we will have to account for our every action. That said, I might have done the same myself, to prevent discovery. What have you learned?'

What had he? 'There are – five people here. Their work is – to explore the ruins – collect items of – pre-Leaving technology, and to try – to repair them.'

'What's their level of understanding?'

'They substitute parts and – try to work out the function. They – hope to find a working Archive—'

Lors said, with a break in his voice, 'Why have they lost so much?'

Lian hesitated. 'I am – not sure. Some was – deliberate – a man named Linn Travassa. He – destroyed what was left. Why, I – do not know.'

'One man?' Alystra said. Lors said, 'But why?'

'One man and his friends,' Thovalt said, blithely. 'How we came to be here.'

'And now. What's the mood? I presume that if they're digging up the ruins and trying to understand what they find, there's been a change.'

'Yes. There is an *isk'dar* . . . She lives in – the old Science Centre. They call it – *caur'isk'dari. Caur* – is house or household.'

'Language lessons,' Thovalt said, 'by Lian.' The others shushed him. Lian continued, 'She has – considerable influence. She had – the dykes built. The people here say – they stay because of her. She – encourages the restoration.'

'Li,' Lors interrupted, 'we have to leave tomorrow night. Our power is low, and that river is going to flood. You can tell

49

us the rest when you get back. Will you be safe there until tomorrow?'

'Yes,' Lian said. 'I will – be safe.'

FOUR

TARIDWYN

Sara sang for the fading day.

Lian heard the wordless coloratura ringing between the stones. He was lying on his pallet, staring at Thovalt's scuff marks on his sanded floor. He felt as though he had struggled ashore through a surf of words. All he could do, at the last, was refuse to let Thovalt consent for him. The Burdanian had tried. Thwarted, he had stalked out, promising to wait with the ship. He did not say for how long.

Lian lay looking at the footprints and listened to Sara sing. He knew where she would be: beside the archway to the sea the garden wall had crumbled into a platform of stones. She used this as a stage. It was part of her self-contradiction. Her demeanour said: I am vain, I am capricious, I do not treat silence as sacred. She pretended not to deceive, yet she did: her singing was a gift for the *kindereen*, whose voices atrophied as they matured. Everywhere, in cells, workshops and gardens, they would pause to listen.

But she was singing a lie. She might have been singing at the end of any of the days which had preceded this, days so similar that they could no longer say on which a particular tiny event might have happened. She was not singing this day, with all its uncertainty and conflict.

Lian got tiredly to his feet and slid his hood over his head. He had not realized how much time had passed. He should at least confirm that Thovalt had gone without further importuning or disturbance. In some part of him, he yet hoped he would see the hover mists thickening and rolling seawards; he hoped the Burdanian's wounded impatience would decide for him. But the sea was still, deep green, the grassy flats calm. Sara stood against the peaceful late sky. He almost missed seeing Thovalt in the shadows of the archway. Then the Burdanian moved and spoke to Sara. She flipped her hands out carelessly in answer and segued into another song, one fast and rippling, a brilliant, testing sound. Lian knew at once that it belonged to the colony. His memories shifted and rendered up new images: a pool full of blue water, fish floating above his head, metal vines, his small reflection in smoked glass, transparent boulles of light floating around his head, an arc of horizon smouldering orange . . .

He came to himself with a shudder. Sara's song had stopped: Thovalt was reaching up to help her down. Although she needed no help, she laid her hand elegantly in his. Despite her earlier anger, she had aligned herself with the intruder. Lian ducked back, and returned to the cell.

He was smoothing out his floor when he heard her voice outside. He raised himself, stepping lightly upon the new-swept sand, and went to hold the curtain aside for her.

He did not know how to greet her. She looked sideways at him from her one, slanting eye. 'Did you like my singing?' she asked.

He should have known; she was a keen observer.

'I taught Thovalt a little, once.' She smiled. '—And you wonder: "What is he to Sara, who marked his cheek?" So I did, and he deserved it. But he said he will wait for you on the beach, so you have given him cause to believe you may come . . .'

He said nothing. She read in his face that he had no answer, yet. 'If you are going back there are some things that it would be irresponsible . . . Ach, Thaorinn's word. But yes—' She segued into sign. *It would be irresponsible of me not to tell you some things I have not told you before.*

Thovalt — told me. About Burdania.

'Ah,' she said softly, aloud.

The curtain tintinnabulated with a draught, and she started slightly and turned her head. Light flickered around the edges of the swaying curtain. Sara watched it settle.

Without turning her head, she said, 'Thaorinn has cast up to me on many occasions that now you have—' Again, when she expressed complexities, she lost him. With an airy sigh, she resorted to signing: *the* innocence *that I, in my youth and naivety, thought I would ensure you by seeing you born and reared amongst the* kinder'el'ein. *But your Burdanian nature proved too strong then, and seemingly proves too strong now.* She reached out and eased her fingers beneath his unresponsive hand, and lifted it, folding it in both hers. 'Lian, why?'

She was holding his hand; he could not sign. He had done nothing, promised nothing, and here she was, pressing him. Trying to dissuade him, it seemed, in her oblique fashion, when all the time she . . . '—sang for him.'

'You mind so?' she said at once. 'I had forgotten what it is to have a discriminating audience.' She shook off his hand, as though he were the one who held her. 'He asked *me* to come, do you know that? I am tempted. Not for Burdania or any such noble cause, but simply to hear speech again. Were it not for Jahde, I would have been talking to the stones long ago. When I was carrying you I used to talk to you; and then I gave birth to you and left you to Telien because I was not rearing you in *silence* . . .' She saw his expression and answered it indulgently, assuring him, '. . . but I will not go, of course.'

He watched her uncertainly, not sure whether to believe her. He did not want the responsibility of this knowledge. Childlike, he had taken his parents' compatibility for granted.

She leaned forward and touched his cheek lightly. 'Have I told you how I came to the jungle the first time?' she said. 'I was working with my parents in the medical wing. Not training; I was too idle for that. They brought in this man who had gone wild in the jungle years before. He looked – he smelled! – as though he'd been buried for most of them. We were astounded he was still alive – let alone that he had travelled the distance he had. He was nothing but bones and two dark eyes watching me from under his caul. He would not even talk, only sign.' She chuckled. 'I learned it quickly then. I wanted him,' she said, in a smoky voice, a woman's perturbing voice.

Aware of his discomfort she put out her hand and patted his lightly. 'Ah, Lian, Lian, it will come to you too in time; I hope. It is the life force . . . I'd never noticed Thaorinn when he was just another tediously brilliant youth. He'd never noticed another pretty, boisterous little girl. But now . . . He'd come, the dear idealist, to his duty by the next generation. He was ripe,' she teased him, in that smoky voice, and this time her son summoned a smile. He did enjoy Sara's stories, though he knew she had a motive for telling this one now. She would come to it eventually, first prolonging pleasure of the performance. She was like Thovalt in that.

'I seduced him; he was surprised,' Sara said, with arch and wicked pleasure. 'I followed him; he was appalled. The more he argued, the better I was persuaded. I never expected that he *meant* what he said about *silence*, when he said he was living without words because that was the way the *kindereen* lived. I cannot say I was not warned. But I would not listen. Thaorinn D'Halldt was a challenge!' she said, with blithe self-mockery. 'You come of a perverse line, my sweet, watchful child. And a strong one.' She traced the line of his jaw with the back of her small, cool fingers.

'It was not easy for me to give you up to Telien, but I knew I could not keep you with me here. To make you my confidant in the womb was one thing, but to bind you to me out of my own loneliness another, and I could not have resisted doing that, and Thaorinn might have opposed me bitterly and you would have been too small to understand, except inasmuch that it had to do with you . . .

'I shall go back some day; not this time, but some day. I still have not given up hope that he will go back with me. But the longer he remains here, the deeper he sinks into silence. For me . . . I don't care for a life of denial; it offends me, though I see the appeal of paring oneself to the very bones of spirit, when the nerves ache so— Perhaps that is what I came to say. I did not know, I only felt I must speak to you before Thaorinn does. I am not the orator he is; I must take what advantages I can find.'

'Thaorinn?' Lian whispered.

'He will see you shortly, outside.'

He was stricken with the need to decide and present his father with a finished, immutable decision. 'Should I – should I go?'

'I can't answer that for you,' she said. *Perhaps*, she signed suddenly, *I have been mistaken in insisting that you speak Burdanian to me. You have not wanted to confide in me. I know I made a mistake in not telling you more about the colony. Despite our gloomy history, one can have a great deal of pleasure from being a Burdanian amongst Burdanians. You had it once, though you may not remember.* She rose, and leaned down to rest her cheek against his. She hummed a single sweet note which resonated between their heads. Then she said, 'If you come to silence, you must choose silence. Your father did, and I chose him. Either one of these choices can be unmade, but unmaking a choice is not easy. I know.'

At the heart of the *kinder'vos* there was a still place, a narrow garden around a pool spread with the gauzy discs of *l'creen*. Neither truly plant, nor truly animal, perhaps not even naturally evolved, the *l'creen* was the most sensitive of native life to empathic flux. It had a spine, of a sort, rooting it in the muddy bottom of the green pond; peristalsis of sorts in the network of sinuses in the stem; ligaments of sorts allowing a swift reaction to unpleasant stimuli, and when Thaorinn D'Halldt came upon his waiting son, the gauzy discs vanished into the green depths as though stones had been dropped upon them.

Lian had been sitting on a boulder beside the pool; Thaorinn had not seen him until the *l'creen* had withdrawn. 'I'm – here,' he said, rising. *You wanted me*, he signed, now he had his father's eyes.

'Yes,' Thaorinn said, in the Burdanian he rarely spoke. 'I believe you are considering returning to the colony with Thovalt Aslinn.'

Every clause in that sentence had a purpose, Lian thought – 'considering', 'colony', 'Thovalt Aslinn' – the superb economy of the master speaker. And the master speaker accommodated his audience, speaking slowly and distinctly. In the pool a wisp of oil floated from the depths, released by the disturbed *l'creen*. It was not toxic, but it was noxious, and the *meer*, which spilled down like pearled lace from the rocks, began to draw back as though pressed by the slightest of breezes.

'Yes,' said Lian.

Thaorinn eased himself down on the boulder where Lian had been sitting, leaving room should Lian wish to join him. A formality, since father and son had not been so close for more than a year. He smoothed his robes with his thin, long-fingered hands.

'Inasmuch as I have any right to condone or not to condone your decisions, I would not condone this one.' He paused, awaiting a reaction which did not come, then said, 'If it is the promise of further remedial therapy for your handicaps, be assured that all that could reasonably be done for you was done before we brought you away. We may be eccentric parents, but we are not irresponsible.'

'I do not – I do not know – why,' Lian said. 'But I feel – I *must.*'

'Must? Obeying compulsion without reason is a dangerous course.' He eased back a wing of his caul with a clumsy gesture, as though he could not summon the interest to do it properly. 'You do not need *good* reasons, only clear ones. If you have no reason, how shall you know if those reasons have been satisfied?'

Or not, lingered unsaid in the air.

He glanced up at Lian, eyes sunken and dark in the shadow of his caul. 'You do not have to tell me those reasons, if you cannot.'

Lian had never realized how much more it would hurt to have his father spare him than demand from him. 'I *could*,' he said in a low voice.

'I shall rephrase,' Thaorinn said. 'You need not tell me if you do not *wish* to.' He indicated the pool with a pass of his hand. 'We forget we might be obliged to ignore evidence of others' states of mind.'

About whom was he talking? Lian wondered. 'I would like – you to understand me—'

Thaorinn turned his head, but raised only his blackish eyes. Cloud-filtered light drained the minimal colour from his face. Small muscles around his nose worked with the effort of inhaling the torpid air. 'It is a trait of the young to wish to be understood. A trait of innocence, if you will; I do not disparage it. You have not learned that there are things about yourself you would prefer nobody know.' He turned his eyes again to the pool, and the noxious iridescence curling on the surface. 'I should not like you, in your innocence, to go to the colony.'

'—not innocent,' Lian said. 'I remember.'

'Unsurprising. Substantial areas of your brain were salvaged intact.'

Lian had not been very long in the *kinder'vos*, before he knew that only thus could Thaorinn distance himself from the accident and its consequences. The knowledge made the chill a little easier to bear.

'What has Thovalt Aslinn to do with this "decision" of yours?' Thaorinn's tone put the word in quotes. Lian did not answer, more because he could not find the words than out of caution.

'He is a dangerous type, Thovalt Aslinn,' Thaorinn said. Black eyes flashed up, then back to the pool. 'He would use you to influence me, without regard as to the effect on you. He wishes to win this debate because he wishes to win *this* debate, at which so many have failed. What will happen afterwards hardly matters. We all have our ways of convincing ourselves of our worth, despite our ancestry. This is his way. I am sure of it, Lian, because,' he stared across the pool at Sara's cell with its sequined curtain, 'I was the same. I *am* the same.'

Lian knelt down beside him, his eyes filling with tears. He had not taken in Thaorinn's every word, but he had understood enough to know what Thaorinn had, at the end, confessed. Thaorinn looked sideways at his bowed head. 'Tears, Lian?' he asked, with a lift of surprise in his voice. 'I survived my failure. I expect Thovalt Aslinn will survive his.'

Lian tucked back his hood to look up at his father's face. 'He'll fail?' After what his father had said, that seemed unbearably poignant.

'He cannot succeed. I see now that that cause cannot be won by rhetoric, no matter how accomplished.' A shadow crossed Thaorinn's face. 'He is very accomplished.'

Lian pleated his robe in his fingers. Was it what Thovalt had provoked Thaorinn to say that evoked the shadow, and made him acknowledge Thovalt's accomplishment? He did not have the courage to repeat the words, and have Thaorinn dismiss them as spoken in anger. They mattered so much to Lian; he wanted them to matter to his father.

'What are you thinking?' Thaorinn asked him quietly.

Taken unawares, Lian said: 'I am sorry – it happened – Thaorinn. My accident.'

'You—' Thaorinn silenced himself, staring across the pool. He would rather not have heard, and certainly not have shown he had heard, but after a moment he continued, 'It was an accident. Certainly you should not have been out on that dome, and certainly it should have been checked for safety. If any one of those branches, or even a tree, had come down upon it it would have offered no protection.' Then he was silent again for a moment. 'None of that matters. It is done.'

He had not understood, and suddenly Lian knew it was important that he *made* Thaorinn understand. 'I am sorry,' he said in a near whisper, which contained the last of his courage, 'it happened.'

Beneath the hood he saw his father's expression become grim. 'You said that.'

'No,' Lian said. '*I* am – sorry. To *you*.'

Thaorinn sat still for a long moment, looking out across the pool, where the first droplets of rain were raising a conchoidal stipple on the oily water and the *meer* was crushed against the rocks. 'How *could* you know?' He swung round, staring up at Lian. 'Who *told you*? Was it Sara? Was it Jahde? *Thovalt?*'

Head down, Lian signed falteringly, *No, it was me. I know.* Thaorinn reached out and lifted his caul, jerkily and not particularly gently, but for the first time in over a year touching his son of his own accord and not when Lian's physical frailty made it unavoidable. At the touch Lian looked up.

'I had not thought I could hate myself more,' Thaorinn said. 'I did not want you to know. It was not rational of me; it was not fair of me; and I did not want you to know. I thought I had succeeded. But it seems I did want you to know, for why else would you insist you are sorry, unless you know – believe,' he amended immediately, 'believe I blame you for it, as though you had anything to do with my ambitions and my delusions.'

'Delusions,' Lian thought, even that could not be gently

58

phrased. 'Which I had no right to blame you for ending . . .' Lian lifted a hand to shelter his face. This was far harder than he had expected, even though he had known. He felt Thaorinn release the hood, and it slid between them.

After a moment's silence his father went on, 'I *have* blamed you,' he said, 'for disappointing expectations which I had no right to have.' Again Thaorinn touched him lightly, his near shoulder this time. Lian reached across and pushed away his arm, but did not let it go. He looked up into his father's drawn face.

'I want – to please you.'

'You cannot please me if I ask the impossible.'

He did not understand; he *still* did not understand. '—sure it's impossible – don't believe— You don't believe – I h-have anything left of a brain.'

'That's foolish,' Thaorinn said. 'Of course you have a brain. You wouldn't be arguing with me if you didn't.'

'*Enough* of a brain.'

There was a silence. Thaorinn looked over his shoulder, towards the archway leading back into the *kinder'vos*. 'Perhaps it is impossible,' Thaorinn said at last, sounding deeply tired, 'for a Burdanian to understand the *kinder'el'ein*. I thought that you might be the one. Born among them; raised by them . . . I expected to fail,' he said, mostly to himself. Lian let go his arm. Thaorinn shifted around on the rock, half turned away, perhaps expecting him to leave. But the ache of his father's failure felt like his own; he could not move, trying to find some comfort to offer.

Thaorinn roused himself. 'I was unfair to expect you to follow my path and not yours, and to blame you for it when it seemed no longer possible.'

'You're sure – not – *possible*. For me.'

'Of course . . .' Thaorinn began, then stopped, insight coming at last. Lian could see him gathering himself – to lie and reassure, Lian thought; he thought he could not bear it. 'You've been severely injured,' Thaorinn said. 'There is bound to be some impairment . . . I am sorry you have been made to feel stigmatized by it. Burdanians tend to be arrogant about their mental capacities.' He closed his eyes briefly. 'And I have

59

inflicted that on you. Please understand, the distortion is mine. Your recovery has been remarkable; your disabilities may be surmountable in normal interaction. And my ... apparent rejection has come of a disappointment of hopes which I had no right to harbour. I ask ... I beg ... your forgiveness.'

'Always,' Lian said, in a voice barely more than a whisper. He could find no comfort in his father's unsparing choice of truth over lie. Nor any irony in Thaorinn's apparent assumption that he, Lian, should accept the disabilities that Thaorinn could not.

Thaorinn pivoted suddenly to face him, leaning forward. 'Do not *go*, Lian,' he said. 'You do not remember everything that happened, while *I* do. I would not like you to be faced with it before you are ready.'

'When will – I be ready?'

'Think what you would be rejecting if you went back there,' Thaorinn said, and then lifted his hands, signing rapidly: *I was twice your age when I first came to a* kinder'vos *and I will live here on sufferance for the rest of my days, for I will never shed my Burdanian modes of thought and perception. You are so different. Let me give you but one example. When I sign, I am translating my thoughts; when you sign, you are expressing yours.*

'I – sign—' Lian said. 'More than I – speak.'

'You sign as one born to it. You may be Burdanian genetically and physiologically, but the *kinder'el'ein* who came to the colony after your accident would not have come for any Burdanian child. You owe your sanity to them. You are beloved and uniquely accepted amongst them. Amongst any community of *kinder'el'ein*, here, or elsewhere, you have a place now and for the rest of your life.'

'We – hurt them—' Lian said.

Thaorinn's hand brushed Lian's hood lightly, and then lingered above his head, not quite touching. Then he drew back his hand, his expression set. *Lian*, he signed, *this will be the last shuttle. We will send a request, from ourselves and from the* kinder'el'ein, *and the colony will respect the* kinder'el'ein *if they will not respect us. I intend to die as a* kindereen, *and when I am dead, Sara may do as she pleases. But as of today, there will be no more shuttles; what disturbances we feel will be of our own making,*

60

and subject to our own choosing. He paused. *You will have no reason to hurt the* kinder'el'ein, *if you choose to live as one. I hoped that you would choose to live amongst the* kinder'el'ein *for different reasons, of the insights you might have gained, but now I wish only for your happiness, your acceptance, which I believe you would find more surely amongst them than amongst Burdanians.*

Because of my handicaps, Lian signed, understanding all too well.

Unsparingly, Thaorinn spoke aloud. 'Even so.'

Lian lowered his head, and looked at the rain-speckled stones before his knees. 'It's not – choice,' Lian said, in Burdanian.

'What is not a choice?'

'Staying. Not to know – if I could be better.'

'Lian,' Thaorinn started, and then turned his head away, restraining his honesty. 'It is raining,' he said at last, though it had been raining for a while, a spattering. Thaorinn rose to his feet, using a hand behind him on the boulder.

A raindrop struck his eyelid as Lian looked up. 'Thaor— Father—' The robed figure went still, uncertain how to respond to this address. Lian scrambled to his feet, starting, *Why did you*, and then breaking off to catch his hood as it slipped. Nothing, no small lapse in propriety, must prejudice his father. *Why did you leave the colony after you almost won the debate?*

Thaorinn's black eyes narrowed slightly. 'Almost won?' he said, aloud. 'Eight votes was no less a loss than eighty. It was all very long ago.' He looked at Lian for a long moment, and when he spoke again, the tone was different, deliberate.

'I put everything of myself into that debate,' Thaorinn said, in Burdanian, watching him to be certain of his understanding. 'I woke and found that nothing had changed, that the heart and spirit which I had laid out for dissection was merely another show in the Archives. No matter how simple it was, how simple the justice, the right of it, the necessity of it, they would not vote to go back. Everything about the colony seemed to me utterly repugnant.'

He paused, and looked at Lian. The warm rain was leaving dark streaks on his headdress and blotches on his shoulders.

'Lone travel through the jungle was more difficult than I

expected,' he said, conversationally. 'I went from having my every need provided for to providing entirely for myself. My second attempt at building a raft was sufficiently riverworthy to start me downstream, though by the time I reached the sea I was paddling my fourth.' He gave his son a sardonic smile. 'I stumbled on *kinder'el'ein* living in an abandoned *kinder'vos*. They looked after me as best they could. When I could, I moved on. I lived four years like that, learning from *kinder'el'ein* who were willing to take me in, and from my own mistakes. Knowing what I know now, I do not think all my encounters were accidents. Eventually my wanderings brought me here. And I realized that here was where I wished to stay. I certainly, at that point, never believed that anyone else would wish to stay with me.' Lian knew he was thinking of Sara. Did Thaorinn know that Sara was tiring of her struggle with silence, and yearning to be a Burdanian amongst Burdanians again? Had he any idea that she had advised Lian to leave, and what would he do if *she* also decided to leave? He would be alone, with his courtesies and disciplines, in his self-imposed isolation.

'Come,' Thaorinn said. 'There is no need to get wet.'

Lian gave him a startled glance, but he had already turned away, leaving, not leading. In the archway he paused and looked back at Lian, thoughtfully, but not as he might look at someone who might soon leave. It came to him that Thaorinn's manner had changed from the moment Lian had asked about his leaving. As though he thought that, by asking how he had come to leave the colony, Lian was letting him know that he wished to do the same.

'Thaorinn!' he said suddenly, half rising. Thaorinn stepped back into view in response. But Lian could not think what next to say.

Thaorinn walked back to him, reaching out his hand, though he did not touch Lian, only offered guidance. The offered hand, and the assumptions behind it, made Lian speak. 'I – can't. I'm – I'm going back. With Thovalt.'

There was a silence. Thaorinn closed his eyes for a long moment, his face almost impassive.

'I – would stay here, but – I would stay – as *we* stay – because

62

– I am not – I am not brave enough – to go back. That is – not choice. Not freedom.' He did not want to tell Thaorinn that Sara had spoken to him about choice: he did not want his father taking the decision away from *him* and laying it upon Sara. And had it only been that, he might not have gone. But to stay here, on *kindereen* sufferance, because he did not dare take his handicaps back to the colony . . . He would not do that.

Thaorinn suddenly reached out and gripped his shoulders hard enough to hurt. Thaorinn's thin lips parted, but he seemed unable to find the words he needed. He simply held him for a long moment, staring into his face. Then he said in a low voice, 'You know what happens to courage there.'

Lian caught his father's wrist, unable to speak, and unsure whether he wanted to hold or push away Thaorinn's hand. The rain fell more heavily around and upon them. The *meer* began to uncrease, to ease out across the pool again, quivering slightly. Thaorinn let his hands slide from Lian's shoulders, and Lian, in automatic response, released him. 'Goodbye,' Thaorinn said. 'I wish you—' He would not lie, but his voice held no hope. 'I wish you well.'

And he turned, and walked away beneath the arch, without looking back.

FIVE

BURDANIA

Lian was awakened by the sound of footsteps outside in the hall. Darkness pressed down on his face. 'Light,' he said. No light came. He reached out for a switch which was not there, overbalanced and put his hand down hard on a silky wooden floor. He lay, hand throbbing slightly, remembering where he was: Burdania.

The darkness was not as absolute as it first seemed: starlight filtered around the canvas over the window. He started to get up, but the blankets restrained him. He had lashed thongs to toggle, mindful of his masquerade. He freed himself, and let the starlight guide his outstretched hands to cold canvas. He thought to untie the hanging until he released the first corner and felt the chill draught wash over his hands. He left that corner folded back, for a little light, and made his way back to the table, found his lamp and a striker, and after too many tries, lit the lamp. His own face wavered before him in the polished metal, sleep-stunned and pallid with cold.

He was chilled, having slept in his insulating underclothes; his feet were numb. He had to move. He pulled on his cold trousers and the sweater, socks and sandals he had taken from the shelves outside, retied the windowshade, folded his bedclothes . . . Recognized that he was stalling, afraid to go out amongst them now that the early euphoria of meeting had evaporated. He paced to the window and back twice, gathering his wits, and lifted the lamp before he remembered the relic in the hall.

He looked over the balcony as the ship-bellied door opened

to admit two cloaked figures, Lara, and a young man with a bulky satchel on one shoulder. Zharlinn and Vylan were there immediately. The young man said, in a restrained voice, 'Where is Valancy?'

'Through here,' Vylan said, and stood aside to let the other pass, and followed him. Zharlinn said, 'Tion; that's a relief.'

Lara said, 'He's the medic I looked for. How is she?'

'Doesn't look any worse than some of the births I've seen, but she keeps saying it feels harder than her first one. Tor's panicking.'

'Tion'll deal with them. And he won't complain about being got out of bed, even if we should have managed it ourselves . . . Hello, Lian,' she hailed him. 'We woke you, did we? You could be in a *carhaun* by the morning.'

Chance presence hardly entitled him to belong to a parental group, Lian thought. He climbed carefully down the ladder, eyes closed, and trailed after them through to the common room.

Valancy sat in the same chair, cushions stuffed behind her back, blankets spilled around her feet. Her hair was pulled out of its braid and spread in a brown tangled veil over her shoulders and the cushions. She was dragging her fingers through it, tugging at the knots. Tor crouched beside her, gripping a fold of her shift and looking white and distressed. He said, 'Tion!' accusingly as Tion paused to unpack several dark-wrapped bundles on to the sideboard beside the dis-mantled relics.

'He came as quickly as he could,' Lara snapped.

Valancy said, blinking back tears, 'Sorry, I shouldn't have . . .'

'I would rather lose sleep for birth than illness,' Tion said, crossing to her and dropping to balance on one knee.

Valancy panted, saying between gasps, 'It doesn't feel right. It's become so hard so quickly.'

Tion felt her abdomen with firm hands. 'Lara says you have not felt well all day.'

'No.' She pulled at her snared hand, and Tion caught it and freed it. 'Somebody find a comb,' he said, absently. To Valancy, 'I would say this baby is well started, which would be why you were feeling unwell. If you want to stay in this room, we're going to need clean sheets, boiled water, all the usual . . .' He looked around at Vylan. 'And soon.' Vylan ducked wordlessly under the rust-coloured curtain. Tion said to Zharlinn, 'That autoclave you made works beautifully: what we now need is a waterproof packaging which does not melt. Waxed paper or fabric is useless.' Valancy made a low sound in the back of her throat, face contorting.

'Nobody's ever satisfied,' said Zharlinn, sounding tense. He bent over Valancy, gently moving hair off her face while he waited for her to relax. ''Lance,' he said, 'do you want to have the baby here or in Tor's and your room? Or somewhere else?'

Valancy opened her eyes. 'Is it all right?'

'Aye,'Lance. It is all right. You are nearer to giving birth than we thought. Where do you want to have the baby?'

She focused on Tor, seemed for a moment not to recognize him, and then visibly collected herself, and said, 'Tor's room, yes.'

'Valancy,' Tor began, 'you should stay here. You shouldn't—'

Valancy heaved herself to her feet. They closed around her, moving to support and then to lift her, Zharlinn at her back, Tor and Lara holding her legs. She clutched at their sleeves, fingers sinking into the knit. Seeing them, together, Lian was assailed by a loneliness which went beyond simply being amongst strangers. He pushed blindly through the curtain. Knowing they would be coming after him, he pushed on, across the little vestibule, through another curtain, moss green this time, and found himself in a kitchen, looking at three steaming pots on a crude stove, and Vylan.

Lian stared at him, making no sense of his face. Fine features, faded hair, unfaded eyes of blue-green. Neither grandparent nor other colony elder. He felt pitched back into his seventh year, when he found himself astray in a full-grown world which knew him far better than he did it.

Vylan gave him a parental look, and then turned back to his pots. 'Have a seat, Lian. I am sorry you were wakened after so long a journey.' As he lifted lids, he talked on, soothingly. ''Lance is fine. Tor is in a fret because his mother died in childbirth; that is neither here nor there. Valancy's already had one child with no trouble . . . she's with her father's kin, up North.'

The curtain was pushed aside. '*We're* not wanted,' Lara said sourly, coming through, with Zharlinn following. 'But 'Lance is asking for you, and Tion's been up half the night already and so he would like an infusion of *cinnaran.*'

'*Cinnaran,*' Vylan said. 'Tion works too hard.'

The kitchen had the same warm, moist smell of compost, overlaid by the mingled aromas of the cords of spices hung either side of the door, and woodsmoke. The sink was salvaged from the ruins, battered but decorative, light green against the plastered wall. There was a tap, but Lian could see only darkness through the window above it and hesitated to ask whether the water was supplied by pump, or hand-carried to an outside cistern. The stove was a neatly fashioned stone chamber with a metal top, tarnished with concentric rings of oxidation where the flame licked from beneath. They must be below his room; little wonder it was warmer than outside.

Zharlinn startled Lian by tracking his gaze, saying suddenly: 'You see where those two branches come off on either side . . .' Just below the ceiling the ridge of chimney broadened and then forked. 'There are three conduits, smoke through the central one, air through the others. They run through a series of bends before they divide to exchange the heat. We can bring the heat down with fans, sun-driven, from parts of relics, or wind-driven, our own design, if the compost underneath isn't enough . . . the whole underside of this building is compost bays. Everything that we can gather in goes to compost, which keeps us warm and sweet-smelling over the winter, and then gets dug in after the flooding . . .'

'Zhar!' Beads of water ricocheted off the stove top. Zharlinn snatched up a cloth from the table and leaped to rescue the smallest pot. Lara lifted a bottle full of reddish powder down from the shelves and measured a small spoonful into a clay mug. 'Not too much,' she murmured to herself. 'He might want some sleep later on.' Zharlinn filled it, stirred it, and topped it with cold water. He lifted it, then hesitated, and said to Lian, 'You take it through. Other side of the vestibule, second right.' Lara quirked a glance at him, but said nothing.

It was a room a little larger than his, lit by four lamps, three around the bed, and one on the table where Tion was carefully unwrapping his bundles. Twists of coarse fabric, several small jugs and a packet of fine knives: the tools of his trade. Vylan nursed the guttering flame of the lamp on the far side of the bed. Valancy lay uneasily on her side, a blanket twisted over her. Tor tried to smooth the blanket; she kicked out irritably against it and rolled away from him.

'Thank you,' Tion said, taking the mug from Lian, and draining it in a single, unhurried draught. His youth surprised Lian: he could be no older than Lara, but his profession had already left its mark. His expression was guarded and assessing.

He glanced down and lowered the mug, its edge caught one of the jugs. Lian reacted just quickly enough to stop it from rolling off the edge. Tion, still holding the mug, looked down at the smear of spilled black liquor and the fallen stopper. He said in a low voice, 'I should have brought a better light.'

It was not an ordinary observation. Lian drew breath, but before he could decide what to say, Tor said, 'Tion!' as Valancy groaned, arching. Lian lifted the mug from his hands, and let him go. He wiped table and jug clean, and put the jug neatly beside the others. That seemed important. Tion was talking in a low, steady voice to Valancy.

In the vestibule Lian gave himself no chance to think. He put the mug on the floor and climbed the ladder, intent on reaching the lamp before his vertigo took a grip. He unhooked the bag and looped it over his wrist. The shadows danced around him.

When he stepped back into Valancy's room all the corners of the room sharpened. Even Valancy raised herself up on her elbow, blinking, to stare at it and him. 'I – thought you might – find this useful,' he said to the young medic.

Tion came forward, hand extended to accept the lamp, face expressionless. The fierce light revealed a milky smear marring both pupils.

Before Lian could react, Lara arrived with a steaming bowl and clean, undyed cloths slung over her arm. 'So that's what's become of it,' she said, of the lamp. 'This what you need, Tion?'

'Lara,' Valancy said. Lara looked a challenge at Tor, and then crossed to take the offered hand, letting Valancy pull her down on to her knees. Tion said, to Lian, 'I have what I need for now.' He seemed to struggle with himself before saying, 'Thank you.'

Zharlinn was sitting at the kitchen table, brooding on his interlaced hands. 'You took your time.'

'Yes – I had an additional – errand.' Lian sat down across the table from him. His shoulder bumped the cords of hanging herbs and bulbs and they whispered as they shifted. Pots burped and steamed. Lian noticed an easing in chest and throat after the dry air outside. For a long moment he and Zharlinn merely sat across from each other at the table. Then Lian said, 'This – evening you were talking about – communications. Over distance.'

'We know it can be done,' Zharlinn said, tightly. 'The Islanders remember; some of them used it even after Linn, but when those units broke down, there were no spare parts. Because of Linn. They work by turning light and sound into a kind of pulse,' he brought his hands together, 'and throw it through the air, or along a transparent wire. I can make the wire ones work, and,' he said, growing animated, 'we've found where the wires used to run along the coast. I've been able to send a signal all the way down to Ardar from the delta, but the wires across Lltharran have been damaged, and we cannot lay them again, even if we could find another leftover . . .'

Lara D'Alna thrust through the curtain. 'More towels,' she rapped. Zharlinn hurried, pulling woven towels from the shelves and flinging them over her arm. They heard a groaning cry from the other side of the house. Lara grinned tightly at both of them, in parting. 'Courage, men. Soon be over.'

Zharlinn said, tightly, 'What were we talking about?'

'Communication,' said Lian. He lowered his head almost to his hands, thinking how utterly unprepared he was for this. He could not shake off a sense of unreality; he *dared* not shake off a sense of unreality. It was his shield. For a long moment, he wished simply to confess who he was and where from, to help them and . . . spare himself from knowing any more. The cry came again. He heeded it; it was all he could do.

69

'There's the rain,' he heard Zharlinn say. Looking up, Lian saw nothing but the blackness of the window, framing Zharlinn's light head as he leaned forward to peer out. His breath left a smudge of fog. 'She said it would ... I don't suppose it will make much difference. There's been enough snow on the watershed to drown the city twice over.' He turned, leaning back against the sink, and said with a weary shift of sweatered shoulders, 'We've held back the river for two springs. But this year – this winter— Even the *isk'dar* acknowledges there's little hope of keeping all parts of the city unflooded, even with double dyking.'

'You think the – the *isk'dar* is wrong – to stay – here?'

'She is the finest of her line,' Zharlinn said directly. 'As you will learn for yourself.'

He is in love with her, Lian thought, and found that that made her more a person. Zharlinn, too. He relaxed, too much, and said, 'But still – the *isk'dar* seems to have too much – authority – here—' Zharlinn bridled. Lian said hastily, 'Forgive me, but I am – trying to understand how Lltharan is – governed. I am an outsider; I do not feel that I can afford – mistakes.' He was rather proud of that little speech, the most truth he had uttered since his arrival. 'If I – disagree with the *isk'dar*, what will happen to me?'

'If it affects only yourself and no one else, it does not matter. If not, then the *isk'dar* decides.'

'And if I – persist—'

Zharlinn measured him with his eye. 'We might ignore you. But if not, we would choose whether to turn you out. If another *caurim* took you in, you could remain in Lltharan, and if not, you would have to leave, or go hungry.'

There was a silence. 'Thank you,' Lian said – but then another question occurred to him, and before common sense could censor it, he had asked it, 'It does not trouble you, being – subordinate—'

'Should it?'

'My people,' Lian said, concentrating on his choice of words, 'decided large matters together, some – spoke for, some against, and the ones who – heard, voted.'

70

'Some people say we did that before Linn Travassa,' Zharlinn said, distractedly.

'Why – change?' Lian said.

Zharlinnn was not listening; he waved Lian silent. Lian heard only the spitting of the rain on the window. Then, suddenly, there came a choppy cry, quick footsteps, and Lara swept aside the curtain and stood bouncing slightly on wide-set feet.

'It's born?' Zharlinn said.

'Long, healthy, male, and black-headed as its father.'

Zharlinn met up with her in two strides and swept her round in a full circle, her flying feet narrowly missing Lian and the table. 'Life, man!' she protested, grabbing his wrists reflexively. 'What'll you be like when it's one of yours!'

Zharlinn set her down. His expression was that of a man whose dearest assumptions were not shared. But he said only, 'I'm going to see them.'

'But Zhar—' Lara began, reaching after him to no avail. She stood, as left, in the middle of the floor. 'So, *you* can help clean up,' she said after him. She gave Lian a wry glance, and cut across to the shelves to reach for a pot. Abruptly, she stopped, one hand hooked over the shelf, and muttered under her voice. Something, plainly, had just come to her.

Lian said, 'He – has children?'

'None to be certain of.'

Her tone was final. She lifted a sealed bottle filled with yellow jelly off one of the lower shelves. 'You can set out mugs and rolls,' she said.

Vylan, Tion and Zharlinn trooped in, Vylan carrying a heavy clay bowl with a cloth spread over it, which Lara glanced at with distaste. He crouched and pushed it beneath the sink. Tion crossed to the stove, and spread wet hands above the hot plate. His sleeves were rolled up to mid forearm and buttoned in place. He glanced aside at Lian and said in a low voice. 'Did they tell me your name and I not listen?'

'Not that I – heard. Lian D'Halldt – upper C'Rynn reach.'

'Tion. Of *tayn* D'Suran and the Medics' Guild.'

His reserve gave Lian's inquisitiveness no purchase. Lian held his peace, thinking again how very young Tion was, to

71

have such knowledge of life and death, and such fears of infirmity. He watched Tion absently rub his eyes, and then look up, sharply aware of Lian's attention. Lian saw tangled denial, hope, and guilt. He would have yielded to the impulse to draw at that tangle, but at that moment Vylan said, 'Tion, there's a bed for you here for the rest of the night.'

'It's foul out there,' Zharlinn added. 'They know where to find you, if they need you.'

'They shouldn't,' Tion said, glanced once more at Lian, guardedly, and went to the table, rubbing his hands together lightly. 'Though I believe I said that of tonight.'

'We could deny you were here.'

'No,' Tion said, sharply. 'Don't do that.'

Lara put a hand on his arm. 'I was joking. I know you'd never allow it.'

'Forgive me,' Tion said, and loosened his sleeves, drawing them down.

Lara nudged Lian aside and served the broth. Tion, Vylan and Lian sat down to drink, Lara stood beside the table, feet well apart, Zharlinn eased his shoulder between cords of drying herbs and sipped one-handed. Quiet prevailed. The broth was sour and more salt than Lian cared for, but the strong taste focused his attention.

Tion drained the mug as efficiently as he had drained the *cinnaran* earlier, rose, and handed it to Lara. 'I will come by in the morning.'

Vylan said, 'Before you go, Tion, take a look through our herbs. You can have any you can use.'

Tion threaded the ropes of drying leaves and bulbs through his hands one by one. Lian asked him for their names and medicinal use, knowing Lors would be interested, and the grave young man told him. Lian knew some from the habitats, and others only from Archival accounts of transgenic plants. More an exercise in aesthetics than for production; micro-organisms and fungi were much more efficient producers. But the micro-organisms required special broths, and the plants only careful cultivation, and so the plants alone survived.

Tion continued his methodical search through the mongrel array of jars and pots on the narrow shelves. Some of the jars were of polymers, or glass, clearly relics; others were clay, quite delicate, glazed an iridescent blue or bronze. Lian lifted a little pot and turned it in his hand, raising the stopper. Crumbled blue leaf scabbed the plug. Vylan reached over and gently pushed the stopper back into the neck.

'Careful,' he said, mildly. 'That's dried *sonol*.' Lian went still, and let Vylan take the bottle from his hands. *Sonol* was one not grown in the habitats: the new leaves were extremely poisonous. 'Not nearly as poisonous as the fresh leaf, but still not the kind of thing wants spilling in a kitchen. I had quite forgotten it was there. Somebody – who was it, now? – left it on passing through last summer.' Lian's murmured apology lapsed as he saw Rathla Zharlinn staring at the bottle with an appalled, sickened expression. Zharlinn's eyes followed it as Vylan held it out to Tion saying, 'Here. It belongs better in *tayn* D'Suran.'

As Tion tucked the bottle away, Zharlinn came back to himself; he glanced up, checking he was unobserved. Lian barely looked away in time. To Tion, he said, 'What does *sonol* – do? Medicinally?' he was inspired to add.

'It's an *Islander* plant,' Zharlinn said, a rasp to his voice.

Tion apportioned small piles of dried leaves, bulbs and powder. 'Correctly prepared, sun-dried and aired, and carefully administered, it is a diuretic; it relieves water retention. Incorrectly prepared or improperly administered, it could kill through dehydration and exhaustion.'

Rathla Zharlinn muttered something brusque and unintelligible, and pushed his way out through the hanging. Vylan noted his leaving, with a slight, perplexed frown. Then set it aside to help Tion gather his takings into his satchel.

When Tion had gone, Lian said, 'He – seems so young – to do – what he does.'

Vylan said, 'Did word come to you about the D'Suran plague?'

As Lian hesitated, undecided whether to feign knowledge, Vylan continued, 'Four winters ago – just at the end of the *isk'dar*'s first year – an illness broke out among the D'Suran. Not uncommon, for wintering conditions, but this one killed nearly all the young children, and more than half of the elder members of the *tayn*. It left Kylara, Tion's sister, as *cal* D'Suran. She brought her brothers and sister to Lltharran, to the Medics' Guild. So many of the others came with her, or left the North, that *tayn* D'Suran no longer exists.'

Tor joined them, carrying his newborn son. He shouldered aside the curtain with care and stood uncertainly before them, holding the baby stiffly. To Lian, more accustomed to *kinder'el'ein* infants than to Burdanians, it seemed a small, improbable scrap, with its blotched, miniature face and minute pad of black hair. In the garden of the *kinder'vos* Lian had gathered seeds larger than its hands. He stood back as Vylan and Lara went to Tor. Vylan guided Tor's hold into an easier cradling. Lara stroked the infant's tiny face, and worked her finger into one small fist. Lian wanted to offer something. He said, 'What – will you call him?'

They turned to look at him, shocked. Tor said, harshly, 'Nors.'

Lian stepped back. Tor's black eyes followed him. 'Yes,' the young man said. 'I have no *tayn*. I am *tarwyn*.'

Tarwyn, Taridwyn, Taridwyni. *Exiled*. 'Why?' Lian said, shakily.

He heard Lara's indrawn breath. Tor's expression tried for scorn, and failed.

Vylan broke the silence. 'He has been unjustly treated. His name should be Tor D'Vandras, and he is from *tayn* D'Vandras, in the mountains.'

Lian started to apologize, and Tor said, 'You have only *said* what others *think* when they hear my name. I would rather have it *said*. Ask me! Ask me what I have *done*, and I will tell you. I am not ashamed. I have held opinions which are a threat to the survival of my people. *Restorer* opinions, in the rarified air of *tayn* D'Vandras. But *here* I find that I am no restorer at all.'

There was a silence.

He said to Lian, 'That is why I go nameless.'

'*Cal* D'Vandras, Illuan D'Vandras, is one of the strongest opponents to the restoration effort,' Vylan said, simply.

'Why does he – oppose?' Lian said.

Vylan had a hand on Tor's arm, gentling him. 'Linn did not cause the ruin of Lltharran,' he said. 'He merely completed it.

Before Linn, something happened, some event of great violence and destructiveness, which reduced Lltharran, the Sor, and Greater D'Alna to semi-desert and ruin. We do not know what happened. Illuan D'Vandras, and others, fear that its cause is still hidden in those ruins, and that in our restoration efforts we may unwittingly come upon it.'

Transceiver held in chilled, resolute hands, Lian waited until the celebration downstairs had faded, and the last footsteps passed his door, Lara's, with an irrepressible skip and shuffle. Vylan knocked on the door, asking if he needed anything. He said not. He blew out his lamp, knowing from the jungle that darkness sharpened the senses, and opened the channel.

'Shuttle, it is I – Lian.'

Thovalt's voice rippled from the speaker, 'I am here, I hear, I heard. So they have put us out of their minds. What an affront to our self-regard! What an insult to all our cherished angst.'

'Thovalt,' Lian forestalled a verbal riff, 'will you – talk to the others – for me?' He remembered Lors' accusation of manipulating mouthpieces. But this was too vital to risk by his own inadequacies. 'I mean to – I offer to stay. I *cannot* – come back now. Not, having begun, having – seen—' Valancy and her son; Tor; Tion D'Suran's clouded eyes; their history as obliterated as their technology . . . '*Make* them – let me stay.'

'Ah, but is it up to us? You are there and we are here . . .'

'I said I – had a pack – supplies – with me.'

'Truth emerges . . .'

'My bag – it is of natural fabric, woven. Like theirs.'

'Hardly,' Thovalt said drily. The bag, a substantial satchel woven of cellulose thread, was decorated with the vast natural palette of the jungle. Thovalt insisted he could hear warp rubbing against woof, chirruping in the darkness of Lian's locker.

'Put plain-clothing. Warm. Anything anyone – thinks I need.'

'Simple though your tastes may be, you aspire very high, impersonating a fisherman amongst fishermen.'

'Some must not – go to sea. And I do not – these restorers will not talk about – what they *know*. They are more interested in – the unknown. If I do not – stay, how can we learn?'

'And if your masquerade fails, what then? We cannot help you. They seem averse to drowning, which is all to the good; but are they averse to drowning *you*?'

'My – masquerade,' Lian said, slowly, 'can – only fail if I am known for – what I *am*. How – can anyone know me for – an outworlder, if – nobody knows that – Burdanians left Burdania?'

There was a silence. Lian listened to the harmonics of the wind in the cracks in the roof. For all his verbal brilliance, Thovalt was not an incisive reasoner, and could be taken unawares by a simple argument. He did not like to be; it inflicted a wound deeper than pride; and he could be cruel in retaliation.

Then Thovalt said, 'Should I agree to put it to them, and should they agree to let you continue, how do we get this pack to you?'

Lian did not answer too quickly, though he had the place chosen. 'Follow – the riverbank until you see the remains of – a sloping paved area with steps, and bays. Leave it – in one of the bays. Nobody lives between there and where – you are. If one of you could bring it – tonight, please. I can collect it as I return—'

'Return from where?'

'If I – talk again in daylight – I might be caught.' This, too, he had thought out. It was strategic; it was also frank cowardice. 'If I – find the pack I will know you – agree. If I do not – I will come back. To the ship.'

'Yes, but Li,' Thovalt persisted, 'I distinctly heard you say the word "return".'

'From *caur'isk'dari*,' Lian said. 'I am going to see – the *isk'dar*.'

SIX

TARIDWYN

Sunset chased them across the jungle. They flew north, and east. Through clear panels by his feet, Lian watched the cushioned canopy turn dusky and then dark. It was so far below it intrigued without moving him. Not like the wrenching, dizzying sight of the *kinder'vos* tumbling away from him. He had been so nearly ill that Thovalt closed the panels and made him look up at the raindrops bursting on the hood. Later, when the clouds broke, unveiling the stars, Thovalt took them so high that Lian could see the arc of the horizon, and the last blush of light. Hidden by that blush was Burdania's blue-white star.

They came upon the dome before Lian knew it. Thovalt gave no warning. Lian glimpsed something pale below, and looked down on a huge, pale swelling, unlit and flecked with fallen leaves. He leaned forward, able to see a sketch of a lattice, and, as they passed overhead, the lustre of the surface . . .

'That's it,' Thovalt confirmed.

In cautious glances Lian took it in. The main complex was beyond the dome, six long buildings arranged three parallel, one across, two parallel, all connected by corridors. Around them were the habitat vaults, each a Burdanian microenvironment. Most were in darkness, with only ground lighting casting fans across paths and patios. But two blazed light, impersonating long tropical days. In one Lian glimpsed swimmers, limbs flicking in water as pale as ice. Jungle-reared, he had found all the habitats cold and alien. He remembered holding snow in

77

his bare little hands, and crying at the ache it left. The experiment had gone unrepeated, too energy-expensive, unrealistic and disturbing, to old and young alike.

He pushed against his harness to look behind Thovalt's seat. The settlement where he had been reared was immediately adjacent to the colony. He could see a dull glint of river, but no lanterns. Thovalt was wearing a waveshift visor, and had earlier offered Lian one; through it Lian saw blue sky, blue jungle, blue sea, yellow sun, and shimmering edges. Unavoidable distortion, Thovalt explained. He thought of it now, but he did not reach for it, would not look for his first home through circuitry. He would see it truly soon enough.

Suddenly the vegetation below gave way to flat blackness. Lian turned his head, knowing as he saw it what he would see. In a sunken hangar as large as the complex itself was the flattened lathe of the one preserved driveship. Illuminated constantly and just enough to show its shape, size and presence. Lights spotted panels and edges, and pieced the fragments together. The colony had been built of the substance of its two siblings, and it had been sealed in its sarcophagus and never boarded since. The atmosphere around it was unbreatheable.

Lian's fingers ached, clenched in his robe. It is only a *thing*, he told himself. Only an instrument. And sealed in and surrounded by poisoned air so that it might never be entered again.

But why not destroyed?

The thought slid into his mind like a lathe. And as though the shuttle had itself run into something like that question, they lurched in the air and stopped, rocking. A blue rectangle switched on beneath them. Thovalt said, 'Nice to know we're welcome . . . Going down.' Lian held his breath, disorientated by the arrays of flickering lights, while Thovalt manoeuvred, then said: 'Release.' They dropped sickeningly, bounced upon air, and settled.

'One accepts challenges as they come.' Thovalt doffed his visor and hooked his arm back over his chair. He looked very tired. 'If you wait here, I'll be up in a moment.'

Humid air washed in, heavy with the smell of new rain. The

78

jungle shouted a many-voiced greeting. Though the sky was almost clear, the landing field was a continent of shallow lakes.

Lian looked out into the living darkness, and inhaled jungle.

'Unless you want to come underground.' Thovalt reached over to key open Lian's harness. Lian climbed down. He stepped over the blazing blue channel. When he turned the shuttle was already sinking. Thovalt, suspended in his illuminated cockpit, sat without moving. The lights suddenly went out, and for a moment the man was only a dim shape in the blue flare and then the flare went out. A moment later the barren platform slid back into place. Muted mechanical sounds continued from underground. Lian was alone in the moon-light.

Sa'stress'eel was at its height, half full; Kré's sliver snagged cloud over the jungle; Kilureel winked through the canopy as the leaves shifted. His moonshadows pulled in two directions, a stout, dark one towards the jungle, a long, pale one towards the colony. He had a third shadow, cast off a single light along the boundary wall. As he looked for the lamps of the settlement, that light glared in his eye.

He thought of Jahde.

When he went to say goodbye to the old *kindereen* he realized that a part of him still longed to hide away while Jahde set things right. Jahde sensed this, for *kin* did not anticipate him, but continued with *kin* pestling. Lian smelled sweet pollen in the air, and the little that spilled was bright yellow.

'Jahde,' Lian said, 'I'm going with Thovalt.'

'Yes.' The word was perfectly timed, neither too soon nor too late. Lian thought of the times the old *kindereen* had waited out his efforts at speech, or nursed him through his headaches, or explained how to recognize fruiting plants though both knew Lian could never use the knowledge.

He signed: *I came to say goodbye.*

Jahde laid down *kin* pestle, Lian thought to sign. But instead Jahde reached out to brush his temples just above where the receptors should be in a *kinder'el'ein* child. Lian closed his eyes, trying to decide whether he might risk an embrace. He longed to feel the hard ridge of *kin* ribcage against his cheek. He felt Jahde's hands on his shoulders, and opened his eyes,

79

thinking Jahde must have sensed his rising impulse and be turning it aside. Slowly, leaning on him, the elder *kindereen* knelt. Lian stared into the liquid eyes, now just above the level of his own, not believing he understood. Jahde waited. Lian raised his hand and with great care pushed back the wings of *kin* caul. There, the empathic receptors lay in a pit of puckered skin. Under his fingers Jahde's skin was as soft as dust. He hesitated; the receptors were excruciatingly sensitive to a misplaced touch. At that hesitation, Jahde's nictating membrane closed and he felt the skin under his fingers contract as the receptors drew in. Lian jerked his hands away, snagging the caul. He quelled the impulse to demand why *he* had been offered this. The *kindereen* watched him for a moment, offering no explanation, then passed a heavy hand over his cauled head, and, leaning upon him, got to *kin* feet. But that was all.

He understood this much: Jahde had treated him as an adult, granting him the parting of equals. He did not know why, whether for something he had done or something *kin* thought he might.

'Still here?' Thovalt said, from behind him. He gathered Lian up with a hand on his back, and started towards that irksome single light. Lian's robe bound his ankles, for want of grass to snag on, and between that and Thovalt's pressing hand he felt on the verge of stumbling. But it was Thovalt whose foot turned on some irregularity, and Lian stepped away as he recovered, and away again as Thovalt reached for him.

'I can – walk—' he blurted.

Thovalt snatched back the hand and started on, stretching his stride. Lian hitched up his robe and hurried over.

They went through a gap in the wall, beneath the light, and up a short path. It was groundlit, and Lian caught himself trying to step up into the hard spray of each light. He had an impression of untidy growth on either side, jungle efflorescence. They reached a closed door; Thovalt touched it, and it opened. The light from inside dazzled Lian. He baulked.

'Nothing's going to bite you,' Thovalt said, equally careless assurance and mild insult.

Lian slid his foot over the step and on to the smooth floor.

The blue-white was beginning to take on depth before him, if not shape.

Thovalt's voice said: 'We're in one of the scientific sections –xenogeography, xenobiology – near this end so novel native samples aren't tracked through the colony. Not so long ago we'd both have been directed to scans, though they *had* graduated past automatic total decontamination . . .'

Lian raised his hood, pulling the hem down over his eyes. He used the edge to blot away dazzled tears. They turned into another blue-white tunnel. This one was glazed along one side, and looked out into a garden. The glaring illumination turned vegetable colours gaudy and made the edges of leaves knifelike. Lian slowed, trailing his fingertips on the chilly glass. He saw that there was glass on the far side, and glass overhead. The lights left flitting voids on his field of vision. 'Tropical habitat,' Thovalt offered over his shoulder. 'Equatorial islands. The real accomplishment is at the other end—'

Near the end of the corridor, the land sank down to a miniature beach. A lava tongue and a small bib of black-bronze sand lay peaceably side by side, with no tide to disturb them, on the shores of a miniature painted sea. 'Come round here,' Thovalt said, and led him around and down to a sunken bay off the corridor, a bubble of glass below the water. 'There,' he said. 'Go down.'

Lian did, step by step, and fetched up against the glass. Under the false sunlight the water had a milky, diatomaceous lustre. The lava tongue was a black silhouette in a pallid veil. His advent had startled away a school of small fish grazing on the algae which mottled the window. As he watched, they returned, moving in precise formation, showing him oblate profiles and then narrow heads and little fins feathering the water. He did not move as they settled into his shadow.

'You do that well,' Thovalt said from behind him. He glimpsed the reflection of a glossy shoulder, the spike of a silver badge. 'I wouldn't let them feel too safe—' Something shot out of the translucent murk towards him, orange maw open. Thovalt rapped the glass, and the browsers scattered like bursting seeds. The newcomer thudded against the glass, and sculled back with a ripple of black fins.

81

'Foxed you,' Thovalt said. Lian turned to him, and he evaded Lian's eyes, a self-mocking smile on his face. 'It'll catch one of them eventually. But there's no reason we should help.'

The predator fish cruised just within the glass, its orange-limned mouth opening and closing ruminatively. It was a heavy brute of a fish, strikingly coloured, with an orange-lined maw fringed with tendrils and irregular orange circles on its flanks.

'You know why they are that colour?' Thovalt said abruptly. 'The little ones, *brach'in*, have a symbiosis with one of the intertidal molluscs. The shellfish – I don't know the name for it – is that same colour of orange around the mouth. The *dris* hides amongst a colony, mouth open; when the *brach'in* come scavenging—' He saw the curiosity in Lian's expression. 'Well, that kind of thing used to appeal to you.'

'You're back,' said a voice behind them. They turned. The speaker was a man of Thovalt's age. His hair was white, unusual in a mature Burdanian, and his eyes the yellow-brown of wet wood, sharp and worldly. He was holding his expression under firm control. He drew breath; and Thovalt pre-empted the moment, redirecting his attention to Lian with a flourish of a supple hand. The brown eyes took Lian in, stained robes, bewilderment, and all; he said, 'Lian D'Halldt. How very good it is to see you.'

Lian could not return the greeting. Lors' white hair reminded him of another face, a woman's face. He could not remember who it was, but he knew it from the time after his injury when his mind was without order or boundaries. He had watched faces desperately, needing them to tell him whether he was closer or farther away from sanity. Other faces showed him, much as their wearers in misguided compassion tried to hide their distress and perturbation. But the white woman's face remained dispassionate and analytical – and abandoned him to his trackless, fragmenting universe.

The young man looked at him curiously. 'I am Lorscar D'Sal,' he said. 'People know me as Lors.'

The quiet, somewhat pedantic inflection was familiar. Lian remembered a little of Lors: he was self-effacing, studious, at times leadenly serious. He had taken an academic interest in Lian's adaptation to the planetary environment and diet.

'When we go back to Burdania, he will be mission medic,' Thovalt said. 'That is, *if* he is still interested.' A challenge sparked between them. Thovalt said, 'Have you run those simulations of the physiological effects of drivestock?'

'Thovalt, I do not need a simulation to be able to tell you that if you place something as exquisitely integrated as a living organism in a field which disrupts that integration, even for an instant, the organism cannot survive. My results will be no different from anyone else's.'

'I'd like,' Thovalt said, 'to see *your* results. Yours, I trust.'

'Thovalt,' Lors said, 'We cannot hypothesize that anything could have survived direct exposure to the driveshock. It is impossible. You will be laughed out of the hall.' Thovalt reared back. Having had the intended impact, Lors continued, 'If we argue that there are survivors on Burdania, it must be on the basis that firstly, the driveshock did not encompass the entire globe, and secondly, the disruption produced did not so alter the environment as to cause complete ecological collapse, or stress our people's physiological adaptability beyond its limit. That argument has been given new strength by proof that our tolerance is far greater than it was believed to be before our parents' generation.' Lian had been following with great difficulty. He started when Lors turned on him. 'And *you*, Lian, are living proof that Burdanians do not need a sheltered habitat, even in an environment as stressful as this one: naturally conceived, born and reared in the native environment. You could be a great help if you allowed me to make . . .'

Thovalt unfurled a long arm across the space between them. 'Ah, if you wish him to prostrate himself beneath your scans, there will be a price.'

'That is surely up to Lian,' Lors said tightly.

Thovalt's eyes narrowed. The tremor around the lids made them glitter fiercely. 'And is *my* well-being not up to me? I would not have believed in a colony this size that one man could so consistently and completely avoid another. You have hidden talent, Lors, not to mention an unforeseen stamina for sulking.'

'I am not sulking,' Lors said. 'I simply find it difficult to *watch* you, suspecting as I do the basis of your behaviour . . .'

Thovalt moved to catch Lors' shoulders; the white-haired

83

medic blocked him with an upraised hand, breaking eye-contact. He stared obliquely down at the drifting shadows on the floor. Thovalt's hands worked at his sides. 'It's not behaviour; it is *I*, myself. The *me* you loved, remember; *me*, Thovalt. Or is it quite simply that you *dare* not love something that's been diagnosed? What was personality is now *pathology*, and *you*, Lorscar D'Sal, cannot be caught loving pathology.'

Lian pressed back against the cold glass. The emotional radiation unsettled him, after his long education in self-containment. He wished to be elsewhere. He was afraid he should be responsible to *vos'neen*.

Lors said, tightly, 'For a long time, I thought it was just you. I thought that it was because my seniors simply did not understand your nature. I needed to believe that one could be as uninhibited and spontaneous as you . . . without penalty.' He met Thovalt's eyes. 'And to a certain extent it *is* the way you are. But now I have a training I did not have, and a responsibility to the colony, to the debate and to Burdania. As a medic and . . . your supporter and friend, I must try to persuade you that your moods, your impulses, your . . . paranoia, have passed beyond normal extremes.'

'If you have such a responsibility to Burdania, where is your star?'

'I am on duty. I think it would be unnecessarily provocative. But if . . . if the debate is as important to you as it is to us, *think* how your behaviour affects it. Our conduct must be un-impeachable. You signed out a shuttle and posted a destination which,' he gestured towards Lian, without seeing him, 'was plainly falsified. The Hall is not another world. People's attitudes to your arguments will be coloured by what they know of you. If you continue to behave impulsively you will undermine your credibility. And at the worst, you may do something which makes it necessary for us to debate a compulsory treatment order.'

Thovalt shuddered, a tremor so quick Lian nearly missed it. It made Lors break off. 'Thovalt, why are you afraid? It is not unpleasant, and it will not change you. It will make you less a victim of your moods, but no less able to . . .' he smiled faintly, with strain, 'indulge in them.'

Thovalt ignored him. 'Lian,' he cast over his shoulder, a gritty smile in his voice, 'I commend your caution. If you disagree with the medics, you are out of your mind.'

Lors said, 'Sweet reason, Thovalt, will you listen to me? You are not out of your mind. You are predisposed to a mood disorder, a neurochemical imbalance which is being exacerbated by the stress of this debate. I have explained to you about feedback pathways in the brain . . .'

Thovalt was beating time, matching precisely Lors' speech rhythms. Provoked, Lors snapped, 'You have no special exemption from the effects of your genetics.'

Thovalt snarled silently at him. This expression was vivid, startling and ugly, and gone before Lian appreciated what he was seeing. He followed it with a brilliant smile, and an elegant little half-bow, both touched with a bitter urbanity. This was Thovalt in performance.

Behind him, distorted by shining water and diffraction, a very tall, stone-coloured figure hesitated. A huge black foot tilted over the step and slid down, toes feeling the drop. Lian started forwad. Thovalt stepped in front of him. Sure now, Lian said, 'Teli!' He pushed around Thovalt and half ran up the stairs to where Telien stood stooping to enter the bay. Before he could think of proprieties, Telien stepped back to stand upright, opened *kin* hands, and he went straight into *kin* embrace. *Kin* held him solidly against the ridge of *kin* sternum, tracing small circles on his temple. Beneath his ear Telien's heart drummed its stuttering triple beat. Before he went away, the heartbeat had come from above. And his fingertips now overlapped over *kin* spine.

'Your nearness in *vos'neen*,' *kin* said at last, 'is like no other.'

A clatter made both look round. Thovalt and Lors had both come out of the bay. Inadvertently or otherwise, Thovalt had knocked over one of the two lightstaffs resting against the glass. Its sliding tip had traced a greenish, downward arc, although the algael fluorescence was quenched by the Burdanian lights. The other Thovalt held, his hands lightly powdered, his expression a mingling of unease, intrigue, and bravado. Lors stood very close to him, his stance defensive. As cloistered colonists, with little interest in their host world, or their hosts, they would seldom have seen mature *kinder'el'ein*. The colony's usual visitors were the sexually and emphatically immature *aneel*, curious, clumsy children not much larger than the Burdanians. Telien's immensity, and alert gaze, were daunting. They could not read, as Lian could, amusement, and even affection, in the planed-down face. They did not know that this was an unusual *kindereen*.

'Thovalt Aslinn,' Telien said. Thovalt's eyes widened, the glitter in them brightening and becoming fixed. Distinctly, he paled. But Telien had already turned *kin* regard on Lors. 'And you are . . . the *aneel*, the son, of Granaith.'

Granaith, Lian thought, his hands closing on Telien's robe. The cold, brilliant, dispassionate presence who had attended and abandoned him. Telien stroked his temple, soothingly.

'I am Lors. Lorscar,' Lors said. His keen eyes shifted to the lightstaff in Thovalt's hand, and its pair, lying on the floor. 'You're here for Lian,' he said. 'You're taking him back.'

'That is so,' Telien said. *Kin* insubstantial voice had a solid, assertive quality to it; Lian sheltered close to *kin* bulk. 'Lian is my son also. I do not doubt,' with a slow, sliding glance of unreadable eyes, 'he will choose to return, in his own time.'

SEVEN

BURDANIA

Morning came in a dazzle. Sunlight streamed around the blind and lay in stripes across the wooden floor and the bed. Lian moved his hand into the light, and slowly closed it, balancing radiance on his fingertips. Sharp strange sounds came through the window, wind against the slats, stone against stone, gravel against stone; less strange ones through the bones of the house: the choppy cry of the newborn baby, and Lara's hilarity.

Burdania. He swung his feet off the bed, went barefoot to the window, unlashed the heavy hanging, and pushed his head and shoulder through. All he saw was light. For a moment he heard only a rushing, as though the light was filling his ears. He tried to draw back, but he was trapped by the window-shade, half-born into this new world. He shielded his eyes, and so the first thing he saw was a shimmering tear spilling into his shadowless palm.

Gradually his eyes cleared. His window overlooked the open land to the rear of the *caur'ynani* over the broad ridgecrest. It was scrubland, patched with bronze and yellow grasses, and shrubs just coming into spring leaf. Only the pattern of growth, the bare lines and flourishing rectangles, hinted at buried foundations. These ruins they had stripped for their building.

Beyond the ridgecrest he could see silver-grey water, quite motionless. And then he realized that it was not the river he saw, but the floodwaters sliding outwards from the breached bank. Their stealth was reptilian. Out of them, to his right, a dark mound rose, steeper than any hill, more immense than any building. Lltharran's Debating Hall and Archives had been a jewel, five great domes on midriver islands linked by bridges. The islands were sunken, the bridges torn away, the domes staved in. All a corroded sienna or a scorched bronze, staining the water with their reflection.

A flash tweaked the corner of his eye. He looked right and up the gleaming slope of the knoll, to the building at its summit. It alone was unchanged, as it was in the Archives of the colony: a plain grey building with two interlocking wings, one partially embedded in the summit rock, one raised on pillars as the slope fell away beneath. He could see the outline of that wing against bright, violet sky, one pillar like a thread supporting it, far too fragile to endure as it had. And there he was bound.

Vylan gave him breakfast, apologies, and instructions. He had meant to go with him, but there was Valancy, and the newborn child. Lian found that going unguided was both unnerving, and a relief. A guide would have informed him, but would also have distracted him. This way, his surroundings would have his fullest attention.

In daylight, he could appreciate the geography of the place. The *caur'ynani* was one of the highest placed, and, by the paucity of lichen on the outer walls, newest, of the buildings. Standing outside the ship-bellied front door, he looked down on five or six rows of buildings, most much like the *caur'ynani*, stone-built and mortar-caulked. Built perversely low to the river, leaving the high land barren. Perhaps they had to be built there, before the land could be cleared. Perhaps it was better sheltered from the wind. Perhaps it was pure defiance.

The dykes seemed not so black in daylight, showing the white and grey amongst their stones, and the grasses growing on their summits. Beyond them the river's currents flexed in confinement. No yellow grass appeared at the base of the dykes on the far side. Lian thought of the shuttle, and shielded his eyes with his hands to peer into the distance. He could not tell the state of the banks, but he thought the shuttle had to be as high as the *caur'ynani*. They were in no immediate danger, and for the sake of his masquerade, he must put them out of his mind. He had an errand and a purpose. The errand was to pass word to Valancy's kin that she had been safely delivered of her son. The purpose was to learn more about the *isk'dar*, concerning whom no descriptions tallied. That was best done at *caur'isk'dari*. By now he grasped that *caur* meant a group-house, be that group united by kinship, common origin, or skill. In *caur'isk'dari*, therefore, he should find the *isk'dar*, those related to her, and those involved in the administration of Lltharran.

Valancy had told him that *caur* Nors was just behind the dykes, and was unique for its hide shutters, and for the field where, in summer, those intrepid enough to cross Lltharran plain grazed their mounts. He worked his way obliquely downhill, trying to seem both purposeful and unobtrusive. Every adult he saw was either already on the dykes, or tending that way. From what Lian saw they were reinforcing the base of the inner dyke with heavy stones, and sealing the upper section with clay and gravel. It was not something he wished to try, for his weakness would be conspicuous.

The oldest buildings – judged, as he had learned in the *kinder'vos*, by the growth on them – were in the third and fourth rows, a comfortable height above the river. The inner dyke would have to be submerged before their flagstones were dampened. Coloured lichen ringed their walls, and fine mosses clung to their eaves. They looked, somehow, more prosperous than the others; Lian took a moment to realize that that was because their windows were glazed. Mostly with rectangles of cloudy green glass but occasionally with irregular transparent fragments, salvage. One building in particular he noticed, for its length, its whitewashed walls, and the number of salvaged windows, placed high not for vision but for illumination. And, especially, its extensive and variable garden. Not all the plants were native: one narrow bed had been deliberately raised, and spread with coarse, sandy soil. The plants had the features of desert plants – spines and thin, tough leaves. Not food crop: too small, too few and too delicate. Tion D'Suran passed him as he stood speculating, turned up the path and went in the front door. This was the Medics' Guildhouse, then, and these the spring crop of medicinal herbs and transgenics.

The building with the painted hide shutters was lower than the others, down behind the dyke. Just beyond it, the dyke turned in across the ridge. A group of labourers were extending

89

the outer dyke further uphill. Between the building and the dyke, a well-tended field of steppe grass was just coming into its summer colour, pale yellow. Lian walked round the building, studying the shutters. They were indeed of animal hide. There was one – he looked away, and then back, slowly – one of a group of people skinning the carcass of a *faunali*, the blood rendered in a raw, defiant orange. An orange that stained knives, ground and hands. *Faunali* were steppe grazers, too large for a microhabitat. Lian had only seen pictures. He could not deny that this was well drawn, the figures fluid and faces individual, even to the single small child hanging back crying. Nevertheless, the rawness of it repelled him.

'I don' care for that one, m'self,' said a husky, slurred voice. He turned and saw a woman at the corner of the building, leaning on crutches and regarding him with head twisted slightly to one side. She started towards him with a dragging gait. He took a step, intending to meet her. She stopped, and looked him in the eye. Hers were a startling shade of gold in the strong light. Her skin was drawn tightly over her bones and her hair was brittle, and gingery in colour. 'No,' she ordered. He waited.

'I do what I can,' she told him, when she reached his side, and started to say something more, but the words were lost in a struggle for air. 'Curse you, don't *touch* me! Best I fall and spill my brains—' She stood braced until her gasping spent itself, and then raised a grey face. 'Apologies.'

'Don't. I understand,' Lian said.

'Hope you don't.' She looked up at the hanging. 'M'favourite's at the back.' He matched her pace to the corner of the house. 'No pain,' she said suddenly. 'Comforts people: there's no pain.'

Lian thought of golden glass breaking, of a vine tearing, of the sensation of falling. Of the terror. He remembered her struggle to breathe. 'Other people – don't know.'

A thick snort of amusement. 'You do? What d'y'know then?'

'Fear.'

She braced her crutches, and stared up at him. But for the crutches, she would have been taller than he. 'Y'r name, dead man?'

'Lian D'Halldt.'

'Arkadin Nors. If I'd pain – maybe I wouldn't mind. Would – want it over.' She turned his attention away with a quick hand gesture. 'There.'

The elements had worn the painting, but it had been made to withstand them, the lines gouged in and the gouges stained in sepia, and the whole painted over with a glaze which had cracked but not fallen away. It was a cliff, a great sweep up from a glittering sea. Handfuls of seabirds scattered across sea and sky. Out on the very horizon was a tiny ship, and on the cliff a woman stood watching.

'Kara's leap, high edge of Ardar down South. Climbed it once,' she reminisced. 'Oh, years ago. Like t'climb it now. Be a good way t'die.'

'No,' Lian said, sick at the thought of that long, pictorial plunge.

'My choice,' she said, freeing her hand to rap his. Her fingers felt like a bundle of sticks. 'Like t'jump off things. Trees. Hillsides. *Faun* – when it's my idea. Oh yes, what I wanted to say. Back there. We only skin the old ones. Or mercy-kill – illness, injury. Y'r not a Northerner, or you'd not look that way at it. They carry us, we treat'em best we can.' She gave him a gaunt smile. 'Like them to put up this old hide, when I've done wi'it.' She raised one wasted hand, turned it. The sun glittered on the thin skin. 'Be pretty. I think.'

'Yes,' Lian said, appreciating her sombre humour. 'It would.'

'Come in?'

'I should not,' Lian said, with unfeigned regret. 'I have errands to run. Valancy Nors asked me to leave word here that her son was born last night, and that she and he both are well.'

'Come back, then. When you're done.'

'Yes.' He saw her back to the front door: the rear had steps and she was not about to accept his help. He waited as she opened the door and negotiated the threshold. The house exuded emptiness. 'You're alone,' he said.

'Able-bodied are dyking,' she said, curtly. 'Do f'myself.' But he knew she watched him out of sight.

He found a level track along the ridgecrest, clear of grass. It might have been a road, once. The path which led from bridge-end to knolltop was fragmented on its lower course, and twice crossed by the dykes which abutted the rising knoll, but a quarter-way up the slope it abruptly consolidated, and climbed steadily. On either side, bronze grass sleeked and rustled like a pelt.

The slope of the hill had been terraced, and the terraces were largely intact. Where they had collapsed the sagging earth had been left to overgrow with the durable bronze grass which grew anywhere that anything could grow on the plain. Cultivation on these exposed slopes required strategy. Stunted trees provided a windbreak, even as they twisted to its direction. Dense shrubs closed in small bays of stillness. Blue and green groundcover matted the earth between cleared rows. Even so late in the spring, the first sprouts had barely broken ground. But somebody was determined: Lian could hear the sound of a blade hacking at the hard earth.

He had to step off the path to track the source, finding it a quarter-way around the hill and below. He leaned over the terrace's broad wall. Below, a lone woman was chopping at the ground beneath a stand of stunted trees. The wind moulded the sleeves of her light shirt around her arms and drew the excess into a thin, rippling wing. Her hair shone russet-brown. One foot was planted forward, letting her derive power from her shifting balance, and she raised and drove down the blade with the ease of long practice. Lian watched her at her task for several minutes, until she rested on her blade, and caught sight of him. 'Yes?'

'I was – just watching. It would be – vanity if I offered – help.'

'Come down.'

That sounded much like an order, but he had found these homeworlders forceful to a one. He followed the wall to the path, and across to where she stood waiting. She was much smaller, face to face, than she had appeared, wielding her hoe. She had loosened the drawstrings at cuffs and neck, and her face and throat glistened with sun-wax and perspiration. Her eyes were an intense, true violet, and for a moment he saw nothing else. Then he took in the rest of a strong-featured, almost overly moulded face. His first thought was: a great need for certainty. His second was that he had seen her before, through the cameras.

'Have we met?' she said, sharply, discomfited by his attention.

'No. I – came yesterday,' he said. 'Lian D'Halldt. Of – upper C'Rynn reach.'

'D'Halldt,' she said. 'That is not a current name.'

'It is mine.'

'From C'Rynn reach.'

There was a silence. 'You have not – told me your – name.'

The violet stare intensified. 'Travassa,' she said. 'Daisainia Travassa.' As though it explained her, which, no doubt it should. 'Why have you come to Lltharran?'

'I – was curious.'

'Were you?' she said. 'D'Halldt.' His name plainly troubled her. 'Where is your *tayn*?'

'I come – alone.'

'Indeed.' She brooded a moment, looking past him into the stubby grass, then her eyes swept up again. 'They need hide no longer, do you understand? Lltharran has changed.'

'That is – what I hear,' Lian said, not understanding.

'But believe?' she returned.

'I – have not been here long enough – to believe anything.'

'Indeed. You have been up to *caur'isk'dari*?'

'I am going – there.'

'Come with me,' she said, handing him the hoe while she pulled down a sweater and cloak which she had draped over a branch.

'I would have thought that – gardening would – be difficult,' he said.

She took her hoe back from him. 'I intend to replant the plain.'

'Would time not do that for you?'

'Would you wait—' she snapped out a hand, taking in the grey, dun and russet vastness, 'for time?' She stalked on a few steps – she had a long, vigorous stride for so small a woman – and then said, 'In my lifetime, we shall decide how it is to be done. I shall be content with that.'

Not according to her tone. Her voice was colourful, richly

93

inflected, becoming more so as she warmed to her subject. 'Living things sustain each other. Shelter, pollination, seed-dispersal, fertilization by decomposition – all those need a certain concentration of life. Once the concentration falls below the necessary level, the links break.' She snapped air with her hands. 'We must restore them with the materials and resources at hand. And do so despite the river.' Her voice was suddenly blackly bitter, her face, when he glanced at it, masked by a disconcerting rigidity. 'But I will.'

'But the river,' Lian said, 'I thought – would fertilize—'

'With our dead.'

He fell behind her, his breath coming short with more than exertion. He knew who she was, now. He should have known from the moment she said her name: Travassa, but whatever he had expected of the *isk'dar*, it was not she, a small, intense woman tilling her garden and speaking of the river with hatred and pain.

The path bent suddenly, and passed underneath the looming southern wing of the Centre: *her* place, *caur'isk'dari*. It sat on two thin pillars and a wedge of shadow like smoked glass. Everything he had seen until then had been ruined and rebuilt of stone and woven cloth and wood. He traced a hand lightly down the smooth wall, dipping his fingers into shadow. On the inner face, he saw a plaque, copper inlaid in grey, still bearing the date of the Centre's building. It had been scored across and across by a determined, but frustrated hand, which damaged but could not obliterate. He stopped; he shivered.

'A distasteful thing,' the *isk'dar* said.

'But – why? What – happened that it must – be forgotten?'

He found himself once more impaled by her gaze. Even if she had not been who she was, he would have found himself holding his breath every time those violet eyes came to bear. He was not afraid of what she might see: she looked from too deeply within herself to see clearly. But there was something consuming about her attention. He held his breath as though holding in his self, as though everything might be sucked out of him and into that deep well of her mind.

This is irrational, he told himself. Of all the things she could do to me, I worry about that . . . But what *that* was, he veered away from defining. I've been amongst the *kinder'el'ein* too much. I am simply dealing with a charismatic personality, and I've done that before. He broke their gaze and looked down. Her fingertips rested on the creamy stone. On the first finger she wore a heavy ring of dull blue metal, cast in the shape of a bird with outspread wings and glittering, faceted feathers. It was huge on her work-worn finger and had been narrowed to fit by a thong whipped around the band. The incongruity of it made him lift his eyes to her face again, and she followed his motion, her hair sliding back from the strong features. He realized how far he had to look down, though he was not himself tall, and thought how young she was, scarcely older than Tion D'Suran. And then, like a lamp being turned on, the force surged back into her eyes, and the impression of diminutiveness and youth evaporated like a dewdrop in a flame. She swung away, the question unanswered.

The path surmounted a ridge, which led, obliquely, to the main door. On its outer side the open slope fell away, and on its inner was a sheltered sunken garden, carefully tended. The far side of the building was not so much built, as embedded, abutting and taking its shape from an outcropping. A natural rock vestibule sheltered the door. Lian started slightly as it slid open, anticipating them. 'You will become used to the automation,' she said, and he could not entirely suppress his smile.

They entered on the mezzanine of a high-ceilinged hall. The nearest wall was the bare, rugged rock of the outcropping, ornamented with metallic cables webbing together its contours. The two long walls were glass panes, none broken and only two crazed. They flooded the mezzanine and the empty hall below with a strong, sunless, shadowless light. It was an extremely sophisticated blind mechanism: the view was preserved, barely unfocused: plain, banded grey, brown, yellow, and the white river rolling southwards, but the sun itself was cancelled, except for a faint halo.

Around the mezzanine was a railing. Near the door it had been coated with nondescript grey paint, but halfway along the paint had been chipped and filed away, exposing blue metal. Facets of engravings caught the light: the vertical struts were dense with names, from floor to top. They were the names of the scientists who had contributed to space science. Somewhere beneath the hard grey paint, still uncovered, were the names of the inventors of the drive: D'Jayna Travassa and Carolinn D'Vandras. Unless they, too, had been eradicated as anathema.

'Ganaskiggle,' a small voice announced from behind him. He started and turned. The toddler hooked a finger over her lower lip and studied him with oval, violet eyes, several shades darker than the *isk'dar*'s. She was an odd, decorative, decorated little creature, in a turquoise tabard over golden-brown trousers. Bodice, collar and cuffs were adorned with intricate embroidery, a twining of leaves and flowers. She came forward, accepting admiration as her due, and smeared her wet finger on to the engraved names. 'Isagliggle,' she added.

'I am Lian,' Lian said, crouching to greet her. 'And – you are . . .'

'She is Crystolan,' Daisainia said, coming to stand over them both. 'Crystolan D'Vandras.'

'Zholan.'

'Crystolan,' Daisainia corrected her firmly.

The toddler clutched his knees and swayed against him, laughing into his face. He could not but smile; her whole being radiated joy.

'Is this – your daughter?' he said, looking up at Daisainia.

The mask slid over her features. 'No. But *isk'dar* after me, perhaps.'

He did not know what to say, so freighted was her tone. He put his hands lightly on the clinging child's waist, but she pouted vividly and squirmed free. She sidled behind Daisainia's leg, clutching handfuls of the *isk'dar*'s cloak, enticing him with her eyes.

Daisainia was not looking at either of them; he followed her gaze to see a tall young woman approaching them with a shrinking, shuffling step. She was a sad, shabby figure. Her sweater was much too large for her, her trousers were faded, the thongs on her sandals trailed. One white hand worked the curtain of her hair, opening and closing a narrow parting. The first surprise was the broad sash around her waist, cluttered with embroidered motifs in many colours, like sketches in an artist's notebook. The second was her beauty. A deeply sunken, spiritless beauty, but unsettling. Lian wanted to cradle it in his hands and gently breathe life into it. The black hair framed a fine sliver of a face, and her eyes were as darkly violet as the little girl's.

Crystolan was still clutching handfuls of Daisainia's cloak. The young woman stared at her, pleadingly, oblivious to either Lian or Daisainia. Crystolan slid further behind Daisiania. The young woman looked abjectly at Daisainia. The *isk'dar*'s face was masked as she stepped aside. The little girl squeaked and darted away along the mezzanine. The woman sagged.

'Chase her,' the *isk'dar* ordered.

'She does not want—'

'To be caught, but she delights in the chase.'

After a moment the woman crept after her daughter. Daisainia watched; Lian felt she made herself do so. To distract her he said: 'Is she – your sister?'

'She is Shivaun D'Vandras.' The *isk'dar* looked sideways at him, her face unreadable. 'If that means nothing to you, then I am glad, and would that it could continue. Those who talk most know least.' She bit off her last words, and turned back to the pursuit. Crystolan dodged the woman's tentative reach, and Shivaun faltered, and turned to look back at Daisainia. Crystolan threw herself against her legs, making her stagger. Clinging to the faded trousers, she laughed up at her. Shivaun's white hands fluttered about her head, not daring to light.

'Come,' Daisainia said, and turned away, leading him towards the shadowed hall mouths. A scattering of luminous panels lit overhead, and the light flowed stutteringly to others as she walked further in. Lian paused. They kindled and pooled about his head, chequered light and darkness. A pattern with pieces missing, like this whole world, like the enigmatic, intense and protective woman leading him.

'Where – are we going?'

Striding on ahead, Daisainia Travassa ignored him. He had just resigned himself to finding out when he arrived, when she swung round, in a tight, powerful motion. The uneven light from overhead dragged shadows down her face. 'You have not told me all.'

For a moment Lian could not breathe, a reaction she did not miss. 'I grant it is your right,' she said, tersely. 'But it is *my* right to seek to change your mind. Linn Travassa disinherited us of our past. Between Linn and myself lie four generations of furtherance, apathy and early death. *My* legacy was one of ruins, relics and splinters: our history worn away to Islander rumours, our knowledge in broken bits of metal and glass, and our people scattered, isolated and suspicious. I would divest myself, and all of us, of *this* legacy. Can we recover the other? I do not know. It may be that it has already gone too far. But every piece of the past regained matters, and perhaps someone, somewhere still lives who can make *sense* of it all.'

'What – kind of sense?' Lian said, unnerved.

She looked penetratingly at him. 'We know that we are not what we should be. The knowledge that has come down to us is not consistent with our experience. We are surrounded by relics which had use, have use, if by chance we make them work again. If I and others so wished, we could tear a building stone from stone, but *melt* the stones themselves . . . no. Something *happened* to us, D'Halldt. And it was *not* Linn Travassa. It began before him.'

'Yet Linn – you said yourself – Linn—' He collected himself with a nearly physical effort. 'Linn was one man. How did he – affect so many?'

'He was *isk'dar*. And he was not alone.' She looked away, at the wall. The grey enamel had begun to blister with age. When she spoke, her voice was colourless and grim, and he had seldom heard anyone so aware of what she was saying. 'Death is the ultimate silencer, and the ultimate persuader.'

'He – killed people who – opposed him?'

She turned her shadowed, consuming eyes on him. 'Need I tell you that, D'Halldt? Need I tell you except to show you that I am not ignorant of it? I *know* that the very ones who have the most knowledge have also had the least incentive to yield it up.'

Oh sweet reason, he thought. How could she know?

He drew breath through a tight throat. 'Who – do you think – I am?'

Anger flashed, but did not speak. 'You are Islander. Burdania has two worlds: the North and the Islands. The North yielded to Linn, but the Islands resisted. To this day, Islander crews ply routes which no Northerner may see. After Linn and Ylid, his successor, we have only their maps to trust. Whole Islands may slip into the sea, or be declared empty. I am no born fool, D'Halldt, and my grandmother was a Shipmaster.'

'What – do you think – is out there?' Liam said.

'As one travels outward from Lltharran, it seems one – moves into the past, by two, or even four generations, to find knowledge retained there which has been lost here. We are in a bad habit of forgetting here. But what we *need* is the knowledge of five or six generations past, while Linn was alive, and Ylid. There were settlements which passed those years in isolation, yes. But, none *known to me* have endured to this present day. Many did not last to the third or fourth generation; we have found their ruins. Others made contact with a world that no longer cared, or feared to care, and so abandoned what they knew. But they could still tell us that that teaching, that knowledge, *did once exist*, that it stemmed from the relics, and may yet be preserved in them.' She had, naturally, the arresting, resonant delivery of a trained speaker. Then he chided himself for assuming that it was untrained. She had been years in her role; she had purpose, and vision, and surely recognized her instruments. 'What we most need, D'Halldt, is to learn how the oldest records were kept. The advantage that Linn and Ylid had was that they knew the structure that they were trying to destroy. They need only push out the keystone of the arch to crumble it. But they could not destroy every stone – the relics which survive prove that. If we can find and restore that keystone, then their cleverness will have undone itself. Any relic is precious, and if someone remembers its purpose, or its use – that, D'Halldt, is knowledge beyond price. And that is what those isolated and hidden *tayni* can bring us, our encapsulated past.' She probed him with a glance, then said, 'And themselves, D'Halldt, their lost names.'

'But – you do not know – what happened. Or why – Linn should impose forgetfulness.' Her hard, watchful silence was a

99

kind of affirmative. He said, carefully, 'And you – regret what – he did. You oppose Linn.' Still she did not answer. 'I – think I – am not what you – think. One man. Curious but here – almost by accident.'

'A long accident, D'Halldt. But have it as you will.'

Her tone belied the words; she was not yet done with him. She led him along the corridors, into the other wing. She showed him room after room of the restorers' scavengings. In every one he looked first at the workstations or wallscreens, and found only grey blankness. She spared them not a glance; what she had to show him was the salvage piled before them, or on top of them, on the benches, chairs, floor, sitting on coarse-woven cloth, or in boxes. There could not have been so many rooms, or so much salvage, but it seemed so: most of it tarnished, battered, dismantled, the personal and domestic appliances of another age. She sketched in their speculations as to what and how, and let him take full measure of their ignorance.

He sensed a change in her manner as they reached the third and highest level. He braced himself, wondering what was to come next. Here the corridors were skylit, and the rooms had windows in walls and ceiling. Some of those windows were broken, and had been rigged with a stained, translucent canvas. She pushed open a door, and showed him into a room so verdant that he thought at once of the jungle. Sprouts in vials on the benches; seedlings in trays on the floor; shrubs in pots against the window. They concealed the outside; the windows were merely there to illuminate them. There were narrow windows between the rooms on this level, and on both sides he could see crowded yellow and bluish green. Daisainia crossed the room and propped her hoe against the wall, alongside several other such implements.

'I will,' she said, 'replant the plain.'

He looked at her amongst her cuttings and seedlings, and could not speak.

She returned to his side. 'I must have done with you now, D'Halldt. I will be needed behind the dykes. You wished to see *caur'isk'dari*; here it is. You may come and go as you please. In quieter times the restorers do much of their work here, and I will have help with my gardens. Most rooms are open, but if you see a wedge in a door, let it lie. We might free you, but it would take time we could ill afford. In places the lighting is unreliable, but there should be lamps placed to assist. On this level in the other wing – those rooms are mine.'

'And – Shivaun? You three are – the only Travassan.'

'*I* am the only Travassan. Others may trace an ancestry; I bear the name.'

'I do not – understand your names. In *caur'ynani* there is – a man who says he has – no name—'

She drew a quick, pained breath. 'That must be set right before his child is born. *Tayni* were not originally constituted by bloodline, but by place: that is the way the newer names are derived. By now, bloodline and place are commonly one. Customarily a child takes the name of the *tayn* best able to provide for him. The obligation of the *tayn* is to provide. The *cal* adjudicates on membership and exclusion.'

'*Cal?*'

'A senior member of the *tayn*, chosen by the others to settle disputes. The obligations change with the *tayn*. The *cal* is responsible for order and well-being within the *tayn*. They are, in the main, well chosen.' There was a bite in her voice which made Lian postpone the obvious question about her own name, and how she was Travassan and Shivaun not.

He said, 'Tor and Valancy's son – was born last night.'

'Ah.' Her sombre, concentrated expression lightened. 'And well? But you would have said if otherwise. So, you are staying at the *caur'ynani*. Then,' she contemplated her ringed hand a moment, 'you may take two messages for me. Tell Vylan D'Caul that it will rain tonight, or tomorrow – I am not sure. But it will be a good rain, worth catching.' She saw his perplexity, and her expression became forbidding. 'As an Islander, D'Halldt, you know what I mean. The other message is to Rathla Zharlinn. You will remind him of the *caur'cali* tomorrow. As the appointed representative of *tayn* Zharlinn, his attendance is *not* optional.' After a moment's silence she said, 'Phrase it more circumspectly, if you will, but he *is* to come.' She swept an eye from his face to his feet. 'Show me your hands,' she said, suddenly. He did, afraid what this unpredictable woman might be looking for. She turned them palm-up with a rasping touch. 'Ah. As I thought. No one hard-winded on the slope could have worked ship. You do not look strong, though there must be some substance to you to have lasted that journey. Unless you were ill on the way—' He could not decide how to answer that, and, crisply, she dismissed the question. 'You need not work the dykes. But if you wish to show us goodwill, you will carry messages as bidden. They,' with fleeting humour, 'or *most* – weigh nothing.

'One further thing—' She turned her consuming gaze on him. 'At the *caur'cali*, senior *cali* from the regions tell me about the state of their *tayni* and learn for themselves the state of mine. It is a courtesy on their part; I have no means of compelling them, but some come every season, willingly. I ask that you be there also. To see how the *isk'dar* deals with her people.'

'I – would be honoured,' Lian said, at last.

In the last hour of the afternoon he went to learn his shipfellows' verdict. Sunlight lay long on buildings and ruins, drawing out fine trembling shadows of grass and long still ones of stones. As Lian picked his way down the fragmenting path to the dykes and the bridge, children were laying dirty branches on the smudge and ash of last night's fire. Nets hung below the near edge of the bridge, to snag near flotsam. Young adults captured that further out with hooked lines. Lian saw Lara straddling the dyke as she played in a weighted log.

From the apex of the bridge, he could see the three settled hills on the far bank, secure against the river, the unsettled ridge, and a little of the ruins beyond. His eyes streamed from looking towards the sun, but if he did not, he would look down at the brown water moving below. He could feel the pulse of it underfoot. He shuffled his hands along the rail, its coarse, flaking surface nibbled at his skin. He was dizzy, but dared not grip, dared not lean. His viscera felt the unsupported moment before the plunge.

When his foot sank into mud, he sat down on the end of the bridge and put his head down. The indulgence was brief: someone asked him if he was all right. He looked up at her tired face, managed to smile. She patted his shoulder, and lifted two gravel-filled buckets. Looking along the path after her, he saw how water oozed into her footprints. People were shovelling dirt and gravel against the seepages. He acknowledged to himself that, conviction aside, he was very much afraid. He was afraid of the bridge, and of the river, but he was most afraid of the place itself, of its ruin, its willed decay, its rejection. The bridge had merely caused a fruiting of his fear. Every strangeness, every encounter, every clash between record and reality had fed its growth. He had thought and dreamed and imagined many things. And left them unexamined because he did not want to come burdened by expectation. And because he did not examine them, and learn his own inner landscape, he found it fraught with mires and traps.

He could feel the river through his spine, and through the palms of his cold hands. The dykes shadowed the path and slope behind them. He would lose the light. He should not draw more attention to himself than he had. Stiffly, he stood. Knowing the shape of his fear did not diminish it. Knowing it was justified did not reassure him. If he found his *kinder'el'ein*-woven bag, if his bid to stay had been approved, he did not know that he had the substance to come back along this path.

At the first ridge the dykes ended, and the ruins stretched before him, open to the river. Between the first, settled ridge, and the second was the ruin of a promenade, four levels of wide corridor with stone benches set into niches. The lowest level had already fallen away. The next lowest was submerged beneath thin, opaque water. The river sucked at the stones of the third. Lian picked his way along the uneven stones, peering into each cluttered niche. He saw no bag.

'Lian!'

He looked up. At the far end of the promenade Lors was scrambling on to the broken, sloping stone. Lian's multi-coloured bag rode bulkily on his hip. They met midway. Lian gathered the bag to him, smelling jungle. Lors retained the strap, pressing his fists together. 'Lian, are you all right?'

'You want – me to stay—'

'*I* assuredly do not. I opposed this.'

Lian summoned his resolve to set a walk along broken stones

and slimy path, alone, above a return to the shuttle, to friendship, warmth and safety. 'If I came – now. How long would – it be before – any of us could – try again?'

'I take your point. Now listen to mine . . .'

'Lors. No.' Lors inhaled, and Lian caught the hand that still held the bag strap. 'Don't – frighten me into – returning. You are too – decent for that.'

'If I can prevent you putting yourself in danger, then enough of decency. You will be alone. I know you have travelled the jungle alone, but you know the jungle. You don't know Lltharran. These people obliterated their history, their technology, and, for all we know, anyone who would not willingly give either up. That *isk'dar* admitted as much. If you are discovered before you are sure that the mindset and machinery for that no longer exists, Li, we will not be able to help you.' He looked at Lian's face for a moment, then said, 'We're been separated for sixty-six years, and they've lost a large part of their medical knowledge. They'll have diseases which you have never been exposed to. And you might be a carrier of variants they've never met, and would have no means of combatting.' Lian heard Vylan saying, '. . . killed nearly all the young children, and more than half of the elder members of the *tayn.*' Lors was holding out a fat tube which Lian recognized as a self-medicator. 'I've had us on anti-infectives and antitransmissives since we arrived, but I've increased your dosage and broadened the spectrum. The display on the injector,' he turned it to show Lian, 'gives the schedule. Adhere to it, I beg you. In your bag are packages of common medications, vitamins and food supplements, and some mild stimulants to increase your resistance to the cold. Remember, you *are* accustomed to a much warmer climate.'

'Could I – start disease?'

Lors looked closely at him. 'If I thought you a risk, I could not, in good conscience, let you go. The colony is an antiseptic environment, nearly free of infectious diseases. You are unusual because of your exposure to the outside and because of your extensive treatment with surgical and therapeutic viruses, but for those very reasons your records are extremely detailed.'

'Lors—' Lian said, faintly, 'if you – wanted to – frighten me – now – you could.'

'I know,' Lors said. There was a silence. 'As you said, I am too decent.' His expression was sour, but his voice was gentle. 'I have done my utmost to safeguard them from you. I wish I could safeguard you from them.' He put a hand on Lian's shoulder, reaching into his own pocket with the other. 'Now, let me see your implant.' Lian bent forwards. Lors' soft, cold fingertips parted his hair, and he felt a twinge around the implant. Then Lors righted him with a light lifting hand. His manner was businesslike. 'I've reset the link to maintain contact at a distance. That will shorten the battery lifetime, but you should be back with us well before it expires.' He looked at Lian, all his unspoken objections in his face. 'I'll contact you if I detect a medical problem, but please, take care of your health. We will be a couple of hours' flight from you, higher land to the north-west, with geographical features which should keep us out of sight. We'll leave the cameras in place. Keep your transmitter active. Don't overexert yourself. Use the self-medicator, and, please, please, be *careful*. Particularly around that *isk'dar*. She's the only one who's challenged you, and given her position, and family history, that makes me nervous.'

Lian thought of the depths in her eyes, of the coarse, light touch of her hands, and of the plants she tended beneath her broken windows. She was Lltharran's spine against the river and the ruins, young, ignorant, and immovable. His fragile resolution settled into place. This needed doing, and he chose to do it.

Lors said, 'Are you *certain* you want to go back?'

'Lors, I – have to.'

EIGHT

TARIDWYN

The lightstaff stained his hands with a gentle, yellow light. Lian watched it, intently, willing it to intensify. He and Telien were standing on the edge of the clearing around the colony, in leaf-fractured moonlight, waiting for his eyes to adapt. Overhead, the lightspray from the habitats stained the underside of the canopy green. Telien contemplated it, *kin* black face invisible, except where a movement of a leaf allowed a shaft of moonlight. 'Patience,' *kin* counselled Lian. 'My eyes need time, too. Burdanian lights are very strong.'

Strong light would be the least of it. Metals and electrical currents were anathema to *vos'neen*; they blinded and disordered perception. Within the colony, Telien would have been severed from the sustaining presence of *kin* own kind, and the familiar resonances of the jungle. Instead, there would be only the screaming incoherence of circuitry, and the unaccepting alien Burdanians. Vaguely, dreadfully, Lian remembered his own experience of delirium and disorientation as he emerged from coma.

'Why – did you come? Not send – a message.'

'And deprive myself of your delight, and mine.' *Kin* voice, like Jahde's, was breathy and timbreless. 'No, *i'vad'neer*, I would not do that. And there are some things you need to know before you come to the high house. Shaleen is home.'

Shaleen. Some *kinder'el'ein*, particularly *kindereen*, could not tolerate the presence and proximity of Burdanians. Telien's eldest child was one. When Sara gave birth to Lian in Telien's high house, Shaleen had left for a deep jungle *kinder'vos*, of a strongly isolationist tradition, and had visited only rarely. He remembered a bulky figure in drab, stone-coloured robes and heavy headdress, who neither looked at, nor spoke to him. Telien said, 'I asked Shaleen to promise that when *kin* became *tris'maeren*, *kin* would give the bond a chance to form with two from our settlement.'

Kinder'el'ein were born unsexed, with *vos'neen* immature, and *en'neen* nonexistent. Sexual differentiation and maturation of the empathies began around the thirtieth year of life, with full maturity attained around the sixtieth; Shaleen was the same age as Lian's grandparents. *Tris'neen* was a threefold bond between a *kindereen*, a male and a female. It was for life. The bond was involuntary, but it could be influenced by familiarity. Telien would want *kin* child to remain in *kin* own settlement. In Telien's voice, regret for the unfair promise struggled with the wish that it be kept.

'I'll – stay here,' he offered, trying to make the offer sound and feel genuine. Shaleen's silent reproach for his very existence would quench any joy of homecoming.

'No, *i'vad'neer*,' Telien said. 'You are my child as surely as Shaleen.' *Kin* swept the tip of the lightstaff in a wide arc, barely stirring the leaf litter on the path. In the diffuse yellow glow the shapes slid and flickered. But Lian's night vision had settled. He could see where the darkness was least dense, where the path wore away the undergrowth. He could see high, silvery patches of moonlight on the leaves and trunks. He could see the narrow curve of Telien's jaw and the liquid shimmer of *kin* eye. Telien sensed his response to what he saw. Without a further word, *kin* started along the path towards the settlement.

The paths which laced the jungle were ancient. *Kinder'el'ein* kept them clear of new growth by sprinking preparations which suppressed germination. Lian and Telien waded ankle-deep through the sheddings of the jungle, and used their lightstaffs to disturb the litter before each step. Some of the small creatures which lived in it carried poison. They went slowly. Lian forgave his eyes their dimness, and, gradually, felt his other senses expand. He could feel the large, heavy leaves sliding away from his feet, and the soft pulp overhead. Tiny feet

107

flickered on his skin. Something flapped through the canopy, with a slopping of leathery wings, and he found himself listening to a startling height. For a year he had lived with the pygmy coastal jungle and the sea, with a moderate height and a great unseen depth. Now the depth was all above. The flyer settled to roost, and a wind moved the canopy. Moonlight poured down a vine-laden trunk and spilled over a fringe of epiphytes. The afterimage shimmered before Lian's eyes, long after the cleft in the canopy had closed.

'I had forgotten,' Telien said, 'that we, also, disturb Burdanians. Thovalt Aslinn and Granaith's child were ... guilty in my presence.'

'They – don't know. About *kinder'el'ein*.'

'No,' Telien said. 'Do they know about *en'vos'neen'el*?'

Lian sensed a purpose in the question, but could not guess what it might be. 'I – don't think – so.'

'Ah,' Telien said.

'Thovalt is – going to – ask to go – back to Burdania,' Lian said, after a silence.

The silence continued, but for the wet pushing of their lightstaffs and ankles through leaves. Then Telien said, 'That is your *en'vos'neen'el*, but it is not a celebration but a ... suffering. It troubles *vos'neen*, and there is nothing we can do to spread it.'

Lian peered at the grey bulk ahead of him. Telien's lightstaff flicked into view, right side, left, right side, left, with an unbroken tempo. Something screeched and flurried past *kin* head, making Telien sway.

Lian said, in a small voice, 'It's – too close to – your *en'vos'neen'el*.'

'Now you feel guilt,' Telien said. 'And you grow inattentive to your footing.' Lian checked his next step and furrowed the litter with the staff. Around its tip, a supple topaz coil unlooped and slid away beneath a leaf as large as Telien's hand. Telien turned to face him. 'I mean no reproof, and you should take none. Burdania was precious to you.'

He flinched away, as he had flinched from Thovalt's insistence. 'I – don't remember. Things – move in my mind. I think – I'm falling.'

108

Telien said, 'I sensed you as you climbed on to the dome. I was afraid for you. I came out of the jungle and saw you.'

Lian caught double handfuls of Telien's robe, as he had when he was a small child. 'Saw me,' he whispered. 'That's why – you came to take me away. You were – frightened. Oh, Teli. Did you see – me fall?'

'I saw you fall,' the *kindereen* confirmed.

The white abyss opened up beneath him. In the year between it had never occurred to him that Telien might have shared the terror and the plunge. He was no longer alone. And it was unforgivable to be so. Telien steadied him without holding him, like a rock or a tree. 'Teli,' Lian wept, 'I'm sorry. Thaorinn – didn't want. Me back here. I – came.' Suddenly he pushed himself away. Telien's lightstaff laid a blush of yellow light down the side of *kin* face, like pollen. His own lay toppled in the litter. 'I – *had* to. Staying there would – have been hiding. From falling. From being – broken. I had to.'

'Every living thing knows its own hatching time.'

Shakily, Lian bent to lift his staff. He held it two-handed, bracing his shoulder against it. 'It – is too close. To *en'vos'neen'el*.'

'My *kindereen*-parent, Jahde, was a child at landfall. Yet you were born into the fifth generation. You kindle and fade so quickly, your people's presence in *vos'neen* changing from one year to the next.' Words were always secondary to *kinder'el'ein*. Even as practised a speaker as Telien answered the unspoken before the spoken. Lian had learned patience with apparent irrelevancies; he trusted that what he was being told, he wished to know, even if he had not asked. Telien said, 'The Burdanians who came are different from the Burdanians who are here now. They thought themselves dying. They had left Burdania behind them. After their great grieving, they were peaceful, quiet in *vos'neen*. Now they are not going to die. Now Burdania is before them and they are not quiet in *vos'neen*.'

'Should we – go back – to Burdania?'

'You are a tragic people,' Telien said. 'We thought we had left tragedy behind. A hundred thousand generations ballast us against change. They know everything that is to be known by the living. Except you.' *Kin* paused, sensing his frustration and uncertainty. 'No, *i'vad'neer*, I do not answer your questions. I do not know how.' The child in Lian thought rebellion at this last, most sympathetic and powerful parent abdicating omniscience. Very softly, Telien sighed. 'Lian, I am *kindereen*. *Kindereen* are not meant to change.' There was a silence, and then *kin* said, wistfully, 'You were such a little thing, when I held you in my hands the first time. A bright, new presence in *vos'neen*.'

'What have – I done?'

Telien did not answer. A few more yards and they emerged from the jungle on to a riverbank, and from the riverbank, could see the lanterns of the high houses on the far side. The low log bridge was wide enough that Lian could come up beside Telien. Telien balanced *kin* lightstaff on its tip and rested a hand on his shoulder. Moonlight flickered on the barely moving river below the bridge, and dappled Telien's robes and the moss beneath their feet.

'You give me great joy, *i'vad'neer*. You always have. I wish we could reach others of your people as we do you. But I see why we cannot. I see it in you. Burdania is now a part of you. Whatever becomes of them, becomes of you, too. And perhaps,' Telien stared up into the trees, finding words with difficulty, 'whatever happens to you, we must share.'

Kinder'el'ein seemed born of earth, not air: dark, soft, slow. Yet they lived at a height: the high houses ringed the trunks of canopy trees above the dense ground growth and its seething life. The veins of the jungle, the rivers, were lined with clustered high houses, each cluster a short day's walk from its neighbours. In this cluster there were nineteen, housing parental and grandparental triads, and children. Some of the trees nearby still carried the marks of dismantled houses, the impression left upon the bark, an outline of platform, roof and struts, carried beneath the moss and parasites. Houses were raised and dismantled to match the number of mature *kindereen*; they were also dismantled as needed to spare the trees. They passed from *kindereen* parent to child, as Jahde's had to Telien, and should to Shaleen.

From the ground, each was reached by a wide stair, which

110

spiralled up around the trunk. The bark had puckered around the inner step and the scaffolding. Moss bearded the trunk, scaffolding and undersides of steps, though the upper sides were as clear as the jungle paths. Lian pushed his fingers through it, digging their tips into every crevice. He felt his way around the trunk, keeping eyes and mind off the drop below. Telien stayed to his outside, and very close, lighting his way with both lightstaffs.

Above his head, the platform of the high house encircled the tree trunk, its struts lipped and absorbed by soft bark. Nets still hung in great pouches around it, sagging with the weight of vines. The *kinder'el'ein* had hung them as soon as he learned to crawl, and at once made for the edge of his known world. They would now be left undisturbed, with all the life they supported, until strand by strand they rotted away.

The last time he had been here, just before leaving for the *kinder'vos*, the vines had been in full flower, long, fat ruffs of white, violet and yellow. Sara had guided him up the stairs to say goodbye.

Through vines, moss and shadow, he glimpsed light, and a weave of white. A child's deep, vigorous voice spoke, and an adolescent's silvery fluting answered. Lian followed the light as the vines closed around him, let it guide him up the final steps and through the hatch in the open platform. The light-bearer was Telien's adolescent daughter, Vaelren.

She he remembered with the sensuous recall of early childhood: a great-eyed face peering into his crib; a thick finger, tentatively given into his grasp. A long body folding over to sweep him into the air. A long arm to play 'snake' with and a deep-ridged ribcage to rest his back against. The feel of warm, dark skin like new-fallen leaves. He knew how her bones and muscles fitted together beneath her skin. She looked much as she always had, extremely tall, black-skinned and cobalt-eyed. She wore a white robe and caul, but her sleeves and hem were green-grey with moss and dirt, and had grubby patches where she habitually wiped her hands. She held a lantern and a bolt she had been shaping: she was an apprentice woodworker.

Though adolescent, still becoming fully female and fully empathic, she was older than Thaorinn.

'Lian,' she greeted him, in her silvery voice, 'you feel like yourself again. You feel beautiful.'

A flush surged up from his footsoles. Vaelren tipped her head to one side, nictating membrane quivering. 'When you came last time you weren't yourself. It became real to me that when you die you will be gone forever.'

He hurt for the pain he had caused them.

'I wanted to tell you,' she said, silvery voice softening. 'I wanted to tell you so I could know you through it.'

'You are beautiful, too, Vaeli,' he said huskily.

'He's not beautiful,' said Vaelren's younger sibling, the *aneel*, Jehane. Jehane and Lian had been infants together. Now he was a diminutive Burdanian young male, Jehane a hulking sexless child. *En* ran a huge hand over his head, dislodging his hood. Vaelren pulled it up for him. 'You're so small,' Jehane said. *En* voice matched *en* close and oppressive size. 'How can you be *maeren* already when you're younger than me? How can you be a man?'

'I – am Burdanian.'

'Do you like my robes?' The child flounced them. They were dyed in streaks of colour, some of which could not have come from the jungle. 'The dyes from the colony are so bright. I make pictures, too, like your parent's parent used to make. I used to make mandalas, but they were just child mandalas, I can do pictures even before *en'neen*.'

Telien clunked the cover over the hatch. They were on an open platform where the torus of the high house had been widened but left unenclosed. The platform was roughly hexagonal in shape, and lightly dusted in moss and lichen. On three sides the hexagon was walled: curtained doors subtending an arc of mossy tree. The rest of the hexagon was open to vines, nets and noisy jungle darkness. Lightflies floated in over the edge, kindling their cool sparks in the dusk display. Vaelren followed his gaze, and turned her head to look back at him, expectantly. Lian remembered what he used to do. He walked forward, towards them. They winked out. He crouched, and spread his hand, and held his breath. After a moment, he felt a trickle on his hand, the insect exploring his pale, cool Burdanian skin. Then there came another, and a third, and presently so many that he could no longer feel individual insects. As one, the flies kindled, and his hand was gloved with pale, shivering blue. He pivoted, very slowly, to show Vaelren.

As he did so, he caught sight of Shaleen standing in the left-hand doorway, the curtain snagged upon *kin* shoulder. *Kin* robe was stone grey, *kin* caul heavy, with wings which jutted like stone wedges. The tremor through his hand caused the insects to quench and disperse like smoke. *Kin* walked towards him with a rustle of robes, stopped before him and looked down at him. Shaleen's eyes were lighter than Telien's or Vaelren's, a distinctive sapphire blue, split by the vertical pupil. *Kin* lifted stiff fingers, and signed a greeting. Hesitantly, Lian signed back. Beyond that, they had nothing to say to each other, not even for Telien. Shaleen stepped back, and glanced down at the platform. Lian's eyes followed *kin* gaze. It had felt smooth under his feet, but he had barely noted it, for stalking lightflies. Now he saw that he stood in an area cleared of moss, and his right foot had scuffed a delicate tracery of coloured sand. It was a mandala, the art of the *kindereen*. He knew Telien's touch with the sands, playful, deceptively simple. This was complex and subtle; it could have taken days to lay. He stared down at his unwitting desecration, dismayed.

'Lian,' Telien said, quietly. 'Come away now.'

Shaleen's eyes shone white with nictating membrane. *Kin* flattened features were tight with revulsion. Lian tiptoed over the moss. He hardly dared look at Telien. He had failed the test as it was presented him. Telien's guiding touch was gentle, and *kin* held the curtain aside for him. 'Teli, I'm sorry—'

Jehane clumped behind them. 'Shaleen doesn't like me either,' *en* said. '*Kin* thinks I am too loud, and paintings do not belong to *vos'neen*, and colours from the colony are hideous.'

The corridor hugged the trunk, opening outwards into the rooms. Most were curtained, but halfway round the trunk was a glass door, which slid easily aside under Telien's touch. Within, blue light rose.

Jahde had adapted the room for Sara's grandparents, calling on skills and knowledge preserved from the first awakening of the empathies to shield outside from inside. Lian had been

113

born in that room, but he felt no affection for it. When he was very young, Telien would carry him here to calm him, staying to talk and sing to him. Telien's singing voice was an improvised affair, a sweet, hooting whistle. But as he grew, he was expected to recognize for himself when he should leave, and subdue his Burdanian nature alone. He had spent far too much time here.

The room was very simple, its furnishings two beds, a table, and, on the outer wall, a painting. Jehane went at once to stare eye to eye with the painted face which dominated it.

The left half was that of a very old woman, the right half that of an infant. Close-braided white hair blurred into the infant's scalp. The old woman's eye was black as space; the newborn's scarcely lighter. Beneath it, a green hill covered an underground barrow, which was crowded with figures indistinct except for a girl in orange and a man in green. A woman, large with child, knelt before the green hill. To the left of the woman was a white city laid out flat, like a child's perspective, on either side of a river. The parklands along the riverbanks were busy. Above a city a building sat on a knoll, one wing embedded in stone.

This was one midsummer's day in Lltharran city, on lost Burdania, as painted by Lian's thrice-great-grandmother, Javir D'Halldt of the ships.

Jehane examined it brush stroke by brush stroke, large round eye nearly on the panel. Telien watched, *en* nostril-slits quivering with amusement.

How could we breed such a one? Kin signed. *It must be the Burdanian influence*.

Lian felt it as a reproach. Pictorial art was rare amongst the *kinder'el'ein*, and an assertive and purposeful interest such as Jehane's even rarer.

En *delights me as* en *is*, Telien signed. *As you do. As Vaelren does. As Shaleen does not, because* kin *will* not. *I was never more surprised than when I knew Shaleen would be* kindereen. Kin *has always resented the imposition of the empathies. At birth* en *resisted the lifebond. Some do. Kin* signs were shaded with melancholy. *Burdanians think* kinder'el'ein *do not know loneliness. I felt it when Shaleen was just born, and I could not make fast* en *spirit. I am not strong in* en'neen; *I thought the failing was mine. All the* kindereen *within a day's walk came. We did something akin to what we do at* en'vos'neen'el, *to bring the* en'neen *close. Even so,* en *would not reconcile to life, to belonging. En cried and would not feed easy, even when we took* en *away from here.*

Vaelren slid open the glass door, and came in, stooping more than she needed to. Unlike Telien and Jehane, she found it difficult to be isolated in here. But she settled herself down on one of the low beds and began to sand her bolt. Its form and grain had to be perfect, and perfection, in accord with structural requirements and *vos'neen*, was a lifetime's study.

Lian was a little surprised that Vaelren had not adopted Telien's and Jahde's herbalist craft. She feared their father's tools, and lacked the special aptitude for their mother's vocation.

Their father was a clothmaker. He drew fibres out of vats of wood digest. The process fascinated Lian, the quickness of the draw, the tangle of thread which grew in the basins of neutralizer. Lian did not get to see the drawing often: children were warned away. Downriver a clothmaker had been scarred from neck to footsole from a fall into one of the vats. Vaelren would not watch her father work.

Yet she would be handling the same enzyme solutions in woodcutting.

Shaleen had studied clothmaking. Lian could not envision *kin* showing *kin* father's elegance at the vats. There was something rigid about Shaleen, not made for dealing with fluids.

Einen was a rarity amongst *kinder'el'ein*: a metalshaper. Burdanians hypothesized that metals disrupted the bio-electromagnetic component of *vos'neen* or – which the *kinder'el'ein* intimated was closer to the truth – retained distorted impressions. Whatever the reason, affinity for inert metal was a rarity. Metalshapers spent days away from the settlements, working with dangerous substances, metal, fire, force, and isolation.

Metals were important. Most high houses had a room like the quiet room, for the protection of young adults beset by the wakening of *en'neen*. Metals were worked into doors and walls,

115

in tradition-set patterns. And – something no Burdanians had discovered before Lian's accident – *kindereen* used metal to treat the disturbed in mind. Lian remembered a mask of silver filigree laid upon his face. Sometimes the thought teased him that all *his* complexity had been trapped in that intricate pattern. If he could get it back, he might restore the person he used to be.

But somehow that mattered less, here amongst his *kinder'el'ein* family. They would accept him as he was.

And then he remembered what Telien had said to him in the jungle, about the debate, and *en'vos'neen'el*. He was still a Burdanian amongst *kinder'el'ein*; he still had an obligation. He would have to go back to the colony, and soon.

NINE

BURDANIA

Morning promised rain. Quilted cloud lay obliquely across the horizon. Scraps of it frayed and scudded before the wind. From the window of the meeting room, Lian watched their shadows, mesmerized by their sharp sliding edges, their darkness. They changed the mood of the plain, making the greys grimmer, the yellows sombre. Even the river, spreading and slick as new paint, turned dull.

The first of the *cali* arrived with a step so quiet that Lian saw his reflection before he heard him. He was a man of Thaorinn's age, perhaps older. His head was narrow and dark, carried with a certain hauteur, his features long and fine. He had the bright, waxy skin of a southerner or islander. He was dressed in heavy grey knits, patterned in cream across the yoke and border of the cardigan and kilt. Beneath the kilt he wore grey trousers, and on his feet varnished reed sandals. On his wrist were two narrow bracelets of the same material, both minutely inscribed, one flaking and discoloured by time. He was clean and well groomed, the only mark on clothing or person an inky smudge on his right index finger.

There was nothing in his look as direct as a question. Lian answered it, nevertheless. 'I am Lian D'Halldt. I have been – invited.'

The newcomer sat down and folded his hands with a dry soft rustle of bracelets. 'Sidor Vassar.'

Vylan and Rathla Zharlinn had each told him a little about the people who would attend today. Sidor was *cal* Vassar, representative of the agricultural settlements in the southern

117

peninsula. Vylan regarded Sidor with mellow affection and tolerance. Lian could already see where tolerance might be needed. Zharlinn was impatient with his indifferent support of Daisainia and her restoration. Both had mentioned that he had compiled a history of the known age, from such accounts as survived.

'Vylan said – you wrote – history.'

Sidor turned his head. His eyes were a brackish brown, his tone forbidding. 'A private project.'

The rebuttal was not unexpected, from what Zharlinn had said, and from what Vylan had not said. 'I am – sorry. History is – important. To Burdania. Because of – the losses.'

Sidor regarded him with a detached curiosity. 'I deprive no one, save of the chance to exploit my work to suit their own agendas. To you history is important. To me it is precious. Do you perceive the distiction, Lian D'Halldt?' His tone said he thought not.

'History puts – perspective on – the present,' Lian said, delicately goading.

Sidor pressed both long hands flat on the table and leaned back. 'The enduring self-centredness of the present: then does not matter, only now. No, Lian D'Halldt, I do not look for perspective.'

'For – removal,' Lian said. 'You prefer – the past.'

Sidor blinked. Lian felt the bright, disconcerting shock of his full attention. In a small, self-contained society, amongst people who knew him, he was unaccustomed to it. He had had it from Daisainia, in the moment of their meeting. He had elicited it from Sidor now. He held his breath, waiting.

'I believed,' Sidor said, 'that if I could but collect enough accounts, I would know the truth. We have excellent memories, and we like to tell stories. That is our failing. We honour truth, we recognize truth, but we change it to suit. I will not have my work become part of the distortion.'

But you did not answer me, Lian thought, intrigued. 'The – truth,' he said, 'about – what?'

'She has told me who you are,' Sidor said, 'and what she thinks you are. It is the present that concerns you. Attend to it.'

Daisainia came in then, her arms stacked with square

118

wooden wafers. She set down the stack and began to lay them out on the circular table. They were patterned with weaving black lines and small boxes. After a moment's straining to make sense of them, Lian saw that they formed a map of the settlement, taking in the river looping around ridge and knoll, the three settled hills, and the ruins beyond the dykes. The dykes showed dense and black between river and settlement. Daisainia's small, strong hands were grazed, the winding on the ring stained dark. She wore a loose undyed shirt, decorated at the throat with some of Shivaun's fine embroidery. The embroidery was a cluster of leaves and she had already collected some healthy green smudges on the cuffs. She said, without looking up, ' 'Tis bad, Sidor.'

'We feared it would be when the thaw was late.'

'I feel – shadowed,' she said, tightly.

'I, too.'

Lian sensed a fuller intimacy here than would show itself before him. More had been exchanged than a few constrained words. Sidor was supposedly an unenthusiastic supporter. But here he came, in this grim season, first to her meeting. And received her confidences as simply as she offered them.

A clatter of sticks in the open door announced Arkadin Nors, leaning heavily on the arm of a big man in a brightly striped sweater. Zharlinn had said she would be coming as second to her absent niece, *cal* Nors. She suffered herself to be helped into a chair, but slapped away the big man's hands as he made to unbutton her cloak. He took it with good grace and sat down beside her. Daisainia set the last tile in place and said, 'Arkadin Nors. I hope my request doest not prove too tiring for you.'

'Ask them that carried me,' Arkadin said. 'As if either'f us cares for tired. When'm dead and there's nothing more t'hear, then'll be too tired.'

'I am well aware,' Daisainia said, drily, 'that should I found a Gossips' Guild, the leadership will go uncontested.'

Arkadin laughed until she wheezed. The big man beside her deftly caught a sliding crutch. His hair was thick, its uppermost layer bleached nearly white. His face was broad, the skin around his eyes seamed with squinting, and his skin tone was rich and lustrous. He had a peculiarly rawboned look for one so

119

mature, as his sweaters – he wore at least three – were all short in the cuffs, strained across the shoulders, and out at the elbows. The topmost was the gaudiest garment Lian had yet seen in the settlement, striped yellow, green, black and purple. Zharlinn had mentioned a senior Islander *cal* entrusted by his fellow Islanders to, as Zharlinn put it, keep an eye on Northerner antics. Zharlinn had spoken well of him, and he looked affable enough, but if anyone were to trap Lian, it would be Ionor D'Alna.

Rathla Zharlinn arrived accompanied by, to Lian's surprise, Tion. He had understood that Tion's sister was *cal* D'Suran. Tion cast a concerned glance towards Arkadin, who flapped a hand at him, still struggling to catch her breath. Still watching her, he said to Daisainia, 'Kylara has a case.'

The *isk'dar* laughed shortly. 'Aye, and by what means did she take that case? I know you, Tion D'Suran. You do not trust her not to quarrel with me, so you come yourself. Either to keep peace between us, or to make her point more subtly.'

'Y'should be glad,' Arkadin gasped. 'She'd'a flayed us both, and need no scalpel t'do it.'

Tion said, in a strained voice, 'I give you my word not to press you about evacuating to the other side of the river, or about relocating to the coast and only summering here—'

'Indeed,' Daisainia said sourly. 'But Kylara would have you remind me of it, nevertheless?'

A tired smile flickered on Tion's face. '*Isk'dar*, will you accept me as second to my sister?'

'Be welcome, Tion D'Suran.'

Tion sat down beside Arkadin and Zharlinn between him and Daisainia. He seemed unaware of this, at first; the realization when it came would have been amusing, had it not been so obviously painful. In delivering Daisainia's message, circumspection had availed Lian nothing. Zharlinn demanded the exact wording. He had objected in fine detail and at considerable length, educating Lian in *tayn* Zharlinn politics, without ever touching on the true and apparent reason. He loved the *isk'dar*. And thought that she was supporting his mother and *tayn* as they tried to reclaim him.

Daisainia seemed oblivious. Lian suspected that she would

subdue her emotions to her own ends. She would do no one else intentional injury; inattention would be her greatest cruelty. Granted awareness, she could be capable of warmth, staunchness, or killing mercy. Had she already practised that on Zharlinn?

She visibly stiffened at the last arrival, and he brought a bracing cold front into the room. Lian recognized the austere, black-haired man who, on the cameras, had resembled Thaorinn. Not so in person. A physical likeness remained: his face was thin, his expression cold, his skin nearly as pale and lustreless as Thaorinn's. His eyes were of a blue so dark as to seem black. But the resemblance ended with the authority of his step and the impact of his presence. Thaorinn muted his projections to fit himself to live amongst the *kindereen*. Thaorinn governed emotion with intellect. This man would govern emotion with passion. The truly cold need not work to seem so. This had to be Illuan D'Vandras, dykebuilder, exiler of Tor, and opponent of the restorers.

He chose his place, directly opposite Daisainia, and sat down. Daisainia favoured him with a nod; he answered in kind. Acknowledgement and antagonism passed between them like a white shaft.

Daisainia leaned forward upon her arched hands. 'My *cali*, thank you for coming. We are as you find us, beleaguered, and I will be calling upon your experience as never before. Of necessity, therefore, this *caur'cali* will be much concerned with Lltharran's state. The river is rising quickly, as quickly as any time on record. The dyke on the far side of the river is leaking; regrettably we will lose what has been planted there. But there is no danger to buildings or people. On this side our outer dyke is holding and our inner dyke nearly complete. I have asked some of you to look to our other concerns: food and provisioning. How do you see us? Arkadin?'

'Th'll be enough to eat. Not fancy, but enough t'take us into summer. Stored properly, too; had them check that. But yes, y'll eat.' She coughed and pressed the heel of her hand against her chest. 'Water stores're high, 'n look clean. Rain'll help.'

'Medical stores are sufficient,' Tion said. 'We have two Guildmembers on the other bank; myself, Kylara and the

121

children here – we will manage. If you would caution people again not to work beyond their limits, we will avoid injuries. But I would,' he hesitated, 'like to suggest that we move as much to the high land as possible. I feel some trepidation about Arkadin, for one, in *caur* Nors.'

'My home,' Arkadin said, truculently.

'D'Vandras,' Daisainia said. The man, who had been tracing a line with his finger, raised midnight eyes. 'What is the risk?'

'There is something more you might do,' Illuan D'Vandras said. He drew a piece of paper from within his cloak and unfolded it with meticulous economy. Daisainia watched him tensely until he slid it across the map to her. It was a sketchmap of the settlement. What it showed, Lian did not see. Daisainia said, 'Ah,' and passed it to Sidor. He laid an inkstained finger on a thick radial line, linking inner dyke to outer. 'You'd block the path between the dykes.'

'If the outer dyke breaches the channel will flood. We will be reduced to a single dyke for the entire length. But if the channel is sectioned, we will only lose integrity in parts, which will be within our capacity to watch and reinforce as needed.'

'That dyke has held for three springs?' Zharlinn said.

'In all the years I have travelled to Lltharran,' D'Vandras said, 'I have only twice had to come by sea. The mountains were quite impassable. This year, and five years ago.'

Lian felt the tension around the table. Daisainia's hand fisted so tightly that the ring stood away from it in a bulky arc.

Sidor said, with seeming inconsequentiality, 'And you did not sail against a current?' He addressed Daisainia. 'I have been compiling the records, weather and navigation: yours, the west coast's, ours, and ships' logs. In winter, a warm current flows past the Ardar peninsular and north-west to the hook of Sor. In summer it follows the coastline north, and brings exceptional warmth to the northern coast. If the thaw is very late, it is brought on by the shift of the current, and is sudden. That happened,' he said, quietly to Daisainia, 'five years ago. A mild rise turned nearly overnight to an inundation.' He shook his dark, narrow head once. 'And that year, the mountain snows were far lighter than this. I agree with Illuan. Exceptional measures must be taken.'

Daisainia looked at Arkadin, who showed her frail, unsteady hands. ' 'Tis not for me t'make work for others. But I'd sleep th'better for it.'

Tion said, 'May I see the map?' Daisainia passed it to him. He held it carefully and studied it. 'You are suggesting six sections. They will have to be built quickly, to be effective. That is a great deal of work. People will be tired.'

'There are ways of lightening the load. Levers. Pulleys.'

Tion sighed, but before he could speak the door behind him whispered open. A young woman stepped in, cast a glance around the room, and stalked to grip the back of Tion's chair with strong, well-kept hands. To Tion she said, 'I changed my mind.'

Rathla Zharlinn had pointed out Kylara D'Suran from a distance, which, he intimated, was the best place to be. Kylara D'Suran had, nearly single-handed, overturned the affluent and settled Medics' Guild and scattered its members across the planet. She was, like Daisainia, a force worth reckoning. Her colouring and dress were as striking as Tion's were nondescript. Tumbling auburn hair with a streak of yellow down the right from crown to tip. She ornamented a shirt like Daisainia's with a deep blue scarf and blue cloth belt, closed by a copper clasp. Heavy copper bracelets adorned both wrists, broad copper rings her fingers. Her eyes were a changeable blue-grey, her glance quick and intolerant. She plucked the paper from Tion's hand and studied it, scowling. She had Tion's firm, regular features, and steady expressions, but on her they set to intransigence.

Daisainia waited, watching her. She did not need to wait long.

'What does it take to make you give up?' Kylara demanded, as though continuing an argument already long begun. 'Our situation is impossible. Winter is killing hard; spring is simply killing, with the work and the wet and the cold, then muck brought down by the river. We cannot grow enough to feed ourselves. And for all that we leave your precious ruins open to the winter and floods. It is all we can do to protect our own houses. *Caur'isk'dari* we cannot understand, and nothing we have done has touched it; it will survive without us, or crumble despite us. For all your talk of replanting the plain, you have hardly broken more earth than your mother. We have accomplished nothing here, except a monument to Travassan obsession.'

Sidor said, 'This is not the time to discuss—'

Kylara narrowed her long, changeable eyes. '*You* would take part in such a discussion; I think not. You would shirk that responsibility, as you always have.' Arkadin rattled a crutch against the leg of her seat. To Daisainia, Kylara said, 'My responsibility is the health of the people of Lltharran. I say we should keep to the high land now, and after the flooding, resettle on the coast. And no more,' she leaned forward to crack her knuckles against a thick black dyke-line, 'of this.'

Tion said, 'Kya, this is not the time . . .'

Daisainia rocked forward on to her hands. Lian could see the fine ridges of tendons along the inside of her wrists. 'I will battle the river to the death,' she said, in a clipped voice. 'And if that death be as my parents', *so be it*. We will all die. You may call that obsession. But remember this, before me, people lived and died in Lltharran. Neither I, nor any other, chained them here. It was their dwelling place, and no winter, no flood, no death, could drive them from it.' Lian stared at her, thinking: she is extraordinary, and equally, our welcome depends on *her*? Kylara's face was white. Lian remembered that she had come south after a plague decimated her kin. Daisainia said, more quietly, 'There is no safe place. Only a place to stand. And I stand here, with those who stand with me.' Violet eyes swept up, holding Illuan. 'Section your dykes, Illuan. And with all despatch.'

Illuan D'Vandras was silent for a moment. Then he said, 'It may be that *cal* D'Suran has the right of it.'

'Three springs—' Rathla Zharlinn bridled, at Daisainia's side. Daisainia's expression was masked, but Lian could see she was shaken.

'In the mountains there were two dams, across the main tributaries. There were also canals and aqueducts to carry the water away. The dams have collapsed now, the canals have fallen in. The water runs over fallen blocks larger than this room. During the melt, the valleys fill with mist, the ground trembles, and the sound . . . Even down on the plain, days away, I heard it in my ears. That is a force we cannot contain.'

Ionor D'Alna tugged at his bright-coloured sweaters. 'If you can't drain the sea, doesn't mean you can't float a raft.'

Arkadin Nors barked a laugh. 'An' raft-building's what's needing here. Need't'last the spring. Then fret about summer. Then the years after that.'

'This,' Daisainia said, grittily, 'is my place. I will stay. You may stay or go as you please.'

Kylara drew breath. '*Isk'dar*, please,' Tion said, more over his shoulder to Kylara than to Daisainia. The lines of Daisainia's face were hard. 'We did not mean to bring it forward like this. But you *are isk'dar*. You have set the conditions of this renaissance. You have affected the lives of all of us here.' Daisainia looked down, at the edge section of the map. 'Whether we go or stay depends upon you. And for many of us, including you,' her head came up. The shy medic hesitated, but only for a moment, 'the coast would be a kinder place to winter.'

There was a silence. They watched Daisainia, whose eyes had closed. Then she thrust herself upright. Looking over their heads, out across the plain, she said, 'Very well. If I last this spring, you may try again to make a wanderer of me.' Kylara leaned over to whisper in Tion's ear, her expression mutedly triumphant. Abruptly, Daisainia's attention refocused. She sat down, with a quick, vigorous movement, a painted tile sliding beneath her hand. 'But first we must all last. And it may be,' she looked challenge at the two medics, 'we shall last so well that you might be persuaded otherwise. Kylara, Tion. One or other of you may go.' Kylara patted Tion's shoulder, and did so. 'D'Vandras, what will we need?'

'Then 'tis settled,' Daisainia said. She eased back in her chair, flexing her shoulders. The tiles before her had been amended in charcoal pencil, denoting sites of the sections, six now, between inner and outer dyke, and the routes for delivery of materials. 'Are any other matters as pressing as the realization of this?' She glanced round the table, her attention for once falling lightly on them.

'Tor,' said Rathla Zharlinn. 'Tor D'Vandras.'

She looked at him. Colour surged into his face and before she said anything, he said, 'He *stripped* Tor of kin, *tayn*, protection, livelihood. He turned him out on the verge of winter. And for what: for having an independent mind.' He looked from Daisainia, around the table. 'Would any of you call that a crime of violence, or endangering the *tayn?*'

'This *caur'cali* does not pass judgement on each other's conduct,' Illuan D'Vandras said.

Daisainia's face was transfigured by a dazzling flare of rage. '*Does it not?*' she demanded savagely.

There was a stinging silence. She looked from Illuan to Sidor, with old, distilled anger in her eyes. Illuan's countenance was icy. The haughty Sidor drew himself up and endured. The tableau held. Then Tion reached out, not looking at her, and fidgeted with the wooden tiles, making a distinct click. Daisainia's head jerked round. She quenched her anger, deliberately and wilfully. Deep and ominous as that anger had been, her sense of justice and responsibility matched it.

Ionor D'Alna said, 'There was a mistake made, yes.' Daisainia's face showed a shock of harsh ironic amusement, quickly erased. Ionor turned to D'Vandras, and said directly, 'Illuan, it was not well done.'

'His views are abhorrent to us in *tayn* D'Vandras. He is therefore no longer of us. And, it is he who introduced himself to you.'

'Illuan,' Sidor said, 'that is unworthy of you.' Heads turned, but Sidor gave no sign that he expected, or welcomed, the reaction. Slowly, Illuan nodded acknowledgement. 'True,' he said. 'None of you need have known. I do not know whether to be glad or sorry he has found such staunch supporters, for it will only prolong his exile. He is *tarwyn* and will remain so until he understands.'

'Understands *what?*' Zharlinn demanded. 'That he cannot argue with you?'

D'Vandras rested his hands on their sides, fingertip meeting fingertip. 'He *did* commit a crime of violence. Against a people – a world – which died sixty-six years ago.' Lian caught his

126

breath at the precision of reckoning, at the authority behind his voice. 'If we disturb their memory, if we try to reconstruct their civilization, such as it was, we are likely to share their fate.'

'We are more likely to share their fate in ignorance.'

'Peace,' Daisainia said, sharply.

'Tor understands,' Lian said suddenly, without thinking.

The night-blue eyes fixed on him. Lian said, 'He argues, ably – and ferociously – against everything he works for. Like you.'

Still an ungiving silence from the man across the table. Lian felt Daisainia's breathtaking stare. 'You come – every spring to – for the dykes.'

Suddenly, unexpectedly, D'Vandras smiled. 'An engineer's pride in his craft,' he said mildly. 'A private indulgence which *cal* D'Vandras should not share.'

Zharlinn said, to Daisainia, 'Do we really need him so much that we dare not gainsay him?'

'What would you have me do?' the *isk'dar* demanded. She got to her feet and, watched by them all, went across to the window. Stopped and turned, heels barely clear of glassed air, the light at her back. 'Whatever you might accuse us of, Rathla, we would not have let Tor starve – for food or fellowship. Nor would Illuan. He trusted that we would take Tor in, and we have. He can be harsh because we are permissive.' She locked eyes with the dark man, who, after a moment, conceded with that small dip of the head. She turned away from them, looking out over the banded grey desolation of her world, or so Lian saw it; what Daisainia saw he did not know. 'This *caur'cali* was begun so that we might keep each *tayn* in touch with the rest of the world. We are not arbiters of each others' law. And yet by the very nature of our relationships . . . by the past . . .' she turned suddenly, her voice strengthening, 'which even now compromises our courage—' She took three strides to Illuan D'Vandras' side. 'I *must* give Tor D'Vandras a public name. Amongst us only the venial and violent go nameless, and I cannot countenance him being so condemned.'

'Hai!' Zharlinn said, and she turned on him, came around the table more swiftly than Lian would have thought anyone would. 'I speak for *myself*, Zharlinn, and myself alone.'

127

'A fine hypocrisy, *isk'dar*,' D'Vandras said. 'You know what you are.'

'And do you remember what you are?' she snapped back across the table, hot-eyed. 'I think not. You have turned *tayn* law to suit you in a contest of will.'

'You have not understood,' Illuan D'Vandras said, with unguarded and authentic bitterness. 'None of you. No matter; call him what you will—' And he looked straight at Lian. 'Tor knows what he is.'

'No,' Lian said, since D'Vandras had spoken to him. 'I do not understand. Is it that Tor – believes that – the old technology – is valuable?'

'Do you truly wish to know, or do you simply wish me to provide arguments to use against me—'

Rebuff was the worst he had expected, not a counter-accusation with unexpected substance. 'It may be – so—'

'It may be?' the dark man echoed. He stood. To Daisainia he said, 'Call him what you want. It makes no difference. Now I must go and do what needs to be done.'

When he was gone, Daisainia skirted Zharlinn and sat down. 'Perhaps other matters may keep until later.'

They took their dismissal promptly, and gathered themselves to leave. She did not move, looking at the map, while Ionor and Zharlinn between them helped Arkadin out of her chair. 'Fool man,' Arkadin opined, crankily. 'Never understood them as would drive away their own.' She recollected herself and shook off the two men. 'Enough of that.'

Daisainia said, 'Arkadin. There is a place here for you, if you wish.'

'Bah. No.' The older woman said frankly, 'This place is halfway t'the afterlife. An' I'll be there soon enough.' She fitted her crutches under her arms. 'Don't fret about D'Vandras,' she advised. 'And let old wrongs lie.'

Daisainia watched her as she made her slow way through the door.

'And let old wrongs lie,' she murmured. 'What must it be to say that with such ease. And mean it, as I believe she does.' She glanced at Sidor, who was studying the amendments to the tiles. But did not press the glance. She turned instead to Lian, catching him watching her. 'D'Halldt.'

He found a question which was askable. 'Is – Tor – Illuan's son?'

'D'Vandras is childless. Tor is parentless. It seemed they were suited. They are much alike.' She let out a hissing breath. 'That man need only breathe to irk me. His affectations of knowledge.'

'He has thought about it a great deal,' Sidor said.

'So have we all.' She snapped to her feet, leaned over and began gathering up the tiles. Sidor stayed her hand. 'Leave them be. We may need to study them.'

Unoccupied, her hands closed into fists. She straightened up, crossed to the windows, and stood staring out.

Tion said, 'I should go and check on Arkadin. Lian?'

In the corridor artificial light fluttered raggedly overhead. Tion led with the pace of a man who had taught himself not to hurry. Lian watched the young, weary face, and remembered the sound of the tiles clicking together. Today he had seen that the machinery of government was embedded in an intricate web of relationships. He knew the colour of some of the strands, but many iridesced with contradictions. And they were tangled into a background weave of history.

'What – happened five – years ago?'

Tion glanced at him, warily. Lian said, 'When – Illuan and – Sidor spoke of – five years ago – there was something in – their voices—' He thought it best not to say what he had seen in Daisainia.

He saw Tion relax slightly, as though what Lian had asked had been less than what Tion expected. 'Ky Travassa and Branduin Vassar drowned in the flooding. The *isk'dar*'s parents.'

'What – happened?'

'Nobody knows. The dykes were not as extensive as they are now. Part of the lower slope of the hill had fallen into the river, and their footprints led there and did not return. They were found tangled in the driftwood netting in the morning. But they were both strong swimmers. It's likely one of them was unconscious and the other could not free them and . . . would not leave them.'

129

'She took – it hard,' Lian said.

'I was not there,' Tion said. Evasion sat uneasily on him. After a moment he continued, 'She was their only child, and they had kept her to themselves. She had no *caurim*. No one to ease her grief.'

'And – Shivaun and Crystolan. Who are they to her?'

They were nearly at the balcony; they could hear voices from beyond the brightly filled hall mouth. If Tion hesitated only a little, and kept walking, he need not answer. But he stopped, several paces shy of daylight. 'Shivaun,' he said, softly, 'has Travassan blood, but her father was declared *tarwyn*, by Ylid, who was Linn Travassa's granddaughter. Shivaun's mother was . . . Morain D'Vandras, who is not . . . spoken of now. Shivaun is very fragile and Cyrstolan is barely a year old, and innocent. Both of them are under the *isk'dar*'s protection.'

Lian heard the warning. He remembered the bright blaze of fury on her face. 'I – would not – like her angry at me.'

'No,' Tion said. 'Nor would I.'

'When you moved – the map—'

He saw the resistance in Tion's misted brown eyes. Resistance and strain. He let the question slip away gracefully. 'Then – Dai – the *isk'dar* has no – family.'

'Just Sidor. Her mother's father.' He smiled slightly at Lian's surprise and stepped out on to the balcony where Zharlinn, Ionor, and members of Arkadin's family were preparing her carrying chair for the downhill journey.

The rain had begun. Rivulets corded and tangled the height of the long windows. Tion saw, said, 'Ah, good. We need this rain.' A thought came to him; he turned back to Lian. 'Lian, has anyone warned you that you must not drink water from the river in flood. Some years the flooding takes poison from the poisoned wastelands; it has been known to be fatal. Filtering or boiling does not remove it. That,' he glanced towards the streaming windows, 'is why the rain is so important. Rain is clean, and we have cisterns drawn from the river which we have tested.'

'Tested?'

'We see if it will allow certain things to grow – bacteria, algae – micro-organisms which grow quickly and are readily killed by

130

poisons. It's something from Linn's time, when the river was worse than now. So drink only from the cisterns.'

'The – *isk'dar* expected – the rain.' Vylan, to Lian's mild surprise, had received the information seriously, although at sunset there was still neither cloud nor haze in the sky. He had sent word to his neighbours, and he and Lian had rigged the rain-catcher – a collapsing funnel of canvas and vanes – over the *caur'ynani* cistern. This morning rain-catchers had sprouted throughout the settlement like some huge, graceless flower.

'Oh yes, she's said to have *shikarl*. Nowadays, it's confined to the Islands.'

Lian hesitated, then risked the observation, 'We – have not heard of *shikarl*.'

'Ah.' He paused to wave to Arkadin and her retinue, who were setting out. She was riding in a canvas-covered chair, with four carriers. 'We all have some weather awareness, if we know how to use it. Humidity, pressure, direction of the wind, the light. Some people have it to an extraordinary degree. The *isk'dar* is one. It is more developed in the Islands and a great aid to navigation and safety; and the *isk'dar*'s grandmother was a shipmaster. So yes, when she says it will rain, she is more often right than wrong. And,' he paused, and Lian saw him weighing his next words, 'if she ever gives you a warning, about anything you are about to do, heed her. Don't . . . ask why; she would not take it kindly. She's one of a very few whose anticipation extends beyond the weather. It is best to heed her and not question.'

'I – do not understand.' She had a powerful mystique, this *isk'dar*.

'No?' Tion looked mildly regretful at having spoken. 'The matter may never arise. Let us find some canvas, so we are not drenched on the way down.' And Lian, though wondering, let the subject go.

131

TEN

TARIDWYN

One day in three, the long planetary day bracketed the shorter Burdanian one and colonists and *kinder'el'ein* shared wakefulness. The day after Lian's arrival was the one. Lian stepped out of the daytime jungle to see the dome fully lit. He was unprepared, preoccupied by what he must say to Thovalt. He looked absently up at the golden glow, and his gaze was caught and carried upwards to the summit. Memory came: hard radiance, a vine tearing away, the plump shape of a single leaf falling with him until the air currents caught it. He shuddered, closed his eyes, opened them again to attend with great care to the present. Its frame looked weblike and fragile, thinned by the upwelling light. Not so the fallen leaves, the coiled vines and fallen branches which mottled the curves. They were dense, black. When the rains came, they would wash down and catch on the struts. His fingertips had trailed in muck as he crawled. He had passed the new corpse of a tree-mouse, a *ta'dess*, still as a furred bud. He took the soft, tiny weight of it in his hand and tucked it gently into his pocket, meaning to return it to the jungle. Or had that been another time, another place, ill-defined enough to have slipped in here, where he lacked a memory?

Timid amusement flickered at the thought of the fastidious Burdanians discovering a dead mouse in his pocket.

The perimeter doors of the colony had once been decorated with the double star. That had been obliterated by the third generation. The doors had not been opened since that time, nor would they be: the jungle had sealed them shut. Lian passed through the wall by a small side gate.

The ground between wall and colony had been a landscaped native garden, neglected as the colony turned in on itself. Jungle refuse filled in the pools and streams, and jungle undergrowth choked the cultivated flowers. Only the chill around the walls and habitats kept it at bay.

The chill enveloped him as he slid through the door: he recognized it as the one he and Telien had left by. He shielded his eyes against the blue light. After the crowded, subtle depths of the jungle, the straight blank corridors were a tyranny on the eye. The quiet was oppressive. Voices had a shocking prominence. Yet nobody spoke to him. They passed with looks, or smiles, or even a murmured greeting, but awaited no reply. He strayed along the corridor, watching and being watched. He felt acutely that he did not want to expend the effort talking to anyone else. All his concentration was on Thovalt.

He fetched up against a grey wall touchplate. Cautiously, he brushed his fingers upon it, remembering the thing Burdanians called the monitor. When he was little, he thought the monitor was Burdanian *en'neen*. It knew everything about them and their colony. It was their integrated management and information system.

Silver letters formed in invitation. Slowly, he deciphered them. Written language had died out long ago amongst the *kinder'el'ein*, and he was out of practice. But an aritificial intelligence was infinitely patient. He traced his question upon the plate: where might he find Thovalt? The monitor told him that Thovalt was in habitat six.

Six was the newest of the habitats, and the most sophisticated in its illusion. It was, in its entirety, a shoreline. The interior was filled with tall yellow grasses, brine scrub, small trees. The outer wall was a wave-washed bay, offshore islands hazy against the horizon. The lacy shambles of the waves seemed patternless, but the seabirds circled ceaselessly above the same rocks, and the same three birds took flight over and over again, without once returning to land.

The ceiling – four stories up – was violet, and backlit. Native sunlight would have filtered very dull. Lamps in hexameric arrays lit in succession one by one throughout the day, impersonating sunshine. Sometimes the lights dimmed, the backlighting was turned off, the projection showed a sullen sea, and water sprinkled down, impersonating rain.

The air was meant to smell of the sea. To Lian it smelled bitter. He wondered if a Burdanian sea had to smell bitter, to one born on Taridwyn.

He tracked Thovalt's voice along the artificial shore.

Eight people sat in a yellow circle of pressed grass, eye-height all around. Thovalt was on his knees, head thrown back, eyes half closed, talking swiftly and rocking as he threw his hands around. His attire would have looked absurd on anyone else: a night-black robe, appliqued with black binary stars.

On his right was Lors, white head lowered, expression tight and withdrawn. On his left, a black-haired woman tapped tapering fingertips on her thighs. Lian did not remember her. She wore a high-collared, hip-length jacket in dark grey, which fitted without a pleat or a wrinkle. Her hair was drawn back into a neat chignon. No grass clung to her. She interrupted, in a penetrating alto, 'This is irrelevant and unproductive, Thovalt.'

Turning to answer her, Thovalt saw Lian. He swept to his feet. 'Lian D'Halldt! Welcome. I never thought to see you again, carried off into the jungle as you were. Meet the rest of our number. Lors, Alystra.' That was the dainty, black-haired woman, who eyed him with irritation. Her eyes were oval and as blue as a *kindereen*'s. Beside her was Thovalt's birthmother, Andra D'Lynnan, as long-boned and supple-handed as Thovalt. Andra, Lian knew slightly, as a colleague of his paternal grandfather. The others he did not recognize. Lian followed Thovalt's introductions around the circle out of courtesy, but when that was done he could not have said their names. He turned to Thovalt. 'I – want. To talk. To you.'

Thovalt widened his eyes. The light caught and glimmered in them. 'Oh,' he said, with a lilt.

Alystra said, 'This is not the time for a private conversation.'

'Not. Private. Make your debate later. *En'vos'neen'el* is now.'

Someone murmured behind him, 'What is he talking about?' And someone else, 'That's the native ceremony at lunar conjunction.'

Thovalt said, confidingly, 'Alystra is our Advocate Adviser.

She is trying to cut us to suit. But neither I nor our subject will be cut to suit.'

'You have no idea of the rigor expected of you.'

Lors lifted his white head. 'Maybe we should listen to what Lian has to say.'

Thovalt ceded the centre with a gesture, but seated himself with a distracting display of spreading his robe and composing his hands. Lian waited until he was done, then addressed Alystra. Thovalt, he sensed, was beyond persuasion. 'You intrude. On *vos'neen*. On *en'neen*. Because of what – you feel. About Burdania. Now is *en'vos'neen'el*. You must – not talk now. About Burdania.'

Andra D'Lynnan leaned forward, eyes narrowed. 'Are you telling us the *kinder'el'ein object* to our debate? That they want us to put it off?'

'Have they sent you as representative?' Alystra said.

'Telien – wants me. To ask.'

'And does Telien speak for – "his" people?'

'*Kin*,' Lian said. '*Kin* is *kindereen*.' Thovalt quivered with amusement. Lors said, 'Stop that.'

'Stop what?' Thovalt said, in innocence. Lors could not answer; he did not know. Lian did; Thovalt was succeeding, by small, well-timed motions, in breaking the others' focus on Lian.

Alystra flicked an empty glance at Thovalt, then looked back at Lian. 'If it were so important to them, why did they not object before now? What did Telien say? What was *kin* message?'

'No,' Lian stopped, explanation beyond him. There had been no message, not as Burdanians understood it. *Kinder'el'ein* would not ask; they could not accept that Burdanians were so oblivious as to need *asking* about something so important. In kindness to him, Telien would not lay upon him the responsibility for Burdanian courtesy. But he knew how glad Teli would be if he took it upon himself to do what they wanted done.

'There was no message,' Alystra said.

'Just because – no message. Doesn't mean. No need. *Kinder'el'ein* are *different*.'

'We are aware of that,' Alystra said. 'We try to be sensitive.

135

But if they had objections they should have raised them before this. We are already committed—'

'Excuse me.' The speaker was a young woman, with dark brown hair braided into a cap. Alystra looked at her; Lian turned. She smiled at him. 'Lian, you may not remember me. I'm Danas Lis.' She had a pleasant voice, and spoke in direct easy syntax. 'I don't know much about *kinder'el'ein* religion, or mysticism. You are talking about the ceremony at lunar conjunction, involving what is it – *en'neen.*'

'*En'vos'neen'el.* Living and – dead together.'

She hesitated before putting her next question. His speech had disconcerted her. 'Could we disrupt it . . . badly?'

He wanted to say yes, but the truth was he did not know. He believed in *en'neen,* as he believed in the colour red, because *kinder'el'ein* he trusted told him it existed. But *kinder'el'ein* did not need to describe *en'neen* to those who shared it, and so the vocabulary to convey its characteristics and vulnerabilities did not exist.

Andra said, 'I have never been convinced that these empathies are real, and not simply metaphor for environmental and spiritual awareness.'

'And why,' Thovalt challenged, rising upon his knees, 'did Telien not put it to me when we met yesterday?'

'*Kin* sensed you,' Lian said. '*Kin* did not – want to.' It was hopeless trying to explain *kindereen* self-protectiveness, and he did not want to say what Telien had told him about how the Burdanians *felt.*

Alystra said, 'So – correct me if I'm wrong – you have not been *asked* to represent the *kindereen.* Telien just yesterday came and went without mentioning it to Thovalt, Lors or any of us. There have been no other objections from *kinder'el'ein.* You cannot know the preparation involved in a debate of this importance, especially this particular debate. These people have been working for over a year – *our* year, not planetary – in amassing data and arguments. My assigned task is to advise Thovalt and his fellows on the best way to proceed to have the proposition accepted. I could not advise them to consider changing the timing of the debate at this late hour, given the psychological cost of this debate, both to speakers and to the colony as a whole.' She paused, briefly, and continued, 'Particularly since the last presentation ended catastrophically.'

Lors jerked a handful of grass out by the roots. The tearing of stems was like a salvo. Everyone stared at the yellow hank and clot of dark earth dangling from his fist. 'For better or worse,' Lors said, 'let us get it over with.'

Then Lian understood what Alystra meant. The last debate had been interrupted by his fall. He drew breath, shaped syllables, but could find no words.

He heard Danas whisper behind him, 'I had no idea he'd been left like that.'

Lian swung round, sent one blind, accusing look at her, and crashed through the grass circle. He fled, not looking back. The mindless cry of holographic seabirds pursued him.

Lian crouched on a chair in Lors' lab, waiting. The monitor had told him where Lors spent most of his time, pursuing his studies. As he waited he laboured on a sentence, setting it out like polished stones before him. Jasper for his demand. Moonstone for himself. Crumbling shale for the past. And obsidian.

On a shelf beside him was a little brain encased into a transparent block. He picked it up. Without warning it fanned into thin wafers, and he had to catch them in cupped hands before they spilled. He patted them into a block again, and drew one at random, holding it up to study the translucent swirls and rosettes. This was the brain, the enfleshment of mind. This was what had been crushed and imperfectly repaired in him.

He slid the wafer back into place, and the block on to the shelf. He got to his feet, straying past screens and shelves. On one of the screens was a schematic of *kinder'el'ein* anatomy, tracing the projections from the receptors into the brain. He found it disagreeable. *Kinder'el'ein* did not dissect Burdanians.

He heard Lors speaking to someone in the corridor. Lors sounded terse, annoyed. He was glad of that, since he did not want to face any of them but Lors. Lors came in, swept a glance around the lab, and, not expecting Lian, did not for a moment

137

see him. Then he checked himself, blinked, and looked again. He came up to Lian.

'I am sorry,' he said, quietly. 'I am ashamed for my fellows. I apologize for myself and them.'

Lian hardened himself to Lors' discomfort. Like Thovalt, Lors had been embarrassed for Lian, and by Lian. He had also been embarrassed by Thovalt, and the others. He pitied Lian. He thought in terms of Burdanians, and did not understand. Lian laid the stones before Lors. Jasper, moonstone, shale, obsidian. 'Give – me – back – words.'

'I'm not the person you should ask. My mother, Granaith, did the reconstructive—'

'No!' The white-haired woman! Lors blinked. Lian struggled to convince him of his rationality. 'She let me – go lost. Be lost. In my head. She wasn't a person to me.'

'She's not much of a person to anyone,' Granaith's son said, neutrally. 'Granaith is a cyborg. She has implants which give her a direct interface with diagnostic and treatment machinery. Without them she might not . . . have been able to save your life,' Lors allowed, carefully. 'But she had them integrated into structures and circuits which should progress non-verbal information and social cues. She knows her lack of effect can be distressing. I . . . could run the tests, and refer them to her. I might be able to direct a basic remedial program. Anything more involved, Granaith herself would have to undertake.'

'Yes,' said Lian, through set teeth. He had failed the *kinder'el'ein* here. He would tolerate anything rather than fail them again.

'We did speak more about it after you left. Danas thought we should ask the *kindereen* ourselves.' Lian flushed, remembering that whisper. He did not want to be grateful; he preferred to be angry and humiliated a little longer. He needed the courage. 'The others did not, I think, want to find out what they might say. Li, we have put so much into this debate. It creates such strain on everyone involved, speakers and audience. If we built everyone up to discuss the issue, had them prepared, and then postponed *now*, it might be enough to cause us to lose. One or two voices could make the difference. If we had known earlier . . . If you want, I will come and . . . explain to the *kinder'el'ein*.'

'I can. Explain,' Lian said, sharply. He could not resist adding, 'To them.'

'I am sorry,' Lors said, again. 'Maybe if we succeed, this time, it will be over.'

'What do you – think – is – there?'

'I don't know,' Lors said. 'I feel we have to go and look. We have to inspect our fears. I study adaptation: how far we can be stressed before we are no longer fertile, before we begin to die prematurely. I think we are more durable than we know. Physically, at least. I think we'll find something has survived; what, I don't know. Adaptation can take some strange and maybe ugly forms. Lian, *for* Burdania, for the case I am trying to make, will you let me do some scans of you? It would help immensely if I could extend the accepted limits of Burdanian tolerance.'

'If you – help. With words.'

Lors' sombre face cleared like the sky after rain. 'Agreed.'

'Jehane is always looking at that picture in the quiet room.'

'Mmm?'

Lian lay head to head with Vaelren on a sandflat where the river had undercut the bank and then withdrawn. Above his head, and her face, was the underside of the jungle's skin, crumbling dark earth held in a sieve of roots. The river bubbled just beyond the fingers of Lian's extended hand. He was soaked in sunlight to the elbow and vastly content. Colonial days he spent with Lors, under study for their twofold purposes. Study of his adaptation was simple enough, if sometimes uncomfortable. He need only sit in a booth and endure whatever conditions Lors imposed, heat, cold, moisture, mixtures of air. Study of his brain dysfunction was exhausting and frequently humiliating. Lors set him psychological tests and intellectual tasks, and scanned him as he worked them. Lors' façade was so earnest and so careful, his efforts to shield Lian so obvious, that Lian let him believe that he succeeded. He did not ask to be told the results; he did not need to.

The one night in three when the jungle was in daylight, he sought refuge with his *kinder'el'ein* family.

Shaleen seemed to tolerate his presence, for the little time *kin* and he would be together. Jehane chattered to him about painting, and the making of colours. Telien showed pleasure in his company, and he took pleasure in Vaelren's. He was delighted that his memory, so fragmented, had preserved so much of her. And yet . . .

He could not trust memory. He knew that. Even in so simple a thing as the light in the jungle, memory was wrong. He remembered green light, yet the light at noon was very yellow, falling on green. And Vaelren he remembered as perfectly attuned to him, to his wishes and needs, without Telien's sense of looking down, amused, from a height. The intimacy was still there, but somehow compromised. She never denied him the answers he had learned to count on, yet they did not come as quickly. There were tiny moments of hesitation, and glancing contradiction. As though she was testing her distance.

As now, 'We are not artists.' Her pronoun, *vos'en*, excluded him.

Lian lifted his head enough that his hair brushed dirt, and looked along her foreshortened form. The crest of her ribcage almost touched the hanging roots, and her robe was dusted with grit and fragments of leaves. Her expression was still and serene, receptors relaxed, eyes half closed. 'Telien thinks Jehane might become *kindereen*. *En* is self-willed. *Kindereen* often are.'

He thought about that, about what it said about Shaleen, and herself. Perhaps the strengthening of the empathies had caused this change in her. He could not think how to address it; he said, a little helplessly, 'But – a *bad* thing?'

'It's new.' She was quiet for a moment, then rolled whiteless eyes up towards him. 'It is not of *vos'neen* or *en'neen*.' There was a silence, then. 'Shaleen is going.'

'Because – of me?'

She blinked with slow sweeps of triple eyelids. The nictating membrane was tardy to clear. He said, 'But Telien – wanted – *kin* to stay.'

'*Kin* cannot. *Kin* cannot live alongside your people.'

He rolled out of the cleft, turned his back and drew up his knees to his chest. He could not think what he had done, or what else he might have done.

The closest he had come to Shaleen had not been intentional: three days ago he had awakened from a doze on the balcony moss to find a beetle exploring his hand and *kin* laying out a mandala nearby. He had done his utmost to lie still and alarm neither *kin* nor the beetle. When *kin* left, the mandala remained, a miniature meditation in white sand no larger than his fist, and of intimidating complexity. Telien said *kin* saw him in it; Jehane said it was funny; Vaelren had studied it, saying nothing. By then the crawling insects had begun to blur the lines, and during the night rain washed it into the cracks between the boards, to join all the years of patterning grains washed before it. He had taken it as a gift, a temporary gift.

He heard Vaelren sliding out behind him. She came no nearer than that. Sunlight lay like a yellow oil on the dark river sands. He thought of Jehane and *en* paints. Jehane was so simple: *en* inflicted hurt and flung *en* arms around him in childish remorse. But when Vaelren did it, she should know better.

'You're turning your feelings in on yourself,' she said, in a strained voice. 'And then pushing them at me.'

'I'm not.'

In his peripheral vision he saw her lift a handful of sand and absently weave a pattern between them. Sand on sand; an unseen mandala. 'You did when you were small. But you didn't know what you were doing then.' Lian, caught between denial and shame, accepted the shame. The wish to force his feelings upon her gave a murky pleasure; the knowledge that he was doing it gave none.

'I can't not feel,' he defended himself.

She breathed in, and lifted her head. Miserable as he was he was struck suddenly by the sheen on her skin. The pupils floated in her eyes like leaves. She caught her breath, and her nictating eyelid flickered across her eye; the inert bluish-white of membrane was jolting. She said, 'A hundred thousand generations in me do not know you exist.'

He did not understand how that pertained, and waited for her to explain herself. He wanted to say to her, 'Is it Shaleen? Is it you? Is Teli not telling me—'

He said, instead, 'Vaeli – that mandala— Did it – was it – what did it say?'

'Mandalas do not say. Telien has told you: Mandalas "depict" the layer's "state of mind". In the *lan'neen*, the solitary mind, or the *vos'neen* or the *en'neen*.'

'What did Shaleen's – depict?'

Vaelren lifted another handful of sand, but made no attempt to lay a pattern as it ran through her fingers. She was not going to answer, he thought, feeling the full weight of his failure to accommodate and protect his *kinder'el'ein* family. 'I tried—' he said. She raised liquid eyes, and he continued in sign. *To make the debate later. They would not listen.*

'I know,' she said. She drew a deep breath and said with an effort, 'It is not only you. It is Jehane, who is loud and improper. It is Telien, who is weak in the empathies, and loves Burdanians. It is Einen, who works metal. It is myself. Shaleen does not belong to us. *Kin* will mate out in the deep jungle, where Burdanians have been asked not to go, where your presence is weakened by distance, and by *vos'neen*. *Kin* will do well enough there. You need not be grieved for Shaleen.'

That last he took for exoneration. It was only later that he wondered for whom he should be grieved.

'Proposition, then: we submit before this chamber—'

'Wordy.'

'We submit that this colony authorize an exploratory expedition to Burdania, purpose—'

'Unnecessary.'

'We must,' Lors said, 'state our purpose.'

'*Purpose,*' Thovalt stressed. 'The purpose, to determine the condition of Burdania and its people.'

Something, Lian thought, is going to happen. The tension was like the tingle before a monsoon thundershower. It would happen between Thovalt and Andra, or Thovalt and Lors, or Thovalt and Alystra: Thovalt seemed the engine of the coming storm.

They had argued about whether he should wear his black costume into the debate itself. They had argued order of presentation, emphasis, moral stance, whether to emulate the

142

most nearly successful approaches or to devise something commensurate with their own personalities. Their disarray unnerved Lian. They were like a sparking fire, scattering their heat. In the few days since he had first met them, he had come to care for them and their purpose beyond the wish that the Burdanians find a resolution and cease to trouble the *kinder'el'ein*. He could see they were paying a price, Thovalt was growing ever more sleepless and glittering; overcaring Lors ever more burdened; Alystra, trying to prove herself in her first major debate, ever more impatient and exacting.

'The proposition,' she was saying, 'is best stated as simply as possible. It is, "Do we or do we not send a mission back to Burdania?" Not, "Are we morally obliged", or "Must we for our own survival"; those issues will emerge during the debate. It should be simply will we or won't we, yes or no.'

'I don't agree,' said Lors. 'You cannot let the other concerns stay hidden—'

'I am not saying that. What I *am* saying is that the proposition cannot be stated as a *challenge*. *You*, Thovalt, like defiance and confrontation. You like to stage scenes. I would advise you to restrain that liking.'

They were in a viewing room in one of the satellite Archives, reviewing previous debates. On the screen, the most recent unfolded, unobserved. Lian sat off to the side, peripheral. Lors had suggested he come along, to listen. Thovalt, once so insistent that he return to the colony, now treated him as a spectre at the feast. Lian had come to accept that any attempt of his to contribute would be derided. He did not know why. He tried not to be wounded. He tried to avoid those glittering eyes.

He looked back at the screen. The records of the debates fascinated him. In one, he had watched a young Thaorinn orating with Burdanian intensity. Thaorinn's voice then had been able to flex and strike like a snake, low, a little harsh, but supple and swift. Unlike the waterlogged voice which time and the jungle had left him. Thovalt had watched Thaorinn fixedly, intently, absorbing every detail. He watched Thaorinn like a rival. And he looked from Thaorinn on the screen to Lian on the periphery with a look of scorn and inexplicable barren anguish.

143

Alystra was saying, 'This is beyond my mandate as adviser, but it seems to me that you have this fantasy of setting yourself against some great adversary, this cruelty and uncaring towards poor Burdania. This is not so. What happened to Burdania distresses us all. We would like to set it right. But we do not know how. These debates should be a sincere examination as to how we go about setting it right.'

From the screen, the woman Proponent's low voice murmured beneath Alystra's. He watched her speak, pacing heavily back and forth across the podium. She was graceless and sincere; no wonder Thovalt was disinterested. The interior of the dome was illuminated by a mixture of daylight and low interior lighting; it was a handsome gold, a joyous colour. Behind her, a screen like this one showed equations and matrices. He heard a distinct, misplaced crack, and thought that someone had trodden on a glass, but nobody else in the room reacted. On the screen the Proponent looked up and lifted her arm as though to fend something off. A heavy, dark blur flashed by and there came another sound, a thudding crunch. The camera jerked and brought into frame a crumpled figure in blue overalls.

'Sweet reason,' Lors cried, attention caught. 'Screen off!'

The image died. They all stared at him, appalled. Lian thought, I even dressed like them. It was his first acknowledgement of what he had seen. In their silence he again heard his own skull shattering. He bent over, trying to get his breath.

On the far side of the room there was a stir, several voices raised in protest. And then an arhythmic series of blunt bumps. Lian surfaced, levering himself up by the chair in front. Thovalt lay sprawled between two rows of chairs. The fading bruise left by Sara's hand stood out starkly against his unconscious pallor.

Lian raised the glass of water to his lips with both hands. On the screen the Proponent stood framed by the drive equations, arguing the safety of a unique driveship for a voyage to Burdania. He read through the equations again, though they were only symbols, distracting himself from the impending

144

moment when she would hear a crack from overhead and look up. He remembered that an argument had drawn him on to the glaring surface, but the record portrayed no argument. She had been talking, and then she had lifted her head and—'

He took a firm breath. He had to watch it through this time. It might be well into colony night – late afternoon outside – but Lors or someone might yet decide to check on him. He had to watch it through.

He heard the crack. She looked up and—

'Screen stop!'

A small blurred golden shape hung midair, a shard of roof. He had not caught it before. He shifted his gaze from it to the woman's face, suspended, too, at the onset of realization. Every time he watched it he saw more. If they met now he thought he would be able to tell her thoughts, trained by the flux of expression across that narrow interval. It was a quite different expression than she or any of them had shown while speaking of the griefs of Burdania.

It seemed his memories were imaginary after all, as the neurologists told him. It had been early afternoon, not, as he remembered, night. There had been no argument, only the Proponent's lecture on some esoteric aspect of physics. He could find her to ask her – she would be attending this debate, if she did not choose to abstain – but he did not have the courage. It would be like facing Telien, another one who had shared the fall.

He looked back at the suspended fragment of glass. 'Screen continue. No – sound.' The fragment dropped from view. The large dark blur followed it, and vanished in silence. The Proponent stared down from the platform, bewilderment turning to horror. As the cameras found the small blue-clad heap somebody's hand appeared before the lens. Through the fingers he saw feet circling round each other and him. Then the screen blanked, and two lines of white print informed him that the debate had been terminated.

He felt drained, having given up more than he had gained. He had hoped the record might complete his memories; instead, it undid them. He did not remember it that way. Daylight, and no raised voices, a quite ordinary brightness, not the radiance which stalked his dreams. Perhaps if he now went into the dome— What would he find? Blood, glass shards, the echo of a cry. Had he cried out? He thought he had. But there were no sounds aside from the breaking ceiling and his skull on the tiles. His voice was not there either.

He heard a sound behind him, like a sob, and swung round. Thovalt sat in the farthest chair of the backmost row, farthest from the light of the screen. Lian got slowly up from his chair and walked around by the stilled screen. Thovalt turned aside in his chair. 'Don't look at me,' he said.

Lian stopped before him. He did not need to ask to know Thovalt had been in the hall on that day. Here was another one who had fallen with him. Perhaps this was the reason for Thovalt's harshness, the unwelcome memories Lian's presence roused.

For Thovalt, as well as himself, he argued, 'It was – dark. Not light. Quarrelling. Not quiet. A leaf falling.'

'What are you trying to do to me, Lian?'

'Nothing,' Lian said, more sharply than his wont. He was tired of people who took offence to his living. '*I* – wanted to – know.'

Thovalt looked up at him, his eyes wide and fixed. 'And do you?'

'Not – this,' Lian said. One side of Thovalt's face twisted. He seemed stripped of posturing, humbled, even crushed. Lian read the bitterness in him, the revulsion, the self-hatred. He wished he could touch the mandala which defined Thovalt, sweep away the warped strands with his fingertips. But Thovalt, Lors said, believed all the strands were hopelessly intertwined, the instability and the brilliance, the fear and the defiance of his colony's fear.

He would not look at Lian. Lian said, 'In the – *kinder'vos*. You – wanted me – back.' Thovalt's nostrils shivered as he inhaled. Lian said, plainly, 'You heard – me speak. There. What is different – now? Is it – the others. Saying. Danas. Lors. Or do you—' He could not finish. He did not wish to know that Thovalt found him repulsive. He feared Thovalt did. He wanted to say, 'I was sleeping and you woke me. You asked me

146

to remember Burdania, and work with you. I need someone to see hope in me, *as I am*. My father sets me against what I used to be. Lors sets me against the norms. Vaelren sets me against *kinder'el'ein*. Only Teli sets me against nothing. I need you.' What he said was, 'What is – different now?'

'Lors told me your results,' Thovalt said. His head did not move; his eyes glanced off Lian. 'Do you want to know? What you were. What you are.'

'I – don't need to,' Lian said. 'I know. Lors – thinks I – don't.' It was a relief to be able to say it aloud, to someone who took no false trouble to hide his reactions to Lian' infirmity. 'I'm bad. Words. Other things better.'

Thovalt gestured towards the screen with a long arm and finger. 'That should be you,' he said. 'You should have been the one to speak for Burdania.'

Lian did not turn to look. He watched Thovalt, steadily. Thovalt was quickly roused by falsity, by the hint of lies, deceit or manipulation. Or by the scent of vulnerability. He said, 'I – will work. With Lors. On words.'

Thovalt leaned his head back and regarded Lian through slitted eyes. The lids quivered, thinly. 'I thought you were curable. I thought if I brought you here, the medics who are so avid about my imaginary instability might do something real.' Ah, Lian thought. Did Thovalt see a parallel between Lian's damage, and his own genetic flaw? Was Lian something he feared becoming, retarded and rejected? Then the insight fled as Thovalt continued, 'But you're quite incurable. Your brain is a fabulous thing of scraps and patches; Lors marvels at it. They could graft, or go in with surgicals, and retrain you; you'd be a project of years, but unless you were virtually regrown, you'd never be what you used to be. What you could have been.' There was a high whine of distress in Lian's ears. Until then, he had been unaware how much he endured the present through hope for the future. And now Thovalt was telling him that there was to be no future. That he was to be as he was until he died. He heard Thovalt say, 'Lors will never give up on you: I can tell you he never gives up; he'll work you until you both collapse.'

147

'But you. Give up,' Lian said, bitterly. 'You wanted. To be – like Thaorinn. You are.'

ELEVEN

BURDANIA

'Linn Travassa,' said Sidor. 'What of him?'

Vylan hid his amusement, for Lian's question had been quite plain, and considered a boulle of dark green flax. It was the evening of the second day after the *caur'cali*, and Sidor had arrived unannounced at the *caur'ynani*, bringing sufficient flax from *tayn* Vassar's fields to clothe its members for a year. It was a rich gift, suggesting either deep friendship towards Vylan, or tacit support of the restorers.

Lian had hoped it might presage a mellowing.

He said, 'I wondered – what picture you have of – Linn?'

'Physically?' Sidor said. He glanced at Vylan, who was rolling a tuft of dark green into a lumpy strand between his fingertips. Sidor pulled another tuft and began to do the same. They were alone in the kitchen: Rathla, Lara and Tor were at the dykes, Valancy and her son sleeping. 'He was not a large man, but strong. He lost one foot in childhood, perhaps during the disaster itself, and thereafter used a wooden prosthesis, and crutches. He was adept with them, swift and agile.' Between his skilled fingers, the strand grew thin and straight. 'His eyes were violet.'

'And – his character? In all – I have heard – I have never heard – why. To – strip his people of – history – knowledge—'

'His deeds speak for his character. His reasons,' Sidor paused, 'we do not know. His own records do not begin in any accessible form until the middle of his life, when his course was established beyond decision or explanation. There is mention of earlier records, but they were destroyed, or censored.'

149

'Can – will you – speculate?'

'No,' said Sidor. He passed Vylan the finely spun green thread, backhanded, and regarded Lian levelly.

Lian said, '*His* – records. Are records – kept since?'

'Of course,' Sidor said, with a degree of chill. 'You can understand that records could be very precious to us, now.'

Vylan tugged gently, then more firmly on the strand and, finding it sound, began to tie a series of miniature mariner's knots. He said, 'Every *tayn* has someone appointed to keep the chronicles. Every ship has a logbook; every *caurim* or Guild its record. Individuals keep personal journals; I am one. Even Linn Travassa could not extinguish literacy, though he tried. He did try.'

'And – may someone see those records who – is not part of the *tayn*?'

Vylan sighed. '*Tayn* chronicles, yes, they are open, but they remain at the *tayn*. Some of the *caurim* are open; Guild accounts tend to be closed.'

'Lltharran is – not a *tayn*? Are there – records?'

There was a silence. Vylan occupied himself threading a free end through a tiny loop. At last Sidor said, 'There are records in *caur'isk'dari*. They are not reliable.' He looked at Lian, brackish eyes challenging. Not all the force in Daisainia's gaze came from the Travassan.

Lian thought, and rethought, and decided to risk it. 'Is that – why you might rather I – not see them?'

Vylan gave him a sharp, blue-green look across the table. But did not speak.

There was a silence. Sidor said, 'It is for the *isk'dar* to give you leave.'

Lian said, 'You say – unreliable. How so?'

'She received you as *tayn* representative. Until tonight I doubted it. But you have asked the questions I might expect. I do not know what stories have come to C'Rynn. I will say this: whatever has happened in the past, it must not contaminate the present.'

The non-answer intrigued Lian. Sidor could have been subtle in his misdirection; he had the sophistication for it. Yet he chose otherwise. Lian studied the narrow, haughty face,

150

noting impatience, irritation and discomfort. Daisainia was the only child of Sidor's eldest and favourite daughter. But this *isk'dar* granddaughter was determined to remake her world as completely as had Linn. That must perturb a man who had made a life's study of Burdania's fragmented history. Even if Sidor were not already nonpartisan. What, in the lived or learned past, might have made him so? What else might an historian discover above and beyond common knowledge . . . ?

For one of the few times in his life, Lian was glad of his marred speech. If Sidor had found allusions to space-faring Burdanians – and if he had not set them aside as fanciful – Lian hardly spoke like the representative of an advanced society.

And, instead of being divided between a wish to ease his granddaughter's course, and a wish not to be involved, Sidor simply might not think Lian worth subtlety.

A little pride in him bridled at the slight, real or imagined.

He said, 'If you know – better—'

'Do I?' Sidor said, bitingly. 'I have come to think that the ones who know best use the evidence of their own eyes.'

'What – do your eyes see?'

There was a silence. Sidor blinked several times. He was probably used to being able to deter by mien alone. But Lian was intent on getting the measure of the man behind the mien, and hardly noticed it.

'I opposed my daughter's liaison with Ky Travassa. It closed a distance my elders had worked a generation to establish.' Sidor stopped. Looked at Lian, and seemed to recollect himself. 'Lltharran, *tayn* Travassa, if you will, is a parasite. It depends upon the goodwill of the true *tayni* for its survival. In past generations it returned nothing but slow oppression, the bleeding away of independence and knowledge. As the islands, the regions were better free of Lltharran, the Travassan, and the Guilds. So I learned from my Vassar and Islander predecessors.'

'And – now?' Lian said, leaning forward, concentrating. 'Your – granddaughter is *isk'dar*. You come to – the *caur'cali*.'

'She is *isk'dar*, yes. And I come.'

'And – do not wish me – to see those – "unreliable" records.'

Sidor watched him, resigned, and perhaps regretting his prior lack of subtlety.

Lian said, 'You could – tell me what – is there yourself.'

There was a silence, not a thinking silence, but one of emphasis, of finality. 'No.'

Dusk was coming in. The sky was dark indigo, and cloudless. The river of stars wound overhead. Haze condensed above the moving waters and the still, as, under a clear sky, the air quickly cooled. Lian pushed his hands into his pockets and walked quickly downhill, shivering. He felt a little ill. He had misjudged. He had not expected Sidor's refusal. He had seen Sidor and Daisainia together, sensed the bond between them, granddaughter to grandfather, connected if not by principle, then by a common love. He had chosen not to consider that transient fury he had seen in the *caur'cali*. What could be between them to make her so furious, and him unwilling to shield her by more than obstructionism? And he had pushed at the obstruction, and so exposed Sidor's reluctance that he see the records that the others would now insist. Had he been left to himself he could have decided that Sidor was merely being possessive of his primary sources. He might have remembered what Sidor had said about the intrusion of history into the present. He had felt the weight of history enough in the colony to *agree* with Sidor. He might have been able to wait, to see some of the *caurim* records, to draw out of people their versions of the story. Tion would tell him. Vylan and Arkadin too. Why had he been so determined to best Sidor? Because of his specialist insight, or because of his hauteur?

And now he would have to *ask* Daisainia if he could see her records, and take whatever answer she gave. He had last seen her on the dykes, as she dropped a plumb line into the water. She had offered him a hand to steady him down from the dyke, and he had watched her walk away, a small, powerful figure in muddy jacket and smeared trousers, her eyes ceaselessly scanning the settlement and the dykes. Her attention to everything and everyone around her seemed more like *vos'neen* than anything Burdanian.

He came to the lee of the dykes, level with one of the cross-sections under construction. They had rigged a pulley to speed the passing of stones over the dyke. The apparatus was lit by six relict lanterns, slung in an arch. Illuan D'Vandras balanced on top of the inner dyke, looking down, face turned into the light. His expression was not unlike Daisainia's as she let the weight sink: intent, aware. He was as much a contradiction as Sidor, this adversary who watched over her dykes.

Of Daisainia he saw no sign. Somebody hailed him to carry two lamps along to the next section, where they were short. The woman in charge there was vexed about awkwardly sized stones, and sent him up on to the ridge, where they were dismantling a ruin, to instruct them. From there he had to go to the Medics' Guildhouse, to fetch a liniment for a strain. And then Lara hailed him and begged him to look over at the driftwood netting beneath the bridge, to see it was not overfull. D'Vandras' project allowed little liberty for wood-catching.

He heard the voices below him as he set an uneasy foot on the bridge. They were standing just below the bridge, between the dykes, without a lantern and hidden by the curve from the nearest workers. He would have called out to them, but the timbre of the voices warned against it. He heard Zharlinn say, 'You allowed just one season . . .' and Daisainia's taut response, 'Time enough for most.' They were standing face to face, Zharlinn gripping her upper arms. She had her hands fisted against his chest, letting him come no nearer. He saw her lift her head to look into Zharlinn's face, the brown hair sliding back from powerful, set features. 'I am *isk'dar*, Zharlinn.' Lian stepped back from the railing, and her voice followed, low and forceful: 'I thought you understood. I may be barren; in six generations my line is all but extinct, and in five years my parents conceived only myself and a son born dead. But it is best that my childlessness seem merely my perversity for as long as I can pretend it so. I must let my people hope. And for that, I need . . . secrecy.' Lian thought, I *must* go. But could not move, convinced that he would be seen. He crouched and slipped a hand inside his jacket to cover the transceiver. Nobody had reason to hear this.

She said, 'I would we had *never*—' and broke her sentence in half.

'Never begun,' he said, heavily.

'I asked you for secrecy, but I did not realize that I was asking you to hide your heart. And that is beyond your capacity. Rathla!' she checked him, said firmly, 'It is.'

'I did what you wanted,' Zharlinn said. It was nearly a cry.

'I know. And I am grateful. Wait! Let me speak. I thought long friendship would make the interlude pleasant, and the ending easy. I thought you could accept that there might be an ending. But it has become plain to me that you *did not heed me*. You claimed years of me for yourself. In this season, I feel . . . most mortal, Rathla Zharlinn. Spring has educated me in loss.'

Lian heard the scuffle of stones beneath their feet. She said, harshly, 'Let me be, Rathla, and listen. It may be that we will have years, in years to come. I shall hope for it. But there are things which I must first do, which you cannot do with me. I cannot hold your heart because I have other things to hold, and I will not let you thrust it into my hands!'

'If you were carrying my child,' he said tiredly, 'you would not be doing this.'

'Perhaps,' she said, but without much expression. 'But I might have come to it yet, and it would have been harder still in a year, or two. I fear for you, Rathla. I can bring you to do things which are not in your nature. If that is because you love me, then I would rather you did not.'

Lian had thought her capable of a killing mercy, and now he had seen it shown. But that last was harsh, and seemed to Lian freighted with experience. What could she have made him do? He heard her say, 'Come back with me now. We have said what needs saying, for tonight at least; I must go, and I will not leave you here.' He did not hear Zharlinn's reply, if any. He watched them climb over the inner dyke, she leading. He watched her look back, to offer an unnecessary hand to Zharlinn, and catch sight of him, crouching on the bridge. She did not react, beyond a single meeting of eyes which made Lian flinch. Her face was white and for an instant, fierce. And then she turned to Zharlinn, and Lian saw how deftly she kept him from looking back.

Stiffly, Lian got to his feet. The sight of a coarse rope, tied in an ornate knot like the ones Vylan had fashioned in miniature, reminded him of what he was meant to be about. As though he

154

could tell whether a net was overloaded. Along the dyke, six arches of strung lights illuminated spars and ropes, backs and shoulders. Fires lit up their own hovering smoke. There was very little wind. Someone was singing, in a hoarse, stubborn chant. On the far hillsides, lanterns pinpricked the night. Beneath him, the river throbbed and rumbled.

He held on to the railing, and bent around it, pulling his stomach in hard so as to make no contact. He looked down on heaving dark water, rucked up against a mass of dripping, jutting and slick spars. The net was bellied under the bridge; he could not see its webbing. The ropes slanted back out of sight. He swallowed saliva, and, very carefully, straightened up.

She came the last few steps to his side and said, quietly, 'What is't you are looking for?'

He had not seen her return; he felt himself blanch with shock. He managed to say, 'Check – the net. Lara – worried.'

Her face was set, not masked, but reserving judgement. 'This is not the place then,' she said. 'Come.'

He followed her; she did not look back. She gave him a needed hand over the inner dyke, and up the slope of the outer, near where she had dropped the plumb line. 'You would be best with a lantern.' Not accusing, merely observing another omission. He could see the strained webbing of ropes binding the trawl to the bridge. The net itself was nearly immersed, merely a line on the water, fringed with caught grass. Broken ends ground against the stones of the dykes. One spar was the width of his spread hands; it had frayed itself to a pale tuft at the end of a shattered spike. He remembered that they had taken the bodies of her parents from such a webbing, drowned and perhaps crushed by flotsam and water. He looked at her, and saw that she remembered it too; but he remembered a fact, and she the event itself. Her eyes looked on nothing living. He reached out, and pulled her head round until she focused on him. It took a while. He expected her to jerk away, but she freed herself with a little tilt of the head, no more than was needed, and presently said, 'Thank you, D'Halldt.'

When she looked back at the river her gaze was sharp and wilfully in the present. She said, 'It may break. It may not. We can do nothing for tonight. The dykes are more important than this wood. A pity: fires warm the spirit, and there will be the naming of Tor and Valancy's son.' Lian had heard Lara, Zharlinn and Vylan planning the naming in their snatched moments together, talking about food, firewood, festive dress. The plans seemed too fragmentary to make sense. Daisainia said irritably, 'We'd have better use for wood than to burn it, but they are the ones to collect it, so who am I to flout Northerner custom.' Then, deliberately, she turned squarely to him, balancing on one hand. 'What you heard was not meant for anyone's hearing. In courtesy to you, I will allow that you did not mean to hear it. In courtesy to myself, and to Rathla Zharlinn, you will not speak of it, not to myself, nor to him, nor to *anyone* else. Do you understand me?'

'I – understand.'

Understanding equalled compliance, in Daisainia's lexicon. She glanced once more at the bridge and the straining ropes, then turned and stepped down from the dyke. This time she waited for him to make his own way. They went beneath the bridge, and climbed the slope of the knoll rather than the inner dyke. Others had before them: the sleek grass was churned and downtrodden. Daisainia said, 'Tell Lara what I have said about the nets,' and started to leave him.

He said, 'Wait.'

She swung round, displeased. He said, 'I – had something to – ask you.'

'Then ask it, D'Halldt.' She waved towards the riverbank. 'I have no time for this.'

'I – spoke to Sidor. About records. He – said you had – records in *caur'isk'dari*. He said I – must ask you—'

There was a silence. Stray light glimmered faintly in her eyes as they shivered and fixed. 'What is't you would know?'

'I – asked Sidor if I might – read his history. He said I – should look to the – sources. As he – had.' He heard his voice fading. He said, 'Dai—' caught himself, '*isk'dar*, if you would rather I – not, then— Sidor said they were – unreliable. He – would not explain.'

'They are unreliable, D'Halldt, because they were kept by the Travassan themselves, or by their lovers or hagiographers. They are apologies, not records. But if you would see them,

156

you may.' She turned away, and said, over her shoulder, 'Tell Shivaun that you have my leave.' She took a step. Stopped and turned back to face him. Her back was straight, her hands fisted, and the mask tightly over her face. 'And, D'Halldt, I will answer no questions. I have not, and never will have, anything more to say. And all the rest are dead.'

'Here,' whispered Shivaun, through her veil of hair.

They were in one of the rooms on the third level which Daisainia had claimed as her own. It was a small workroom, still furnished as it had been seventy years ago, except for a single, wooden chair. The stringently ordered clutter seemed characteristic. Rock specimens, cuttings pushed against one of the light panels, a pot with a sickly-looking creeper whose roots were muffled in flax. Components in one box, floor plans of ruins in another. Papers stacked on the desk, diagrams, sketches, in a number of different hands. The detritus of an active mind. Or, less charitably, a possessive one.

Shivaun started to sidle back through the door. He said, 'But – where?'

Reluctantly, shuffling her feet one past the other, she entered the room and indicated a stack of volumes on the shelf behind the desk.

They numbered at least two dozen, broad, heavy books. Some had been covered with hide, others with heavy fabric, two, the bottom-most, with black synthetic. Three sat away from the others, isolated by a wooden strapboard filled with loose sheets. The shelf was dusted with paper flakes. He hesitated, then he lifted the topmost, eased open the cover, to the first brittle black-writ page.

Shivaun said, 'I wish you wouldn't do this.'

Startled, he looked at her. She locked her hands one in the other, but still they strained against each other.

Gently, Lian closed and replaced the volume he had opened. Flakes clung to his hands. 'What is – in them?'

'Sickness,' she said, her voice high and trembling. 'Malice. Death. Evil. Don't let it all out.'

'I will not – let anything out. This is a – good place. I would not – threaten it.'

157

She sighed, stirring a few strands of hair, and shuffled to the door. He looked up, having not heard her leave, and smiled. One violet eye watched him. Then, trailing a white hand on the wall, she vanished, and the door closed.

The records shelf housed two other items, a blue glass goblet and a carving. The carving was a bird with a woman's head, the shoulders and breast fused to the long arc of wing. The wing was smooth and polished, featherless, but the face was minutely detailed and individual. Lian lifted it down into his lap, turning it in his hands, stroking it. It asked for stroking. It had been carved by someone with a strong sensuous awareness. He wondered whether Daisainia was aware of this. He remembered Zharlinn and Daisainia behind the dykes, and, disconcertingly, eyes like pupilled sky. With a smile at his simplemindedness, he set the carving down, and turned to the records.

As he surmised, the two synthetic-bound volumes were the earliest. The writer was Krysanin D'Caul, follower of Linn. They began in Linn's middle life, and they made grim reading. They were a systematic account of Linn's aims and strategies. Written by someone who loathed both, and hated himself for his compliance. There was still no explanation of Linn's motivations, except for the fact that Linn claimed total amnesia of his childhood prior to the destruction and the loss of his foot. Had he found that a blessing, and thought to share it? Or found it a blessing, and feared to lose it? His monomania was such that he could impose his own condition on a whole world.

Lian had intended to read the records chronologically, but by the end of the first volume he had had enough of Linn and Krysanin. Neither Daisainia nor Shivaun had returned, and he felt the oppression of deep night and silence all around him. The window reflected the room in on itself, darkly, and he looked back at himself out of staring pits. Needing diversion, he reached for the three volumes which were set apart. As he anticipated, they were the accounts of Ky Travassa's years of *isk'dar*, as recorded by Branduin Travassa.

Daisainia's mother had deplorable handwriting. He interrupted himself to check the loose sheets in the strapfile. As he thought, there could not be a greater contrast. Daisainia's hand

158

was small and erect, almost cut into the paper. Branduin's feathery scrawl arced across the page. She stuffed the margins and the spaces between the lines with crabbed, vital sketches. 'Branduin Vassar – Chronicler to Ky Travassa, *isk'dar* – 14 Tirnon 56. High summer. Fine weather, little cloud. Scrub-growth well established around on the far side of the river; the plain in the distance has taken on a hint of living colour. Ky has brought me samples, *thail*, of course, *k'drii*, a species of *allys'drii* –' tiny marginal sketches, '& descriptions of where he found them – we need to know how they grow where they do.'

Settling, he read her account of her pregnancy and the birth of her daughter; of her and her Companion's possessive adulation of that daughter; of contentious *caur'cali*, and crop rotation; of her father's slow relenting towards her lover. So much *life*, he thought. So much joy. Almost involuntarily his hand sought the third of the three volumes. They had been bound when complete; he found the entry on the last page, two lines in the small cutting hand. 'The *isk'dar* and his Companion drowned Lltharran, night of Talanis 7, 62. The bodies were recovered—' the paper had torn, and been dragged by the nib, as though the writer had not noticed, or had not cared, 'day of Talanis 8. The pyres burned down and the ashes given to the river, by the *isk'dar*'s instruction.'

Lian put his head back briefly. When she returned her parents' ashes to the river, she was no older than he had been when he fell through the ceiling of the dome.

He looked for the next volume, expecting Daisainia's next entries. Instead, the thickest of them all began, in a large, painted script: 'Talanis 29, Morain D'Vandras, Chronicler.'

The name was familiar, yet he could not recall where he had heard it. He turned a page, then another, finding more of the painted script, not yet committing his eye to the page. A word caught his eye, then a whole phrase. He read the sentence around it, then the paragraph, and then turned back to start at the beginning.

Morain D'Vandras had founded the Restorers' Guild. She saw the need to use the relics of the past. Error, she wrote, taking Lian's breath away, was not crime. The crime was in the knowing misrepresentation of events and the destruction of

159

knowledge. Lian read quickly on, thinking, what else does she know? She never said, though she returned to that theme frequently enough. Something of the tone of the argument disturbed Lian, but not for long. He had to work too hard to understand. She used language with the ruthlessness of the prodigiously intelligent. She speculated widely and with great originality as to the nature of the ruins, and the relics they freed from them. Her curiosity seemed both demanding and fearless, and he read on, scanning sections where she repeated herself – she returned often to the evils of destruction of the old knowledge, as though in self-justification – impatient with his own slow wits, and compelled by a growing sense of dread. He remembered where he had heard the name: from Tion speaking of Shivaun's mother, 'Morain D'Vandras who is not . . . spoken of now.' What could have brought so able a woman, one so like-minded to those living here, to infamy and silence?

It was, again, the last entry, dated early autumn of that same year. The nib had caught the paper and dragged it as though the writer had not noticed, or had not cared.

'Morain D'Vandras died today of *sonol*, taken from my hand. Daisainia Travassa, *isk'dar*.'

TWELVE

TARIDWYN

. . . Then I left him, Lian finished. *I came here.*

His hands trembled with fatigue and the spilling of everything he felt and thought about Thovalt, Burdanians, and himself.

Vaelren knelt above him on a felled tree trunk. Split lengthwise, it was still higher than Lian was tall, fringed with vines, lichens and fungi. Grey-green, musty coils of exhausted vines lay in its shadow. Throughout his telling, she had merely watched his hands, in silence. Her eyes had stayed clear, but he could not see her receptors for her protective caul. As though aware of his eyes, she reached up with a gloved hand and stopped herself just before she brushed it down the caul.

It was a shocking cruelty, she signed at last.

It was only the truth. I had to know, he said, he lied. He knew she would feel that he felt otherwise. He wanted her sympathy. He wanted her to approve his leaving Thovalt, leaving the colony, coming here.

She lowered her head, as though returning to her work. Then she hesitated, yielding to his need and said, 'Come up.'

Only at the top did he realize that he was up, and the ground was down. He glimpsed the dappled heave of it and stepped back. '*Watch*,' she said, sharply. 'That will eat through your shoe—'

He shifted away from the deep, moist cut in the wood, feeling suddenly, frangibly, merry.

In the canopy the wind toyed with the leaves, and the dappled sunlight shifted on her shoulders and hands. Her coarse overall moulded itself over her heavy shoulders and curved spine. On the far side, the other half of the trunk lay, shrouded in vines and seaweed, for preservation, and beyond that were several more trunks in various stages of segmentation.

'Tell me if my line is straight,' Vaelren said. 'You are good at that.'

Of all people he did not want her kindness. Slowly he moved to Vaelren's side, and looked along the cut.

'It looks – straight – to me.'

It might take her a quarter of a year to split the trunk, by controlled enzymatic digestion. There was no hurry: the building of a new high-house was a years-long process. If Telien were right about Jehane, perhaps Telien's line, through Jehane, would start this house.

Why don't you put a rope along it? Lian asked in sign.

'I was taught to do it by the eye and by the *vos'neen.*'

Kindereen *rope their gardens.*

She did not answer. She steadied her tube in the cleft, and began pouring the thin, yellow mixture into it. The tube itself, a hard, treated reed, was beginning to soften. Lian eased himself to his feet, and, careful to step where the moss seemed green and healthy, collected a fresh tube from her neatly arranged supplies, and laid it down beside her. She neither thanked him nor objected, but once her tube had drained, set it aside, and lifted the new. Lian sighed. All adults had their work, all had their means of contributing; all children, once *maeren*, were inducted into one of the traditional skills. But everything had to be done with due attention to the *vos'neen'el*, and he, lacking *vos'neen*, could live only as a guest or as a dependent child.

As at the colony, where he would be a handicapped adult.

Where would there be a place for him?

Vaelren laid down her tools and rested her hands turned up on her thighs so that her fingers would not come into contact with wood or fabric.

'I am disturbing you,' Lian said.

'Yes,' she said. 'We will talk for a while, then I must ask you to go.'

'Go where? Where can I – belong?' he burst out. 'All I know

162

are lacks. Intelligence. *Vos'neen.*' Her figure swam in shadows and tears. 'I'm going!' he said, before she could insist.

'Why?' she said. He bridled at her cool inquisitiveness – and sensing that, she said, 'I prefer the way you feel now to the way you felt before. You seem already – better focused.'

Iridescent joy swelled and burst within him.

There was a long silence, and then she began to peel off her gloves. 'Lian,' she said, 'why did you come to me?'

'Shouldn't – I have?'

She moved her head slightly, but did not raise it; he glimpsed the movement of her mouth as she said, 'I am not Burdanian.'

He did not understand the rebuke; he had not been asking that she be Burdanian, rather the opposite.

She got to her feet, and gathered up her tools and the pot of enzyme solution. 'I – don't want you – Burdanian,' he said, as she passed him. She did not respond. He watched as she stirred in the inhibitor, rendering the solution dark and harmless.

'You're not – cutting – more?'

'Come down to the river, Lian. I need to wash.'

The river ran along the edge of the work area. He followed her through thinned undergrowth, between the draped hulks of cut trunks. She knelt, and slowly, ritualistically, cleansed her hands, and spread her loose tunic to inspect it for stain and perforation. The droplets sparkled against her dark skin, even in shadow. She pulled her sleeves down and turned to him.

'What were you doing?' she asked.

'I—' he said. 'Watching you.'

She clambered to her feet, shaking water off her hands. 'I have food; we will not need to go back to the high-house. When I am cutting, I forget to eat. I will suddenly find that the light is so poor, that I have been proceeding by touch and by *vos'neen.*' She paused, and then looked at him. 'You resent *vos'neen.*'

There was no lying to a *kinder'el'ein*. *There's nothing for me to do!* Lian signed, hands flashing. *I have no words, and I have no* vos'neen. *Burdanians have no more need for me than you do. Everything living has a purpose and I have none!* 'Teach me!' He broke into words suddenly. 'Teach me!' *I can cut as straight a line as you. Straighter! You can tell me where to cut, and I will not deviate, Vaeli, I swear it. Please teach me. Please.*

163

Her nictating membranes quivered at the inner corner of her eyes. For that moment he did not repent, nor did he try to mitigate his emotion. How could she know how much he needed this unless she felt it?

'I will talk to Teli,' she said. 'Teli will think of something.'

Telien would, and *she* had offered. He smiled at her radiantly.

You will have to learn quietness again, she signed.

I will, he promised. *Here, I will.*

They settled side by side on a buried root bole of a tree nearest the river's edge. Subsidence and erosion had exposed the root system, a brownish, twisted cage, jutting out into air. Roots plunged downwards, sinking into the water. Once he would have sat with feet dangling above the clear water, letting Vaelren pass food out to him. He glanced at her, wondering if she had the same image.

'Smell first,' she said, offering him a tuber and a handful of wafers. 'I did not pack for Burdanians.'

Once vegetables began to ferment Burdanians needed supplementary enzymes to prevent poisoning. Lian, reared native, relied on selectivity. Everything she handed him smelled, albeit faintly, of fermentation. She would have chosen vegetables already softening, to spare her weaker jaw.

It does not matter, he signed. But, irrationally, it did.

They ate without further conversation, he the wafers, she the vegetables. He clambered down to the water's edge to refill his water sack; he was intensely thirsty, and the wafers had left a slight musty taste. He did not know whether this was unusual, or whether it was compared to colony food. The river water, too, tasted strong, of earth and jungle. He dragged himself back to his place, and lay down, beside her. The heat left him no strength. His skin prickled with perspiration and moss and insect feet.

He was drifting off to sleep, to the cacophonous lullaby of the jungle, when he felt her move.

'I must go back,' she said, when he opened his eyes.

'May I – come?'

She stood up. He, having not had leave, did not. 'Lian,' she said at last, 'you blind *vos'neen*. With you standing by, it is like-trying to see phosphorescence in sunlight.'

164

Again that iridescent bubble of joy, swelling, and, as he fully understood, bursting. *You want me to go*, he signed.

She was silent for a moment. Her eyes were indeed the colour of the sea, from a height, from the shuttle.

'Why aren't you *kinder'el'ein*?' she said.

It was as though she spoke his own thought.

She reached out – with himself sitting on the bole and she standing beside it, they were at a level. He watched her hand come, a slow, warm darkness, and shifted forwards to meet it. A moment before he felt her touch he felt the warmth of her touch. And then she snatched her hand back.

'What are you making me do?' she demanded.

He jerked away, hurt. The hurt deepened as he saw that he couldn't argue with her: he had wanted her to touch him. Even though *kinder'el'ein* ways were very different and he had learned so in his cradle. For a moment he stared at his lap, willing her to leave him there with his shame. From the corner of his eye he saw her hem shift and his head came up without his volition.

She had not moved. Her dark skin had a yellowish cast. He could see the drawing of the skin about her receptors.

'Vaeli –' he cried. 'I'm sorry.'

'You've grown up,' she said. 'Your father felt this way to your mother.'

He didn't want her to tell him what he felt like and turned his head away.

'All the time it has been growing stronger, and I could not recognize it.'

She stepped back; he felt it as surely as if he had *vos'neen*. His head jerked round and she stopped. Or he stopped her. He was not sure that he could bear it if he had.

She said: 'It used to make me feel – very strange – sensing that from him. And then when you were born—' Something – aversion – came into her voice, and she stopped. 'I didn't expect it in you,' she said, her voice going high. 'Stop it, Lian! I'm trying to make it better! I haven't known how, all these days. I still don't know how.'

He hugged his arms round himself, feeling betrayed by

165

himself, and even more by her. 'Go away, Vaeli.' Hearing the accusation in his voice.

'Shall I?' she said. When she did not answer, he saw her hem vanish. Then despite himself he looked up to see her departing back, and his grief and desolation at the sight of her leaving surged after her and swung her again. Her nostril slits were flickering, but it was not laughter; it was the trapped breath forcing itself in and out.

'Vaeli,' he whispered, 'I'm sorry.' She lifted her hands between them, staring over her fingertips with dilated eyes. He saw Shaleen in her, repelled by the alien. Not the alien's intrusion, or its importuning, or any deed or thought or emotion of it. Simply by what it was, the one thing it could not change.

He covered his face and sobbed.

After a moment he felt her take his head in both hands. He could not speak, so he shook free to sign, *Don't stay. I don't want to hold you.*

Her hands remained poised for a moment, though her face was still a sallow hue. Then she signed: *I am not held, Lian, except as I love you and would not wound you. I would not.*

He did not breathe for a moment, staring into her sea-coloured eyes.

'It's funny,' she said at length. 'You feeling like that about me.'

'It is not *funny*,' Lian cried.

'I don't know about Burdanians at all,' she said. 'I thought you chose pairs by smell.'

'By *smell*!'

'Or taste,' she persisted. 'You have no *vos'neen* and no *vos'neen'el*. No *kindereen*. Just man and woman.' She hesitated. 'I thought it was chemical. I didn't see how it could involve me.'

If it was knowledge she wanted, even he could give her that. *Chemistry decides whether two can have children alone*, he signed. *If the cycles of fertility match, or if doctors must help. Tastes and smells maybe should – maybe once did – help us pick. But we don't know that. We just pick people we like – 'love', know well and think are – beautiful—*

'I was afraid,' she confessed. 'I thought you had no choice.'

166

'It's not *tris'neen*,' Lian said. 'Probably I'll grow out of it.'

'You could have children,' she said, in wonderment. 'I played with you in your cradle, and I was already becoming *maeren* then.'

'Vaeli,' he said again. 'I'm sorry.'

'No,' she said, soothingly, but not personally, as though he were a wild thing strayed from the jungle. 'I didn't – understand. I thought you didn't have any choice, and I thought that meant—' she glanced away from him, into the jungle, 'I thought that meant I didn't either.'

Remembering her touching him, remembering her turning back to face him, he said nothing.

'When you were born—' she said, 'I thought it was a – horrible thing.'

He stiffened, certain she could not intend 'horrible', even after what she had just said. But he would not know until she went on, and that would be too late. She turned her elongated head and looked at him.

'I had just found out that I would carry the children for my *tris'neen*,' she said. 'Then Sara came to have you. It was so different from any birth – to even the animals. It was so close and – so violent. Such pain – such feelings. You with no *kindereen* to guide your passage. I thought you would die. I thought you *had* to die.'

'I'm sorry,' he said, thinking he must quiet her. He did not want to understand why she was telling him this. She inclined her head, sensing him; he glimpsed the bravely dilated pit of her receptor.

'Telien brought you to show me.' she said, very softly. 'You were so small, crumpled up and raw; your hands and feet – pulsing, trying to clutch at things. You looked more like an organ than a baby. Something torn out before it was finished.'

There was a silence before she went on, 'All the time you were being born – it was like a mockery of – my own new, my own *precious*,' she said reproachfully, for the adolescent self so badly used, 'new possibilities. But there – you were. Different. Alive. A new presence. So strong to have come through it all alone. You moved it all away from me again.'

He signed, tentatively, *Vaeli, I don't know much about*

kinder'el'ein – *bonding*— *Does it always – work? Does anyone ever get left out?*

'Sometimes,' Vaelren said. 'They are often strange ones – unbelongers – from the start. But still, it is sad. The *tris'neen'el* never comes.'

And – three of those couldn't come together if they chose—

'Without *tris'neen'el* they would not know each other,' Vaelren said, her silvery voice shy and precise.

Even living together for a long time, even with vos'neen—

'They will never know each other. And they cannot have children.'

There was a silence. Lian wondered why he was so determined to know, when his ignorance meant either he had forgotten or Telien had chosen not to tell him. He distantly remembered heaving himself up off the balcony planks in indignation, 'I'm *never* doing *that*,' and *kin* snuffling laugh.

But no, he knew why he was determined to know. It was his only way of asking: 'Must it be this way?'

You want – children?

She looked down at him, unoffended. 'Of course. Don't you?'

The thought had never occurred to him. He tried to picture a Burdanian woman who might have his child, and failed.

Do you – ever think about who your partners might be?

'Oh, often,' she said. 'Thinking about it might mean that it goes the way we want.' She anticipated his next question, 'Some think it will, and some think it won't. Nobody knows if thoughts even *touch* that deep where the bond germinates. But – it has to, hasn't it, because everything's interconnected throughout the mind. Isn't that what you say?'

We don't know anything about vos'neen'el, *or* tris'neen'el.

'*I'd* like Tenar to be my male, and Estareel to be my *kindereen*.' There was a silence; she looked at him. 'Don't feel like that, Lian,' she said, wistfully.

I can't not feel just like that.

'You will always be special,' she said. 'To me and my mates. Our children will have four parents. But you mustn't feel like that, or you will make my children cry.'

168

It's not fair. I didn't even know that I felt – I didn't feel or do or say – anything – and now it's – spoiled.

'Lian,' she said, a shiver in her silvery voice.

'I'm sorry – no,' he said, then signed, defiantly, *No, you know I'm not. I am and I'm not. If you – know about things inside me before I – It will happen. It will.* He had enjoyed thinking of her, remembering her, watching her. Was that any more imposition than her pulling his embryonic feelings out of him, and making him see them through her alien eyes?

'Wil you – talk to Teli?' he said suddenly; when she did not answer he implored, '*Please.* About teaching me. Finding something—Letting me stay.'

Vaelren did not answer.

'I won't bother you—' *But I don't see why it has to be this way,* he burst out, in handsign. *You told me you loved me.* Her eyes went white, under the onslaught of his emotions, and he stopped himself, holding still his trembling hands.

Must I tell you? she signed slowly. *I do not want to become one of the unjoined. Kinder'el'ein do not know why the bond takes or does not take. I belong to a family that is already strange to en'neen'el because they know Burdanians so well. This should be a time of peace, of expansion, of looking into infinity. We dare not look, because you are always there. You have divided our family: Shaleen, who should come with kin mates to our high-house, will go to the deep jungle and mate with two we have never seen. Telien thinks and worries about you, your Thovalt and your debate, not about en'vos'neen'el. Kin is weak in en'vos'neen'el, as though en'neen withdraws from kin. A hundred thousand generations which are part of us, part of me, do not recognize you at all.* She stood a moment, sensing him; then she signed, with finality. *They do not even know you exist.*

169

THIRTEEN

BURDANIA

From somewhere above his head the voice said, 'Where is she?'

He smelled dry leaves and resin, tasted old ink. Paper pressed against his cheek. Letters swam away from his opening eyes.

He lifted his head off the book, brushing against a cold, stiff hand, which removed itself. Illuan D'Vandras was bending over him, heavily cloaked, his face and hair damp. He was in Daisainia's room, her last volume open before him, the other records piled around him. He had been looking for . . . looking for explanation, justification, latterly even confirmation, of that single line. He thought he had found it. He had only been dreaming.

D'Vandras' fingertips rattled upon paper. He said, *'Do you know where she is?'*

Lian breathed a dusty word, 'No.'

Before he could draw breath again, D'Vandras was gone, leaving only a whiff of floodwaters, mud and sweat. Lian heard his footsteps receding down the hall. Then silence.

He looked down at Daisainia's account of a summer's day nearly a year ago. Her entries were never longer than a page, but meticulous. Births, deaths, boat arrivals, rainfall, water testing, the health of her garden. To every arrival, departure, or accomplishment, she attached a name. Except that she herself was absent. She seldom used the first person. Her record and Morain's cast each other's omissions into relief. Both were compelling, and gave an illusion of completeness, but when he set them side by side he found Morain as overpresent as

Daisainia was effaced, Morain's world as empty as Daisainia's was crowded. Nowhere in her account did Morain mention Daisainia's name. And nowhere else did Daisainia mention Morain's.

But why kill the woman, obliterate her name, yet keep her records where any might see? Although they had objected to his seeing them, for this very reason, they had not prevented him. But for Daisainia, *Daisainia*, to kill . . .

He could not say why the thought so appalled him, or left him so disbelieving.

Somewhere out in the night was the shuttle. They would have heard him amongst the records. They would expect him to call in, it being night. If he contacted them now, if he told them, they might insist on returning for him. The river had them unnerved enough. He had no faith he could unpersuade them. They would take him with them, and all his questions, all his delicate explorations, would come to nothing. But if he did not contact them, he might learn more, learn that it was not the atrocity it had first seemed. Would seem to them. But there had to be more.

He got shakily to his feet, and pressed his face to the window, cupping his hands around his eyes. He could see nothing but the glimmer of his own eyes. Where was the dawn? How long had he been reading, and after that, asleep? Where was Daisainia?

In the corridor, he listened hard. Perhaps, from some other corridor, he heard Illuan D'Vandras' firm, urgent tread. Perhaps it was merely imagination and fatigue. He had to think where she would be, if not in the settlement, or anywhere Illuan might already have come to her. These rooms, she had said, were hers. He suspected Illuan would not trespass. He wondered how far he himself might. He suspected not very far. There were five doors between this study and the end of the corridor. He moved from door to door, knocking on each, and quietly, saying her name.

Before he knocked upon the fourth, he thought he heard someone speak. He knocked; there was no answer.

Slowly, he brought his hand up to the touch panel and keyed open the door.

The air inside was very cold. There was only light, welling from a panel beside the door, and spreading in a diffuse fan across the floor, illuminating the interior and casting heavy shadows upon the far wall.

No dust lay on floors or furniture. Behind the vents, unseen fans filtered the air clean, and then, with a shock of ions, discharged themselves. On the table, a desiccated sprig crumbled across a half-finished sketch. The ink in pen and pot had long since dried. A model sailing ship sat beside it, half rigged, casting a peaked web of shadow on the wall behind. A contraption of wheels and levers leaned against a trestle, its purpose unfathomable.

The bed was unmade. On it, there lay a long shift, dirty at the knees, and a litter of papers, covered with feathery scrawl.

The room itself neither surprised nor, at first, disturbed him. He had sensed it within her, this closed room of the grief. It lived on in her home as Burdania lived on in the Archives of the colony. Hopeful, repossessed of the living Burdania, he had more patience with shrines and shrinekeepers. In time, the living would fill this place, and even if they did not, it was such a small place, against the immensity of Burdania.

Then he saw her.

She was sitting on the floor on the far side of the bed. Only the crown of her head caught the light. He could see her still, darkened profile. Uninhabited, the room had seemed insignificant. Enclosing her, it seemed ominous. He entered it as he would have entered a lair, without sound, barely treading on the dustless floor. Without looking up, she acknowledged him.

'D'Halldt.'

'Yes,' he said, and crouched down, letting one action carry into another. She turned her head. They studied each other in silence. The neck of her shirt had been torn open, the thongs snapped. One shoulder was nearly bare. Her small, powerful hands had been scrubbed clean, although all her fingers were scraped or cut, and the middle finger of her left was bandaged. She had tied back her hair with a thong, but it was too short to remain secure, and slid forward to bar one eye. Her expression was sombre, haunted.

'You've hurt your hand,' he observed.

172

She shifted the bandaged hand, and gazed down upon it for a long moment before she realized a further effort might be required. 'D'Suran says it is not broken.'

He relaxed slightly, in relief at so straightforward an answer. That was a mistake. He lost momentum. He crouched, looking at her, unable to think how to proceed. That hanging lock of hair disturbed him intensely. He reached out and pushed it back. He kept his touch as transitory and impersonal as possible, but the feel of her skin so impressed itself on his fingers, that it seemed the next thing he touched he would feel through her skin.

He pushed aside the impression. Seeing her he could not believe that she might have killed, and written about killing. In her presence, that line in the records seemed a warped fiction. 'Illuan D'Vandras is – looking for you. I think it – may be important.'

She drew, and let out, a shaking breath. 'I will not be ruled.'

'By – Illuan?'

'She went down to the river.' She bit through the word. 'But not to warn. She went to die. I will not be ruled. *I will not.*'

'I – do not understand.'

'I see a crumbling wall,' Daisainia said harshly. 'But I will not be ruled.'

He could not, in good conscience, tax her about Morain when she was like this. She had to be nearly exhausted; she looked it. The cameras had recorded her on the dykes or in the settlement day and night for three days before he came. He said: 'I do not know what other people – think of, leaving you like this. Perhaps you make them – believe that all they – can do is leave you – but you cannot make – me.'

A very slight smile flickered across her face. And went. 'I will not be ruled. I will not be led to the riverbank, to the ends of things. I am not she.'

'Who – are you talking about?'

'Knowingly—' she whispered and bowed her head towards her bruised hand.

He crouched beside her, feeling her suffering. As he brushed the bedcovers, the papers rustled, drawing his glance. He recognized the scrawl; it was the same one as in the records. 'Is "she" – Branduin Vassar? Your mother?'

173

'Knowingly,' Daisainia whispered.

He drew a deep breath. 'Daisainia, please, you cannot – believe she – could have known – you cannot or you will never forgive—' He reached out to touch her hand; this time she reared back. Her expression silenced him: She had never forgiven; she believed that there had been a betrayal and had never forgiven that. This was beyond his experience. 'Daisainia – *nobody* dies except in – ignorance. We are none of us honest – about our mortality – we each hope we – are the exception—'

She looked at him as though the language he spoke was not Burdanian. 'Do you not know the story?' she said in a white tone. 'Did you not read it in her records? How she foresaw my father. Foresaw me. Foresaw her death. And went to meet it. Because her own mother likewise foresaw her death, sought to avoid it, but came to the sea in the end. Do you not have it in your Islands? It is called *shikarl*. The best of shipmasters have it, in a lesser form. It tells them how the weather lies. It helps them know the routes they may take, and the ones they may not. It is my legacy. And my curse.' She said to the floor, 'I see a crumbling wall. But *I will not be ruled.*'

'Oh, Daisainia,' he murmured. A great need for certainty, he had thought, at their first meeting. This was the form it had taken, seeded by an imaginative mother, and rooted in unaccepting grief.

'Y'think me mad, D'Halldt?' He caught his breath and sat immobile, wishing he could turn off the transmitter. No one should be listening to this. But before he had decided what to say, she lifted her head again and said, 'It does not matter. I am all Burdania has.' He suddenly saw her as she might be in twenty years, at the onset of her hard old age. Endurance would replace vigour and grimness her passionate intemperance. She would have obliterated all visions from her mind, and all that she would know would be that some things would rouse her to a black fury, followed by an even blacker remorse, and all her brooding would not tell her why. She would do well by Burdania, but the young woman before him would be sacrificed to that. *Isk'dar* that she was, she must know she could not go on this way.

'Daisainia,' Lian said, to the young woman, 'I cannot speak

174

– for your mother. But I will not accept – that what *you* feel – is anything but – knowing the river – the dykes. Illuan – came for you tonight. Perhaps – he sees the same.' The only movement in the room was a slight flexing of the windows before the wind and the quivering of dead leaves of paper. Did she feel ghosts in the room; did he? He thought of the river, of the fires burning behind the dykes. Of her leaning out over the water to drop her plumb line into the depths. He said, quietly, 'If you – neglect – your intuition, and a dyke fails—Already you carry too – many burdens. If you warn – them—' He saw her flinch around the eyes. 'If you warn them – and nothing happens – you will not mind – being wrong – and your people – safe.'

There was a silence. She looked at him, an abstracted, unseeing look, her eyes seemed very violet. 'Yes,' she said, leadenly. 'Whatever will serve must be used.'

'I did not mean—' he started, dismayed at what she had taken from his words.

'Did you not?'

'No. I do not – believe in *shikarl*,' he said, there being nothing else to say. '. . . believe you – should suffer so for—' he hesitated, summoned his courage, 'imagination.'

'D'Halldt,' she said starkly, 'I know the landscape of my own mind.' She pushed herself upright, hands laid on the floor. 'Nevertheless, I thank you for showing me that – even that might be harnessed to necessity.' She got to her feet, and, looking down at him, said in a soft voice, '*Must* be.'

He started, clumsily, to rise, but she paid him no heed, and words would not come. He knelt looking after the erect small figure for long after the doorway was empty. The draught of her passing had started one of the wheels slowly turning. A ratchet clicked, and clicked again, loudly.

He eased an unsteady hand into his pocket, and withdrew the transceiver.

'Lian, where are you?' Alystra said. He tried to envision the close, polished interior of the shuttle, high in the mountains. The image would not come into focus.

'You heard what we – were saying? Is it – possible?'

There was a silence. 'Before we met the *kinder'el'ein*, Lian, we would have said empathy was impossible. But prescience,

175

no, I would still say that is not possible.' He leaned his head lightly against the dusty bedcovers and closed his eyes. 'No,' he murmured. 'Not possible.'

'I should have thought to warn you about tendencies to magical thinking in a degenerate culture.'

'Their – culture is not degenerate,' Lian protested.

'Whatever ... Lian, don't overidentify. From my own experience I can tell you it is not easy, but you *are* an observer, and you must keep a consistent perspective. That is your value to us. You must maintain perspective. What did you find in those records?'

He said, faintly, 'I – will make a summary. When – I have read more. Much – is still – unclear.'

She sighed. 'Collect what information you can. We're considering moving to monitor the agricultural settlement, Sidor Vassar's origins. Or some of those Islander settlements. Based on what people have said to you, they would seem to be the best prospects. But we could only do so if you felt secure enough to have us move further away.'

He swallowed dust. Alystra seemed to find nothing unexpected in his silence. She never had given him long enough to speak. 'Lors asks me to remind you to use the autoinjector he gave you. He is extremely concerned about you.'

'He – need not be.'

'So are we all, Lian.'

She closed the contact. Lian stared at the wall. A small line of black flecks marred it, like insects, but motionless. He leaned forward to see them. They were insects, sketched on the wall by the merry pen of a dead woman. He bent over, forehead nearly touching the floor. What he needed, the others could not give. He was alone with his experience. And he had kept the core of that experience from them. He had kept this night's knowledge from them.

But it would be wrong to judge the homeworlders by colonial standards. In the crucible of the Explorers' fire, they had been transformed. Perhaps it was they who were the truer strain of Burdanian.

But could even that exonerate or even explain that one line in Daisainia's record?

176

As soundlessly as he had come into the room, Illuan D'Vandras bent over him and lifted the transceiver from beside his hand.

In his other hand he held a knife, a long shaft of metal worked to a thin point and wrapped in rope and skin at the hilt for gripping. They all carried them, for cutting rope, cutting food, scraping and levering. Implements, Lian had thought until now. D'Vandras turned the transceiver to look at the double star emblazoned upon it.

'Emblem?' Illuan D'Vandras said. 'Or conceit?'

His face was cold, the skin around his eyes blanched with fatigue. Twin tiny images of the emblem floated in his eyes.

The contact-requested light flashed once, and went dark. D'Vandras said, 'I knew there was something about you.'

Lian, who had started to struggle to his feet, stopped in half crouch. 'You – knew.'

'Oh, yes,' Illuan said. 'I know what they say: Illuan D'Vandras fancies himself. But I am of Camnor D'Vandras' line.'

Camnor D'Vandras had been one of the main adversaries to Exploitation.

'But you might know that,' Illuan D'Vandras said. '*She* is descended from Carolinn D'Vandras and D'Jayna Travassa, the authors of it all – d'you wonder her line would rather forget? And you, D'Halldt? In the thousand who left, there could not have been so many of your name. Could yours be from Javir D'Halldt, and her lover, Vavarian Nors? Who was, by my accounts, also a ship's captain.'

He needed no spoken affirmative. 'So. Shall we play this out to any better end than six generations ago, do you think? The D'Vandras have expected this for sixty-six years. However Linn Travassa deluded the rest we knew you would be back. We did not think it would take so long; we had begun to hope—Your colony must have been exceptional. Viable, at last?'

'Y-yes.'

'Then why didn't you stay?'

'Biologically – viable. Its spirit—'

'And what about our spirit, D'Halldt? Will you crush it out of us again?'

177

The contact light was flashing again through D'Vandras' fingers. D'Vandras glanced down, saw, lifted his inky eyes. 'Will you talk to them?'

'They cannot – help me,' Lian said, mustering his resources. 'Will you give me a chance – to persuade you of our goodwill?'

'Goodwill? Lian D'Halldt, this will need more than goodwill.'

'Goodwill is – indispensable. We bring what – we bring. You—'

'You give us no choice,' D'Vandras said starkly.

'You cannot deny us—'

'The chance to finish what sixty-six years ago you started. I would deny you that if I could.' Meticulously, he handed back the transceiver, and sheathed the knife, making sure that Lian's eyes followed every movement. Then, deliberately, he reached down, gripped Lian's arm and pulled him to his feet. And let him go. 'There is no one on this planet to whom violence is a greater anathema. But I thought to kill you.'

Lian closed his eyes and drew a slow breath. He had to think. 'What – will – you do now?'

'React,' Illuan D'Vandras said. 'That is all you have left for me to do. I cannot be author of my own fate; we cannot determine our own destiny. You have taken it into your hands, Lian D'Halldt.'

'No. We are the – supplicants—'

'Don't mock me.' With energy, almost enjoyment. 'You have everything – knowledge, technology – the stardrive which did – this.' He gestured outwards. Lian's eyes followed the gesture, helplessly. 'We are the victims of your choices. Do not delude yourselves that there is equity, whatever indulgence you offer.'

'Please! Do you not think – we have learned, even as you?'

For the first time D'Vandras hesitated before replying, though his face, the bitter cold of his expression, did not change.

'I would not have said, a little while ago, that I had learned anything. Learning can be unlearned; it can indeed— What have you learned? Coming here in secret, lying to us— What have you learned?'

'Would you believe I meant – well by it? I meant to – spare the old injury as best I could.'

178

'Whose?'

'Both!' Lian said, with passion. 'Yes, I – have done wrong by my deception – but I will not – let you say that I have done harm by it.'

'Yet,' Lian heard him almost say; it would have been the obvious rejoinder. Illuan D'Vandras was no adherent to the obvious. Instead he turned his chiselled profile to Lian. 'An interesting distinction. I almost believe that you are the innocent you seem. But then I am moved to wonder what kind of people would send an innocent into this, and would be forced to conclude that they are fools. Which is not possible— What subtle game is being waged here?'

'I am – not – an innocent,' Lian found that his hands had fisted; he unfisted them with an effort. As soon as he began to speak, they closed again. 'I – fell when I was a child – through the colony dome. I suffered – grievous brain damage. Believe me a – fool—'

'Too easy,' Illuan D'Vandras said, looking at him again. 'Great guile can look like folly.'

'I don't—' Lian began. He sensed the readying counter-strike, and broke off. 'Could we have – done it another way?'

D'Vandras let a silence lengthen, keeping him under the stare of those light-flecked eyes. 'I will tell you what you can do,' he said, almost gently. 'Go back to your colony. It is viable. This, I assure you, is not. What has happened between us will simply be played out again between our peoples. I have felt the impulse – more than the impulse! – to murder in my hands. You cannot justify what you have done. Not because you are a fool – or inarticulate. You are most – persuasive. But because it is unjustifiable that you should dismember our spirit to heal yours. You know that, Lian D'Halldt. If you were anyone other than who you are I might think you a good man. But you are what you are, and my feelings are . . . what they are. Now you have seen what your ancestors left . . .'

'They – were not alone – in doing!'

A slight lift of a black eyebrow; D'Vandras' adjudication of that response. 'True,' Illuan D'Vandras said, again almost gently. 'But it will make little difference.' He paused. 'Imagine

179

what might have happened had you told Daisainia Travassa why you do not believe in *shikarl*.'

'I think – better of her—'

'Of course you do. But whether you think well or ill of her, that does not alter reality. Daisainia Travassa would have someone to blame for her marred world. I do not think, even after so short a stay, you underestimate her influence. Were it not for her, they would be content still to retreat to the hillcrests and wait out the flooding. She is the one with a vendetta against the river, but most of them have forgotten that now.'

Lian remembered D'Vandras at the council meeting, his council meeting, his bruised hands resting on the table, and the transient rapport between them.

'I – do not agree. It is necessary for – morale, for heart, that the river be – withstood.'

Illuan D'Vandras conceded, silently. 'Be that as it may,' he said, 'accept that you are facing a woman who understands leadership, but who will use that understanding to serve not merely her own ends but her own needs – and who has a need to blame. Consider that she can turn such hate against a mindless thing which simply obeys the seasons and the contours of the land – and imagine what she might turn against the living descendants of those who laid Burdania waste.'

Lian shivered at his own perceptions reflected from a darker mirror. He might argue that their children would eventually insist upon the homeworld they were denied. Would a generation change anything but the players . . . Daisainia's line perhaps ended by an infertility these people could not cure. D'Vandras' line – the man had no children. To whom would he pass on his knowledge? And he, himself, ending his days in exile under Taridwyn's dim, hot sun. A wanderer, perhaps, like Thaorinn, at peace neither in the colony nor, any more, amongst the *kinder'el'ein* . . .

He closed his eyes. Be honest, he told himself. Separate your need from everything else, from all judgements. But knew he could not, and knew that there was no one else he could offer this dilemma to and say: choose for me. He opened his eyes again. On Daisainia's shrine to her dead parents. 'No,' he said. 'No. I – cannot – accept your version,' he said. 'But I am not – I

have not made mine.' He turned to face D'Vandras. 'I beg time
– to reach my own decision. Will you – give me that time – talk
to me again?'

'You will persist—' the man said, in a voice like breaking ice.
'I've never known arrogance look so like humility. Why ask me?
I'd not tell anyone, and I'll not harm you, though I'd rather
otherwise.' Lian flinched at the harshness. 'You've left me
nothing; don't you think I know that, despite your indulgence?
But by all means, speak to me again. By all means.'

'It is not indulg—' Lian caught himself, as Illuan D'Vandras
turned to go. 'We need your goodwill.'

'No,' Illuan D'Vandras said over his shoulder. 'That you
cannot have—'

'Then you will – help disaster—' Even as he spoke he knew it
was wrong, but could not moderate either tone or sentiment.
The tall man pivoted. The desiccated sprig flew from the table,
shedding fine leaves. Watching it, he lifted his eyes too late.
D'Vandras' hand dashed the transceiver from his. Black filled
his vision, and he felt himself seized and shaken until his head
snapped on his shoulders. When the force released him, he was
blind with dizziness. He reached out, found something to hold,
and held on. And when his vision cleared, he was looking into
D'Vandras' eyes. Illuan D'Vandras looked far sicker than he.
Lian, against whom no man's hand had ever been raised in
anger, felt virtually nothing.

He looked down at the hands that gripped Illuan D'Vandras'
cloak. He let go. Blackness moved away. When he lifted his
head again, the doorway was empty.

The transceiver lay at the base of the far wall. He had not
heard it strike. All its lights glowed, static, unflickering. When
he spoke into it, the lights did not change. And when he
listened, there was no answer.

FOURTEEN

TARIDWYN

Lian had never seen the dome from inside. From the door, he looked in on a dark golden cavity, like the hollowed rind of a fruit; it looked wrong, inverted. He was seeing from the inside what he had only seen from the outside. And, perhaps, fleetingly, from above.

He should get no further. Protocol said that only those proven able to appreciate and provide complex arguments were admitted. The admission debate usually happened in or around the seventh year, Lian's age. Nobody had suggested that Lian try. Instead, Lors, now standing on his left, and Danas, on his right, had insisted Alystra petition for special dispensation. She did not approve; her straight, narrow back said as much as she walked forward to meet the Determinant, arbiter of procedure for this debate.

People eased past them, courteously, in ones and threes. Some smiled; a few wished Lors and Danas well. Others merely acknowledged them; and one or two radiated such silent hostility that Lian shifted between Lors and them, as though Lors were *kinder'el'ein*. Lors was aware of little outside his own miserable skin. His face was nearly as pale as his hair. His lips were white with pressure, and the skin around them green-tinged. For Lors, public presentation was an ordeal; he had passed his admission trial only on the fourth attempt, and then, he said, with bittersweet amusement, only under threat of ordeal by Thovalt if he did not.

From the middle of the floor, the Determinant looked towards Lian. All three heard him say, 'He has not passed his trial.'

'And never may,' Alystra said. Her low, creamy voice was unusually sharp. She was vexed and edgy, put upon by Thovalt's erratic behaviour and Lors' and Danas' intransigence. She glanced back, saw Lian watching, and turned her senior away with a respectful touch. They bent their heads together. Lian looked straight ahead, keeping his dignity. He heard Thovalt's voice, from somewhere within, racing and elated. The Determinant frowned towards Lian, and then, Alystra trailing, approached them. His was a distinctive face, wide, mobile, and for a Burdanian, very dark, with skin like a newborn *kinder'el'ein*. He and Lian shared the ancestress from whom the trait had come: Javir, the painter from the ships, had been as dark. His eyes were brown as pebbles; there was warmth and humour in their glance as he said, 'I suppose if I don't let you in, you'll join us the same way you did last time.'

Lian felt his skin prickle with Lors' and Danas' shock. He saw Alystra caught between offence and her reflexive approval of all her superiors said and did. Lian himself felt a sudden lightness of spirit, a release from the drag of his tragedy. He said, 'No. I – won't.'

He expected the Determinant to say more, to test his capacities. But the man only watched him with shrewd eyes. 'If you draw any attention but once, you'll be put out. I'll tell you where to sit, you sit there and you sit still. Keep your hands off the touchplate by your chair. Understand?'

Lian understood. The Determinant did not speak like a rhetorician at all; he was direct and simple, and his face was mobile and easy to read. And Lian understood subtext as well: he had been tested, and he had passed, though he did not yet understand how. Between Lors and Danas, he entered the hall.

The hall had been built to seat the full complement of the three ships. Not daring to envision the future, the builders had scaled it by the past. Five hundred and thirty-five Burdanians were presently eligible to sit, each in a place which, like a *kindereen*'s cell, was granted for a lifetime. Their names, and the names of those who had sat before them, were shown on the greyscale touchplates beside each chair. As Lian climbed up the rows, the names dwindled from six, to four, to two. He looked in dread at the high middle seat he had been directed to, afraid it would carry but one name, but there were four, and the last was Raman D'Halldt, Thaorinn's brother and Thovalt's father.

The rising tiers of seating cut away the base of the golden dome on one half. The other half had a crescent-shaped dais along its base, equipped, with monitor/archive port and curving screen. Thovalt prowled the dais back and forth, murmuring to himself. He wore black, marked with small, waxy stars, and on the black, his emblem sparked. Alystra caught him, making him bend down and listen to her. She was still trying to instruct, Lian saw; she thought them unready. They were the rawest speakers, and Thovalt the youngest Proponent ever to bring this proposition before hall. And that, Lian now knew, was his doing. There were people in the audience who had spoken for Burdania three or four times. Who had been standing on the dais as he plunged through the ceiling to near death and mental ruin. Of those experienced speakers, only Andra and Alandras had consented to contribute this time, though Thovalt had approached them all. Lian's accident had shattered a thin, but durable and accomplished tradition.

People had noticed him, seated high in the back, and drawn their neighbours' attention. He tried to look healthy, alert and intelligent; pleasant, but not overly approachable. If anyone tried to speak to him, it would abolish the illusion of his recovery. The Determinant caught him at it, and pulled his mobile face into a caricature of Lian's expression. Lian had to laugh. His laughter softened the gazes of the people watching him. Except one. From a seat on his level, but at the extreme horn of the arc, a white-haired woman stood studying him with no regard for his ease. She was the cyborg surgeon, Granaith D'Sal. He saw not merely dismissal, but annihilation in her eyes. She knew everything about him; she had delivered the final judgement. It took a supreme effort to turn away, not to stand resisting futilely with his eyes across the room.

From the floor, two new arrivals waved up at him, and then climbed quickly up the rows towards him. They were Sara's parents, Iryssan Nors and Varidian D'Halldt. They were bioscientists who migrated between the four scientific outposts, studying the Taridwyni fauna, including *kinder'el'ein*. From Iryssan, Sara had inherited her delicate build, her slanted eye, her fey humour. From Varidian, Sara and Lian took the smoky grey of their eyes. The tight lineages of the colony made Varidian half-brother to both the Determinant, and to Granaith. Varidian's skin was dark, like his, his hair white, like hers. They all were of the third generation, the generation which Thovalt characterized as having turned away from Burdania. Iryssan said, 'Lian, we heard you were back, but we hardly expected to see you here. Have you been admitted, then?'

His courage failed him; he did not want to disperse the pride in their eyes by speaking, by answering. He raised his hands, and signed, *For today. Just.*

'You're in this?' Varidian said, casting a glance over his shoulder. 'Yon Thovalt's a troublemaker. He does not appreciate what he's asking. He brought you back to show off, no doubt.' He caught Iryssan's eye, and between them passed something as tangible as words, a reproof. He sighed, then smiled, grey eyes lightening. 'I cannot blame you for the faults of your friends, can I?'

Lian watched them back to their seats, troubled. They were the ones whom Thovalt had to convince. And if they, and others like them, thought Thovalt a troublemaker, and Lian merely something on display . . .

He came back to himself as the Determinant stepped up on to the dais and raised his hands. As naturally as he had pulled faces at Lian, he commanded attention. Lian appreciated the elegance and simplicity of his signal. Even Thovalt was contained, though his fingers tapped on his thigh and his toe tapped on the dais and the light jumped and jittered on his emblem. Lors blanched further. On the screen, the roll of attendees appeared. Seven abstained by nonattendance, amongst them Thaorinn D'Halldt, Sara D'Halldt, and Kryssanin D'Vaul, the previous year's Proponent. Lian felt, or imagined he felt, Granaith's chilling attention again. Would she challenge his presence, display what had become of him?

The Determinant welcomed them briefly and ceded the dais

to Thovalt. Lian saw a last tremor run through Thovalt's frame, a last flicker on the emblem; then Thovalt stood rigidly before them, more motionless than Lian had ever seen him. He said, huskily, 'I am Thovalt Aslinn. I have come to put before this hall the proposition that we send a mission to Burdania.' Lian released a slow breath. He was not alone. None of them had known what Thovalt would say when he stepped upon the dais. Thovalt, aware of this, bestowed upon them his sweetest smile. 'I am going to tell you a story.'

This was one risk they had let him take, to stand out there alone and tell the story, without records of any kind. Tell it not in the words of the past, but in the words of the present; tell it as he, child of the fifth generation, saw it. It was a risk. Thovalt was facing people who had rejected not only Burdania, but himself as Proponent. Whether he could humble himself, efface his anger and scorn, nobody knew.

The story was the one Thovalt had told Lian. Lian felt fleeting resentment, that the challenge Thovalt had delivered him alone, so personally, should prove to be merely a rehearsal. But instead of goading, Thovalt's tone was gentle and confiding, almost too much so. He spoke as a member of the fifth generation might tell the sixth, with apology and incomprehension. Lian sensed the unease in the audience. He thought he knew what Thovalt was doing, trying to make them hear anew a story they knew all too well. He wondered whether Thovalt knew what he was doing, whether it was a considered strategy, or a kind of petulance. So much of Thovalt's brilliance seemed heedless and unrefined.

Only at the last did Thovalt change his tone. He threw his head back and delivered his challenge in a ringing voice. 'We are going to prove, to the satisfaction of scientists and specialists, that Burdanians survive on Burdania. We are going to prove that we have a homeworld to go back to.' Quickly, he stepped to the edge of the dais and dropped to the ground, striding to his temporary seat. Dropping into it, he sat as immobile as a creature in camouflage.

Tarian D'Sal, Lors' elder half-brother, walked out on to the dais. After Thovalt, his was a very ordinary appearance. He was a warp physicist, a theoretician. Lors and Lian shared an awe of

186

him, Lors for his imposing intellect, Lian for his imposing silences: during the preparations he had spoken maybe twice. He had looked for accommodations in the drive equations which would allow them to argue with annihilation. On the screen, equations formed, and trundled upstream. Lian's hands went cold, and he tucked them into his sleeves. He was unable to resist an upwards glance, but could see nothing, no shadow creeping along a strut. The lights left blue-ringed blots on his vision. This was now, he told himself, this was now.

Tarian summarized: 'What the equations tell us, in essence, is that although we have the power to perturb the universe, we have no power to alter it. The drive effect is extremely nonhomogeneous: warp and normal space-time interpenetrate. Boundary conditions must be accommodated, which means that after removal of the perturbation, what remains must be contiguous with normal matter, energy and time. It is a powerful restorative force for normality.

'Between the regions of profound perturbation, there were nodes, when the business of the universe continued as usual. They would have been quite unaware of the driveshock, until the effects, as propagated through the medium of ordinary matter, stone, atmosphere, reached them. Within those nodes, survival would be assured.'

'Momentary. Survival,' someone said from the audience. That was the start of the challenge; the discussion became one of specialists, esoteric. Lian listened instead to the tone of the voices, learning their emotional spectra, trying to guess who supported, and who opposed, and who argued for the sake of pedantry. The Determinant rose to close discussion, referring those who had the interest and background to the Archives, where they could access the detail omitted by Tarian.

Tarian gave his place to an earnest Danas. Her speciality was atmospherics; she was to speculate on the physical effects of the aftermath. Hers was an unforgiving task: the mercy extended by Tarian's nodes might be capricious but absolute, and most of the audience must take its terms as given. But Danas must project hope despite all the outrages of a traumatized planet. Those were disasters of a dimension the audience well understood. She was challenged, and challenged

187

again, by specialists of all stripes, medics through physicists through Archivists.

Shaken, Danas yielded her place to a mist-coloured Lors. For the first time in Lian's knowledge, Lors was wearing his emblem, one of the few surviving originals, preserved through his antecedents. He started falteringly, 'I have . . . a hypothesis to offer. Concerning the success of this colony and . . . also pertaining to the possibility of Burdanians surviving on Burdania. As far as we know, we are unique in our survival as a colony. Yet all previous settlements were on planets more like Burdania than this one.

'It has been suggested that Taridwyn is so inhospitable, we maintained an enclosed habitat environment, instead of trying to adapt, and for that reason, prospered. I disagree.'

He shifted his feet, settling into his stance. 'Burdanians originated on a marginal world with a brittle ecosystem. To survive we needed endurance, tenacity, and fecundity under adverse conditions. We, and Burdania, became victims of our own success. So, we imposed constraints upon our own biology, particularly upon our fertility. For over a thousand years we lived comfortably, without having to apply much conscious thought.

'But the changes were imposed upon an organism which was, and is, a survivor. Challenged by an inhospitable environment, the fundamental traits reassert themselves.'

He looked round them as though expecting argument. None came. He said, 'Ease of conception correlates with exposure to the Taridwyni environment.' A graph appeared behind him on the screen. Lors said, 'I have asked people, examined records, drawn . . . inferences from additional data; I think the trend robust enough to overcome the uncertainties.'

Iryssan Nors got to her feet. 'Intriguing,' she said. 'But,' with an undertone of whimsy, 'fecundity *does* tend to run in families, along with behavioural traits, such as roaming around the jungle.'

'I have discriminated according to lineage.' The graph changed. 'The trend remains. I have additional evidence, more detailed examinations of individuals. The mother of my most intriguing subject lived outside for the duration of her pregnancy, and he himself has spent more time outside than in. Lian . . .'

Granaith D'Sal interrupted. 'Lian D'Halldt is an atypical subject, given the micro and molecular interventions required after his fall in this dome a year ago.' *No*, thought Lian.

'There are others,' Lors said, tightly. 'I have prepared them for examination.'

'I shall,' Granaith said, turning aside to the plate. One hand tapped and stroked the surface, while the other absently parted the white hair above her ear, exposing the socket, a dark blue metal circle. Lian had a sudden image of Vaelren's shadowy receptor, an image, and a comparison, which made him queasy. But the hall was unequipped for Granaith's modifications; she smoothed her hair, and returned her remote gaze to her son. When Lors was done, she bent her white head over the touchplate, shutting out the proceedings. Lors watched her from his place in the opposite horn, apprehensively.

Alandras followed, speaking about psychological effects of disaster, and individual and collective modes of coping. Lian had avoided the psychologist, remembering too many humiliating cognitive and adjustments tests. Despite Alandras' years of study, he could not apply what he knew to himself and the people around him. Nevertheless, his case was meticulously presented, detailed and authoritative. He deserved the murmured congratulations he drew from the others.

Thovalt kept on to the dais. His colour was high, his movements dramatic. Lian saw the others tense: they recognized the warning. Thovalt flung out the challenge: 'Burdania is alive. Burdanians live. We are Burdanian; we *belong* on Burdania.' He swept a long arm in the direction of the landing field. 'Out there, there is a ship. It is not a monument, but a living ship. It is not entombed; it sleeps. We have not killed our past, but held it in stasis, for this time, now. That ship might cross the whole galaxy, but the only place we want to go is Burdania. We have the designs for the prototype which left Burdania in safety all those years ago. Out of the ship which sleeps in the landing field, we might rebuild that prototype.' He gestured sweepingly to the screen. Schematics appeared, unleafed the ship section by section like the little brain in the lab.

Lian's thoughts drifted. He regretted how little he could appreciate their arguments, or weigh their laboriously given facts, but listening exhausted him. What he could measure with little effort was the emotion in the hall. It seemed . . . insufficient. Their audience was too still, unengaged, unchallenged. When they spoke, Lian heard interest, curiosity, irritability. But these were petty emotions. He remembered the debates led by his father. There had been passion there, passion and anger and furious argument. Here the argument was about experimental fact and scientific detail. Their emotions and energy were diverted from Burdania, towards their specialist interests. Lian could hear none of the stress of minds being changed, of energy and emotion being released to engage with Burdania. It was too still.

But that was merely an intuition, unprovable, inexpressible. He did not know whether he was imagining an absence. He had no *vos'neen*. Perhaps calm was what they needed, now, calm and a quiet hearing.

He stared up at the faceted golden arch overhead as Thovalt presented their projected navigational calculations. Outside was late afternoon: the *kinder'el'ein* day moved ahead of the short Burdanian. One night to *en'vos'neen'el*.

Granaith's flat voice checked his reverie. 'I have some further observations on the medical data.' Lors, looking beset, stepped up on to the dais. 'I have examined the data,' she said, 'and found certain additional traits which also correlate with ease of conception. Monitor, display. In view of those correlations, it is a fallacy to ascribe the ease of conception to environmental conditions.' She sat down.

There was a silence. Lors swallowed visibly. 'But – but clustering of traits is inevitable, given the small numbers of . . . founders. And the people who can survive won't *all* have come on the ships. The question is not *why* . . . the question is *whether* . . . Whatever the reason, if we could survive here, Burdanians should—' Lian saw his fleeting, unthinking glance towards Thovalt. So did Thovalt. Like a wave, he rose upon his toes, and swept around Lors, ending before him in a half crouch. His eyes glittered. 'I am bored, bored, bored by all this punditry. This is not a symposium, it is a debate. It is a debate about Burdania. So let's talk about Burdania.'

Lian felt the change in the hall, like a change of wind. Like the still before a tropical squall. He saw people shift in their chairs, heads bent towards each other. Lors whispered over Thovalt's shoulder. Heedlessly, nearly striking Lors, Thovalt flung his arms out. The binary star spat light across the hall into Lian's eyes. 'Burdania, remember,' Thovalt said. 'The planet we left, five generations ago. There is a ship on the landing field which could take us back. There is life there, or could be, but does it matter whether there is or could be? We could go home, if we dared. We are going to go home: why else keep the ship, while we burn the emblem off all our doors and crush our stars? It is inevitable; it is our destiny. It could be a magnificent destiny.'

His face tight with distaste, Varidian D'Halldt got to his feet. 'I think not,' he said bluntly. 'What magnificence is there in a world dead or altered beyond our tolerance? The Explorers' original mandate was not to collect planets like so many coloured balls, but to find sentient life. We have found the *kinder'el'ein*. Maybe *they* are the reason we survive to this day. Perhaps the presence of the *kinder'el'ein* sustained us. What would it mean to us to lose their forbearance?

'We idealize our homeworld; we forget how precarious life was there. You already accept that Burdania could be greatly changed. It is implicit in your carefully prepared justification for adaptation. Consider the form of that adaptation, then, behavioural as well as genetic. In the past, survival has taken barbarous forms – territorial wars, ritual killing, infanticide, geriatricide. All appear in ancient records; all justified by insufficient resources. Could you look squarely upon those? I do not believe we left Burdania unharmed or lightly stricken; I think the damage was grievous and I think we would let that damage destroy us. We would, in fact, feel *obligated* to let that damage destroy us.'

There was a ripple from the hall. Varidian said, 'I am of the third generation. I knew the last of the first, and the first of the fifth. I have seen all the ways we used to sustain ourselves against exile. I have seen the crusaders and the suicides, the

191

scholars and the nihilists, the accusers and the apologists. Burdania polarizes us. But my sustenance is not Burdania, not the matter in our Archives – it is my family, my love, my work and my friends amongst the *kinder'el'ein*. Shall I risk those to pay a debt which is so long overdue that it is unpayable? I have seen what Burdania has taken, even at this remove, from my family.' There was a silence. He looked sideways, and up at Lian. Stripped of its rhetorical force his voice was as soft and light-timbred as Sara's. 'I stand in defence of the only home and family I know, and my life's work and the Explorers' true and original intent. I wish I did not feel that it was either the one or the other; indeed, we should go back, because we've taken more than we've left, and perhaps in fifty years, we will be able to. But none of you will now acknowledge the price we will pay.'

'But the worse it is,' Danas said, 'the more we are obligated to help.'

'If you cannot swim, do you try to save a drowning man?'

'You *learn*,' said Lors with some spirit.

'In the thirty years I have lived,' Varidian said, 'I have seen no indication that we are learning.'

'How *dare* you!' The voice was Thovalt's and nearly unrecognizable. 'Burdania has taken things from your family . . . As though that excuses your indifference. Lian is the one who suffered and Lian . . . Lian suffered because he *cared* about Burdania. How dare you make that an excuse to do nothing. It should be a reason to finish what Lian D'Halldt cannot.'

'Thovalt,' Lors said, stepping forward.

Unhearing, Thovalt raked the hall with a bright, hard gaze. 'For five generations we've told ourselves that we cannot, or we dare not, or we should not, or we ought not return to Burdania. We have told ourselves that there is no one there to help; or if there is anyone there, they do not need our help; or they would not want our help; or they *should* not want our help. We have told ourselves that the Burdania left could not be anything like the Burdania we knew and left; or it would be *too* like the Burdania we knew and left; or it would be not enough like the Burdania we knew and left to be worthy of our attention. We have created a perfect little Burdania here, whole miniature

192

seas and continents according to our design, the ecosystems depend upon us, the day, the night, the rain, the pseudo-sunshine. We may be breeding, but we're dying still, dying as Burdanians, as authentic, spontaneous, living creatures. Look at this event, this ritual; we might be holos in the shrine for all the freedom, the reality it offers us. It is all preordained: who speaks and when, what they might say and how; the scientific proof and the debate and its supporters and its detractors.' He pulled at his collar; the fastening gave with a tear. 'I'm stifling in it,' Thovalt shouted. 'I'm stifling in our good manners, our formality, our propriety. *We destroyed Burdania.* We destroyed Burdania and then we turned our backs on it for fifty-nine years. Our ancestors pared us down to fit our planet. We have built ourselves a habitat, and pared ourselves to fit in it. We are starting to believe this is the world. Well, I don't want to live here any longer. I want an authentic life; I want a life with space . . . I want . . .' His voice broke. He said, hoarsely, 'I want to know what happened to Burdania. I want to know so that I do not have to feel this – this immeasurable sense of wrong, this . . .' He looked up at Lian, and Lian saw that his eyes were glittering with tears. 'I want to stop feeling evil,' Thovalt said. 'That is our legacy, the taint of evil, of being part of a terrible, terrible wrong. We are all stained by it. You have built a little Burdania and try to pretend it is the world, and maybe most of you can, and if you can, I hate you. *I hate you,*' Thovalt shouted. 'Because . . . I . . . cannot. And *there*,' he pointed straight at Lian, 'is someone else who cannot pretend. He bears the legacy of it. Not because of anything Burdania said or did, but because of what you said and did. You tried to pretend that this was the world, and Lian D'Halldt was not deceived. He had to know what else there was, and when your rules barred him from entry here, he crawled out on to the ceiling, and fell, and was nearly destroyed. How long is it going to continue, this destruction? How long?'

FIFTEEN

BURDANIA

From the path Lian could see the night thinning over the horizon. Under the stars, the floodwaters glimmered, broken by islands of darkness. Overhead, the river of stars flowed, slowly turning. Lian paused on his way down, and peered towards the mountains. He saw nothing, but lit water, blackness, and stars.

Behind the long hook of dyke lanterns swirled and clustered. Figures scrambled up and down the rear of the inner dyke. One by one the arches of relic lamps sagged and were gathered in. Dark shapes threw shafts into fires, and sparks surged. She had roused them indeed. They would be too busy tonight to look for him. Thovalt could land the shuttle on one of the uncultivated terraces, on the far side from the settlement. The noise would be covered by the river's roar. He could be long gone before they found its marks on the grass, if they ever did before the wind combed them out.

And then . . . ? What would they think of him, Daisainia, Vylan, Tion and the rest? What would the others think of them, of *her* hearing what he knew? What would become of the healing they had hoped for, in coming?

And if I go down, he thought, knowing that Illuan may already have told her . . . if I offer myself, will anyone understand that I have, and why? Or will I simply become . . . an enemy? Daisainia *could* kill an enemy of her people, and she would. Me? Illuan D'Vandras had withheld harm once, but again . . . ? How would Thovalt and the others treat them then?

But if I leave – assuming that I can – and never give her the chance . . . ?

He held the silent transceiver in both hands and brought to mind everything he knew, every sense he had, of her. He remembered her speaking of the river, remembered her amongst her seedlings and nurselings, remembered her laying the map of the settlement, remembered the coarse, ragged hand gripping his, and the pupilled sky of her eyes. He had to set that against records. He smiled in the darkness. The decision was his alone, to be made on his terms. And those terms had brought him here, in trust and in hope.

He said, 'Thovalt. Alystra. If – you can hear me. I am – going down to the – settlement. To – see what I – can do.'

He pushed the instrument into his inner pocket and started quickly down the path.

When he saw her she was standing on the dyke directly below *caur'ynani* shouting at the clustered people to spread out and watch along the dykes. In part of his mind he was pleased to see Rathla Zharlinn beside her, crouching and holding a lantern towards the inner dyke. Pushing against the movement of people, he collided with Lara. She steadied him on his feet; her greeting was quite ordinary. 'The *isk'dar* and Illuan are worried about the outer dyke. We're to spread out along the perimeter.'

'*Illuan?* Where is he?'

She blinked at the urgency in his voice. 'Down there.' She pointed. 'Checking.'

To be trusting and hopeful on a hillslope well above it all was one thing; to be trusting and hopeful, and confront Illuan D'Vandras, was another entirely. His blood felt like mercury slamming through his veins. He barely heard Lara call his name as he started forward, scrambling gracelessly up the lee of the dyke. If there were to be a confrontatiaon he wanted it *over*.

As his head came level with the dyke, he heard a stone fall.

At the base of the inner dyke, several strides along from him, Illuan D'Vandras straightened from a crouch, stepped back quite collectedly. He turned, as though to speak to Daisainia,

195

but before he saw Daisainia, he caught sight of Lian.

Daisainia said, sharply, 'Illuan. 'Tis past time.'

Lian saw disorientation and deep indecision in his expression. Not the cold ultimatum of their conversation. So D'Vandras had not told yet her. Had not yet broken the silence the D'Vandras had maintained for sixty-six years. Perhaps never would have, had Lian done as D'Vandras asked, and gone.

At D'Vandras' back, shadows moved beneath the stones. The *stones* moved.

Daisainia shouted, 'Illuan!' She swung a leg over the dyke, reaching towards D'Vandras. Rathla Zharlinn dropped his lamp and caught at her shoulder, pulling her back and nearly overbalancing himself. The lamp clattered down the dyke, spattering burning oil on the stones. Illuan D'Vandras suddenly came back to himself, and took a stride towards her.

And the outer dyke tore along its length like paper. Daisainia, caught with one leg still on the flood side, cried out wordlessly.

Water and boulders crashed against the inner dyke. Lian felt the shock against his hands, shins and bootsoles. Gravel and small stones rattled within the dyke and down the inner slope. Spray rained down upon him. A little away from him a hand reached out of the foam to claw the stones. Beyond the hand Zharlinn got both arms around Daisainia and heaved her clear. Then the surge ebbed and Lian saw Illuan D'Vandra' face rise out of the foam, streaming mud and blood, eyes rolled back and white as a *kinder'el'ein*'s. He gathered his feet beneath him and threw himself forward, landing on stone and transceiver. Blind and suffocated with pain, he groped for the hand, and found it slipping. It dragged him with it. He dug his fingers into crevices, gripping with his legs and feet. He could hold himself, but he could not raise the drowning man's head above the water. 'Daisainia—' he said, more a whisper than a cry. He grazed his face on the rock, turning it to look for her. Daisainia was on hands and knees, shaking her head slowly from side to side. Zharlinn crouched beside her, eyes for her alone. 'Zharlinn.' The hand in his was slipping, slipping, with water, with his weakness, while his anchoring fingers tore on the rock.

196

He averted his head, so as not to see how near and helpless help was. Voices surged and faded, surged and faded, like a tide. He thought of the slow, green tides of Taridwyn. He thought: I can stand this. I have stood worse. Just let me hold on. Even as he knew that no amount of willingness could compensate for the simple weakness that, until this moment, had seemed so harmlessly humbling. Was a man to drown because he was too weak? I can do no more than not let go. No more than that—

Hands wrenched at him – he cried out in protest. People were shouting – he thought he heard Daisainia, and turned his head again, looking for her. Somehow the rear of the dyke had filled with people. He saw lanterns throbbing, and faces rose past his, immense and livid. Bodies blocked out the light, and he felt the burden lighten. Hands caught him around the waist, heaving him down on to the slope. He slid feet first, juddering, until he dangled by the arm which still clung to the drowning hand. Someone broke open his grip and Lian folded bonelessly into the angle between dyke and land. A lantern was pushed so close to his face that he could smell the fishy smoke of it. He weakly turned his head away. 'Lian!' Lara's voice appealed. 'I'm sorry,' he whispered. 'I have to lie down.'

He came back to himself lying on his side in the mud with wet grass against his cheek and gravel coarse-polishing his bruises. Somebody – Lara? – was sponging his face with water. He felt the icy creep of it across his throat and down the crest of his shoulder. Tion D'Suran crouched over him, saying, 'Lian, I want to move you. It will be unpleasant.' He gestured, and Lian realized he was not to be offered an option. Ready hands slid under his shoulders and chest. Tion said, 'Don't pull on his shoulders.'

'No,' Lian said thickly, 'I shouldn't—'

'Shouldn't what?' Tion demanded, rather more sharply than was his wont. Lian did not answer; he did not know what he should not do. As Lara and Tor got him to his feet, he saw Illuan D'Vandras being laid out on a stretcher under Kylara's close eye. The left side of his face was raw and bloody and Lian could not see him breathing. He was distracted from looking closer by the sight of Daisainia, leaning against Zharlinn, fingertips digging into her left thigh while her eyes went from face to face, desperate for distraction. Below the knee her trouser leg was sodden. Her gaze met his with the usual, palpable shock; then she waved to his supporters, a clawed gesture of dismissal.

He managed not to pass out again until he was laid down in *tayn* D'Suran, the Medics' Guildhouse. Then the light went greyish-green, and although he was aware of his cloak and boots and sodden jacket being removed, the events did not connect.

His jacket! The transceiver! He caught the hem as it whisked across his field of vision. 'No. *Need* it.'

'*Lian*,' Lara's voice said. 'It's soaking and filthy. We'll dry it, brush it and give it straight back.'

'Need it now,' Lian said, distinctly.

'Oh *c'arch*, Lian.' She capitulated as he tried to sit up. 'I'll hang it here—' She hooked a chair with one muddy boot and slung the coat over the back. 'Take twice as long to dry.'

She did not know it, but she could have won her argument then, for the nausea had only been waiting its chance. Lian was drooping over his aching shoulder, mouth filling, trying to decide whether to swallow, or not . . . A greyout spared him the decision.

Tion was standing over him, pulling up his sweater and vest to probe his bruises with cool, smooth hands, then helped him sit up and examined chest and shoulders, arms and fingers. Lian, more accustomed than he knew to body scans, found the touch disconcertingly intimate. Not the least because Tion's fingers probed around the dark straight mark left by the transceiver casing. But he made no mention of it, simply said, 'Nothing broken, I think. Bruises and muscle strain. I'll see you have something for it.' Then he was gone, with his studiedly unhurried tread. Lian slumped back.

'Lian? Lian? Come on, Lian. You have to be awake before I give you this.' A mug, descending, with Lara behind it. 'Something to relax you. From Tion.'

Lian reached and flinched as racked muscles protested. 'Jacket?'

She pointed. 'There! She must have been really something,' she said shyly. 'Or he.' Lian stared at her through aromatic

198

steam. 'Whoever gave you it.' Slowly, Lian appreciated what she meant, but Lara coloured slightly and started to rise, saying, 'You drink that.'

He raised the mug to his lips as a diversionary tactic. Tion's brew did not taste unpleasant, and it shouldn't do him any real harm. He sipped cautiously, avoiding conversation, until things began to grey out again.

'Daisainia?' he said.

'Nothing broken,' Lara said. 'A rock: bruised muscle and bone. Illuan's bad. He must have hit that dyke hard, jumping . . . combination of inhaled water and concussion . . .' Her voice was getting blurry around the edges. Blurry? Blurry was visual. Edges were visual. Voices went – the word was— He felt the mug being taken from him and a calloused hand slipping behind his neck to ease him back. But I – he thought, and at the last moment: Tion's mixture! He hadn't expected any effect.

Beyond the door of his room, people came, people went. He heard Daisainia's voice say, 'Whatever *possessed* Illuan? To scatter his wits like that?' He could have answered; he did not. Outside the window, daylight matured. The little room was warmer than any he had been in, the warmth supplied by relic heatlamps, similar to the lights, placed in brackets upon the wall. He could feel the warmth from the one on the left, and turned his face into it, dreaming of green jungle and yellow light. He half woke when someone came in to draw the blind. Daisainia's voice again, from the door. 'What do you make of him?' Her voice sounded tight and clipped. Tion's sounded frayed. 'He seems healthy, but in unusually poor condition for an Islander; I can't quite see how. I suspect he's been an invalid in the past. If he heals well from this, I'll see what I can do about his muscle strength . . .' He went out the door, pulling it to behind him. Daisainia's step, following him, was uneven.

Lian awoke, feeling refreshed. The feeling lasted until he tried to roll over on to his side. From shoulder to hip, his pale skin was blotched with ochre, brown, dark brown. His shoulders flared into pain with each movement. His fingers were tender, his hands scraped and stiff. But the steep sunlight around the blind told him it was near midday. He reached first for his jacket and relaxed only when he felt the weight in its

199

inner pocket. It remained silent. His throwing himself down on it had doubtless finished what D'Vandras had begun.

He stood a moment, listening. Wind. Rumble of the river. Voices from the dykes. Voices, hardly louder, from down the corridor. Surely it would feel different if he had been unmasked. It would certainly feel different if the shuttle had arrived, sweeping down out of the east. So, they had not come. Telemetry from the implant would tell them he was alive and passably well. Possibly, through the cameras still mounted on the far side of the river, they had seen the dyke collapse, and his deed. Would they think it courage, or recklessness? Cautiously, alert to sound behind him, he drew the transceiver from the pocket and snapped open the casing. Nothing looked loose, or broken. He rocked it gently in his hand. Nothing shifted. He entertained a brief fantasy of passing it off as something he had found in the ruins, and asking Vylan's help. But it was a brief fantasy. Somehow that seemed too venal, even before he considered Illuan D'Vandras' passionate, icy judgement.

He had therefore to assume he had been trusted, by decision, or abandoned by indecision. Time to find out what he had been abandoned to.

On the chair beneath were folded a shirt and two fresh cardigans, all warm, both front-fastening. He was thankful for that consideration. He took one painful pass with his fingers at his hair, and left it as it was, matted and in disarray. Barefoot, he slipped out into the corridor.

In the shuttle they had remarked upon the Medics' Guildhouse without knowing what it was: the handsome, large building in the third row with glazed windows, and flaking white paint. The main door was towards the end, and opened into a spacious public room. The medics' own quarters were upstairs, and the remainder of the ground floor was treatment and recovery rooms. The treatment rooms faced south, for light, and had glazed windows set high in the wall. The recovery rooms faced north, towards the river, and their windows were lower. Lian had been laid down in one.

Across the corridor, the doors were offset, but the nearest door was slightly open. The floor was bare and sanded to a silky finish, and a woven blind filtered the light. Illuan D'Vandras lay

200

on a pallet too short for him by half a shin's length. A longer mattress was propped against the wall. One high cheekbone was hidden by swelling, the eye swollen shut, the brow blood-encrusted. He was breathing, slowly. Lian's eyes shifted from the protruding feet, tenting the blanket over air, to the battered face. He had received a stay of execution, but he would rather not have it this way. D'Vandras had been unconscious too long.

Tion, seated in the public room, had seen Lian emerge. He came quietly to join him, and looked in to the room. Before Lian could speak, he said, 'I don't know.' He glanced at Lian. 'You can't do anything more than you have, Lian. Nobody can, except wait—' He looked at the battered face and the jutting feet, and sighed.

'And – the *isk'dar*?'

'I am much less worried about her. There will be no lasting damage . . . if she will but rest it.' He caught sight of someone behind Lian, and his expression lightened perceptibly. 'Medicines all delivered, Fia?' Lian turned to see Tion's younger sister standing behind him, windblown and flushed from running. She was a waif of three Burdanian years or so, a delicate-featured child with Kylara's fiery hair and Tion's gravity of mien. Despite her youth, she was already well into her apprenticeship. Tion saw her glance towards D'Vandras' open door. He said, 'No change, Fia. I'm sorry. Go and sit with him for a while.' The little girl slipped past Lian, giving him a slanting glance from beneath her lashes, and into the room. Surreptitiously she eased the door closed behind her.

Tion said, 'For some reason she is very fond of that—' He might have said *cold*, he might have said *forbidding*. Instead he sighed and rubbed his eyes with his fingertips. He was parent and teacher as well as brother. He said, with an effort at lightness, 'I have no idea how it came about, but one day last autumn they were suddenly thick as two old Islanders. And after that it was Illuan D'Vandras says this and Illuan D'Vandras says that, and this spring, she had to go down to the landing stage morning *and* night to ask if he had arrived . . .' The lightness faded. 'Perhaps he fills an empty place; she can hardly remember our father. She was just beginning to crawl when . . .' He did not say it, shook his head slightly to cast off grim thoughts. 'She would never stay where she was put – we kept finding her curled up in her own little nests. And maybe that saved her life. She never contracted the plague.'

Lian watched the stoic, very young face, finding himself, for once, impoverished in response.

'I worry about the restorers,' Tion said.

'How – so?' Lian said, after a moment.

They went into the public room. It was strongly lit by the north-facing door – a transparent, sliding relic – and side window. Its focus was a massive round table which could seat twelve and was the centre of Guildhouse life and work. Tion steered Lian to a seat, with wordless subtlety, and moved round him, gathering up scales and pots of medications, scraps of paper, instruments and whetstone. 'My eldest brother was the first person to contract it. He insisted it came from a ruin down the coast, an *old* building with vaults and a . . . strange symbol on the doors. We were sure he was wrong. Until we came here and . . . one of our teachers said the symbol was sometimes used as a warning of infection.'

Lian felt cold. 'How – did it look?'

Tion glanced curiously at him, then dipped pen into ink and sketched the encapsulated coil which marked facilities for the preparation and containment of surgical viruses.

He heard Tion say, 'Lian, what is wrong?'

Of course it was possible. Surgicals were a powerful therapeutic tool, and potentially, *theoretically*, harmful if unmonitored. With the knowledge gone and the containment broken . . . He felt Tion at his shoulder, Tion's cool fingers on his throat pulse.

He gathered himself. Pushed lightly at the young man's wrist. 'Sorry. I moved – unwisely. Hurt – myself.'

He felt the young man's scepticism. 'You – think,' Lian said, his voice sounding remote to his own ears, 'the restorers might – find something – like – that.' Tion moved away and went back to his tidying up. He said nothing; his silence was beyond courtesy, or even rebuke for Lian's evasion. Belatedly Lian recognized his own unwitting cruelty. Tion knew he had not seen him move; wisely or unwisely. And he could not trust his own eyesight.

If only he could say something to give Tion hope.

He said, 'You – will have warned them. What – to look for.'

'Yes,' Tion said. He walked to the rear of the room and pushed instruments and sheets of paper into the lattice of storage slots beneath the stairs. When he came back, he wore his usual steady expression. He said, 'I should go probably and look in on a few people. Now, while it is quiet. You may stay if you wish – or go back to the *caur'ynani*. They are preparing to name Tor and Valancy's child tonight. Tell them I said you are not to do any lifting. If you have much discomfort, Fioral will know what to do . . .'

The sliding door jarred open. Tion's younger brother, Toring, tumbled through. As soon as he saw Tion, he drew himself up, and stood with his back to the light, panting. Toring was the misfit of the family, an overstrung, overimaginative youth who was appalled by suffering. Lian had seen this for himself, having met Toring and Fioral over the bedside of a woman suffering from heart pain. Toring had been nearly hysterical. Lian had intervened to make his knowledge serve Fioral's steady hands until Kylara arrived at a run. Fioral's eyes implored his silence as Kylara complimented their work. Neither Tion nor Kylara was willing to give up on their brother.

Tion was usually the patient one; but now he said quite sharply, 'Where have you been?' He did not wait for an answer. He said, 'You've been leaving your writing around again. If you *are* going to do it, could you do it more circumspectly? You know what Kya will say.'

Toring gripped the woven packet he carried against his chest. It rustled faintly. One trait he shared with the rest of the family, absorption in his work. In Toring's case, playwriting. He left a trail of scrawled paper behind him.

Tion lifted a cloak from a hook by the door. 'Your papers are with your other notes in your nook. I have to go and see Valancy Nors, Arkadin and some others. Illuan D'Vandras is still unconscious; Fioral is sitting with him. If she calls for help, go to her immediately. She is too small to manage with him physically. Kylara was called across the river; I do not know when she will be back. I need you to prepare some *cinnavar*, also some *vannil*. There are instruments and dressings to go

203

into the autoclave. Make sure that the wrapping is intact. If the *isk'dar* comes by, she may need the strapping on her leg changed . . .'

'I've seen her,' the boy said, in defiance and triumph. 'She's asked me to be Lltharran's chronicler. To keep the *records*. I won't be staying here.'

Tion's hand went still on his shoulder, holding his cloak on it. As he drew breath, Toring burst out, 'I shall drown myself if you do not let me go! I shall go mad!'

Tion said, with strained firmness, 'You will not go mad if you can learn not to see yourself in every patient. You overidentify. With time and with experience, you . . .'

'No! She's taking me. I'm going with her. I'm not staying here.'

'You are *needed* here,' Tion said harshly.

'I will drown myself,' Toring said, his voice shrill.

Behind Toring, Lian saw a figure through the frosted glass. He knew it at once by the vigour with which it laid hands on the handle and shoved it aside. Daisainia limped through the door, took in brother and brother, and said testily to Toring, '*I* was to tell him.'

'It is not your place,' Tion said.

His tone was unexpected enough to make even Daisainia hesitate. She gave him a long look, and then said, 'He will make a better chronicler than he will medic.'

'A chronicler,' Tion said, 'is a luxury. He is needed here.' He faced down the *isk'dar*, white-faced. 'You have no right to intervene in Guild matters.'

The raised voice had brought Fioral from Illuan D'Vandras' room. She had, Lian noted, carefully closed the door behind her, and now stood in the corridor, fist pressed to mouth, green eyes wide.

'D'Suran,' Daisainia said, 'what is it with you?'

Tion's hard, distraught expression warned Lian of something harsh and perhaps unforgivable in his answer.

'His eyes,' Lian said.

Tion stared at him, in shock. Lian started to elaborate, but Daisainia surprised them both. There was an unlit lamp sitting on the table. She lifted it, keyed it on, and limped round to hold it up to Tion's face. He flinched and would have looked away; she brought her hand up under his jaw and braced it. His face was waxy under the revealing light.

'Ah,' was all she said.

Without warning, Tion buckled. He did not faint; he simply abdicated from the effort of standing upright. Daisainia caught him, one-armed, fumbling the shining lamp on to the table beside her. They lurched, weight coming down on to her injured leg, and she gasped with pain. With Lian's tardy help she sat Tion down. He folded his arms and laid his head on them. Daisainia dragged up an adjacent chair and sat down beside him, without touching him. Lian, who would have touched him, was constrained by her restraint, and stood at her side, awaiting a lead. Fioral put her arms around her brother, burrowing her forehead into the crook of shoulder and neck, her hair spreading down his back in a feathery flame.

After a long moment of tortured indecision, Toring put his hand on the doorhandle. Daisainia sensed the motion, and the intention. 'Stay.'

At that, Tion lifted his head. His face was still white, his eyes staring and dry. 'I apologize for that display,' he said.

'No need,' Daisainia said. She sat considering him. 'The question now is what I can do for you.'

'You do not need to . . .'

'You are precious to me,' she said, her voice clipped, 'and I would not leave you in despair.'

Tion looked down at his hands. 'You can take Toring,' he said.

'I'm sorry,' the boy blurted.

Tion raised his fingers to his face, and said, through them. 'I am sorry, too, Toring. I should have known that it was more than a matter of time.' Tion looked over his hand at Daisainia. 'I will not be a burden.'

'That I will never allow,' the *isk'dar* said, her face troubled.

'There is nothing you can do,' Tion said, plainly. 'But I will still be able to use my hands, my ears . . . I will have others' eyes to use . . . I can teach and learn, and spare my fellows the preparative work . . .' His voice thinned to absence. He looked past Daisainia into nothingness.

205

Clining to him, Fioral started to sob. He slid his hand up her back, his expression numb.

Lian was watching Daisainia. She had much in common with Tion, the youth, the responsibility, the realism. In the stark view of that realism, there was nothing she could do. She was not facile with words, or ready with emotional support; any help she gave had to be concrete. But still she sat beside him, offering her silent presence.

Could someone capable of such patience and compassion have poisoned a woman without regret?

He thought about the pages written in that small, cutting hand, the dense factuality, the lack of authorial presence. The missing explanations. Was her appointment of Toring acknowledgement of her own inadequacies? Had his probing prompted it? But Toring hardly seemed to have the spirit to keep an independent account. Was he meant to; was he merely a tool? Or was it simply a mercy to Toring?

And then the thought came to him, that maybe he and she had more in common than he thought. He was inarticulate in all things; she in particulars, in reflection and in the language of emotion. He had seen it with Rathla Zharlinn; now he saw it with Tion. Perhaps it was not a wish to hide that led to the omissions in her account, but simply that she did not know the words.

Tion was lightly stroking Fioral's hair, but so lightly that she would hardly feel it, would not be lifted out of her weeping by it.

Lian said, 'It is – no offence – to – grieve your – losses.'

Daisainia looked at him; Tion did not. Lian said, 'You will be – as good a medic. You will – make yourself so. But you – are losing the – beauty – of sight. And much – trust. In yourself.'

Tion's flawed dark eyes lifted. He was listening. Fioral felt his motion, and lifted her head, peering past his shoulder with drowned green eyes. 'I lost – language. I – learned to use – sight. I learned to – know people. I manage in – the world. You will. By hearing. Smell. Touch. Asking. But beauty which – other people know – you will not. And – commonplace things – you cannot do. Those you – will grieve.

'For myself – I have – more than enough – beauty to give me – great joy, even if – language is never beauty – only struggle.'

206

He included Toring with a look, and let himself show some of the awe he still felt for the word-crafty. 'But – but I – lost – confidence. Though I – see that – everybody has their own – incapabilities – more than half the time – I forget.' He stopped, deeply shaken by his own words. He had never seen it that way himself. Because . . . he probed the insight cautiously . . . he had never talked about his own condition as a state *of being*. As something to be remedied, compensated for, or alleviated. Or not at all. He had not envisioned what he was. He had fallen into a kind of diffidence of spirit without recognizing it.

Quietly, leaning on the table, Daisainia stood. She looked down at Tion, then at Fioral. Lastly, she measured Lian with a glance, inside and out. Then she limped to the door. 'Come,' she said to Toring. 'We leave your brother in surer hands than ours.'

SIXTEEN

TARIDWYN

'How *could* you?' Alystra said. Her voice was cream and bile. She had a lifetime's training in formality and she drew on it now. Not a thread, a hair, or a fold misplaced, her posture straight and her hands folded, she projected a pitiless authority. 'We lost this debate; we lost it by twenty-eight votes. And before any of you are tempted to utter the words *next time*, which I assure you would be nothing more than a pitiful attempt to salvage your pride, I suggest you examine why. Starting with *you*, Thovalt, and that exhibition of yours.'

Thovalt sat on the floor, back against the dais, his long legs drawn up and his glossy head lowered. He did not move. He flinched at her voice, but not, Lian saw, at the words, only the tone.

Lors sat on the very edge of the dais, leaning over Thovalt. His hand kept lifting, hovering, wanting to touch, and then settling to his side again. When Alystra moved threateningly towards Thovalt, he stepped between them. Finding a fitter target, she said, 'And you, you were supposed to be monitoring his condition!'

Tarian said, 'This will not help.'

Lian stood on the edge, trying to find words for them. Something had changed when Thovalt spoke his heart. In the deliberation recess they kept to their seats, speaking quietly in twos and threes. There was no intellectual discussion, just a quietness, as at a death. Burdanians had stopped talking. In the silence, there should be thought, and feeling. He looked at Thovalt's bowed, glossy head and thought, if. If.

As though reading his thoughts, Thovalt raised his head, his eyes slitted as though against pain.

'What did you think of it? Twenty-eight down's not bad, is it? Not bad at all.' He goaded him to accuse. Thaorinn had warned him of this; it was this aftermath which had driven Thaorinn into the jungle, to live or die. But Thovalt had no such escape. He was trapped, here, in the colony, with his failure, with them all listening.

Lian took two, three steps forward, and crouched facing Thovalt.

'There will – be again,' Lian said. 'We *can*, again. You – *changed* it—' He faltered. He and Thovalt shared no language which described the change of texture of a silence, the timbre of a voice heard across a room. Thovalt did not perceive these things. And yet, all unheeding, he had changed them.

'Oh, indeed I did, didn't I?' Thovalt said, with a sudden, iridescent smile. Lian tensed. Thovalt took his words as a cruelty, as an accusation. He drew breath to deny all accusation, but Thovalt said airily, 'You have no idea how much I can change things. Shall I show you, before I fly away into the starry black?' He scrambled to his feet, forcing them back. 'Shall I show you how I changed things for you?'

Alystra snorted, daintily, and turned her back. She crossed to the touchplate and laid a small round hand on it. Darkness stepped down upon them from the upper rows. Thovalt started for the door, borne on his mercurial energy, and in it, turned and gestured for Lian to follow. Lors took a step towards him; Tarian held him back, his hand closing on his brother's arm. 'There has to be a limit to your concern,' he said, as though stating a physical law. Lors wavered. He appealed to Lian, 'Be careful.' So Lian went after Thovalt alone.

He caught up with Thovalt in the foyer of the Archives. Thovalt was staring at the vortex of Javir of the ship's last painting. A grim and gory composition of bars and swirls, with a glaring yellow well at the centre which trapped the eye. It was a pictorial mapping of the triple-drive waveform, a memorial, an indictment. After it was done, the artist of the ships had painted nothing more.

When Lian was small he had populated it with strange

209

creatures whose eyes gazed back at him, whose movements made the lines waver. Even the yellow well became a pool under the midday sun. Now the lines were tangled and incoherent, and the yellow well reminded him of his hallucinations, when the *kindereen* shone beams of light into his eyes to anchor him.

Whiteness leapt out of blackness. Thovalt's fist drove into the centre of the painting with a hollow thud. The plastic did not yield; Lian was still looking at it when the tremors died out. Thovalt clenched his right hand in his left, his shoulders hunched in pain, his breath coming out in grunts. Lian watched him, in disbelief and incomprehension.

Thovalt leaned his forehead against the glass, eyes closed, until his breathing quietened. Finger by finger, he opened his hand. The skin was split, the blood smeared on the swelling joints. Without lifting his head, he said, to Lian, 'Go on. Go back.'

Lian did not move. He knew the painting. He knew the smoky internal doors. He knew what he would find inside, the chill, the hush, the listening air, the memories. He turned away from Thovalt, and with his motion, the smoky doors opened into the Archives, where Burdania was kept. He had been here before, many times. Nowhere else was preserved so completely in his mind. One left transient footprints on the soft, lustrous floor, as though on sand between tides. High above three skylights showed Kilureel, outblazing the stars. But at a word, the ceiling space below the starlights would become filled with other stars, Burdania's stars. He had stood amongst them, on the balcony. He had been small, pushing his face through the wrought railings, stretching out to grasp one. He remembered his shock as his fingers snuffed the star. He had jerked away, and when the star rekindled, begun to cry. The star drifted away, unmoved. But he knew he had put it out. Nothing, no knowledge, act, or awareness, could be truly undone.

On either side of the central aisle were the doors to the viewing rooms, and between them, decorative terraria. Caught between the sudden brightness outside and the twilight inside, orange flowers had closed untidily. A lizard clung to the inner glass, presenting suckered toes, and bluish belly. Lian watched its tiny breath swell and collapse the thin membrane of its chest. He could have spread his arms halfway around the microhabitat.

In the next habitat, a desert *toran* raised its plumed tail in alarm. Air feathered the plume, while the others behind it dug into the sand. Evolution was indifferent to the bred-out of any species, but instinct had gone further in the *toran*, giving the old the willingness to sacrifice themselves for the young. Even when only the dimpled sand remained, the old *toran* waited, grizzled tail erect, body stiff.

Lian stepped back from the glass. A tremor passed through the *toran*'s tiny body and slowly, very slowly, the erect tail softened and curved down. The sand heaved and one of the others scrambled from its refuge to sniff noses: there, you're still here.

The stars were above. Burdania was here, in the booths and displays of the Archives. The ghosts were below, in the shrines. Holoimages of generations of Explorers waited to recount their voyages. Images without presence; voices without mind, no matter how subtle the emulation. Yet worse was the glimmering of living vitality, the vestiges of real spirits, which could be wounded, Lian thought, irrationally, by his necessary conviction that they were not real.

He knew why Thovalt had brought him. He remembered. He whispered, the sound carrying in the silence, '. . . You – told me to say, "I am Lian D'Halldt. I ask to hear – Islain Nors"—'

'It seems a long time since anyone asked for me,' the voice said. 'Maybe not.' And from the air, as before, he appeared.

He had hair the colour of the sun at noon, and the most haunted eyes Lian had ever seen. Lian had forgotten the eyes. He did not look at his face, but at the binary star motif worked across his breast. Thovalt sat on the chair in the centre of the booth, gripping the arms. He seemed unaware of his own jolting tremors. Lian stood against the wall. He could have touched the man with no stretch. Nothing would have induced him to try. He tucked his hands against himself as the image's eyes sought out his audience. But when they came to rest, they looked straight at Thovalt in the chair, and Thovalt stared back, transfixed.

'Lian D'Halldt,' he said. 'You've called on me before.' Lian shrank back from this too personal observation, misdirected as it was. 'And you're young, aren't you? Not seven yet. Or so the records say. Perhaps you now know – as we can only surmise – what we left behind. Perhaps by the time you ask this our descendants have had the courage to go back.'

Lian caught an involuntary breath, as before. Thovalt did not move. The image hesitated, inclined its head, in an uncanny listening.

'Perhaps,' Islain Nors' ghost said, 'it is as terrible as we fear.'

There was a silence. The image wavered slightly, as though with emotion. Then firmed.

'It is in a way ironic—' and now his eyes went beyond Lian again, 'no, let me rephrase, it is supremely ironic, that we have accomplished one of our great goals, contact with another intelligent species. The very vindication we sought, and no one to know it.

'We would have left Burdania – in peace!' a sudden burst of passion, of self-defence, quickly over, 'because over generations we had become a society in ourselves, living according to our own priorities, and we *resented* the intrusion of the larger society.

'Yours is the twenty-eighth colony established, the one hundred and fifty-ninth planet visited. Seventy-nine ships went out, ten were lost . . . Are those only numbers to you? For two hundred years we failed in our quest, and now, when the quest seemed bred into our bones . . .' He broke off.

'What am I doing? *The quest* . . . as though I can make our flight from our society into something worthy. Once I thought it was. The woman I loved, Javir, was my window upon the world. She was an artist; I saw Burdania through her eyes. But I did not recognize that I used a window, and that so many others had none.

'Briefly, Lian,' with a crisp impartiality, 'these are the events: in winter 1609 began a series of debates inquiring into continued exploration, given that we had been unable to found a viable colony. The thrust of the opposing position was that the gathering of scientific data alone was not important enough to justify the current expenditure of talent and resources. In

212

short if we were to be planet-bound by our biology, space was an exotic hobby. I think it was only then that the degree to which travel was in our blood revealed itself.' He smiled, without humour. 'We had been sequestering precious minerals from the worlds we had visited for generations, and a large part of our cache was confiscated. There was great bitterness over this, on both sides.

'This might have gone nowhere, except that Carolinn D'Vandras and D'Jayna Travessa developed the theoretical foundation for a stardrive free of the fundamental limitation of the tunnel drive: we did not have to have a spatiotemporal map of our destination.

'A prototype was built and embarked along the outer track where seven of our ten lost ships had gone . . . and it returned.' Those green eyes came to life for the first time. Forgetting, Lian reached out.

As his hand touched, the image stuttered and vanished. He jerked his hand back. Thovalt stared through the image at him, shocked. Islain continued unaware, unmoved: '. . . visit a sufficient diversity of environments, to support ourselves in space; we need never return. Unknown to the designers or the outside world, we began construction on three larger ships. It divided us sorely: families which had been Explorer for generations rejected the prospect of leaving Burdania forever. But they told no one: they were Explorer.

'The ships were all but complete when the designers learned that we had built *three*, and came to me. They were my dear friends, and they were candid: the space-time stress of a single drive fired in space was more severe than they had let be known, for fear the testing would never find approval . . .

'You know how tragedies build to their climax,' he said in a detached tone. 'Knowledge goes unshared, circumstances unforeseen; people who might reconcile never meet. I promised my friends that those drives would never be fired but singly, and well outside any planetary system. I will never know whether they believed me, or whether in the end they understood the fragility of even the best-meant promises. I will never know whether they were the ones who brought down an impounding order upon the ships and upon the Explorer's

213

spokespeople. I resisted: it seemed unreal, even at the moment at which I was forcibly subdued, and certainly to the moment at which I awoke, aboard the ships.' There was a silence.

'We did not *intend* that the drives be fired simultaneously, and so close. We did not, until someone – and I suspected my friends, for nobody else knew the systems so intimately, but I do not know; I can never know – but *somebody* attempted to override the drive control. What compelled them to so endanger all aboard the ships, I do not know; were they under threat of the same kind of violence I had seen? I do not know.

'And perhaps,' in a very soft voice, 'it was precisely because I believed *at that moment* that my friends were responsible, and I was hurt in more than body, not rational – perhaps that is why I did not listen to their warnings—'

Lian stifled a scream. Before Islain there appeared, just for an instant, the image of a planet, with a glowing ring swelling across the surface until the whole planet had a pale corona.

Then there was only Islain. 'I'm sorry,' the image muttered. He looked round, through and past Lian again. 'I – I'll try again. This wasn't very . . .'

Blood pounded in Lian's skull. Sparks whirled around him as though he had wandered into the heart of the starscape. Someone said his name. He thought it was Islain, and threw himself against the door in panic. A black vine snaked past him, and the door slid open, and it seemed the whole floor followed it, tilting and falling away beneath him. He grabbed at the vine, knowing even as he did so that it would not hold, that it was rotten. His hand slipped away, and he pitched forward into brightness, towards the bony crunch of landing. This time Thovalt caught him, and held him on his knees. 'Lian, Lian, I am so sorry.'

Sight returned. And the sound of whispering voices. Lian looked up at Thovalt's face, stripped of poise, of Thovalt's complex glamour. Beyond Thovalt, ghosts moved, filling the corridors of the shrine, crowding in on anyone who came to see them. Lian closed his eyes. He felt Thovalt release him, carefully, setting him well on balance.

Lian said, 'I – saw him. Before.'

'Yes,' Thovalt said. 'Before.'

Before he asked to be admitted to the debate, Lian thought. Before he was refused. Before he climbed up on to the dome. Before he fell. Before. Thovalt had shown him this, before.

The whispering around him stopped. He did not open his eyes. So this was what Thovalt had carried, what had informed his bringing Lian, his abandoning Lian, his anger at Lian's prognosis. Thovalt, like Thaorinn, bore the guilt at what had happened to Lian. Bore it, nurtured it, cherished it. Lian was suddenly furious at both of them. They were what they were, they could do no better than was in them. Their guilt was useless to him, worse than useless, a burden. *He* was the one who had climbed up on to the dome, *he* and no other. If it was because of the knowledge that they had dealt and kept from him, so be it, but the deed was *his*. He had nothing else; they should not take that away from him.

He opened eyes smoky with an uncommon anger. The corridor was empty, of the living and the dead. Thovalt had left him in the shrine.

The anger ebbed, and anxiety replaced it. Thaorinn had warned him of the aftermath; it had driven Thaorinn out into the jungle, to live or die. But Thovalt had no such escape: he was trapped in the colony, with his failure.

A fragment of a phrase came uppermost in his mind . . . *before I fly away into the starry black.*

Thovalt had made a study of the ships. He had styled himself their navigator. Lian stood in the silent shrine, cold to his bones. He thought, I am being foolish. But in his mind, the chamber loomed, its occupant a few sketches of dim highlights, a sleeping monstrosity. I am being foolish, he told himself, even as he started up the stairs from the shrine. I shall stand looking out over moonlit barrenness, and feel very foolish indeed. Lors will have come for Thovalt; he will have been waiting outside. Lors will take care of Thovalt, and then I will speak to Lors. Maybe Lors will understand how it changed in the hall.

The moonlight jolted him. The three moons hung high and golden, each missing the barest sliver from the base. It was the night before *en'vos'neen'el*. Telien and – his mind flinched from her name – *kin* family would be starting out on the day-long walk to the Andeer. All over the planet, by day and by night, *kinder'el'ein* would be gathering along the banks of the rivers, the veins of the world. Lian was the only Burdanian ever to attend *en'vos'neen'el*, as a toddler carried there on Telien's back. He remembered a river as vast as a sea, flat water disappearing into luminous mist.

There would be no more *en'vos'neen'el* for him. He was stained, irrational, prey to sudden frights and obsessions.

He had so nearly persuaded himself of his foolishness that he did not see the figure leaning against the glass of the chamber for a long moment. And in that long moment Thovalt saw him, and ceased his stroking and murmuring to the glass, and opened the outer door of the airlock.

A lightburst set the hazy air glowing, and stained the sleeping canopy bright green.

Lian ran forward, blinded. He slammed hands first into the clear wall, and felt along it. Behind the glass, Thovalt waited for him. Through stinging eyes, he saw Thovalt's wild smile, and his supple hands pantomiming flight. Lian's fingers slid on the edge of the door; he scratched and beat upon the crystal surface. The frosted shadows of a binary star emblem slid over his skin, and beyond it, Thovalt laughed hugely at him. He saw Thovalt's fingertips caress the panel controlling the inner door, and understood then why Thovalt laughed. He, Lian, could not do so simple a thing as open a colony door. The pale yellow gas came out of the inner door like two huge wings, and folded Thovalt in. He took three steps forward and collapsed in a shambles of unruly angles. A siren screamed.

Near blind with floodlights and desperation, Lian pounded upon the door panel. It felt strange, warm and barred; he looked at it at last and saw that it was covered by a hand, an immense, dark hand. Telien pushed him gently aside. He clutched at *kin* robes, and *kin* put his hands away. He saw the huge chest swell, collapse and swell again. *Kin shouted* something at him: he saw the effort, felt the force of it, even as the siren deafened them both. Then *kin* took a final deep breath, and opened the door. Lian screamed, unheard.

The siren swooped and swelled. The hangar lights synchronized, blooming and bursting. They made nonsense of motion, catching onrushing people mid stride, mid shout, mid gesture.

216

Lian stood without moving. He felt disconnected from himself. Thovalt had gone into poison, and Telien had followed, and he had not been able to prevent either. Nothing he did would have any effect on anything. He was nothing. People jolted against him, pulled at him, gabbled at him. He said nothing.

'Stand back!' he heard someone yell. 'It's coming out.'

It, Lian thought. He knew *it* meant something. The crowd rippled, and drew back from the door as it opened. A very tall, thick-bodied figure emerged, staggering beneath a black roll folded over its shoulder.

It. Burdanian has no pronoun for *kindereen*.

Lian reconnected. He thrust people aside with all his strength and no heed, and reached the front as the door closed. Somebody caught his arm. 'The gas—'

Telien went down on one knee. Lian wrenched his arm free. A dark hand hung groping in the next flash. He grabbed and tried to brace it as the black roll slid inwards on Telien's shoulder. He gasped something incoherent to Telien, and got a whiff of gas which scalded his throat. Gagging, he released Telien's hand and heaved on black fabric. The weight beneath slid away despite his grip. Then the lights stabilized and there were people around him, helping him drag the black off Telien. He glimpsed Thovalt's face, inverted and bluish-grey, blood and yellowish fluid leaking from his mouth. He pulled on the sagging Telien. Telien looked up into his face in bewilderment, *kin* pupils almost circular. But yielded, trying to stand. Both felt the jerk through *kin* frame, and recoiled at the sound of tearing fabric. Lian dropped his head to see Telien's foot caught in a band of material. He started to reassure, 'It's just—' and then a shift of Telien's weight warned him. *Kin* eyes gleamed bone white. Lian cried out as the immense body toppled, bearing him down.

'A different biochemistry, *i'vad'neer*,' Telien said.

They sat in the bay beneath the lagoon. In the colony it was near midnight, outside, tending towards daybreak. Telien rested *kin* cauled head back against the glass and looked up at the fish nibbling algae overhead. *Kin* colour was terrible, nearly yellow. 'Far less noxious than the distress of so many

217

Burdanians,' *kin* said. 'I understand Shaleen better now.' With a visceral shock, Lian remembered Telien's eyes in the bleaching light. The rim of Telien's receptor puckered, the exhausted *kinder'el'ein* had sensed his shock.

Teli, he signed, *let me take you home*.

'Soon,' Telien said, closing all three eyelids on the sight of his fussing hands. 'This is as near to a peaceful place as can be.' Telien drew a slow, luxurious breath; he watched the massive chest expand. 'Watch the fish, Lian.'

Not understanding, Lian shifted himself around, to obey. There was a slight pearly cloudiness to the water, which made it seem brighter than clear. The fish were like embers or flowers, bright, tropical. He watched an orange-mouthed fish lipping the glass. Slowly he brought his finger up to meet it. The fish bumped glass again, its quartet of dorsal fins fluttering. Lian lured it towards Telien. A second of its kind joined it.

'Ah,' Telien murmured. 'I suppose it is just that you remind me that some of those little minds are predators.'

Lian stared at the orange-mawed fish. He saw now that it was the kind that Thovalt had thwarted of its prey. *Dris* was the name Thovalt had given him. Thovalt was alive, barely. He was on detoxification and life support, Granaith's remotes nudging their way through his bloodstream.

Telien said quietly, 'Forgive me.'

He looked blankly at *kin*.

Telien said, simply, 'I felt your anger.'

An instant later, Lian felt it surface from the depths, a tide of heat across his skin. *You could have died!*

'*I'vad'neer*, you *would* have died. I would not have that. You are too precious.'

'I am *not* – *precious*. I am – useless. I could – have said – something. For – Thovalt. I could have – stopped— Listen to me. I could – not have done anything. I cannot do – *anything*.' He doubled over, plunging his face into his hands, and gave himself up to grief, fury and frustration, for Thovalt, Telien, and himself. Telien's warm hand moved gently up and down his curved back, its pressure unwavering. Emotion spent, he was deeply ashamed of himself. He braced himself to

218

straighten, to look Telien in the face and appreciate the distress he had caused.

But before he spoke, *kin* said, 'Come with me to *en'vos'neen'el*.'

It was the last thing that Lian expected. His heart contracted with joy and pain. Vaelren! 'Now? After *this*?'

'Do not confuse speaking with doing,' Telien said, precisely, but with long pauses between phrases. 'Come. Show my people how your difference can enrich as well as grieve. Declare yourself to us. We have lived too long as strangers on our one planet. If we are to live together . . .' *Kin* sensed his reaction and rolled *kin* cauled head to look at him again, slit pupils floating like leaves in blue. 'If we are. If you people cannot find the courage . . .'

'They *must*,' Lian burst out. Mended his mood and tone: 'I was at *en'vos'neen'el* – before. Nothing changed.'

'You came as my charge, not to take part. This will be different. You will be the focus of a – you will be the focus of our attention, our – I do not think you have ever been taught the sign . . .' *Kin* signed, and Lian thought he glimpsed some meaning in the inflections, but none in the whole. 'There is no verbal form. It is a . . . gesture. An inner gesture. Exercise?' *Kin* shrugged heavy shoulders, despairing of language.

Will it change – me? Lian signed.

He expected denial but *kin* said, 'Perhaps.'

There was a long silence. He stared at Telien, believing yet knowing it was impossible, trying to discipline his Burdanian curiosity and his un-Burdanian love.

'I am not asking you to try to be other than you are,' Telien said. 'The *en'neen'el* contains many brave and resilient spirits. They will respond to you. They might teach—' *Kin* voice faded. 'Teach those of the present hour something.'

Lian did not know how to answer. Telien's eyes were closed again. 'This is a peaceful place. The water and the living things in it filter your people's – passions. We would sit here between watching over you.'

'Telien, *why*?' The one question he needed to ask. 'It was not – chance you were – there. Were you coming – for me – again? Were you – compelled – to help?'

219

Kin pushed away from the glass to look straight at him. 'I was not compelled. I chose.' *Kin* leaned back again. 'I cannot explain to you in words, even in sign; I would that I could. When I felt your debate end I knew that it was time to change the relationship of *kinder'el'ein* to Burdanian. I came to ask you to come to the *en'vos'neen'el*. I was diverted. There was no compulsion, but neither could I have ignored what I felt. Do you understand?'

'No,' because he could not lie. 'It doesn't – matter, Teli. You – did not die. Thovalt will – not die.' He slipped an arm behind the inert, heavy body, drawing up the tenderness he felt towards *kin*. He remembered lights winding down the trees and threading along the paths beneath, departing for *en'vos'neen'el*. He was fascinated by this *kinder'el'ein* thing which the others found so important, yet which Telien was prepared to forgo on his behalf. He schemed to persuade his guardian to leave him. For years he had been delighted with his infant cunning: not only had Telien gone, but *kin* had carried him along. It had not occurred to him that Telien had *kin* own ideas.

He felt Telien's body relax, *kin* respiration unconsciously pacing his. He slowed his breathing so the *kinder'el'ein* would not hyperventilate in the colony's richer air. He remembered how it felt to know himself loved and comforted, and he tried to offer that to Telien. Injury, infirmity and handicap had kept him self-centred for too long.

When Telien, spoke, *kin* sounded stronger: 'When the Burdanians came,' *kin* said, as one who had been musing upon the subject, 'they thought they had come to die. They were the first sentient peoples we had met since we went out exploring—'

'Teli! You never told—'

'It was before *vos'neen*, and even further before *en'neen*.' *Kin* held up a hand to secure his silence, and signed: *I am going to tell you something. I hope you will understand when I am done. It is about the beginning of the empathies.*

Kin rested a moment, gathering strength. The fish clustered in *kin* shadow, mouthing the glass, predators and prey alike. Two Burdanians strolled past the bay's mouth, glanced in, and then hurried on.

When first they came, the empathies looked like madness to the ones before. Kin used a pronoun that Jahde had applied to a school of fish, washed up dead upon the beach, *aer'en* – the sundered, lost dead of insensitives. 'E'en *could not live as* aer'en *did – as you do – in close company, amongst metals and electricity. There had always been a few who were particularly sensitive – in the early years, they were holy people, spirit touchers. Then the empathies – the madness – the mutations and the sterility – visited more and more in each generation.* Aer'en *were frightened.*

'They didn't know,' Lian said, uneasy. If this were a pleasant tale, Telien would have told him it long since.

I'vad'neer *if that were all, I would agree. But scientists found the genes which were changed in 'the madness'. This made it possible to choose which unborn children should live, and which – should not.*

Lian stared at *kin* in horror and disbelief. 'But those would be *kindereen*.'

'We know that,' Telien said, also speaking aloud. 'They did not. They saw those children as flawed; they thought it best to eliminate the madness.'

Flawed children like himself. Lian shook. Telien said, gently, *They did not know,* and lowered *kin* hands, waiting for him to recover his equilibrium.

But the empathies lived, Lian signed.

Before the empathies, the people believed in universal creators with purposes, and that the creators meant us – the people – to see en *purposes through. Kin* watched him for a moment, sensing questions, but none cohered. *Others were simply disturbed by the thought of killing so many. They thought if it were so easy, other traits might be chosen for change or elimination—*

They did that to Burdanians, Lian said. *Once.*

Are you easy with that thought?

Lian brooded. *I'm here* because. *You are here* despite.

Telien reached out and brushed his temple with *kin* finger. *People learned to understand instead of change. They saw that the madness was caused by the surroundings, not the empathies. They learned to live with low technology, in small communities. There the first children were born as empathic mated with others. They were also empathic.*

Kin sensed his relief. *Do not look too soon for resolution. Even those who revered the creator would not accept that the creator would push them and all their accomplishments aside. They knew they would have to choose between their civilization and their children. They were very proud of their civilization. So they tried to change their children, using surgery to destroy the receptors. But the common mind, the* an'neen, *strengthened. The common mind could better withstand assault.* An'neen *was aware of the damage being done to the 'environment', the 'ecosystem' vos'neen. It became a struggle for the world. The empathies do not teach us to live – do not allow us to live – in any other way than their own.*

'Sometimes,' Telien said, aloud, 'your people recall those days to *en'neen*.'

Will en'neen *ever accept us if we are like them?*

You are like, but you are not them, Telien signed, meticulously. He basked in *kin* pleasure at his understanding. *That is what we will show* en'neen.

'With *me*?' Lian said.

Kin looked down at him for a long moment, receptors dilated to the fullest. Lian wanted to urge Telien to be more self-protective, even with him. And grasped, in a new way, why his headlong dashes for the edges of things had so unnerved his foster parents.

'If you need certainty,' Telien said, 'you should have been born into another universe.' *Kin* eyes lidded, first the nictating, then the two outer eyelids. 'I do not know what is going to happen; I do not know all I am asking you to do; I am only asking you to come, with all the courage you have in you, and all—' eyes closed, *kin* touched his temple lightly but accurately with a large finger, 'all the love.'

SEVENTEEN

BURDANIA

Lian eased aside the canvas hanging on his bedroom window and looked out into the night. At what was, in summer, the garden of the *caur'ynani*, marked out by ruined walls. It looked even more derelict for the heaps of dried floodwrack piled in the corners. Starlight gleamed on stripped grey wood. Tatters of leaves dangled, twisting in the wind.

He had come back to a house dressed for festivity, swept and dusted, hung with coloured nets, streamers and carved wood. Lara bossed him into borrowed finery: a dark brown robe with decorated border, and a hood which was comforting. In the midst of disaster, they intended to celebrate Tor and Valancy's son. Lian wanted only to lie down and worry. About Illuan D'Vandras, who remained unconscious. About the shuttle, somewhere unknown out in the night. About that sentence in Daisainia's record, and what it meant to the present, and the future.

'Lian!' Lara pushed open the door. 'Come *on*. He's started.' She caught him by the arm, in her high excitement not noticing his wince. He moved with her to spare his shoulders, across the hall, into Vylan's room, which was draughty with the blind removed from the window.

Over the gate into the garden hung twin loops of fire, torches being spun overarm at blurring speed. Dimmer lights dotted the darkness beyond the wall, brushing upon a hand, a portion of a face. People lined the walls, watching.

The whirling fires stopped, held by outstretched hands. The torchbearer dropped lightly into the gate, sweeping the torches, twin bunches of tapers, overhead as he landed. He collected both in one hand and executed a one-handed cartwheel to the edge of the bonfire, paused teasingly, and bounded on to the nearest low wall. He detached a taper, tossed it right, another, tossed it left. Oil-laced floodwrack caught, illuminating his grinning, soot-streaked face.

'Rathla?'

Zharlinn ran along the wall towards the *caur'ynani*, tossed a paper into the nearest heap, and disappeared, with a leap, down the far side of the building. The torches moved and jostled, trying to follow. Lara darted across the hall into Lian's room. Lian stayed where he was, eyes half focused on the lit bonfires, admiring the recklessness, the agility, the display. He wondered if Daisainia might be watching from behind one of these torches.

Lara scrambled back into the room. Across the hall, his wide-flung window framed fire. All his hoarded warmth escaped, and the room full of smoke. Perhaps he should take Tion's offer of a heatlamp.

Zharlinn reappeared upon the near wall, whirling his tapers. He tossed one into a corner heap, and disappeared in a gout of smoke as damp wood caught. He slipped off the wall, staggered clear to collect himself, doubled over, coughing. Then remounted, leapt and skipped to the front wall, and presented a taper to one of the children. Lamps followed him along the wall to the other corner. He mimed a great show of indecision before surrendering another taper. The taper dipped, but an older child caught the young one's hand. Zharlinn strutted back to the gate, and neatly vaulted down. The lanterns stilled. Lara drew a breath. Gently and precisely, Zharlinn lobbed the torches before him into the heaped mound in the centre of the garden. They scattered, the oil burst into flame, and Zharlinn ran at the fire, leaping through the flame and landing, unscathed, on the other side, to applause.

The night moved around Lian: flames and flying sparks, torches in hands. Children carrying tapers and burning sticks tried to imitate Zharlinn's mount on to the wall. Around the central fire, people had begun to dance. Lian pled ignorance.

224

'I'll teach you,' said Fioral D'Suran, delicate and poised in a a circlet of small white flowers. Likely she could have detailed the properties and prepared the appropriate elixir. Small glass beads twinkled on her tunic. 'Gather dances are confusing, but we can story-dance here.' Idly, Vylan drummed a one-handed beat on his thigh. Fioral watched her feet through a simple square-step. She made a cradle of her arms and tilted her head. She danced several beats so, then leaned sideways as though passing a baby to someone else, pivoted around her arms and drew the imaginary baby in. Her feet described a wider, springier pattern, and she tossed the baby before passing it on. It was then – as her steps became more solid, and she held the baby firmly, but looked beyond it towards the horizon – that Lian realized that she was dancing Daisainia. The steps before had been Valancy and Zharlin. The fourth she danced was, clearly, Lara, and Lara saw, and laughed. The fifth was Vylan, who smiled at Fioral's impression of himself. The sixth moved uncertainly, but lightly, and held the baby with tenderness and sadness. Did he look like that to her, to them? The seventh was Tion, grave and sure-handed, and the last was proud and withdrawn Tor. She stood blinking, and panting slightly.

'That's us,' she said, 'welcoming Valancy and Tor's baby.'

'I – saw. You are very good.'

Kylara D'Suran scoffed. At Lian, not at her sister: she dealt the crown of Fioral's head a light cuff, deftly sparing the circlet. 'Where are all the Islanders who can *dance*?' She was flamboyantly dressed, with full sleeves and bloused trousers. Slats of polished copper dangled from her bodice and flashed like knives when she danced.

'You stand like this,' Fioral said, to Lian. 'Now you step forward, step sideways . . .' Lara and Kylara followed suit for a while, then started their own improvisation. 'Then you can do this—' Side, together, forward, back, other side, together, forward . . . Kylara spun in a whirl of blades, Lara mirroring her. They slapped palm to palm and thrust each other in the opposite direction. Vylan broke off his beat to shake stinging hands. At his side a small boy tried to fill in with stick on wood. Vylan said, 'Cymail, would you get my drums from the common room?' As he watched the little boy dart away, Lian caught sight of Arkadin sitting on a wall, leaning forward on her splayed crutches. She waved to him. Lian stepped right when he should have stepped left, and jostled Fioral. They looked at each other. Lian said, 'I think – I will go and sit on – the wall with Arkadin.'

'Good gather!' Arkadin extended a hand for him to take. 'Used t'dance the strongest of'm t'their knees. B'lieve me.'

He settled beside her. 'I believe.' He hesitated. 'Arkadin – were you – here five – years ago?'

'I? No. M'brother brought me autumn'fore last, thinking the young D'Suran might ease me. But 'twas he went back north 'nd died.' Grief touched her face. After a few heartbeats she recollected herself. 'Why?'

'I have been trying – to find out what happened – with Morain D'Vandras.'

'Why'd y'want to do that?'

'I am a stranger—' he began, and then sighed and looked down at his hands. 'I have this – habit of – stumbling into – the heart of things and – risk whatever I find there. But – the more I learn the more I need to learn.'

'That doesn't make a powerful lot of sense,' Arkadin said, matter of factly. 'Y'sure you're only looking for what you want to know? Hidden *tayn*'n all.'

'No,' Lian said. 'I – cannot be sure.'

'It's not a story for gatherside. Not one I'd tell, left to m'self. Matters to th'young Travassan. Knew her father in th'North. Many years now.' She gave him a sidelong glance full of wickedness, reminding him of Sara. 'Knew him *well*. R'member him well, too. B't it's not an old woman's gather tales y'want . . . What I know, I'll tell.'

Fioral tore up to them. 'Rathla and Tor are dancing Steppe and Sea.' Lian looked to Arkadin for enlightenment. She waved an unsteady hand. 'Old horrors c'n wait. B'sides, I need to get my breath.' Fioral hauled him through child-sized gaps in the gathering audience. 'Nobody'll mind you being in the front,' she assured him. 'Just sit down.'

The heat was scorching, the fire dazzling. Through the fringe of flame, and the shimmer of fired air, Lian could see Zharlinn and Tor, limbering to dance. Fioral said: 'It's supposed to be about *my* grandfather. It's not what really happened, though; it's sad— Ooh, they've got drums.' She bounced on her knees, her firelit hair bouncing with her. 'Vylan's taking one – they're giving the *isk'dar* the other!' He saw Daisainia trying to fend off the offered drum, but her people surrounded her and pressed her, until she took it and knelt with it gripped between her knees. The firelight raised the russet lights in her tangled dark hair, and the skin of her face and hands was like Kylara D'Suran's copper. He could not read her expression through the shift and shimmer of the superheated air, but he thought she was smiling. He watched her ease into the beat set by Vylan. The two drums negotiated tempo and volume, playing off each other. Then, gradually, they settled into two distinct beats. Zharlinn and Tor began to dance, Zharlinn to Vylan's drumbeat, Tor to Daisainia's. The dances were athletic, exuberant – the audience around Zharlinn had to yield space – with elements of mime. Zharlinn set sails and pulled nets; Tor, less flamboyantly, mounted and rode unseen *faun*.

Gradually the drumbeats interwove, and the feet passed the pattern, one to the other and back again. The two men circled each other. Hands touched, grasped. Fioral whispered, 'My grandfather was an Islander; he and Taryn D'Suran loved each other. They couldn't have children with each other, so they could only pair for a year. That's custom in the North.' One whispered in the other's ear – 'My grandfather wanted Taryn D'Suran to come away with him' – and the other, Tor, flung him away.

There was a breathless silence. Then the beat began again. Zharlinn raised himself from the stones. The two men circled back to back, moving apart. Each danced with phantom partners, Zharlinn on the edge of the fire, Tor in the cool outer firelight. The drums beat against each other; Lian, son of a musician, appreciated the skill, even as he tensed against the irresolution. The two dancers danced, separately, sometimes tenderness, sometimes happiness; Zharlinn twice mimed a baby in his arms. Yet at intervals one stopped, and stood still, looking towards the other.

The pulse quickened. Zharlinn danced the setting of sails.

227

Vylan drummed in swelling rolls like the sea. Daisainia's drum faltered, skipped beats. Tor faltered. He brought hands to his chest. Zharlinn leapt from his boat, across the little space between them, as Tor fell and lay still.

Silence again. Only one drum sounded, a slow deathmarch. Zharlinn turned to the fire and mimed the lifting of a branch, and the laying of it on the pyre. With his hands, the smoke rose. Vylan's slow beat went on. Zharlinn gathered ashes, and lifted his hands and opened them up to the wind: Daisainia slid her hands across her drum, an amplified whisper. Vylan gave a soft, shivering little roll, and silenced it with a palm.

'What *did* happen to your grandfather?' Lian asked Fioral, as they worked their way away from the fire, as the dancing had spread to a merry frenzy.

'He left but he went back. He had children by Astarian D'Suran. My father was the oldest. Taryn never had any, so he wanted my father for *cal* next. When they were old they lived together again. They died in the bad winter. Why do people make unhappy stories, even out of happy things? It's not that it's a bad story, even a boring one. Toring's the same.'

'Is Toring happy being chronicler?'

'Oh yes,' Fioral said. 'And he'll be good.'

'D'Halldt,' Daisainia said suddenly, appearing as though from the smoke. 'Good gather, Fioral.' The little girl bobbed her head, floral circlet slipping. Daisainia said, with some lightening of her expression, '*Cinnavaul*, I see. Well, 'tis abundant enough.' Then to Lian, 'Walk with me.' Her tone did not allow refusal or even negotiation. She led him through the throng, through the gate. Beyond the gate, out of common view, she favoured her left leg. He stopped before they had gone beyond the standing wall, so that she might sit if she wanted to. Not unexpectedly, she did not. She looked towards the Guildhouse, where light shone golden behind one woven shutter. 'Toring *will* be good, Toring D'Suran. He has patience with words on paper. I have always preferred the act to the accounting.'

Was that, he thought, a message?

She faced him squarely. 'I have much to thank you for. Tion D'Suran, for one. I saw him again before I came here, and

228

found him easier in his mind. For Illuan D'Vandras. Most of all, for last night. You challenged me to think what mattered more: my liberty, or my people.'

'That was – not what I meant—'

'D'Halldt, if will or disbelief could undo it, it would be undone. But even you are part of it: when we met I had the sense that I know you, or that I *will* know you. I have the sense that you are, or will be important. Imagination? Or an intuition from what I already know of you . . .' And then the violet eyes challenged his. 'This hidden *tayn* of yours . . .' He thought: *Illuan*. And recognized belatedly how skilfully she had trapped him. But she closed the trap lightly. 'It has been known,' was all she said.

'A—' Relief made him gasp. 'A – little – more time is all I ask.'

She fixed her gaze on the garden of fires. Sparks spiralled to the rooftop of the *caur'ynani*. 'You cannot know how tired I am of *surviving*. Instead of working on the relics, my restorers will spend the spring building dykes and clearing mud. We are chained down in a dark cleft with a small sight of the sky. Perhaps the D'Suran are right and we would be best on the coast, summering in Lltharran. But it would so . . . *vex* me to yield.'

He had no answer for her.

'D'you think me cruel to Zharlinn?' she said, suddenly.

'Cruelty – is not in your – nature,' he said. It sounded absurd. She had poisoned a woman.

'To what would you abscribe it, then?' she said bitingly.

He said nothing. He might call it an act of mercy, and of fear. The intensity of Zharlinn's attachment had taken her unawares. He did not have the daring to call it so to her face.

She said bluntly, 'I need a child, D'Halldt, and soon. I am *isk'dar*. I am Travassan. I should be succeeded by a Travassan child.'

'Why not choose – your successor from – the most capable?'

Visibly she bridled. 'My child would be *isk'dar*.'

'And you would not trust Burdania to anyone else's?' he completed her thought. It took her aback. 'No,' she said, nearly defiant. 'I would not.'

There was a silence. Laughter spilled over the walls like froth. It seemed very far away. In thinned starlight her eyes were not violet at all, but black.

She stepped back. Unthinking, he stepped forward. She stiffened and drew herself taller. Then and only then did he see her as apart from him, starlight on her shoulders and the beginnings of a frost around her feet. Then and only then did he realize that he had moved with her.

He stepped back, starting to say something. She spared him from finding out what by catching his arm. He felt the Travassan strength jolt his bones, and stared back at her. Uncertainty hardened her face and she let him go. That, he felt in his bones and in his spirit, too.

Nothing he felt for Vaelren could have prepared him for this. This woman was a stranger, his uncertainty of her profound, his knowledge of her scattered over a handful of meetings. Vaelren he had known in substance; Daisainia he seemed to know only in outline, by her impact on her world. Yet it did not matter. He remembered how, when he returned to the colony, he had always had the sense of knowing more than was in his consciousness. Of Daisainia, he knew more than was in his mind; he knew more than knowledge.

He thought: this is dangerous.

'I have known Rathla Zharlinn all my life,' Daisainia said. He thought the moment had passed. He drew away slightly; he thought she did not notice. ' 'Twas easy; perhaps I deceived myself.' Then those dark – violet, he was sure that he could see the violet – eyes came up and snared him. 'Do you understand what I am asking, D'Halldt?'

'No.'

She brushed the thigh of her injured leg. 'I will not make old ashes, not as *isk'dar* on Burdania. There are too many dangers, here, and where I must go, travelling to bring my world together. When my time comes, I will have no warning, for I will *not* run to meet it. But a child of mine, an *isk'dar*, is essential to Burdania.' She lifted upturned, half-clenched hands, gripping air. He felt her desire to make him understand, like something palpable. The gesture distracted him; he could not translate it. It suggested an inarticulate, unyielding

230

strength. 'I am unity; I am the pole which attracts or repels. Burdania needs that. Linn and Ylid Travassa destroyed our past and splintered us. I and mine must right that. But my child will bear the Travassan legacy, and *shikarl*. I cannot spare him either. He will need a father, and *tayn*, who will shield him from them. He will need people who do not keep him apart, who refuse him when he needs refusing, and make him see that things do not *have* to be simply bcause he might wish it, or he might dream it.' She looked away again, lowering her hands. 'Here is too full of ghosts. It is at the cusp of past and future, and sometimes I do not know which is before me . . .

'You would tell me,' and here she brought her head up, and stared at him with monochrome eyes, 'and rightly! that it is a terrible thing to leave a child in a place which I cannot myself endure. But I must, for Burdania, and for those who have been *isk'dar* before me. I will *not* let what they have done go to dust because of my nightmares. I will do for my child as much as I can. If he must live in Lltharran, and with the *shikarl* in his blood, I will leave him amongst people who can lead him through the murk of premonition. Make him see that things do not *have* to be. I cannot.' And here she looked away again, 'You have done that already for me, I who am rotten with *shikarl*. You would not let a son of yours grow up rotten. Perhaps if there were someone who fastly doubted, and reasoned away the frights and darknesses; perhaps—'

He stared at her, stunned. She expressed herself nearly callously, and with calculation; how much calculation he did not know. Yet she did so now, and not at any other time, as though she sensed, or shared, his feeling. He told himself, you are projecting what you feel on to her; it is simply that she now has the opportunity. She— then he finally realized what she *had* asked. And realizing it, realized that it sounded neither selfish nor callous, but the raw expression of basic desire. And it touched something raw in him.

Children had always been something for the future, for after Burdania. For after Vaelren. For such time as he could mute his expectations to reality. He was amongst the youngest of his own generation; he had an alien upbringing and socialization; he had involved himself with Burdania; and he was aphasic.

Genetically he might be suitable, otherwise he had to accept a life of subtle exclusion. There were no Saras amongst his own generation. And certainly no Daisainias.

He said, with some urgency, 'You – did tell him -- Rathla – that you – hoped for years.'

'Aye,' she said. Paused before she decided to speak. 'But I am not made for intimacy, and I have . . . darknesses of spirit that I should be always holding down lest they . . . corrupt him.'

Was this, he thought, another of her strange imaginings, or was it perhaps a confession? And of what? 'Am I – not corruptible?'

She looked at him with inky, introverted eyes. 'Perhaps. But you have held against my conviction that you are other than you are. You have held against my belief in *shikarl*. And you can do what needs be done. At the dyke, you saw to D'Vandras' greater need, while Zharlinn was distracted by me.'

'Only – because he – was closer to you,' Lian said. 'I am – drawn by you, Daisainia. By your people – your place. But I may not – be able to stay.'

She turned her face into profile. He saw the hard mask against the fire, and realized that somehow he had hurt her. She said, quietly, and with dignity, 'So be it. I will not ask the reasons for your coming or the reasons for your going. I would much prefer it, though, if you said farewell.'

She turned and walked away, towards the path to *caur'ynani*. She was limping. He could not hear her footsteps for the festivities, and yet he hardly heard the laughter, either, for listening. Cold starlight shone on her hair, and on the damp heel of her boots. Briefly she was outlined against starlit floodwaters, in tarnished silver; then she became only a moving shadow against the knoll.

He tracked the shadow, examining word, tone and texture, motion and emotion, every aspect of the encounter. He was shaken by how much he perceived only in retrospect. And how much he still could not understand.

He thought, with fragile amusement, that if he had nothing else from his father, he had Thaorinn's susceptibility to living enigmas. As Thovalt's fascination with the *kinder'el'ein*, so his own fascination with Daisainia.

And he shared Thaorinn's cowardice before the dark core of the enigma. He had a sense he had entered a pact with her, that she would not interrogate his secret, if he did not interrogate hers. How he had come to accept such a pact he did not know, but this he did know: Daisainia did not like her pacts broken. Zharlinn was suffering that.

He remembered her wordless cry as the dyke gave way. Not an order, not even a name, nothing from her disciplined, denying mind. Her parents' deaths were still very much in her present. And as that dyke failed, her own must have seemed very close. But one of her pacts with her people was that they never see the abyss beneath her feet, and never pull her back. Not when in her eyes hers should have been the hand which held Illuan's.

Oh, Daisainia, he thought. How could you kill?

EIGHTEEN

TARIDWYN

The sky was barely lighter than the jungle when Telien and Lian set out. Lian had to change into his grey robe and sandals, Telien to collect provisions from the high-house. Telien cast a worried glance skywards: they would have to travel through the stifling midday. Lian knew not to dismiss *kin* concern, but set himself to endure.

The settlement was largely empty: most of the *tris'neen'el* had young children, and had embarked earlier in the night. Telien collected lightstaffs, watersacs and drymasks from the high-house, gave Lian a drink, and tied a mask over his face. *Kin* had devised them for Iryssan, who was prone to vapour inhalation pneumonia. The desiccated mosses prickled fiercely, and Lian yielded more to Telien's yellowed hue than to wisdom.

He said, voice slightly muffled, 'Do – *kinder'el'ein* – know I am – coming?'

'We have thought this through long since,' Telien said. 'It was left to me, since I know you as my son, to decide on this time, or another.'

'Does – *everybody* agree?'

'Everybody will accommodate us. A *kinder'el'ein* cannot resist *en'neen*, or *vos'neen*.'

'Aren't you—' He couldn't find a word to ask how Telien could presume so. How *kin* could be sure *kin* was not abusing it. That *kin* reasons were good. He could not believe that a majority of *kinder'el'ein* favoured letting a Burdanian intrude on their most sacred ceremony. There must be more like Vaelren, *good* people, who found Burdanians difficult. And

234

there would be others like Shaleen, cold, isolated *kindereen*, who could not endure them. What would happen to *kinder'el'ein* who wanted to keep their distance from Burdanians? The further they travelled along the deep jungle paths, the more it oppressed him. 'Who – *lets* you do this, Telien?'

'What gives me the right, you mean?' Telien said, surprisingly in Burdanian.

There was a long silence. He had to break it. 'Some – *kinder'el'ein* would not – would rather Burdanians – not be – near.'

'*I'vad'neer*, that is unnatural for *kinder'el'ein*.' Telien stopped and turned to him. Enough new daylight was filtering through the jungle to cast a soft sheen on *kin* features. 'What we share is beyond 'agreement', beyond 'consensus.' *Kinder'el'ein* are meant to be together, within ourselves, within our world, our time. Our distance from you distresses us more than your presence amongst us. Some of us have been changed by knowing you. Others cannot change, because they resist knowing you. That has created distances between us. I am *kindereen*, I am a guardian of the body spiritual of the *kinder'el'ein*. That is what gives me the right. I am not strong in *vos'neen*, but I *know* that the Burdanian can be accommodated. Others have let me guide them. *I'vad'neer*, I *know* what I am doing is right.'

'Vaelren – said we made you – not strong. *En'neen* pulled away.'

'Foolishness,' Telien said robustly. 'Vaelren is *maeren*; she does not yet know. The *an'neen* needs the weak and the strong. We are all part, we all contribute.'

'Does Vaelren love me?'

'You know the answer to that,' Telien said gently.

He would remember that walk to the end of his life. He thought it was like slow drowning in honey: the downwelling yellow light, the heavy sweet scents rolling in from either side, the rising moisture from underfoot. Telien plied him with water, made him sit down and changed his drymasks. *Kin* strengthened as they put distance between them and the colony. *Kin* colour became darker, *kin* step lighter. *Kin* sang to

235

him in a sweet, hooting whistle. Sequins of sunlight slid down the trees to light upon the littered path; lay there briefly, and then began to float upwards again. High above the bright flecks of sky turned a deeper green.

They reached the Andeer just before sunset. Lian hardly noticed the rich, red light, until they stepped out of the jungle beneath the glaring eye of sunset. A smouldering track led out into the river; on the far bank, a black canopy supported the hot, orange ball. It purged his eyes of shadows. Gratefully, he reached up and untied the drymask, drawing a breath bright with the smell of fresh water.

Along the red-lit bank, *kinder'el'ein* stirred. He had not noticed them, for seeing the sun. Now he looked along the river sands and saw pale robes tinted by the sun, dark hands and faces which were only smudges. He felt their attention upon them. He felt their stillness around him. For the first time, ever, he felt the isolation of alienness. He swung round to face Telien, and checked himself. Telien had doffed *kin* caul; *kin* held it loosely in one hand, watching him. *Kin* receptors were like scars on each temple, not circular as he had imagined, but elongated back towards the well-formed pinna of *kin* ear.

He said, 'No – already. I'm not – ready. I'm – tired.'

Telien reached out and pushed back his hood, and with a feather touch stroked his hair back from his temples. 'You have been readying for this all your life, though none of us knew it. Come.' Telien gathered him with a hand on his back and guided him down to the middle of the sands. There, waiting, were Telien's mates, and Jehane, Shaleen, and Vaelren. Shaleen kept *kin* head turned away, face obscured by the heavily winged caul. Vaelren watched him with steady, cool eyes. Her black scalp, a flawless dome, gleamed; she wore the sun's image centred on her forehead like a topaz. She would not let him hold her eyes; she looked away.

Lian knelt, turned from Vaelren, into the sun. Telien knelt, facing him, *kin* shadow filling his lap. His hands plunged into it, and gripped each other for reassurance. He braced himself for the beginning.

'Lian, tell me who you are.'

He stared at *kin*, disorientated.

'Lian *eith*'Sara *a*'Thaorinn *aur*'Telien, tell me who you are.'
'D-D'Halldt. Lian D'Halldt.'
'Where are you from?'
'Burdania,' he said. 'And here.' His hands leapt up into sunlight. *Why are you asking me these things, Teli?*
'Trust me, *i'vad'neer*, and tell me. Tell *kinder'el'ein* how their world looks through your eyes. Speak or sign; it does not matter. Talk to me.'

He did, stumblingly. The light was falling, so he talked about Burdanian eyes being made for blue light, seeing blue, and blind to red, while *kinder'el'ein* eyes saw red and did not see violet. He talked about how the heat tired him. He talked about how the jungle looked to a Burdanian eye, and how rank it smelled to a Burdanian nose. He talked about Iryssan and Varidian studying native wildlife while they tried to abide by the strictures of *vos'neen*. Then he found his hands moving of their own volition, and as he lapsed into sign, he no longer made comparisons. He described the *kinder'vos*, the fern-shaped corridors in the shelter of the pygmy forest, the stillness in the inner pools and the weaving of light by the sea. He described the high-house as he remembered it as a toddler bumbling around its confines. He took walks through the jungle in his mind, and talked about Thaorinn punting down the river on his disintegrating raft. He grew husky and Vaelren brought a flask full of river water for him. He fell silent, watching her walk back to where she had been sitting, and thinking that he had almost forgotten her.

Telien let him watch *kin* daughter until she reached her place, and then spoke again.

'Tell me about Telien.'

At every stage in his life he had seen a different aspect of Telien. To the infant and toddler, *kin* was the sky-bridging parent. To the young Burdanian, oppressed by courtesies, *kin* was a slow, ungainly creature who could be wounded by a thought. To the injured youth, recipient of *kinder'el'ein* courage, Telien had been healer and accepter. *Kinder'el'ein* did not change: Burdanians said that of them, *kinder'el'ein* said this of themselves. The empathies barred change. What offended *vos'neen* was not done, what went unrecognized by *en'neen'el*

237

was not accepted. Yet here was Telien, *kindereen*, bound by *kin* race to *en'neen*, asking *kin* race entire to recognize Lian D'Halldt, Burdanian, and through him, all Burdanians.

The truth would have been: I am frightened by Telien. I am awed by Telien. But it was a forbidding thing to say to someone one loved.

He remembered the sound of the triple beat of Telien's heart.

'I – love Telien,' Lian said.

'Telien knows,' the *kinder'el'ein* said. 'And Telien is glad.'

Though Telien never tells me what is happening, Lian signed.

Telien's nostrils slits flickered, he was sure. 'Telien is penitent.'

But he thought he was beginning to understand. They did not want fact of him, or even his impression of their alien environment. They wanted feeling, the full repertoire of his emotions as the question evoked thoughts and memories. And the *kindereen* would sense him, *were* sensing him, and then what?

Telien interrupted his thought: 'Tell me about the high-house.'

His memories spread out in a web, and caught his hand gloved with lightflies, a gift for Vaelren. He fell silent, in fright.

Kin said, 'Tell me about the *kinder'vos*,' and left him to tread the curving corridors past cells with curtains shredded by the years.

Dusk smothered the bank. Along the bank, lanterns blossomed. Vaelren came down to set one beside Telien. There were lights across the river, shimmering slightly in the currents of air. He had not realized that there would be *kinder'el'ein* on the far side. The *kindereen* of Jahde's *kinder'vos* would be waiting to light their lamps, for night would not have touched them yet. Did that mean that on the far side of the planet, dawn would be washing over the sensing *kinder'el-'ein* – and who chose the moment and the hour?

'You and I,' Telien said, out of the darkness, answering a question he did not know he had asked.

The questions began again, harder questions, now. 'Tell me about the colony,' said Telien. Lian described the straight,

238

white corridors, the habitats, the work that must be done to maintain the microecologies. He spoke about the dome, and the Archives. After a moment's hesitation, he described the Explorers' shrine, and the ghosts who filled its corridors.

' – And Burdanians,' Telien prompted gently. He spoke about Thovalt, the man for whom Telien had risked life and equilibrium, despairing of making a Burdanian, particularly so extreme a Burdanian, understandable, or even less than repugnant to the *kinder'el'ein*. He found himself speaking about the others, the protective Lors, the remote Granaith, Andra of the Archives, Danas of the clear physicist's mind and clumsily effective kindness. His grandparents, Iryssan and Varidian; his parents, Sara and Thaorinn; in their various self-chosen exiles.

The three moons rose behind Lian, one by one. The canopy's tiered shadow withdrew across the sand. With each moon's rising, it became thinner.

'Tell me about Thaorinn,' Telien said.

He looked at *kin* in mute appeal.

'Tell me about Thaorinn.'

He told the story about the sinking raft, and that led back to the young Thaorinn of the records, and the Thaorinn of Sara's stories . . . but Telien was not satisfied. 'And you,' Telien said, gently, insistently. 'Tell me what *you* know of Thaorinn.'

'I – am – his son,' Lian faltered. 'I – look like – him. I – fell. He – did not want – me – after. I – turned towards – Burdania. He – did not want – me even – before.'

That sounded stark, and unfair. Lian closed his eyes, trusting them, trusting the moonlit peace of this night. For the first time he looked down through green-fractured impressions. He found the robed figure of his father, sitting on a moss-eaten log and pointing to one thing and then another. *He taught me the way the moons came together, what the* kinder'el'ein *called clouds and stars; he taught me names – he taught me the names of plants, birds, animals, and how to see in the jungle with Burdanian eyes.*

'He taught you something else,' Telien said.

He stared at *kin*, who was still limned by moonlight, *kin* dome scalp thinly gleaming, face shadowed. There was such certainty in Telien's voice.

'Who told you about Burdania?' Telien said.

'You – did.'

'No, *i'vad'neer*. I would have. But I did not. Tell me about Burdania, now. Tell me.'

Stumbling again, he told *kin* about the meticulously preserved history of his kind which was so fleeting beside the half-remembered epochs of the *kinder'el'ein*. He told Telien about Islain Nors' confession. He described the debates, the one that he had fallen into and the other that he had witnessed. He tried to explain what he felt had gone wrong in Thovalt's debate. He tried to explain why Burdanians could not do the simple, just thing and go back. It was as though they had been created with a limitless craving for knowledge, so that, like the empathies for the *kinder'el'ein*, it could be both their greatest joy and their greatest curse. They thought it natural until they met the *kinder'el'ein*, who craved not knowledge, but harmony. Could they ever find the wisdom to return, and look, and be unbroken by what they saw?

He was standing, signing as fast as his hands could move, his face burning beneath tears. He was hardly aware of himself, or of the river or of the lights up and down the bank. The three moons cast triple shadows around him, making a chaos of his signs on the smooth sand.

He heard – he did not know whether he remembered or imagined it – his father's voice. He thought it might be a memory, for it seemed to be coming from a point above him, as it would if he were a small child listening to an adult. And yet his marred memory had never delivered up so much entire: 'I lived with an ideal, a promise – Burdania. I argued for return because I wanted to see Burdania once, once more, it seemed to me, though I have never seen Burdania in my life. I knew the Burdania of our Archives, of our collective yearning. I saw only that. One passes over a divide when one becomes aware that we would not be going back to the dream, but forward into the horror of the present. I came to understand why the others voted against me, because I came to appreciate what it would mean to me to find not the Burdania of the archives and habitats, not the Burdania of the memories, but the Burdania that would have been left behind when we left. And yet I recognized that we will go.'

240

He trembled, recognizing who had been speaking to them through him: Thaorinn, unburdening himself of ten years' silence to a child barely old enough to understand and far too young to demand why, if those were his thoughts, he was not still on the debating floor.

Lian understood the extent of his father's sorrow and error, that he had looked to the *kinder'el'ein* to train him in the detachment and the serenity which he thought he needed to complete his journey in safety. And had learned only an intensified loathing for his people's nature, and therefore his own, set against his perception of *kinder'el'ein* virtues, indeed, to Thaorinn, perfection. Lian thought for a moment that Thaorinn should know what Telien had told him about the history of the empathies, about the *kinder'el'ein* persecution of their changing people. But he recognized that Thaorinn would not think that it had anything to do with the *kinder'el'ein* who lived now. Would allow, as he would never allow for Burdanians, that that had been a different people in a different age. Would resent Lian for telling him. Thaorinn D'Halldt needed perfection. In their turn Burdania, his son, and he himself had all disappointed him. Now he had the *kinder'el'ein* of more durable virtue.

How could he make that so clear to Lian, and yet not see it in himself? Or if seeing it, how could he resign himself to it and not try to change it, for it had given, and would give him, such grief.

Telien knelt gently moving a thumb against the flow of his tears for some minutes.

'Now,' *kin* said softly, 'I want you to tell me about Vaelren.'

He heard, from the *kinder'el'ein* within hearing, a collective, indrawn breath.

Perhaps at the feeling the name had evoked in him.

He found he did not care. He had shown them the Burdanian spirit in all its remorse and confusion. Let him own it all. He felt giddy with defiance, and in defiance, he turned and looked across the golden sands to where Vaelren sat, behind her small light. He loosed his heart to go to her. The moment stretched, and stretched; and then she reached out her hand and covered her light, bowing her head forward.

241

Lian said: 'I love Vaelren.'

Telien spread *kin* hands, signalling an end, signalling release. Lian acknowledged to himself that he was spent, that he could go no further; that he dared to learn what else he might do. Along the bank the living shadow behind and between the lamps was still.

Telien offered him a waterflask, a simple, ordinary gesture. He stared at *kin* hand, and the flask dangling in it, in refusal, or simple lack of acceptance of the commonplace.

'What – happened? Did it work?'

'Burdanian,' *kin* chided him, and pushed the flask into his hand, steadying it until *kin* was certain he had the wherewithal to keep his grip. 'What we have accomplished here will take shape in time,' Telien said, getting unassisted to *kin* feet. 'We have the main part of *en'vos'neen'el* to conduct now. You may stay with us, or rest as you will.'

'Then it worked!'

'Aye,' said his weary parent, 'if you had but patience—' *Kin* touched his temple in the old fashion and drew a finger down his cheek. 'But that is unfair. What has happened I cannot put into words – shall I ask you how you draw breath? – but you are recognized.'

His eyes were caught by lights shifting in his peripheral vision, and he looked round before he thought, straight at Vaelren, watching him. The moonlight flowed down her face, and he could not tell, if he ever could, what was in it. He wanted to cry, remembering his last defiant assertion. She might never speak to him again, now that all *kinder'el'ein* knew by proclamation, and not by ordinary, forgivable overhearing.

He looked imploringly at Telien, but Telien offered him no guidance, either in expression or gesture. He had the impulse to dash away along the sand flats . . . an impulse so intense that he felt the packed sand under his feet, the thin water splashing ankles and robes. But when the impulse and its impressions passed he was still standing there.

He heard Telien sigh – release from his attention, perhaps – as he took the first step towards Vaelren. As he reached her she began to turn away. He hesitated; she looked back over her shoulder. 'Come with me,' she said.

'It is – all I ever – wanted,' he said.

'No, Lian,' she said. 'It is not.'

They went down the riverbank to where the flats widened. Lights and figures drifted aside and around them; Lian glanced backwards and saw them gathering, lights, patches of moonlight on bare heads and robed shoulders, densely plated shadows upon the sand. And a widening stretch of pale, footprinted sand between. He knew suddenly that she had taken exile upon herself. He stopped. She turned, white showing in the edge of her eyes.

'Go back,' he said. 'I don't want—'

'Don't want what?'

He flung out his arm. 'Leaving *en'vos'neen'el*. Because of me.'

'I am not leaving,' she said. 'Why are you angry at me? I do not understand how Burdanians—'

'I am not "Burdanians"!' Lian flared. 'I am Lian.'

'Yes. I know.'

'I – cannot help feeling!'

'I do not understand why you are angry,' she said again.

'I don't want – to be with you if I can't be – with you.'

'I don't want to be without you,' she said, suddenly. 'But I want *tris'neen*. I *want* mates. I want children to grow in me. Your feelings get all tangled up with mine. You confuse me, Lian. I don't know what is me and what is you in me. If it were not you, I would know, but you are you. It's as though you've been *part* of me. I don't want to be strange. I don't want to do strange things. But it seems I already am strange and doing strange things. I was there when you were born. I grew up with you. I felt you fall. All those days after it was as though *you* were *dead*, and in me was a place of dark confusion. And then you came back, and the place of dark confusion was full of light again. But then you started wanting Burdanian things of me, splitting me off from *en'neen'el*, and I was afraid. I am *kinder'el'ein*, and I always will be, and you are Burdanian and you always will be.'

'Can't – we make something – different – ourselves? It doesn't *have* to offend – *en'neen*. Not if I'm recognized now. I *am* recognized?'

'*Something* happened,' Vaelren said. Her eyes whitened, he

243

did not understand why. He was calm, delicately hopeful, but calm. She blinked away the whiteness, and caught up his hand, spontaneously, not seeming to notice how he reacted. 'Come!' He followed her strides, his legs tangling in her robe, his heart racing. 'Is it – them?' he gasped, not really understanding his own question. She did not answer, but broke stride to stoop down and lift the lantern off the sand and hand it to him. In the sea light he saw that her nostril slits were wide with excitement, and her receptors fully dilated. She covered his lips with sandy fingers and hers moved, but it was a moment before she remembered how to make sounds. 'No more words,' she said, and pulled them in amongst the *kinder'el'ein*.

Their eyes had already begun to whiten. Shutting off sight, that sense he shared with them, invoking the sense he never could. Even Vaelren was lost to him as soon as he had begun to hope she could be gained. He freed his hand from hers and eased himself away from her, and looked out between robed bodies. All along the riverside, his was the only light. The *kinder'el'ein* had no more need for sight now than did trees in the jungle.

Lian wondered what he had done when he was one year old, alert and demanding. He suspected Telien would have to tire him out so he slept through the meeting. But he was older now, awake and concerned, and he would have to make do with what senses he had. Recognized or not, he was the only Burdanian here. He eased the rest of the way out of the *kinder'el'ein*, and knelt alone on the sand. The light of the three moons glazed the sky. He could not even hear the *kinder'el'ein* breathing. He looked back at the heavily robed figures, looked no higher than the crest of the ribs, which seemed not to be moving, lest he look directly at those white eyes. He had not expected it would be like this. He had not expected to feel his alienness most acutely at his moment of acceptance. Whatever was taking place within *vos'neen* or *en'neen* was unseen to him. He had expected to at least be aware that something significant was happening, but instead he knew nothing.

Through the luminous glaze, even the brighter stars were dim. Thaorinn had taught him their names, this he could believe. Thaorinn had taught him the motions of the moons

244

and the names of the plants and wildlife around him; a Burdanian intimacy. But Thaorinn had taught him about Burdania, out there in the veiled stars. Lian shivered. He thought memory made the man, that having lost so many parts of his memory, he had lost those parts of himself. Even retracing the steps of that past would be insufficient, without knowledge of what he was retracing. And yet retracing those steps seemed to be recreating him; though he was incapable of recognizing his past its influence worked on him still. Thaorinn, Telien, Burdania and *kinder'el'ein*.

For Burdania was as much part of the Colony as the *en'neen'el*, the *kinder'el'ein*. The colony had a collective memory as much as did the *kinder'el'ein* except that it was recreated every generation, as his memory had been recreated. Burdania was as much present and part of the colony as if they had never left. As Telien had said, the debates were a form of *en'vos'neen'el*, a form of touching what had been left behind. There was no letting go. The negative vote changed nothing.

No, Lian thought, with a sudden dazzling focusing of thought. Life is not fragile. His life was not fragile, he should have been destroyed and was not. If it were an error to believe that because he was not dead or vegetative, Burdania should not be either, then he would make the error, because belief was what was needed, belief to defy logic.

What a premise, the Burdanian in him mocked; that because the one is not, the other follows. They will laugh you out of the debating hall for that.

He had a flash of arguing voices, bright light, falling. He leaned forward on the sand with both hands, knowing that that flash, and the records he had seen, refuted his conviction. He was capable of believing the error. *Believing* the error, in a way that he would still act upon it. No matter what he had seen on the record of that debate, what was real to him was an argument and a long fall from darkness into brightness. The two were irreconcilable; he was certain only that he would act on what was, to him, real.

He felt a light touch at his temple, and then a hand rested against his shoulder. He craned his neck but still could not see the face of the *kinder'el'ein* directly behind him. He breathed

245

again. Presumably this was as the *kinder'el'ein* intended, that he should join, physically, if not in spirit, their meeting. He wondered at the ceremonies of feeling which must be happening, unsensed, unseen, across the planet, in darkness and in daylight. He closed his own eyes, and extended his senses, trying to find something *between* sense, something which was not sight, hearing, smell, touch, bodily awareness, thought, memory. Some other conviction or experience. He probed and interrogated each sense: light showing as a thin slit beneath his restless eyelids; the nocturnal chuckling of the jungle; the sting of perspiration on his face, the damp heat of the *kinder'el'ein* hand on his shoulder; the slight fatigue, frustration and satisfaction at his reflections; the green fragments of his past, and the tangled growth of his present. It all seemed frighteningly full, and complete. He was incapable of knowing more.

He felt the *kinder'el'ein*'s hand tighten on his shoulder, and then, across the bank, a lamp sparked into being, and from further up the bank, a baby cried. The *kinder'el'ein* holding him released him with a little forward push, and he felt *kin* thrust by and break out of the gathering, half running. He recognized the heavy stone-coloured robes, but not the shape of head until *kin* caught up a caul from the sand and pulled it on, the sharp-winged caul of Shaleen's kinder'vos. Cauled again, *kin* stared at him across the sand for a second, and then swung away and plunged into the jungle.

Lian stood without moving, shocked.

Telien appeared from the group at his shoulder, blinking as though waking, with slow sweeps of *kin* three eyelids. 'Nothing for you to feel responsible for, *i'vad'neer*. *Kin* will come back.'

'But what – happened?'

'You sensed nothing?' As though *kin* thought it should be otherwise. As though now that he understood and was reconciled to experience as offereed by five senses and a single consciousness, *kin* chose to blur possibility. But Telien knew *kin* error swiftly enough. 'It was *en'vos'neen'el*. Unlike any before, and unlike any hence, I trust; I trust you will forgive me. Yes, it's "worked".'

'It seems,' Vaelren said, 'impossible that he could not know.'

246

She spoke more to Telien than to him, in simple wonder and without defensiveness. Her generosity of tone made his heart contract painfully and conspicuously with hope. He saw her sense it. What passed over her face was not precisely a flinch, but she did not look at him.

'But – what *happened* to me. I was – dreaming. I was mad! To have—' His face burned numbly as his thoughts finished the phrase in advance: to have said aloud 'I love Vaelren.'

'I knew no better person to come amongst the *kinder'el'ein*,' Telien said. 'We knew you as a little child, when you were not always trying to behave. And we nursed you when you were so badly hurt that you did not know we were there.'

'I – did,' Lian protested.

'I trusted you,' Telien said in a gentle, final tone. 'As I would have trusted none other. And you trusted me, in a way that leaves me humble. Yes, something happened.' He sensed quiet, intense excitement. Vaelren leaned forward, receptors wide open. 'Perhaps it was what Burdanians would call an "artefact", a consequence of the experiment we had conducted with you. Nevertheless, in experiments artefacts must also be reported. Or so Varidian and Iryssan tell me.

'Sara came to us when she was carrying you, to ask if I could sense you the way I could sense my own unborn. She asked – a great deal of a *kindereen* who knew her so well, and whose empathies were not strong. Like searching out a firefly in sunlight.' Vaelren's own metaphor, Lian thought at once. 'Even with my receptor against her skin, I had no sense of you, until a moment before you moved – rather violently, it seemed. But for that moment I recognized a tiny spark in *vos'neen*.

'That was what we sensed. A tiny spark in *vos'neen*.'

'What – was it?' Lian said. 'A – baby?'

For answer Telien pointed, down the river over the curve of quivering lights. Lian let his gaze travel outwards from the forefinger into the murky night. *Vos'neen* gave an advantage over sight. He looked at *kin* in bewildered reproach. Yet *kin* continued to point, adjusting the direction slightly upwards, towards the stars.

He thought suddenly of Thovalt, pointing out a violet star rising above the sunset horizon. Understanding glimmered, understanding which terrified him with its potential. 'Leaves?' Lian said. 'Birds? Trees?' Throwing one wrong guess after the other with pauses for refutation as narrow as any Burdanian's. 'Something flying? Clouds? The sky? Stars?' Telien was looking at him, pupils huge, nictating membranes quivering on the verge of closure. But with joy reflecting his joy. They both knew he understood.

Lian whispered: 'Burdanians.'

NINETEEN

BURDANIA

'Young Zharlinn's na' happy with you,' Arkadin Nors said by way of greeting.

He had been aware of Zharlinn as he tried to weave his way back into the gathering. He had seen him evade Kylara's attempt to recapture him for a dance and shift around the fire to keep Lian in his line of sight, looking for something in Lian's demeanour which Lian hoped he would not find. He looked bruised and a little bitter, the triumph of his display extinguished.

'I know,' Lian said, sitting down beside Arkadin. Then he remembered the secrecy Daisainia demanded, and looked up into Arkadin's sparkling eyes. She laughed. 'Nothing t'do but look, these days. But'know what t'look for. He's moody as a *faun*. She's stiff: like her father won't chance getting seen naked. An'I don't mean just skin. Not that he'll take warning. Not that you'll, either.'

Lian drew a deep breath. 'You did promise to tell me about – Morain D'Vandras.'

That checked her. She leaned forward on her crutch to stare into his face. 'Y'trying for a cure?'

'No,' he said, not sure.

'Got a better one,' she said. 'Me.'

Lian started to laugh. The colony had no Arkadin, either. He managed to catch her hand and say, 'Thank you, Arkadin.' She was robust enough to return, 'Long time since any *laughed* at me,' and to relate a rambling tale of one who had, during her impertinent, precocious youth, until he recovered his composure. He held on to her hand, although the thinness of her fingers tugged at him. She was another one whose time was limited.

She spoke first, seriously, 'R'member it's past. That's all I can say.'

'Please,' he said. 'I – need – to hear it.'

She sighed, and let his hand go. 'Trust you'n that, I will. I wasn't there, but m'brother told me. *Cal* Nors, he was then, an'part of it, to his regret. Sad and sordid story; guilty and innocent change with the telling. Parents drowned; she might's well have gone down with them. There was a void and Morain filled it. Moved into *caur'isk'dari*, with her daughter – th'daughter's Travassan, from one of the ones exiled by Ylid –a poor spiritless thing, even then. Morain was *isk'dar* in all but name. In autumn Morain asked th' *caur'cali choose* th'*isk'dar*. Other *tayni* had choice and why should 'vrything we'd done fall to the mad? She wanted it; that was stark clear to all. But not much of an alternative, was there? The *cali* agreed.' She stopped to get her breath. 'C'n y'believe I danced all night; while I ruin a story in the telling?'

'If you would rather—' Lian said reluctantly.

'Oh, hush, man. You asked. Where was I? Th'agreed. Morain said she'd keep Travassa. Sidor said no, he'd take her. She'd not go. Hid in the ruins, talking t'the young people, people who'd known her, and her father, stirring up discontent. Th'blood that was shed, that's on her hands. But who's to know there wouldn't't'a been stained hands, otherwise. Grant her that. What we know is that the ones she'd roused followed her to *caur'isk'dari*, to take it back by numbers. Numbers met numbers; there were words exchanged, and Morain ordered hers to hold Travassa, hazard t'herself and others. An'they did. 'Til one of *hers* struck out . . .'

She fell silent a moment, her gaunt face grim in the firelight.

'Y'see, Lltharran'd never seen anything like it. There was death in daylight under Linn Travassa, and things done in th'dark under Ylid, but that was more'n forty years ago. Burdanian didna' fight Burdanian. Four died that day; others still carry th'scars. Th'say when Morain and Daisainia met again, Morain said only, "It's proven." *Cali*'d set out for their

250

homes just the day before, and runners had gone to summon them back. Neither o'them would leave *caur'isk'dari*. In the morning when the *cali* came back, th'found D'vandras waiting across th'table from Travassa, plainly sickening. And it was then that Travassa told them all what she'd done. There's a Northerner salad leaf, *kalfid*, looks much like *sonol* plant. T'use *sonol* for medicinals, have'ta dry and whatnot before; th'leaf's itself lethal. Morain was not herbwise, not th'way Travassa is; she'd others do the gathering for her. After th'trouble, Travassa'd mixed *sonol* with *kalfid* in Lltharran store. Those as were there said th'telling was the most frightening thing they've ever heard. Morain was four days dying, an' when she died, they say all Travassa said was, "Burdanian is mine."' Lian shivered, violently and involuntarily. 'That's the story y'wanted,' Arkadin said brusquely.

'Yes,' he said, hunching over to stare between his hands. 'Please – the rest.'

'Not much else. Lltharran was hers: none of Morain's stayed out the deathwatch. Nobody else t'be *isk'dar*, with Morain a corpse and Shivaun's mind cracked wi'the horror. *Caur'cali* split to impotence, with some wanting to accept, and some to condemn, and one t'put her to stoning, but all afraid of what else might issue from it. She set Lltharran in order, an'when that was done, she turned to Burdania. An'from that day on she's been as y'see her now, and done nothing anyone can cast against her but that one thing.'

Now he understood the transfiguring flare of rage which had answered Illuan's, 'This *caur'cali* does not pass judgement . . .'

He understood that now. 'I need a child,' she had said. 'I should be succeeded by a Travassan child.' And yet: '*isk'dar* after me, perhaps,' she had said without bitterness of blithe little Crystolan, Shivaun's daughter, Morain's grandchild. Now he knew the story, or knew, at least, the *events*; yet so much seemed unexplained.

Or maybe it was there, and he was simply refusing to see it.

'Was – Morain in Lltharran when – Daisainia's parents died?'

'Y'r not the innocent I took y'for,' she said, with a hint of sharpness. 'But no, sh'was North. Th'd met, she an' Ky

251

Travassa. Took t'each other like *faun* bucks in spring; too much alike, maybe. An' Brandy Vassar wasn't one t'cross, either. She stayed quiet in th'North until they died.'

'What was – Morain like?' he asked, in a defeated voice.

Arkadin brushed his forehead with her hand, and then he felt the dried-wood lightness of it settle on his head. 'Folk told me things about men I loved—' His head came up, she said, 'Saw you and her, together.' Shook her head as he drew breath to say something – anything. 'No. R'member. Y'know what you can weather; it's for nobody else to say. Otherwise there'll be nothing left at the end but regret, an've known too many go t'that. Heed the wisdom of an old woman.' She tapped his cheek with her sharp fingertips, and he took her hand in both of his.

'Thank you,' he said. 'For – for telling me. For understanding.'

She snorted. 'Bah. Understanding! That's for sweet people like you. Travassan are harder on lovers than on enemies, and enemies they poison. An'if poison's not t'y'r taste, there's always salt.'

He smiled. 'Tell me, how was – Rathla Zharlinn involved – in this?'

Her face lost its light. 'I'm saying this only t'you, and t'nobody else. Y'must know something, since y'r asking "how". I think dearly of him. But aye, he told me he was the one brought her th'*sonol*, when she asked.' There was a silence. Heavily, Arkadin said, 'He wouldn't, at first, thinking it was for herself. So she told him it was to save her life, not t'take it. He loved her from a child, y'see.'

And thus, Lian thought, she corrupted him, and brought him to do what was not in his nature. How could *Daisainia*, with such clear awareness, murder Morain in such a fashion? Or maybe it was the murder which taught her about corruption.

Arkadin said, in that same, burdened voice, 'An'Rathla may be Crystolan's father, too.' For the first time she looked old, and in need of comforting. Lian had not expected this, but he was not much surprised. Shivaun was beautiful, violet-eyed, Travassan. And Zharlinn had brought the poison which killed her mother. If she had not stood in Daisainia's stead, guilt and pity might have been enough.

252

'Zhar went North after th'death; *caur'cali* thought it best, even if they didn't know his blackest part, he'd fought for her. Shivaun went North two years ago. Wandered th'North, taking hospitality and work when sh'could, came to *tayn* Zharlinn. Tamin put her out for th'trouble she caused amongst the young men: y'don't take lovers by fours in *tayn* Zharlinn, an' at that time, she had them by fours. 'Twas a great shock t'Tamin when Zharlinn went with her, but then she's never had sense about her son. Sh'doesn't understand yet that it was always th'*isk'dar* and not Shivaun. It's near a season's journey from th'Sor to here, and Crystolan was born but days after th'came. But th'babe's taken after the Travassan, so there's no way of knowing.' She leaned forward on her crutch and twisted to look at him with a tawny eye. 'So y'be fair to young Zharlinn. Or as fair as y'can.'

'Do – you think Daisainia would – ever – do it again?'

'Who's to say? You? I? She's settled now; who's t'know what'd happen if crossed?'

'But she cares – for Shivaun and Crystolan. She grieves what she – had Rathla Zharlinn do. And she – keeps Morain's record – openly—' But something across the fire had distracted Arkadin. Following her gaze, he found a close huddle of Tion, Kylara and Fioral. Tion's expression was worried, Kylara's sharply attentive. Fioral looked distressed. 'Looks bad,' Arkadin said.

Lian got to his feet. Eyes on Fioral, he picked his way between dancers and wanderers to where the little girl was standing. When she saw him, tears welled up in her eyes. 'Tion thinks they have to operate.'

'Can he?' Lian said.

The tears overflowed. 'It's dangerous.'

Kylara put a hand on her small sister's head and watched with approval as she struggled to compose herself. Then, with a gentle pressure, she turned Fioral in the direction of the Guildhouse.

'How can you?' Lian asked of Tion. The objection was as much on Fioral's behalf as on Illuan's. Surely they would not make her watch. 'Without—' Without scans and remotes, he almost said, and barely checked himself. 'You will kill him.'

'It is a last resort,' Tion said, tiredly. 'But he is sinking.'

After the warm firelight, the light of *tayn* D'Suran was harsh. Even the vibrant Kylara was haggard under it. Illuan's decline was shocking. His face was grey where it was not bruised and sunken where it was not swollen. To Lian's unpractised eye, D'Vandras looked moribund, and from Kylara and Tion's grim expressions, his eye was not wrong.

The two medics moved round him, dancelike, handling him skilfully. Tion broke the silence suddenly, but for several phrases, Lian did not understand what he was saying. Then simultaneously he recognized what they were doing. They were testing Illuan's reflexes. Lian's skin remembered the touch of fingers and instruments from long ago. Tion's voice was lapped and overlapped by other explanations prompted out of memory. A small part of Lian's mind stayed clear to compare Tion's explanations with those he remembered. The larger part was dazed with horror and compassion.

Fioral, standing half in front of him, listening intently. Unseen by either of her seniors, she kept an aching grip on two of Lian's fingers.

Tion and Kylara stood back as one. Their eyes met. Kylara said, 'There's definite weakness in the left side. That puts it,' she leaned forward and touched the bruised side of D'Vandras' head, 'there. If we trephine here, and see if we can drain . . .'

Fioral's hand tightened.

Were they planning to open his skull blind? Lian drew a breath to protest. Kylara shot a spitting look at him. Tion intercepted the look. He said, patiently, but sounding very strained, 'We have an idea from his reflexes which part is affected. What we don't know is whether it is a clot, swelling, or bleeding. We don't know whether that area is affected directly or whether it is being pressed upon by an adjacent area, or how deep the injury is. The least dangerous course is to release any blood or fluid just within the skull.' He paused. 'People do survive this kind of injury. The bleeding stops on its own, or the clot dissolves. But there can be lasting damage. A paralysis or a speech or memory impairment. The sooner we act the more likely we are to spare him that.' He stopped, seemed to weigh his next words and said, humbly, 'Wouldn't you?'

Lian's vision greyed. He pulled at his hand until it came free, and made for the remembered door. He glimpsed flashes of orange hair and yellow hands. Voices talked at him. He was thrust through into shadow and found himself sitting at the great table in the lamplit living room, resisting the pressure of Tion's hand on the back of his neck.

'I am – all right,' he said. Tion drew back the hand, but Lian leaned forward until his vision cleared, and the grain on the sanded floor resolved in all its intricacy.

Tion said, 'I'm sorry.'

'Don't be,' Lian said. Carefully, he straightened up. Several sheets of paper had been spread across the table, covered in anatomical diagrams in Tion's neat hand. Tion reached out to gather them up, but Lian already knew what they were. Tion's notes planning the operation on Illuan. He made his choice.

He knew it was reckless, but to choose otherwise would be callous, and in Lian's eyes, immoral. He knew what impairment meant, from within. He had no one to advise him, and he must again seek his own guides. To speak out, to involve the shuttle and Lors, would be indefensible in the eyes of the colony. He could endure their censure. Not to speak out would be unforgivable in the eyes of the Burdanians, in Daisainia's eyes . . . and in his own. That he could not endure. He lifted his head as Tion started to rise, saying, 'If you think you will be all right—'

'Wait!' Lian said urgently. Stood, pushing aside fleeting dizziness. 'Tion. There is help. For you. For D'Vandras. If I can find a working transmitter. Illuan—' the irony was sour in his mouth, 'broke mine.'

Tion's expression was perplexed. Lian hardly blamed him. He tried to organize his sentences. 'I am not – from Burdania. I am Burdanian, from a colony – elsewhere. Another planet. There is a shuttle of my – people in the mountains. There is a medic: Lors. He has equipment – like the relics,' Lian said, inspired. 'Working relics which can tell you precisely – where the damage is and what – you must do. He has remotes – tiny tools which can go into a body and do repairs. He can help Illuan!'

Tion grasped that, and pushed aside other questions,

though Lian saw them stirring. 'How do we send for them? How will they come in time?'

'With this,' Lian said, pulling out his transceiver. 'Only it is broken and I – I do not know how – to fix it.'

Tion took it, as much for something solid to grasp as out of any purpose. The loosened cover slid aside under his fingers, exposing the circuitry. Tion blinked at it, in unexpected recognition. 'It is full of those little things that Vylan studies,' Tion mumured. 'Where Fia? Fia!'

Fioral came uncertainly out of the corridor. She had taken off her floral circlet and beads, and put on a clean, coarse-woven smock. Her feathery hair was tied back, and her fine, bare face looked even younger. She looked at Tion in bewilderment as he pushed the transceiver at her. 'Take this to Vylan—Do you mind, Lian?' Lian saw the sense of it, though he quailed at the though of it being carried openly into the midst of the gather. Already this was out of his control. 'Tell him he *has* to get it working again. I can't explain, because I hardly understand it myself, but Lian has offered us a miracle and I cannot let my own slow wits stand in the way of seizing upon it!'

Fioral hesitated, and looked at Lian. Lian said, 'I – have a friend, a – medic. He knows – how to help Illuan. If – this is fixed. I – can ask him.'

Fioral gulped and ran. 'Don't drop it!' Tion shouted after. He turned to Lian. 'He has it all?' he said. 'All the lost knowledge?'

'As much as we – could bring. We did not know – what we would find.'

'I must tell Kylara—' He stopped suddenly. 'But if we cannot repair the transmitter? What happened to it? How did you come to be here and they there, and why not tell us?'

Those were the questions which he had pushed aside. Lian was reluctant to answer them, reluctant to surrender his claim to be a miracle or to quench the amazed joy in the young man's face. For the first time Tion looked his youth. He said: 'Even if we – cannot fix – there is a way.' His implant was, as far as he knew, still working. Any injury would be registered on Lors' scans. But he had been battered, bruised and terrified for his

256

life, and that had not brought them out of hiding. What would? He determined he would not think about that until it became necessary. 'There is a way,' he repeated. 'I would – rather not have to – go to it.'

Tion looked closely at him for a moment, but after that moment did not ask. They went back into D'Vandras' room. Kylara, bending over D'Vandras, scowled up at him. 'I had to put up with Toring's vapours. I will not put up with yours.' Then she saw her brother's face and straightened up sharply.

'Tell her, Lian,' Tion said.

He would rather not have. Tion had been easy to tell: he was patient, and he needed telling. Kylara's tongue was her sharpest instrument, and Lian knew he was not, in her eyes, the stuff of miracles.

'I – have a friend who could – operate on – *cal* D'Vandras without – risking his life.' Kylara drew a sharp breath. Tion said, 'Hear him out, Kya!'

'And where is this friend, C'Rynn?' Kylara said. 'A season from now this man could be nothing but bones.'

'Lors is – in the mountains. We have a – an aircraft. He could be here by this afternoon – if—'

'Ah,' Kylara said, folding her arms. 'An if.' She flicked a glance towards Tion. 'This goes above and beyond any story that Toring tried on us.'

'Kylara,' Tion said. 'He had a device – it looked like one of the relics, but it was *new*. There was an emblem on it, but the enamel was not chipped.' Lian was impressed by his observation. 'It was broken and I have asked Vylan to repair it so he can contact his friend.'

'Bah.' She pushed back her yellow-streaked hair, looking unhappy. Tion's belief disturbed her. But she would spare him the scorn she would not have spared anyone else. She gestured abruptly towards Illuan D'Vandras. 'Watch him,' she said to Lian, and to her brother, 'I want to talk to you.'

Lian sat down on the small chair beside D'Vandras. Kylara and Tion's voices murmured from outside, Kylara's timbre was sharp, but when Tion spoke, she listened.

Lian let his eyes stray around the room, seeing it as Lors might shortly see it. Bare stone barely plastered over, free of pictures and hangings; wooden planks and beams. There was a door instead of a curtain, in that door a rhombus of blue glass, unflawed except by a starry crack at the apex. The furniture served, it did not ornament, it did not inform. Lian remembered a wall's length of screens, Thovalt in multicoloured effigy. He remembered colours playing across Granaith's face and points of light glinting in Granaith's pocket. On the table beside D'Vandras' head there was a lamp, a bowl and instruments bundled in a cloth. The pointed tip of one had cut free.

Kylara came back in, followed by Tion. She skirted the bed, and came around to Lian. He got to his feet, unsure as to what to expect. 'Tion says your clothing is peculiar too. Show me what he means.'

Lian pulled off his jacket and let her examine the fabric. Then he sat down and removed one of his boots, offering it up to her. Tion joined her and turned it in her hands. 'See. It is not hide: there's no grain, no fibre, and there are no seams.'

Lian looked up at the medic's flawed eyes, shaken. 'You knew.'

'I saw there was something different about your clothing while I was looking after you.' His shoulders shifted slightly. 'You had not invited me to look, and I knew that you would explain in your own time.' Kylara looked from one to the other with a thin smile, which, turned on Lian, became acid. She half stooped and dropped the boot by Lian's foot. 'So,' she said. 'Now what?'

'If Vylan can fix—'

'Tion says Illuan broke it.'

'He – broke it, yes.' Too late it came to him that he might have plausibly claimed it broke when he threw himself down on the dyke wall to catch Illuan.

'Illuan knew what you are, then? He, as well as my discreet brother.'

'I did not know, Kya,' Tion said, peaceably. 'I had merely noticed a few things. Occasionally I do that.'

Kylara ignored him. 'And Illuan did not like it. I would not have expected him to,' she said, a little sourly. 'Nevertheless, I have never known Illuan break so much as a mug, even by accident, and certainly not on purpose.'

'I – do not know if he intended to break it,' Lian said.

'Where've you come *from*?'

'A planet – a planet many systems away along – the outward track. We call it—' He hesitated. That name was too revealing. 'We are the only colony we know to survive from the years of exploration.'

'And it has taken all this time for you to come back?' Kylara said.

'Yes,' Lian said.

'Flying ships in space are Rathla Zharlinn's obsession, not mine,' she said. 'I'll be convinced this is not all florid imagination when I see this medic, and not before.'

'But – you won't operate on Illuan—'

'If he gets any worse, we—'

'No,' said Tion firmly. Kylara looked at him. To her he said, 'We won't operate on him.'

Vylan shouted open the door behind them before Kylara could retort. He was breathing hard and his hair was windblown. He still wore his celebratory robe, which smelled of smoke and had several ember-burns on the dark green fabric. In his left hand he held Lian's transceiver, in his right a satchel of yellow cloth. To Lian he said, 'I have been told a very brief but astonishing story—' He caught sight of Illuan, and broke off. He took a step closer, and saw that Illuan was already beyond being wakened by a raised voice. He crossed to the table, crouched beside it, spreading his workcloth, with purposeful movements. He glanced once at Illuan's profile, now level with his eyes, and then began to speak, setting the little oblongs upright as he did. 'These were what I had to hand. If they don't suit someone will have to go up to *caur'isk'dari*. Lian, surely you know how this is put together – surely you *saw* it being put together, or do your people have Guild secrets too—' He looked up at Lian's abashed face. 'Well, I will replace everything I can recognize and let you test it and we must hope. Can you at least explain how it works? It might let me make an intelligent guess.'

Lian tried. Vylan worked, detaching and examining element by element, asking questions and often proposing answers himself. Lian wondered what might have happened if the

259

colonists, like Telien, had given him instructions instead of theory, had let him learn through his hands. Could he have achieved the same ease with colonist techonology as he had with *kinder'el'ein*? Instead of being fit for no more than to turn the transceiver on, speak into the void and listen to silence, and pass it back.

'It's not going to work, is it?' Tion said quietly from above them.

They had gathered the lamps on the sidetable for Vylan's work. Illuan did not need them. Tion's shadow lay across Illuan's face, which was grey and black beneath it. Kylara sat on the far side of him, holding his hand in a firm, challenging grip. Fioral stood on the far side of the table, pressed against the wall, silently eyeing the small spread oblongs. Vylan looked at her, at Kylara, at Tion. He said, 'I will keep trying but if you have any other ideas—'

Tion said, 'You did say that there was another way.'

Lian got stiffly to his feet. 'Feel behind my ear.' He guided Tion's hand. 'Yes, there. That is – a monitor. It relays my – state – to the shuttle. I think you should – cut it out. I think – that should bring them.' He looked around the ring of faces, and did not say, *because then they will not know whether I am alive or dead.*

'Let me see,' Kylara said, skirting the bed. Her probing was firmer than Tion's, and she bent him forward so that she could see. 'Under the skin, and mobile. That's easy.'

'But they would arrive thinking something had happened to you?' Tion said.

Kylara's fingers had continued to explore. 'You've scarring here,' she said suddenly. 'Very tidy, but quite extensive scarring.'

Lian pulled away. 'I was injured – younger.'

'Let me,' she said, holding him by a handful of hair. He submitted, unhappily. 'Those would have been serious injuries,' she said, in a hushed voice.

Lian flushed. It was ridiculous to feel so exposed by her touch when he had been stripped to his molecules and pinned up on a wall.

She drew her hands away. She stepped back. 'Whoever

treated you must have opened up your skull and gone directly into your brain.'

'*I* opened up my skull,' Lian said, straightening. 'I fell from – higher than your rooftop.' She looked up at the ceiling. 'It took – everything our medics had to – put me even as – together as – I am.' To Tion he said, 'I – could not tell you.'

'I believe you now.' She looked awed and a little stricken. Her hands, which had touched him, she held with spread fingers at her sides. Vylan watched her, looked at D'Vandras' inanimate face, and then at Lian. 'It seems,' he said, 'we need the help. If you think it will bring them, and you are willing to let them take this monitor out, then you can explain when they get here.'

'Yes,' Tion said. 'But it will hurt. We can numb the skin, but—'

'It does not matter,' Lian said, hiding the visceral twinge at the thought. 'I will have known worse. You can – control bleeding and – prevent infection?'

'I should hope so,' Kylara said, recovering. To Tion she said, 'You, or me?'

'It is Lian's choice.'

Lian looked from sister to brother. 'Tion,' he said.

Kylara lifted the package of instruments. 'Next door,' she said.

Next door was a smaller room with a high table in the centre, and a series of cupboards along the side, labelled with paper scraps. On a shelf above the bench was a cluster of cloth-covered lumps, which shone through the slats of the shelf.

He sat on the edge of the table as Tion stripped the covers from the lights. The wood had been sanded and resanded to a silky smoothness, but a faint smell of caustics attached itself to his hands. The floorboards, likewise sanded, were lightly spotted and stained. Lian reminded himself that Lors would be able to correct anything that they mismanaged. Nevertheless his attention was jumping and skittering with fright. When he lay down, prone, his heart thrust again wood and backbone.

Above him, Tion said, 'You are sure?'

Lian took a grip of the edge of the table. 'Yes,' he said.

Kylara draped his head, finishing with his face, so he saw

only a stippled brightness, with murmuring shadows beyond it. A chill liquid touched the skin over the implant. Tion said, 'I'm going to prick your skin a number of times—'

Kylara's voice said, 'Vylan, what is it?'

In the quiet left for the answer, a thin thread of speech unwound. Lian heard his own name, spoken in Thovalt's voice.

Gingerly, Lian sat up, shedding cloths, feeling an icy dribble track down his neck. Vylan stood just inside the doorway, cradling the transceiver in both hands, much pleased with himself. Lian accepted it as offered, holding the loose cover in place. 'Thovalt?' he said, dry-throated with tension.

'Li! Where've you been? What happened to your transceiver? The last Alystra heard you and Illu— Are you alone?'

'No,' Lian said. 'I am not alone.'

'Are you all right?' That was Lors.

'Quite all right. Lors, I— A man – is hurt. Head injury. I have – I have offered your help.'

There was a silence. Thovalt said, 'I suppose it is too late to suggest further discussion.'

'Yes.'

'Lian,' drawing the name out to two syllables.

Lors' voice overlapped his. 'When you say head injury, what do you mean?'

Lian passed the transceiver to Tion. Tion held it below his lips like two handfuls of water. Kylara came to his side. 'Introduce yourself,' Lian prompted.

'Tion D'Suran,' Tion said, stammering slightly. He had no experience of conversations without visual cues. 'The man is Illuan D'Vandras. He was caught when the dyke collapsed—'

'Last night,' Kylara said.

'Kylara,' Tion supplied. '*Cal* D'Suran. Medics' Guildleader.'

Diffidently, Tion offered what they knew. Kylara amplified it. To most of Lors' questions they had no answers. Some they did not understand. Lors simplified or went on to the next. Lian heard Alystra's and Andra's voices beneath Lors', followed by Thovalt's, doubtless provoking even as he soothed.

'My diagnosis would be no better than yours at this remove,' Lors said, by way of conclusion. 'May I speak to Lian again?'

Tion returned the transceiver. 'Li,' Lors said, 'we take your vote in favour of this as a given.' Quarrelling voices rose behind him. 'Give us a little while.' He broke contact. Sparing him, Lian realized.

He lowered the transceiver, forgetting the cover, which clattered to the floor. Tion bent and handed it back. 'Take care of my work,' Vylan chided.

Tion said, anxiously, 'They will come?'

'Lors – is like you,' Lian said. 'If they will not fly him, he – will walk.' He spoke more optimistically than he felt, not on Lors' account, but on the others'. Lors had committed himself with his first question. Andra would oppose it. The drama would appeal to Thovalt. Alystra might be equivocal. But all knew that if they refused, the Burdanians would know. In damaging Lian's transceiver, and making him ask for help in repairing it, Illuan D'Vandras had done himself more service than disservice.

'Why should they not come?' demanded Kylara.

'Why should who not come?' said Daisainia's voice from the door.

She must have been down behind the dykes, because there was fresh mud on her shoes and a long smear of it on her cheek. She carried her cloak slung over her arm, and her sweater sleeves had been pushed back, showing her strong forearms. Her colour was high, her eyes brilliant. Lian could not imagine how he could, for the past moments, have forgotten her.

He saw by the other's faces that, except for Vylan, they too had. And that they were shocked by the omission.

Daisainia was aware of their shock, if not its cause. She stepped into the room, addressing herself to Vylan. 'Lara D'Alna tells me that Fioral Nors came to you with a strange artefact in her hand and a plea that it be fixed so that Lian D'Halldt could bring help for Illuan D'Vandras.'

'Yes, she did. I repaired it.'

Daisainia turned her gaze on Lian. Unable to speak, he offered her the transceiver, turning up the binary star. She lifted it from his hand. But she showed no interest in the emblem, sliding aside the cover to inspect the components. She glanced at Vylan, then back at the clustered circuitry. 'What does this mean?'

263

'I – have friends who may be – who should be – coming from the mountains – soon.' He collected his wits, not easy under her eyes. 'Daisainia, I am not – from the Islands. I am – not from Burdania, though I am – Burdanian. I come from a colony – a *tayn* – from a planet – far from here. I regret my – deception, but I – but when I met – Lara and Zharlinn – we had not yet decided to – tell you we were here. We have a shuttle – waiting in the mountains. Our medic can help – Illuan and – he can be here in a little time.'

'I presume,' Daisainia said to Tion, 'that they *can* help, given the evidence of this,' she tilted it, 'and shuttles.'

Before Tion could answer, the speaker hailed Lian from her hand. She started violently, but tightened her grip. Lian saw the casing yield slightly. Thovalt's voice chirruped through her fingers, 'Invitation accepted. Find us a landing space. Oh, and Andra wants your tattered cortex for a sponge.'

'So *this* is what you would not tell me,' the *isk'dar* said.

TWENTY

TARIDWYN

'It has been an education,' Thovalt whispered huskily.

He lay confined by a narrow tube of a bed, shoulders raised on a sloping platform. Behind him on the screen, his effigy drew breath, blue-white blooming in his chest. His heart pulsed bright yellow.

Lian disdained the Burdanian reliance on scans, images and graphics. His experience was tactile, authentic. But for eight days he had looked in on this room, on this image, unchanging and stale, and Thovalt lying inert beneath it, sustained by machinery, waiting for a new heart and lungs to be cultured to readiness. The blue-white and yellow meant life itself. They were more Thovalt than the crushed shell of the man. Who said, with a feeble, gasping earnestness: 'I never realized how it might be for you—'

Lian jerked his eyes away from Thovalt's glowing heart, irked at the reiterated theme. Thovalt's skin seemed as transparent as Sara's; his eyes sunken, unglittering. 'My mind used to be like a spider's web. It shimmered; everything was all caught up in everything else. Do you know, I used to see words in colour; I used to be able to taste sentences. I could smell music. Synthesia, it's called. Now, I feel like I'm roped to a stinking corpse. I'm dragging it through grey fog. My mind's full of a foul chemical fog. That's their *cure*. I can't believe Lors would do this. I cannot believe he betrayed me like this. What did I do to him that he would let them to do this to me? Was he jealous of me?' He stared at Lian, pleading. 'Why did he let them do this to me?'

265

'He – tried to stop—'

'Tried. Tried. If he had meant to, he would have stopped them. He thought I was mad, too; he was glad, yes, that is all. He was glad they finally took charge.'

'He pleaded. But you – frightened them. Too badly.'

Thovalt's eyes moved around the edge of the room. Lian remembered doing that himself, remembered the hours of senseless looking from corner to corner, searching for the ghost of something past. Lors had insisted that the treatment would not change Thovalt, would not make him less capable.

Lian said, 'Thovalt, we – must think – about Burdania. Burdanians live.'

Thovalt moved his head from side to side. 'You *have* to!' Lian said. 'You can. When you spoke – it all went still. They *thought*. *Kinder'el'ein* sensed Burdania. Thovalt! You have to.'

'I'm not Thovalt any more. I'm a sack of chemicals.'

'They – cured *me*,' Lian said.

Thovalt's eyes started open. He grasped what Lian had said; then he grasped that he had grasped it, and a weak pleasure at his own intelligence lightened his features. He breathed a laugh, then gasped with pain. One hand slid up the covers to press his chest.

'Lian,' he whispered. 'I feel terrible.'

'When you spoke – it was the only time – it focused. Thovalt, *listen*. You have to – listen because I – don't have words. And I am – not wrong. When you spoke – about feeling – evil, about wanting to – go back—'

Thovalt turned his head away. 'I can't,' he said. 'It's not in me, any more.'

'Burdanians live,' he said. '*Kinder'el'ein* sensed them. You touched – hearts. You are *important*.'

'I am nothing.'

Lors said, 'What did you expect?' His fingertips rapped the edge of the touchplate, speaking his hidden anger. 'Whatever you perceived,' with a faint, stinging emphasis on the word, 'the only thing that matters is the outcome of the debate. And that was catastrophic.'

Lian could not speak. Lors' fingers drummed more slowly,

as his anger ebbed. He turned from his station, and looked up at Lian with gentler tawny eyes. 'I'm ... sorry Thovalt was difficult. He has undergone major surgery. He's still suffering toxic aftereffects. Physically, he's a mess; it's no wonder his mind's not working. He *would* blame it on the stabilizing treatments. But Li,' Lors said, with a twisted expression, 'those haven't even *started* yet.'

'He does not – know.'

'He knows. But he is immovably convinced that we are tampering with his mind. I suppose it is that that has finally persuaded me that Thovalt *needs* the treatment. It does not matter if he hates me for the rest of his life, as long as ...' His voice trailed off before he could say what he wanted for himself and Thovalt. 'The confusion, the sluggishness, all those will go as he recovers, and he will feel so much better in comparison that he should not notice the treatment. Which is by no means drastic. All they want to do is retune the sensitivity of some of Thovalt's neural circuits so he is not so ... volatile. That can be done pharmacologically and by ... conditioning.' Lors' voice was tired and heavy. Those things which he said did not matter, mattered profoundly. 'Lian, please leave aside the subject of Burdania. I did not say anything to you before because I thought what you had to tell him might help. But it seems not. So leave it be.'

'But – the debate—'

'Given the way our appointed Advocate Adviser – and most of the others – feel about Thovalt, I very much doubt if there will be another debate for him.'

Lian touched the very corner of the plate. He recognized Lors' private project in progress: a collation of scientific evidence for the existence of the empathies. Lors looked at his hand, looked up at his face, sighed. 'I cannot see this will be any use. We can explain *vos'neen* half convincingly, at least ... the bioelectric and biomagnetic sensitivities are well established. *Kinder'el'ein* learn to interpret them in terms of emotion, stress, living state. But *en'neen* ... though I have a theory about *en'neen*. The *kinder'el'ein* exchange information through bio-electricity, biomagnetism, as well as through the other senses. The higher cortex dedicated to the "empathies" is immense, compared to other senses. Even our visual and verbal processing is not so favoured. So, because of this intensity of exchange, *kinder'el'ein* act as a gestalt. The way this works across generations . . . and here's where I'm speculating: there's been much less study of *kinder'el'ein* psychology than of physiology, but it seems as though *kinder'el'ein* memory is structured quite differently. There's much less . . . episodic and factual recall. What I am wondering is if . . . *vos'neen* has its own memory. We have a *kind* of racial memory in the Archives: each generation has access to the sum of knowledge of all previous generations. *Kinder'el'ein* have access to their parents' and grandparents' . . . emanations, for want of a better word, directly, through the living source, but they also have access, through the living, to their stored impressions of previous generations, as received through *vos'neen*. Which is what I think *en'neen* is. Not some ethereal presence but a bank of stored impressions, some of great antiquity, passed down through the generations, via *vos'neen*, and placed in this special memory. Access seems limited for individuals, outside the collective ritual of *en'vos'neen'el*. *Kindereen* . . . I find it hard to explain *kindereen*, since from the admittedly limited data we have they are not neurologically distinct; genetically they can be either male or female, so the locus determining *kindereen* is not a sex locus, but somehow sexual maturation is curtailed or . . . rerouted. Actual data on *kindereen* is scant. It may be that theirs is a ritual empowerment, supported by a kind of training and rein-enforcement. They are influential, witness Telien taking the radical step of getting you "recognized". But . . .' He smiled suddenly at Lian, and said in a different voice, 'You look pained. I *know* you would like us to take it on faith, and not probe too impertinently into the mysteries, but Li, we are Burdanian. We rely upon logical argument and evidence. And that is what I *cannot* provide. I can explain how *kinder'el'ein* might carry the presence of their ancestors within them. I can explain their gestalt. What I cannot explain is how they might have sensed a living planet eight thousand light years removed. Even collectively. Even having just "read" your emanations at maximum collective sensitivity. I know you believe it. I would like to believe it. But liking to believe it, and being able to convince the rest of the colony of it . . . I will not give up,' he promised. 'I have a passenger's place on the next provisioning shuttle to Station Three; I'll talk over the phenomenon with Iryssan and Varidian. Yes, I know they are opposed; I am counting on scientific curiosity, and their faith in you as a reliable witness. You might like to consider joining me.'

Lian said nothing. He had returned from *en'vos'neen'el* so full of hope, convinced that the others would believe, would want to believe, what the *kinder'el'ein* had sensed. To find Thovalt despairing, the others splintered and blaming Thovalt and each other, and insisting on a scientific justification for the miracle.

'Well,' said Lors, at last. 'I'll keep working on it. Li, while it's on my mind, I wanted to discuss with you the . . . possibility of your making a contribution to the germ-line banks. You are young, but you . . . will be spending more time outside than most of us, taking greater risks and exposed to a wider variety of parasites and toxins. It by no means precludes your having children within a relationship, but it means that if anything . . . fatal happens to you before you do . . . your traits will not be lost. You are the only descendant of both your parents, and your mother's grandparents, and your father's brother is dead and his son . . . is Thovalt. We . . . have to begin being more careful than we have been so that we do not produce the kind of predispositions which have caused Thovalt so much suffering. You show no trace of them, despite the traumas you have experienced.'

Lian looked down at his hands. He did not know why the suggestion seemed so threatening. It was logical; his father had done it; he supposed that, from a Burdanian point of view, he did take risks. As Lors said, it did not preclude him having children within a relationship. But it did not make it necessary.

Lors said, quietly, 'It is your choice.' After a moment, he added, 'I, myself, am a chimera. I am Granaith's son, yes, but on the other side I carry genetic material from three people who had no fourth-generation descendants.'

'But that is – for the colony,' Lian said, voicing part of his unease. 'Children – here. What about – Burdania?'

'With Thovalt as he is. With us, divided as we are. With your

269

hope, unprovable ... Li, I cannot see us being able to do anything for Burdania soon.'

His days took shape in study in both the colony and the settlement. He continued with his remedial exercises, under Lors' tuition. Lors encouraged him to organize his knowledge of the *kinder'el'ein* for the Archives, as an exercise and as a contribution.

Of Thovalt, Lian saw little, less than chance would allow. This was Lors' doing. Subtly, ruthlessly, he kept them apart. Once he was discharged, Thovalt avoided the medical area: from the window, Lors and Lian often saw his lanky figure passing by on the overgrown outside path. Lors, of course, always saw Lian within the medical area, and at the end of each session walked him to the edge of the jungle and saw him away. He seldom discussed Thovalt, save to say tht he was recovering well, and had gone to work on the computational support of Archives and colony, intellectually demanding, emotionally steadying work. Lian might not have yielded to his machinations. But he saw that Thovalt and Lors had made a tentative reconciliation, and he knew how fragile such a reconciliation could be.

He would have said, when he was with Vaelren, that he was complete, and happy. When alone, he knew it was a trick of the mind; he saw how he had curtained great parts of himself in response to her wishes, to her subtle withdrawal. For Vaelren, *en'vos'neen'el* had accepted Lian as an individual; it had not accepted the Burdanians. She accepted him as Lian; she did not accept the Burdanian in him. He learned not to seek her out on return from the colony. A good day's labour on the structured Burdanian language locked his thought to a rigid lattice. A bad day's work left him exhausted, hope and spirit lacerated. In the cool room he disciplined, decontaminated and cloaked his spirit. And despaired of the impossibility of it all. Until he walked out on to the sunlight-dappled platform and saw her there. A great stillness settled on him; the Burdanian in him slept.

Telien took him as *kin* apprentice with wholehearted joy. They rambled the jungle paths together, usually in the slight cool of early morning. He spent hours belly down in the fringes of the undergrowth, examining bulbs or stems with minute attention. Minute attention was his best substitute for *vos'neen*. His visual recall improved; his sense of smell became exquisitely discriminating; his touch became fine and acute. Telien seldom corrected him when he decided at last whether to harvest or leave, and he trusted that this was not indulgence: Telien was instructing him seriously, to stand by his skills amongst any *kinder'el'ein*. As they strolled and gathered, they talked. About the trivial, the material, and the spiritual. Lian told Telien about the change he had felt when Thovalt spoke. Telien tried to describe what *kin* had felt when *en'vos'neen'el* received a Burdanian. He became used to the failure of language; he grasped that a name, a description, was not permission for existence. That even if he could not express, he *knew*.

Three-quarters of a year after he returned to the colony, Lian asked to be put to Trial.

TWENTY-ONE

BURDANIA

Daisainia handed him back the transceiver. 'Silence this,' she said.

Thovalt huffed. Lian took the transceiver, and, held by the consuming violet eyes, turned it off.

'Come with me,' Daisainia said.

She left without looking for him to follow, turning her face away from him, and from the others. They heard hard footsteps on the boards, and the door sliding open and closed. Tion gently lifted the cloth draped across Lian's shoulder, and used to it daub at the line of chill on his neck. He did not meet Lian's eyes. His evasion was not hostile, or rejecting, but equally disconcerting: it was humble. Kylara frankly stared, demanding. Vylan seemed the least changed, but the most troubled. It was he who glanced at the open door, and back to Lian, telling Lian where he should go. It was he who stepped forward to steady Lian as he eased himself down from the table. Lian laid the transceiver beside the cloths, propping up its cover, and followed Daisainia.

Outside, he found the same night. The same fires burned high around the *caur'ynani*, their smoke layering along the ridge and drifting down into the valley. The dancers danced to the beat of drums and sticks. Silhouettes leaped and lunged across the flames, and on each side, firelight shone off slick faces. The same waters lay restlessly under the starlight, plied by the wind. The same stars, Burdania's stars, flowed in a turning river from north-east to south-west.

Daisainia stood, looking up at the stars. Starlight limned a contained, intense interest. 'Where?' was all she said.

He looked up himself. Too quickly; tension, and motion, put him offbalance; the stars wheeled in white streaks and he had to shuffle his feet. When the stars came to rest, he was lost. Pattern recognition was one of his subtle deficits. He wanted to answer her. He knew where to look, and what to look for, seven stars in a circle, with a faint red one in the middle. But he could not find it. He felt her insistence like the heat of a flame. 'Daisainia, I – *can't* see.'

'I am *isk'dar*, D'Halldt.'

Her rebuke brought his awareness back into focus. Stars did not matter, to either of them. He brought his eyes down. Her strongly moulded face was distorted with highlights and shadows. He saw the flicker of her eyes within the deepest.

'What do you *want* of us?'

'We – have been away – so long. We want – to know you are – still—'

'But it was before Linn you went away. While,' she gestured, 'there was life in the white ruins, and the plain. While those great dams and ducts of Illuan's still stood. You have airships, while we have only the rusting relics. You talk through the barren air – Rathla will be vexed. Or, no, perhaps not. Perhaps it is sufficient for him to have the use and not the making.' She shook herself slightly. 'You might turn Illuan back from a straight path to the pyre. What could you want from us.' It was not a question. Even had it been, Lian could not have answered it. He hardly heard the words for listening to the shiftings of her colourful voice. It seemed that she had already said everything which might be said about the impact and effect of their coming, and what she said frightened him almost to muteness.

He said, 'Did you – ever hear that – Burdanians left – Burdania?'

'Never. I find it inconceivable.'

He knew he could not let her ask the next question; he must avert it. 'Our thice-great-grandparents. They were – Explorers,' he said. 'They – travelled.'

'So long,' she said. 'Did you care for Burdania?'

He closed his eyes, briefly. He saw the habitats, shining

273

daylight into the Taridwyn night from their shifting arrays of lights. He saw the synthetic shores and cultured grasses. He thought of the Archives and the domes. There was so much he wanted, needed, to tell her. He wanted to say, we cared. He wanted to tell her why they had stayed away so long, what they had feared to find on their return. He knew he must not, not until he knew why she received his news so blackly.

'*Isk'dar*,' Lian said, 'they need – a place to land. The shuttle is – not large, but it needs – solid ground.'

'And if I give you no place to land,' she said, 'what then?'

He had never heard that metallic tone from her before. He said, 'Why – should you not?'

She drew breath in a shallow gasp and pointed stiff-armed past *caur'ynani* to the ridge. 'There. Let them land there. And trouble me no more.'

'Will you – wait with me?' Lian said. 'Will you greet them?'

She did not answer.

'Please,' he said. 'When you were speaking – I kept hearing – anger, fear – things I – could not imagine. Daisainia, you said I – helped you see what you would not. Help me to see what I – cannot – what I will not. I – so long for this to come out *well*. I have to know what – might go wrong. *You* know.'

She closed her eyes, and swayed slightly. 'Know? I do not know. You yourself said I do not know. But I knew you. You were the centre. I thought I knew you as my mother knew my father. You stood as clear as sunlight, and I thought that for once this thing, this curse, would offer me joy. But no, this is why I knew you, and there are shadows all around you now.'

'Oh, Daisainia,' he whispered.

He remembered the last time they had spoken, this night still, about the child she wanted, the child that he, too, would have wanted. Was it the personal betrayal she resented, the knowledge that having shown him what was most precious to her, she had been repaid by mendacity? Daisainia was not one to believe in 'would have', any more than he was capable of expressing it. His handicap confined him to the past, and the present. He must start from where he stood, to re-earn her trust.

'I am not – asking about – *shikarl*. I still – do not *believe* – in

274

prescience. But I – believe in *you*. You *knew* about the wall – because you – know the river – you know the building. You *know* about Burdanians, about *Burdania*. This has – you frightened, and I – do not know why.'

There was a silence. He heard her tight breathing.

'What purpose,' Daisainia said, 'would that serve? Leave my shadows to me. If they are unreal, best they go unrevealed. If they have substance, then time will show. Come. Before your people arrive, mine must know.'

She set her back to the central fire. Only her hair stirred, caught by the draught. Rich light flickered on her raised hands, and on the hard edges of her face. Silence came quickly for her.

Daisainia said, 'We have long known that the stars were suns, like our sun, which had planets, like our world. The knowledge was merely a curio; the stars . . . remote from our struggles and our sufferings.' There was a silence. The fire heaved and snapped. Ragged light fringed Daisainia's tight face. 'Many of us have long believed that the ruins and the relics represented something real, coherent, and lost. In a little while, an airship will arrive from the west. Before the plain was razed, before Linn Travassa became *isk'dar*, Burdanians left Burdania to explore the stars. They have escaped the years which have so ravaged us. Now their descendents have sought us out.

'What their coming means I do not know. I sense change, great . . . change impending. The shape of that change I cannot know.'

'Head's full'a smoke.' Arkadin Nors' mutter reached Lian's ears. He managed to look away from Daisainia as Arkadin dragged her crutches into line beside him. Her tone was sceptical, but her thin face was intent.

Daisainia said, 'They will land their craft on the ridge above. For safety, no one must cross it, until after daylight. We will receive them with the same courtesy we have shown the first of them to come amongst us. That one . . . is Lian D'Halldt.'

A sap-filled stick burst behind her. She pivoted to slap embers from the back of her leg. Rathla Zharlinn stepped in to steady her and draw her away from the fire. He said something

275

in a low voice. Daisainia looked up at his face, and said, dinstinctly, 'It is so.'

'But you said you were from the *Islands*.' Lara spoke out of the fire-streaked darkness.

'I – was not meant – to meet – anyone – in the ruins. When – you came – I could not think – what to say. Then you – said my name was – Islander and I – said yes.' He stretched his hand a little way across the distance between them. 'Forgive me, Lara. One of my – forefathers was – from greater D'Alna.'

'Greater D'Alna is a wasteland,' someone said.

'Not – then.'

'Who was he?' Lara said.

The voices seemed clear, yet remote. His shock, and theirs. Through it, he could feel them. Arkadin, behind him, was an amused, sceptical presence. Lara was already looking for a reason to forgive him. Daisainia, before the fire, was a black intensity of attention. Zharlinn, at her side, was watchful, brittle, defensive.

Lian answered Lara, 'He – was Islain Nors.'

The young woman stepped forward to confront him, stiff-legged. 'Is that the truth?'

He wondered what was coming. 'Islain Nors had a son,' Lara said, staring at him hard. 'That son was *my* great-great-grandfather. And you say you come from another planet.'

Vylan said, quietly, 'He does. He held the transceiver out to Lara, sliding back its cover with one hand. 'This is Lian's.' She tilted it towards the firelight, which caught and shimmered on the circuits.

'Why did you lie to us?' Zharlinn flung at him from Daisainia's side.

'My – people had – not decided yet to – speak. You are—' He looked at Daisainia. 'You are much changed.' The *isk'dar* stared back at him. He regretted his misuse of their time alone. Silenced by his own fears of what she might ask, he had not told her what she needed to know.

'That is not our doing,' Zharlinn said.

'It is, in part, Linn's,' Daisainia said in a shadowed voice.

'Please,' Lian said. 'Let – the past be. I would – rather that than – anything.' He saw the challenging lift of Daisainia's head, and knew that she understood, even if she did not believe. He took a cautious step forward, then another. He pushed his voice to carry. 'There are – four coming. Lors – Lors D'Sal is the medic. He is a kind, good man – cautious – conscientious. Alystra is – the eyes of the colony. We – do not have – an *isk'dar* or anyone like. We debate – we vote. We try to reach – consensus. Alystra D'Caul is the – guardian of consensus.' They had drawn closer to hear; he felt crowded, a little threatened. But they could not hear him from further: he was unaccustomed to addressing a crowd, and the fire was too much competition for his light voice. He made himself stand firm. 'Thovalt Aslinn is – our pilot. He is a great rhetorician. He is – impulsive, thoughtless; do not – let him offend you. Some call it an illness, some call it only – his nature. Andra D'Lynnan is an Archivist. A keeper of the – records of the Burdania our – forefathers knew.'

'And what are you?' Zharlinn said. In closing around him the Burdanians had left a clear passage between himself and Daisainia. The *isk'dar* was standing quite still, watching her people deal with him. Her firecast shadows lapped against his feet.

'I am – nothing much. I helped them – as best I could.'

'He told us,' Vylan said, quietly, 'so that he could ask his people here to cure Illuan D'Vandras.'

'But why *hide* from us?' Lara said, coming back to him with transceiver held before in both hands. 'We *showed* you what we were trying to do with the relics. You must approve of that.'

From the fire, Daisainia said one word: 'Linn.' She was turning the heavy faceted ring on her finger. They all looked at her. 'His legacy marks us to D'Halldt's people, as it marked us to the North and the Islands, and to hidden *tayni* for four generations. I was not so wrong about D'Halldt,' she said in a clear voice which hurt him to hear. 'He was indeed from a hidden *tayn*. He was wary, as many before him have been wary, seeing Lltharran as Linn left it. I understand his wariness. I cannot rebuke him for it.

'D'Halldt generously says, let the past be.' Lian winced at the edge to her voice. He had not let *her* past be. 'I do not think that it will be as easily done as said, as easily willed as wished.

277

Nevertheless, I look to you all to demonstrate to D'Halldt's people that we have shed Linn's legacy and mindset. They are no different from those amongst us who braved warnings, oppositions and old grim stories to come to Lltharran.'

The transceiver chirruped. Lara, who was inspecting it by torchlight, started and nearly dropped it. She swung round, boots grinding on the stones, and looked at Lian. It chirruped again. Lian held out his hand. She gave it to him. Watched by them all, he opened the channel.

Thovalt said, 'What're you doing down there: trying to dry off?' Lian held the transceiver very still, and looked up, through the bright smudges of smoke and lightspray. Slowly, he swept his gaze west. High in the western sky one star shook loose and drifted downwards. Following his gaze, Lara pointed, two-handed. Beyond her, Daisainia stood silhouetted against the fire.

Thovalt said, 'Lian, have we a landing site, or should we aspire to a buoyant frame of mind?'

'D'Halldt.' Daisainia closed on him in four strides. She had seemed so far away. Her voice was tight, her face inscrutable. 'Tell him he must wait for our torches.' Over her shoulder she said, 'Take torches. Encircle the open land.' She swept an ellipse in the air with a stiff arm, then swung round to face him. 'What size is this craft? Larger than one of our – but you would not know. Larger than *caur'ynani*?'

'Not – as large,' Lian said. 'But Daisainia – Thovalt can – land. He has – night—'

'You asked for a welcome, D'Halldt,' she said, with the first hint of pleasure he had heard in her. 'We will give you it.'

Behind her, torches were pulled from bundles propped against walls, and passed hand from hand to those nearest the bonfire. Arms dipped torches into the flame and passed them outwards, trailing ragged fire. Rathla Zharlinn came forward, carrying a torch for himself, and one which he passed to Daisainia. She let it be placed in her hand, not once releasing Lian's eyes. In the torchlight her expression was one of grim challenge.

Lian lifted the transceiver. 'Thovalt – the – Burdanians are going to – mark the edge of the – field with torches. They – will be *holding* the – torches. Take – great care.'

278

'Not a hair stirred,' Thovalt vowed. 'Coming in.'

Lian closed the channel, incoming and outgoing, assuring them privacy. '*Isk'dar*, thank you. What you – said was – generous.'

She turned her forbidding face away from the torch. 'I did only what was needed.'

Along the edge of the sky was a band of indigo. Torches encircled the ridgeline, peaking and pleating with the contours of the land. Their thin smoke threaded the open space within. The fires in the garden of *caur'ynani* blazed abandoned, casting diffuse wild shadows.

Daisainia, on Lian's left, held her torch high, two-handed, immobile. Her face remained grim and sombre in the flickering light. Arkadin, on his right, had hooked a lantern to one stiff hand, so it rattled against her crutch and splashed light across her thigh. Her breathing rasped, but her yellow eyes sparkled.

Rathla Zharlinn stood on Daisainia's far side, his torch level with hers. Sidor, torchless and bare-headed, was behind her. Vylan nulled the swing of a netted relic lamp with a palm. Valancy carefully pleated a fold of blanket back from her son's face.

On Arkadin's far side, Fioral tried to take up the lantern bumping against the crutch. Arkadin rumbled at her. Kylara looked skywards, mesmerized. Only Tion spared a glance for Lian, peering through the shifting and difficult light.

Thovalt did not hurry his descent. He teased them; he flirted with the air. He kindled all the shuttle's landing lights, rocking in the air so the fierce, tight spotlights played across the watchers. He let the downdraught brush them, making their torches flicker, looping the threads of smoke around their heads. He spun the shuttle overhead, displaying its lines. Lian thought he would faint with tension. He came close to opening the channel and urging Thovalt to have done – through he knew he should not, of Thovalt. Perhaps succumbing to a revolt within the shuttle – or perhaps merely sated with display – Thovalt centred the landing beams on the middle of the open ground. The shuttle seemed to balance upon stilts of swirling

279

light as it slowly, delicately descended. Its legs extended to span the uneven ground. The Burdanians stepped back as the wind rose, pulling at clothing, flames and hair, flinging dust, and then sand. They held their torches to one side, as the flames snarled and streamed, and in twos and threes, blew out. Lian half turned away, shielding his eyes. At the edge of sight he saw the shuttle enfolded by a grey cloud of dust and its own lights. The extended legs were taken in as the body settled, Thovalt quenched the underlights; the engines whirred to silence.

The ragged circle of Burdanians straightened, drew themselves up, and began to relight the extinguished torches from those which had endured. Reflections flecked the sides of the shuttle. Somebody on the ridgeback yelled wordlessly and flipped a torch into the air. It might have been Lara. Lian watched the flame whirl upwards, spraying sparks, and fall . . . to be snatched in mid fall. Around the circle other torches flew, to be caught, or bounce untidily on the ground. People began to dance, passing each other hand to hand in circles or in untidy chains. The euphoria of the bonfires reignited.

Between the dancers, though, groups of torches remained still. As did the one around Daisainia. They knew her far better than the dancers. Stiffly, as though waking, Daisainia lowered her torch. She squinted at the shuttle as though not quite able to draw it into focus. She looked not at it, but at its edges. She found it in the way; it blunted her gaze. 'It is . . . not what I expected,' she said, to Zharlinn.

Fioral dodged round in front of Arkadin. 'Where's the medic?' she said, urgently.

On the far side of the shuttle, there was a sudden, contagious stillness. A finger of light stretched from the shuttle into the crowd, and at the end of it, a tall figure danced alone, while the Burdanians withdrew. He danced on, vividly, wildly, catching up two fallen torches. Points of firelight twinkled on his body and sleeves. The sight jolted Lian into motion. He ran across the choppy ground and ducked around the shuttle, sliding his hands along its slick, space-scarred flank. It felt strange, after the stone walls and dykes. 'Thovalt!'

Thovalt swung round, spraying sparks. He stopped, balanced on his toes, quivering. His face was ecstatic, dangerously radiant. 'But nobody will *dance* with me, Lian.' He thrust a torch at Lian; Lian had to take it or be ignited. Thovalt's eyes laughed at his discomposure. 'Hold it, hold it high. Andra! Lors! Alystra! Come out and dance.'

White-haired Lors appeared in the shuttle's lit doorway. With a visible gathering of resolve, he stepped down on to the rough ground. 'Lian,' he said, 'are you all right? We were extremely worried about you. Your telemetry registered acute physical trauma and continuing pain and stress . . .' Lian swayed on his feet, yielding to the effect of sleepless nights, bruises and strained muscles, and unremitting worry. Yielding to the relief of having them there, at last. Lors steadied him and muttered against the others for having prevaricated when Lian's transmitter went silent. That shocked Lian out of yielding. Relief was premature. He opened his eyes and saw Daisainia measuring herself against Thovalt.

'Daisainia Travassa,' she said. '*Isk'dar*.' In that moment he saw a likeness between them, and why each held him in thrall.

'You? Is that all there is to you?'

Lors stepped quickly around Lian and crunched across the wasteland to join them. He said, 'I'm Lorscar D'Sal, the medic.'

Daisainia gestured without looking back. The gesture brought Tion and Kylara to her side, Fioral between them. 'These,' she said, 'are Tion and Kylara D'Suran. Medics of Lltharran.'

Lors turned to Thovalt. His voice had a thin, hard edge to it. 'I am going to need help with my equipment.' Thovalt watched him a moment, gauging his seriousness. Then, with a flourish and a smile of distilled mischief, Thovalt handed Daisainia the torch and whirled to obey. After a moment, more slowly, Kylara followed him. Tion and Fioral stayed as they were, Tion's hand on Fioral's shoulder. His sight would be unreliable in the shifting light. Lors took a step forward as he saw Kylara heft a case from the shuttle door. 'That one's heavy.'

Kylara said mildly, 'No, it's not.'

She passed her brother and the watchful *isk'dar* with a steady step and a straight back.

Thovalt leaned over to murmur sweetly, 'Adaptation,' as he followed her.

'D'Halldt, your warning was . . . most appropriately given,' Daisainia said, austerely, as they watched Kylara lead Thovalt downslope, with Lors, Fioral and Tion following. The Burdanians had opened a torchlit channel for them.

Alystra heard as she stepped down. Lian saw a disconcerting suspicion in her glance at him. It was swiftly erased as Daisainia heard the crumbling of gravel underfoot and swung to face her. Alys wore a plain brown jacket, grey slacks and boots, without emblem or ornament. From a distance, like Lian, she could have been one of the crowd. A high step above her, Andra stood braced in the doorway, white arms outstretched and rigid. Nothing would move her. Her black eyes darted to the source of each voice or motion.

The clear area around the shuttle had shrunk under the pressure of the Burdanians' curiosity. Alystra, unlike Lian, was unperturbed.

'I am Alystra D'Caul,' Alystra said, addressing Daisainia in a voice pitched to carry. 'Advocate Adviser assigned to the Proposers, and observer for the colony at large. You, I suspect, are Daisainia Travassa, called *isk'dar*. I expect you will be no more familiar with my status and occupation than I am with yours. I would appreciate a chance to rectify that. The better we understand each other's process of decision-making, the less chance of disharmony.'

Daisinia acknowledged that with a tilt of the head. She said, in her ordinary tones, 'Why did you hide from us?'

Lian had always admired Alystra's equilibrium. The Adviser answered without a hint of hesitation or uncertainty. 'Our mandate, upon which our colony voted, required us to survey only the planet. We were not mandated to make contact. That was an omission which seems,' her voice lifted, 'preposterous, now. Lian D'Halldt's encounter with your people was accidental.' Lian felt the brush of violet eyes, but when he looked at Daisainia, she was watching Alystra. What she thought, he could not tell. 'Respecting our mandate, he concealed his identity as best he could. The flooding forced our departure and left him stranded. We remained in contact until his transceiver was damaged, and then the next we heard was a request that we come to the city. What he did was both decent and inevitable.'

So, Lian thought, that is our version. He was glad he had not tried to answer it. Such seamless readjustments were beyond him.

'You left,' Daisainia said, tightly, 'before *this*.' She took in the wasteland, the ruins, the flood, with a flick of her hand. 'Why have you stayed away so long?'

That made Alystra hesitate. But only briefly. 'Burdanians do not fare well offworld,' she said. 'We are the only survivors of nearly thirty planetary colonies. For three of the . . . five generations we have been away, our own survival has been in doubt.'

'And what could *you*,' Daisainia said, 'wish of us?'

'Burdania,' Alystra said.

Daisainia stiffened. Lian looked quickly at Alystra. He saw a fleeting satisfaction. Despite the windbreak of bodies, and the hot breath of the torches, it suddenly seemed cold.

'Survey the planet,' Sidor Vassar said, out of the shadow between two torches. 'And make no contact. Did you not expect us to be here?'

Alystra blinked, but recovered. 'We had had . . . no communication,' she said. 'We did not know what might have happened.'

'And what do you wish of Burdania?' Daisainia said. She might keep expression from her voice, but unlike Alystra, she could not add false coloration. Her people stirred slightly at the timbre.

'We are a colony, not a large colony, on a planet very unlike Burdania. We do not know how many generations we will be able to sustain. We would like to have the option of returning to Burdania. We have preserved knowledge that would be of great value to you.' There was, in the cool, creamy voice, a hint of a question.

'If you'd value it,' said Andra, from above. 'I do not see why we should help you, with your wanton destruction of artefacts and suppression of knowledge.'

Daisainia's face lit with anger. 'That was not I. Nor these here.'

283

'What about you, then?' Andra said. 'You're in the same position as we are. Lian forced your hand. I, for one, would never have agreed to contact until we knew far more about you than we do.'

Alystra raised her voice. 'Forgive my colleague: she is an Archivist and she is having difficulty coming to terms with Burdania as it is now. As are we all.'

Daisainia turned her head to look at Lian. Ribbons of smoke drifted across her eyes, but through the smoke her gaze held his, deep and penetrating.

'Very well,' she said, 'we must all come to terms.' She looked back at Alystra. 'Look around you. Satisfy yourselves that the "wanton destruction" has ceased. Speak to whomever you please. And we shall speak to you. We will meet again.'

'You have been very silent,' Daisainia said, to Lian.

They were in the large room of *caur* D'Suiran. The equipment cases sat upon the table. From one of the inner rooms, he could hear Lors' dry didactic murmur. A wan, resentful Fioral was crushing and mixing herbs. Lors had barred her from the operating room.

Daisainia had cut him deftly from the crowd, taking him away with her on a cursory inspection of the dykes. She did not speak to him. Sunrise brought them back to *caur* D'Suran, to wait for news on Illuan. She rapped her bandaged finger on the hard casting, not looking at him. He watched her in some trepidation. He did not have Alystra's agility with wording.

She said, 'Silence may betoken many things. Complete agreement. Or complete disagreement. Unease which dare not speak. Or a decision to watch, rather than participate. Which was yours, Lian D'Halldt?'

'It – was not my – place to speak, *isk'dar*.' Her eyes shifted to him, at the unexpected title. 'We decide by reaching – consensus and seldom let – crisis override consensus. I – placed myself in – a unique situation.'

'And do you *regret* what you have done?' Daisainia said, returning her gaze to him. The personal challenge took him unprepared. Each one of his choices had served that moment's good, and since he would do so again, he could not disavow

284

any. But in not disavowing them, he chose his choices over consensus, and made himself responsible for their consequences beyond the moment.

'I – did what served – the moment,' he said. That was no answer. 'I – would do the same again.'

She gave him a long, narrow stare. 'Vylan D'Caul tells me that D'Vandras *broke* your instrument. Did he know what you were?'

Lian felt icy. 'He – knew. The D'Vandras – passed the knowledge – down.'

'And that explains much,' Daisainia said. 'About Illuan D'Vandras and about,' her throat closed on the name,' Morian D'Vandras.'

Lian did not move.

'I know you have read those records. She had knowledge,' Daisainia said, very quietly. She was watching Fioral's hands, which worked, hesitated, and worked on. 'Now I understand whence that knowledge came. Perhaps you do not understand how she used it. She used it to drive me from Lltharran. She used it, as some say I use it, as an instrument, as a lever.'

Fioral's frightened green eyes met Lian's over her head.

Daisainia said, not looking at him, 'Do you understand, D'Halldt?'

TWENTY-TWO

TARIDWYN

'I am so sorry,' the dark-skinned Determinant said.

His voice was quiet; the stillness of the debating hall absorbed it. The twenty other Advocates were gone; he and Lian were alone in the hall. All but a few of the lights had been turned out, and the rich, strange light of the Taridwyni morning, filtered by the dome, filled the air. Lian would always remember the hurt and the golden light.

The Determinant sat down on the edge of the dais. He had to speak up to Lian; this, Lian knew, was not accidental. 'We thought very hard about whether or not we should admit you. Although this sounds like my trying to justify myself, it is not. I wanted to make the exception.

'You see, Lian, you would have to have been an exception. For most of my fellows the question was whether to compromise their standards, the standards of admission which were established upon Burdania.' He sighed. 'I think that is the essence of it: Advocates, like Archivists, are tradition-bound. Burdania is something sacred and immutable. They will permit no lapse in standards. You did better than expected, but you did not, *could* not, attain the standard. You surprised us with your insight, but you did not develop complex argument as the formal debating style demands.

'I know, most of us know, the extraordinary effort you have made. But extraordinary effort should not be needed. For you to contribute would demand continued extraordinary effort, detrimental, perhaps, to what you might do elsewhere. You are one of the colony's experts on the *kinder'el'ein*, a precious

286

resource. In any decision involving the *kinder'el'ein* you will be consulted. You will have an informal input into any debate, because you know everyone involved . . .

'As I said, I wanted to make the exception, regardless of your disabilities. In some ways, you are very sophisticated. I think you could contribute. It may be that in time we will need to include *kinder'el'ein* representatives in our decisions, if our colony continues to prosper, and our relationship with the *kinder'el'ein* to warm. Then, standards will have to change. I only regret that we cannot change them for you.'

The monitor told him where to find Thovalt, in the Archives.

Through the door of the viewing booth, he saw a blurred golden figure. He stroked the door; it slid open. Thovalt sat inside, profile to him. The screens behind and to his side were silver-blank. In the centre of the booth stood a young man in grey, struggling to speak. Only a faint translucency betrayed his unreality.

Lian saw himself as they had seen him. Dressed as he was now, standing as he had stood on the dais. His skin like white sap, except for the gilt touch of daylight along cheekbone and brow. His grey eyes stared, narrowed, at a middle distance, searching out words in the air. He held his hands flat to his sides; his voice was worn thin and nearly inflectionless with struggle. Lian could not understand him. He spoke, but he did not communicate, not even with his own self.

Lian let out a slow breath. His mastery of words was illusionary. What he had learned was compensation, the ability to take meaning from context, gesture, emotion. He could understand. But he could not speak, not for Burdania, not even for himself.

And here was the one who could, perhaps the only one who could. As Thovalt watched Lian's image, oblivious to the living, Lian watched Thovalt. Thovalt unawares was Thovalt naked. His face was tight with suffering; he lacerated himself with Lian's ruin. Lian felt a bright shaft of anger and bitterness. Thovalt had everything, the eloquence, the authority. But he could not use it. Something within him was disconnected, and he could not measure what he did. He could not hear the stillnesses he made; he fled the truths he spoke; he seized upon false guilts. He, the colony's favourite child, had begged them to free him from the *evil* of his part in Burdania's neglect and ruin. There had been a stillness . . . Lian had heard it as clear as a singing note in the air. But had Thovalt heard it, he would not have abandoned it, and himself. He would not have gone in to the poisoned chamber of the ship, to his near death and dispossession. Sheltered in the Archives, stabilized by consensus command, he was no favourite now. And yet he still had the power of articulation, the power to move them all.

Lian stepped forward, bracing himself for a collision of body on body, which never came. The image blinked out, and he stood in its place.

Thovalt had started violently when Lian stepped into the image. He closed his mouth; then stood up and without warning, thrust Lian hard back against the wall of the booth. The image re-formed, grey and white. It had spoken two words when Lian's outstretched hand negated its existence. After a moment, the booth cautioned Thovalt that the projection field had been interrupted. Did he wish to continue? Thovalt measured Lian with slitted eyes. 'No,' he said.

Even in dress, he disdained conformity. Archivists customarily wore white; his shirt was yellow, streaked as though by water, his trousers dark brown. He wore a heavy necklace of strung shell and unpolished amber, and a belt of topaz beads on woven thongs.

He stretched, and tucked his hands behind his head, defiantly at ease, except for the quivers of tension which showed as shivers in the soft fabric. 'A brave, but ultimately pathetic performance.'

'Yes,' Lian said. 'I failed. My father – failed. He left. You – failed. You left. You left – it to me. Will you – leave it to – me still?'

Thovalt smiled. 'Will you leave, too?'

'No. But I – cannot – be Proponent for – Burdania.'

The smile wavered, and rekindled. 'That's true.'

Lian said, 'Will you?'

Thovalt whitened around the lips.

'I ask – you to speak. For me. Because I cannot. And you –

can.' He wanted to say: you showed me Islain Nors' testimony, and maybe because of that I chose to go on to the dome, and maybe because of that I fell, and maybe because of that I cannot do what I want to do. Except that you would take away the maybes and create a heavy chain from my merest thread. But I want no more than you the responsibility of injuring someone else's life. I am not demanding a penance from you. I am asking your help. He said, 'That is – *all. You can.*'

'They won't let me back in hall,' Thovalt said, so quickly the words were nearly unintelligible.

'They – cannot – exclude you.' He paused, organizing his clauses. 'They set – the terms. You went into the ship. *They* decided – you were ill. Not – intending ill. You were – treated. Their terms are – satisfied.'

Thovalt gave a thin laugh. 'If you thought that out between the hall and here, they have misjudged you indeed. What makes you think I can do any better now? Except commit suicide more efficiently: I know the mistakes to avoid there.'

'Display,' Lian said. 'Show – screen – hall in the – final recess of the last debate on – Burdania— No! First – Thovalt Aslinn – his words, "How – *dare* you!" '

Thovalt spun in his chair as the small, canted screen behind him illuminated with his own image. One hand hovered above the screen, as though readying to strike. The other hand pulled at his collar. His breathing was harsh. Lian crossed the booth on stalker's feet and stood beside him, close enough to feel Thovalt's warmth and Thovalt's shivering. He did not touch Thovalt; Thovalt resented touch, and would wilfully mis-interpret it, provokingly or seductively. Together they watched Thovalt cry out against the little artificial world they had made for themselves. When the image tore at his collar, the living Thovalt snapped his hand away from his throat as though burned. He interlocked his long, supple fingers and pulled upon them until the image leapt from the podium and ran out the door. Then he said, 'Display, stop.'

'No,' Lian said. 'Continue.' Thovalt swung the chair. Lian did not move, did not yield him the space to turn away. Thovalt's legs jarred against his. His hazel eyes were fierce with anguish.

Lian said, breathlessly, 'You failed. You say so. Everybody – says so. But – *there* – was where you – best succeeded.' Involuntarily Thovalt glanced over his shoulder at the stilled hall. He slid a hand around to adjust the viewing angles; panned a synthesized viewpoint over the gathering. Found the others, clustered before the dais, Lian held in front of Lors. The others faced inwards, towards each other. Lian's face alone turned out. Thovalt focused in on that searching young face, as it sensed a nameless change in the silence. Lian spoke for it. 'Until you spoke – it was – ritual. All – things – said before. Moving to – the same decision as – before. Better here. Peaceful here. Then you spoke. Fifth generation. Touched. Hurt. Angry. Burdania does not – sleep – in us. It does not – go away. It mars. You. Me. All of us. Who never knew. Who had no part. You are – the best of us. Young Proponent. Beloved one. Even you – are touched. Thovalt, did – you not even *hear*? What you said. How they – heard it?'

Thovalt drew the viewpoint back from Lian's face, continued panning. 'All I can see,' he said, in a brittle voice, 'is that I shocked them.'

'They needed – shocking,' Lian said. His mouth was dry.

Thovalt sketched his wild smile. 'That, I can do.' He leaned back in his chair, in feigned repose. Lian felt his tension like a static charge. 'So, you propose I shock them so profoundly that they send me to Burdania to be rid of me.' Beneath Thovalt's yellow-clad arm he saw the Determinant cross the floor to join them. What might have happened if they had not assented to his offer of an early vote? If they had recognized the change in time?

'No,' Lian said. 'You must – make them – see what – having Burdania – unfinished – does to us. We – this little Burdania – this artificial world – is *cruel*. Makes us – keep suffering. It is a – cruelty we – make for ourselves. We *cannot* forget Burdania. We have not – left Burdania. Like you – watching me. I *am* – what I – am. *You* will not forget me.'

Thovalt slammed to his feet. The turning chair bruised Lian's knee. He rapped out several commands. The booth was suddenly crowded with figures, rustling with voices. Lian recognized speakers from the debates: Thaorinn, Krysanin,

Thovalt himself. They winked out and into existence as Thovalt paced through them. Lian thought he looked distraught, and frightened. The whispering voices, and the image of Thaorinn, pushing into and out of nonexistence, were distracting. He wanted them off so he could see Thovalt clearly. Frightened, *why*?

He held still against the pressing ghosts, and waited.

Thovalt suddenly stopped, swung round, cleared the booth of phantoms with a word. His eyes were very bright, his breath audible.

'And if I cannot? Is this some kind of revenge upon me, Lian?'

'No.' Thovalt waited for more. Lian offered him nothing but his steady gaze. Silence, when he could use it, was stronger than any argument.

Thovalt swept across the booth in a stride and a sweep of water-streaked yellow. He spun the chair, dropped into it. 'What is this about *kinder'el'ein* sensing Burdania? Lors has some intriguing files amongst his records—' he glittered up at Lian, daring him to comment, 'and I do not mean his private journals, either, although those are an illuminating study.' He gave Lian an inviting glance.

'My record of – *en'vos'neen'el* is in – *my* records.'

'How I have missed your subtle scolding,' Thovalt said, impenitent. 'Lors remains unconvinced, as I am sure he has told you. But how much *did* you omit? How much did you decide Burdanians ought not to know?' He turned a glittering eye on Lian's unease. 'Come, Lian,' Thovalt said, silkily. 'For *Burdania*. Convince me that we have a world to go back to . Or better,' he said, caressing the word, his face lit with malicious merriment, 'take me to those who can.'

Telien was waiting for them at the bridge. Lian had half expected it, and intensely hoped for it; Thovalt was quite unprepared. He had been all but treading on Lian's heels all the way, while Lian swept the path with staff tip and paused to let those he distrubed squirm or scurry aside. When they came to the opening around the stream and saw the bulky figure waiting, Lian abruptly felt the pressing presence behind him fall away. Telien collected *kin* robes in a single, neat gesture, and, holding them high, crossed the bridge. *Kin* moved carefully, evenly, managing *kin* height and bulk. *Kin* face was smooth and planed, but *kin* headdress was well forward and the skin on *kin* temples shiny with tension. He looked back at Thovalt, who was standing immobile where path met riverbank. The light shivered in his wide eyes. Lian had managed to persuade him into headdress, for courtesy; but with a sudden snatch he pulled it off, and stood bareheaded before the massive *kinder'el'ein*, the grey cloth and headband dangling from his hand. The gesture had a desperate honesty to it. Lian thought it both unbelievable, and characteristic, that Thovalt would not anticipate meeting this one *kindereen*.

Telien checked *kin* walk only momentarily to brush his temple in greeting. '*I'vad'neer*,' *kin* murmured; and went forward to greet Thovalt. *Kin* did not touch him. 'Thovalt. Thovalt *eith*'Andra *a*'Raman.' A slight pause. *Aur*'Burdania.' Lian caught his breath. Thovalt only blinked once, quickly, and Telien did not respond. *Kin* stood over Thovalt, rocking slightly so that *kin* moss-coloured robes swayed. *Kin* said, in Burdanian, 'For Burdania midwifed you; Burdania is a presence in your thoughts; and you gather in Burdania's name. You are a most distinctive presence in *vos'neen*. You conceal nothing of what you are, and little of what you feel.'

Lian found that he was holding his caught breath. He had never known Telien to conduct such an assault on a Burdanian's fears and sensibilities. To confirm to *Thovalt*, of all people, that his elaborate defences of malice, perversity and disrespect were as nothing. Thovalt mustered a wan, tarnished smile. 'Then that should make this easy.'

'Perhaps,' Telien said. 'you would do us a courtesy, though, if you would come along the riverbank with me.'

'Ah!' Thovalt said, brightening. 'I thought distance did not matter.'

Lian glided slowly to one side until he could see them both in profile. Tendons stood out on Thovalt's neck and a white line showed along Telien's inner eye.

Telien said, 'Distance, no. But living presences shield and attenuate.'

'I leave a bad taste, do I?'

Telien blinked slowly, with sweeps of all three eyelids. Lian guessed it was the only way *kin* could yield to the reflex without it being obvious. He was becoming angry with Thovalt, angry at Thovalt's refusal to recognize the effect he was having on the *kinder'el'ein*. Telien sensed up Lian's anger before he recognized it: *kin* took a step back, and turned to look at him, with wide, fixed eyes. 'Go downriver, *i'vad'neer*. I would like to stain some sands; see what you can find for colorants.'

But . . . Lian thought. Telien's eyes flashed white, and Lian yielded, stricken that he was no kinder than Thovalt. He stepped down on to the dark river sand and loam, and had started to walk away when it came to him that Telien's lapse had been deliberate. He swung round before he thought, and looked accusation at his parent. Telien turned *kin* cauled head, and signed back, *It is so.* And returned *kin* attention to Thovalt.

From a safer remove, Lian paused and looked back again. Thovalt's body was eloquent, but contradictory. He seemed to relax from stylized posture into natural expression; and then abruptly to revert to posture. Telien's body told him nothing. *Kin* hands were silent, without even the fragmentary sign *kin* often absentmindedly sketched. He realized, as Thovalt turned a pale face in his direction, and immediately stiffened in a pose, why Telien had sent him away. He was too much audience for Thovalt. Reluctantly, he took himself out of sight into the jungle, pushing into a heavy downgrowth of vines. Experience told him deep shadows and tree roots were ideal for the fungus source of his favourite bright yellow.

Telien found him uncertainly sniffing a fungus, a large, bulbous excrescence nearly the size of his head. He could not concentrate well enough to decide whether its musky scent was aged enough for him to harvest it without offence. *Kin* levered aside the vines with some difficulty, looked down at him kneeling and said, almost apologetically, 'Too fresh, *i'vad'neer*. We have not yet come into the season.' He accepted *kin* hand up. What he liked about having Telien as a teacher was *kin* courtesy towards his ignorance. He helped *kin* push through the vines. Thovalt was standing outside on the riverbank, looking along the cleft in the jungle. He greeted Lian with a studiedly opaque stare. Neither spoke to the other as they walked back to the ford. Telien touched his temple in parting, and turned towards the settlement without a further word. *Kin* walk had lost its evenness; it was heavy and trudging. Lian kept his back to Thovalt, lest Thovalt see and be pleased by the futile anger in his face. He furrowed the litter with his staff, walking deliberately slowly, daring Thovalt to push at his back. Thovalt was oblivious to pace and anger. He did not speak until they were in sight of the colony walls.

'You will be pleased to know,' he said, in an ordinary tone, 'that I did do the courteous thing, and thank *kin* . . . for my life. I would have done it earlier, had I been sure I appreciated the gift. But,' he said, growing arch, 'as to the objective of our errand: am I convinced? Well, no. Telien seemed to think that it did not matter whether I believed or not. *Kinder'el'ein* put scant effort into trying to convince one: I found that restful.' His studied tone said he was disappointed, but Lian heard a deeper unease: Thovalt needed the energy of friction, to warm him, to mark the boundaries of his self. He demanded and provoked it. From Telien, he would have provoked nothing but sharper insight. Lian had a better sense of what had happened in his absence, now. Far from Thovalt wearing Telien down, Telien would have made clear the futility of his defences and manoeuvres. With a small malice of his own he said, 'Telien – knows you.' He felt Thovalt check slightly and fall back; then the Burdanian said, 'I believe you are jealous.'

Lian stopped, and swung round, jamming the staff tip into the ground between them. 'You – took – my telling – the courtesies and – misused it. Telien saved you. No need to hurt. No need – to offend.'

'You are jealous.'

'You do – not *deserve* attention.'

Thovalt put his head to one side. 'But I have it,' he taunted. 'Telien thinks I matter.'

Lian's empty hand closed on, not robe, but the grey synthetic he had worn for his Trial. All the hurt and humiliation he had set aside suddenly uncoiled and bit. He twisted away from Thovalt, and started for the side gate, sweeping his way with wide, jerky strokes. He found the wall by the feel of shadow across his face. Thovalt caught up with him just inside. Without waiting for him to speak, Lian turned on him. He absorbed an image of Thovalt's gleeful, deeply unnerved face, and then half closed his eyes so as not to see. To the tall blur before him he said, 'You – matter only – if you – *do* something. I have *done*. Telien has – *done*. It was – hard for – *kin* to talk to – you. You – foolish and – *cruel* – cannot stop *kin* knowing – you. Burdanians – *must* go back. *Kinder'el'ein* want – them to. For peace here. Peace in *vos'neen*. Peace in *en'neen*. We disturb the *peace*. Nothing to be – pleased about. Telien believes you – matter. So, *will* you matter?'

He opened his eyes again, looking full at Thovalt. He felt lightheaded with heat, humidity and racing heart. He could feel his nerves tingling. He saw the fear in Thovalt's face. And, in that moment of heightened awareness, saw something in Thovalt he had never seen before.

Thovalt *had* to act to prove he existed, through his effect and others' acknowledgements. He acted upon impulse, craving significance and attention. He did not analyse or anticipate outcomes. He simply let what happened happen, and gloried in it. The consequences took him blindside, terrifying him. He did not dare imagine, and because he did not dare imagine, everything took him unawares.

Lian had a sudden impression of the olive, black and gold painting in the Archive vestibule, the chaos equations. It seemed an apt portrait of Thovalt's internal landscape. What must it be like to lack a fundamental belief in the sense of the universe? To feel entirely at its mercy.

Lian said, hiding his pity, 'Telien knows – you matter. *Kin* would not – attend – otherwise. *Kin* has – special feeling for – Burdanians. Would be *kindereen* to – us, too. Trust – Teli.'

Thovalt suddenly smiled, a wide, glassy smile. 'Oh, I do. And may my twisted gods help me, I trust you too, with your innocent, reproachful grey eyes.' His face relaxed into ordinary, wicked anticipation. 'I do look forward to telling Lors. He will want to dissect you, Lian.'

'Lors – cares,' Lian said, knowing it was futile.

'But what does he care *about*? That I exemplify and validate *his* view of the universe: that there is nothing which is not fundamentally reasonable and curable, even *me*. He does *ask* for it sometimes, Lian; and so do you, with your irritating philosophy that creation is basically good and everything will work out well. I could simply sink my teeth into the both of you.'

Lian folded his hands atop each other on the staff and rocked against it. He was oddly comforted that Thovalt was once more his own difficult self. 'I – do hope,' he said.

'Really,' Thovalt said, 'you should not.' He swivelled lightly on one foot, and strode across the grey paving towards the nearest entrance to the colony.

Lian was with Vaelren in the woodshapers' area when Lors came after him. It was early evening, and the shadows were already thickening. Lian was preparing an enzyme solution, under Vaelren's eye; he felt her lift and turn her cauled head. He knew her well enough to read the minimal expression on her face, the sudden distance in her deep blue eyes. 'A Burdanian comes,' she said, and took the utensils from his unwilling hands. He knew better than to ask who it might be; he hoped it was not Thovalt. She did not look up as he climbed to his feet. He picked his way between rows of seaweed-wrapped planking, and low tables of utensils, between the huge carcasses of newly fallen trees. When he saw Lors on the path, he wondered at Vaelren's reaction: Lors took seriously Lian's instructions on courtesies, and on his infrequent visits was always carefully respectful. Then Lors caught sight of him, and lurched to a stop, gasping for air. Lian saw that his face was suffused with overexertion, white hair clammy beneath a hastily donned cap. He wore his colony overalls instead of the light robes he usually affected in the jungle. And his anger came at Lian like heat.

'You,' he managed to say. He bent over, coughing. Burdanian lungs were never suited to Taridwyni humidity. Lors should know that better than anyone. And Lors should know not to come crashing in amongst *kinder'el'ein* in a passion. Still bent over, Lors said, 'Thovalt tells me you and he are going to pursue Burdania again. That you are designing your approach around that . . . exhibition of his on the

296

platform.' He straightened, face suffused, fist braced against his chest. He delivered whole sentences entire, with breathless pauses between. 'You suggested to Thovalt that his reactions are a sensor of the suppressed emotion of the colony . . . You propose that he reexamine, that he *use* emotions which a year ago nearly caused him to destroy himself. . . . You propose to reopen records of an incident which irreparably damaged his standing amongst us . . . Naturally, *he* is enchanted with the idea. He was right all along, not ill, but . . . sacrificed. He has no insight – *wishes* no insight – into his own condition. Have you any idea the danger you are placing him in? Have you any idea of the consequences to him of failure? Have you looked squarely at your own motivations in this?'

Lian felt a little vertiginous. Lors' accusation was fair. When he put his argument to Thovalt, Lian had not considered Thovalt's weaknesses, only Thovalt's powers. He had not even been aware of them.

'You are not *kinder'el'ein*,' Lors said. 'You cannot sense emotions. You read nonverbal signals expertly, but they can be misleading, and you can be wrong. Whatever you saw was their inevitable shock and pity at seeing Thovalt break down before their eyes.'

But Lors, in protectiveness and frustration, saw only Thovalt's weaknesses. He had motivations, too. Motivations for Thovalt accepting his illness, taking no risk. As Thovalt had said, Lors could not love an unsafe Thovalt.

And there was Burdania. It was larger than any of them.

He said, 'No. It *changed*. In the – air.'

'Sweet reason, Lian, you must know how Thovalt feels about you. He thinks he *caused* your accident. He believes *you* could have been Proponent for Burdania. That is why he feels he must do it.'

Lors pleading was worse than Lors angry. Lian found he was gripping fistfuls of his robes. He shook his hands out. 'But – I cannot. And – he *can*.'

'Then *you* will be responsible for the consequences.'

'That – offends,' Lian said. 'Thovalt thinks he did damage to me. You think I do – damage to Thovalt. We think – we do damage to Burdania. I am a – person. I *choose*. Thovalt chooses.

We will choose. Consequences, too. Thovalt watched me. In hall. He had me – playing when I – came in. I did not – make him think. Of me. *He* thought of me. Nothing is – forgotten.'

'I will have no part of this,' Lors said; Lian saw that he had not been listening. He had come with a set mind. 'Or of you. I do not want to see you again. Our work together is finished.'

Lian stood in the small works area. Vaelren had gone. Everything had been put away, the pots of enzyme sealed, the brushes and trowels cleaned, the woven seaweed pulled over bare wood. The thoroughness of it was cruel. The reproach was absolute. She might never have been here, nor he with her.

TWENTY-THREE

BURDANIA

Lian squatted to catch his breath in the middle of the forecabin. It was the only space left him: Alystra sat at the scan station, and Thovalt and Andra took the two auxiliary chairs. Lors stood nearest the outer door, hands jammed in pockets, white hair windblown and face preoccupied.

Alystra, acting in her capacity as colony representative, had summoned them to confer. Their original mandate was to observe. This, they had already exceeded. Where should they now set limits on their involvement?

Through the arching front screen Lian could see *caur'isk'dari* on its knoll, brilliant in the midday sunshine. Beneath it, the slopes rippled and glowed bronze. When the door closed, shutting out sunlight and wind, the cabin seemed airless. He steadied himself on his hands, panting shallowly, and reasoning with his claustrophobia.

Lors said, 'I hope this will not take long.'

'It should not,' Alystra said. 'Lian, did you or did you not tell anyone about the drive?'

'No,' Lian said.

'I thought not. Have,' she looked hard at Thovalt, 'any of you?' Thovalt feathered the air with his fingers. Over his spangled overall he was wearing a dark blue cable knit sweater. He had spent his morning exhibiting the shuttle to the restorers, and then gone up to *caur'isk'dari* with them. Alystra stared at Thovalt until he gave her an airy assurance that he had not. Andra, nearest him, grimaced at the smell of seawater and spices wafting from him.

299

'I would recommend that, for the time being, we do not. That we are circumspect in what information we do give . . .'

'Alystra,' Lors said, heavily. 'This morning I operated on a man with a haematoma, assisted by two medics who are little more than children. One of those medics has a progressive visual defect – etiology unknown.' Lian set out a slow breath. He had hoped Tion would trust Lors. 'I have seen conditions which should not exist outside historical archives. Genetic disorders which should have been corrected prenatally or in infancy. Degenerative diseases which require gene therapy. The medics have an excellent knowledge of anatomy, gained by dissection of corpses.' Thovalt lost some of his high colour. 'A basic knowledge of cellular biology and biochemistry, and precious little genetics, virology, or molecular biology. It will take, I estimate, some twenty years to make full provision of trained personnel and diagnostic equipment, *if* the effort is given priority. So, you see, I have little patience for the niceties of hall protocol.'

Alystra contemplated the back of one small, round hand. 'None of us,' she said, neutrally, 'were prepared for the extent of degeneration. Andra, tell them what you told me about the archives.'

The Archivist folded her arms. Her uniform looked more natural: the sleeves were soiled and the pockets bulged. 'There's nothing left of Lltharran Halls and their archives. I've examined the Science Centre archives—' It took a moment for Lian to realize she meant *caur'isk'dari*. 'Hardware's in a remarkable state of preservation, given the state of everything else. Some of those rooms are deathdraps with half the door circuitry and all the lighting down or dismantled. Thovalt can tell you. Interfaces and power are still there, but I can't access, I can't do diagnostics and I can't clear memory. I can neither access a resident system manager, nor upload ours.'

'Could you link to our system?' Lors said.

'No!' Andra said. 'Nor should any of you. We can't have *any* direct signal transfer between any equipment on Burdania and ours. Those archives are so thoroughly inert that I'm beginning to suspect they were deliberately corrupted. To do that on a system of that size would probably take a self-perpetuating deletion protocol.' Thovalt sat up straighter. Alystra's hands settled neatly on her thighs. She fixed Lors with a steady, dark blue stare. 'I've been wondering about this absolute loss of knowledge,' Andra said, with a grim smile. 'Planetary Archives were networked. A protocol started at any point, here for instance, would spread throughout the net.'

There was a silence.

'If there's something like that in that archive, it could corrupt our complete ship's database, navigational information, medical instrumentation ... everything. It would be catastrophic. I've given specifications to the program designer aboard the parentship for a minimal interface with immunity. It won't be anything you recognize, but it should get me in. Until then, *nothing, no transfers* of any form.'

Lian studied the textureless, featureless grey floor. He did not want to tell them about Krysanin D'Caul's account of Linn Travassa's depredations. Not when that sat so close to Morain's and Daisainia's own records.

'I,' Alystra said, 'have been examining the political structure. I am sure that none of you are surprised to hear that it is essentially authoritarian: inclusion within kin and support structures – a matter of life and death, here – depends upon arbitration by individuals. Generally the appointment of these individuals is by some degree of consensus. Lltharran is a perilous exception: the arbiter here became so by direct inheritance, while yet very young. She is well entrenched. Few decisions are made without reference to Daisainia Travassa. She maintains her position by considerable personal charisma, occasional intimidation, and judicious control over resources, a prime resource being knowledge. I draw your attention to the fact that skills and disciplines are also under authoritarian control, though the Skills Guilds. Which, according to my source, were one of the original mechanisms through which undesired knowledge could be filtered out, and innovation suppressed. It is no accident that Daisainia Travassa is herself considered head of the affiliation working directly upon reestablishing the old technology.'

Lian was beginning to feel distinctly sick. Daisainia had warned him. He had defended his people to her as sincerely as he could, without, he thought, moving her, and without believing her. He trusted Daisainia's immense self-discipline and robust practicality. She would subordinate her feelings to her people's needs. And she would know how to make the shuttle crew's knowledge serve those needs.

He had not thought that the others might reject *Daisainia*. Not for anything that she had done, because they did not know what she had done, but because of what she was. He had been naive, he saw, in his understanding, if not in the instinct which had kept him from telling them about Morain. They would threaten Daisainia because Daisainia threatened *them*. The knowledge of old Burdania had been lost, but not displaced. They could put it back. But the structure and spirit of old Burdania had been displaced. The halls had melted and sunk beneath the floodwaters, and Daisainia stood unyielding in their place. Alystra and the others were still too raw in their discovery of Burdania's alteration to forgive her.

'Have – you spoken to – Daisainia?' Thovalt's slow smile told him that more had passed between Thovalt and the restorers than talk of technology.

Alystra tilted a hand towards the scan station at her back. 'The interview is on record.'

He remembered his first meeting with Daisainia, the consuming concentration, the sharp possessiveness as she spoke of Burdania. She would make sure Alystra knew the Burdanians were under her protection.

Dear life, Lian thought, what do I do? If I tell Alystra about Morain, it will only harden her antipathy. But if I do not tell her, and she provokes Daisainia – Daisainia has *warned* me.

'Alystra, I – please, be – careful. If you—' He sought for a word which would mean 'offend' but would not offend. There was none. He felt, though he was not moving, as though he was slipping. What *did* he think Daisainia might do? He said, hiding hard thought and selective wording in his hesitations, 'You – will – go – too fast. People will – resist. They are – accustomed to – being autonomous—'

'Autonomous?' Andra said. 'How can they be autonomous?'

'It is not – simple – between Daisainia and – the people. They are – hers, but she – is theirs. She *is* – theirs, and –

anything you take – from her you take – from them. Anything you take – from them you take – from her. Daisainia is – part of Burdania. You must contend with her.'

'We're not here to *contend* with anyone,' Lors said. 'We are here to return to Burdania what was taken from Burdania. We *owe* these people our knowledge. If we want to absolve ourselves of responsibility for what happened sixty-six years ago, then we are obliged to yield it up, whole, no terms, no conditions. And even if we start now, there'll be two generations of of casualties beyond this one.'

Thovalt stretched and said casually to Lors, 'If you can transfer specs for the equipment you think essential into the portable archive, I'll put the restorers on to it.'

'No,' Alystra and Andra said together.

Alystra continued: 'You have no mandate to commit resources—'

'I'm not,' Thovalt said sweetly. '*They* disinterred the relics, they'll put them together.'

Alystra said narrowly, 'We do not yet know enough about these people to give them access to our knowledge. We are custodians of the very technology which wasted this planet – would you turn that over to them?'

'If we can be trusted,' Lors said, 'then why not them? They know the consequences.'

'Our mandate is to obtain data, and I think that mandate may be the saving of us, because it is an anchor to caution. Yes, these people need our help, and conscience and compassion demands we give it. But survival demands we temper compassion with caution, and not let our contribution be used to empower a regime which is antithetical to everything we believe in.'

'I am not sure,' Lors said irritably, 'I object to empowering Daisainia Travassa. I, too, spoke to her, albeit briefly. The first thing she did was to draw my attention to Tion D'Suran's deteriorating eyesight. No, before that, she asked after Illuan D'Vandras.'

'I am sure,' Thovalt said, slyly, 'Lian is pleased to hear you say that.' He looked at Lian with sparkling innocence in his hazel eyes. 'You do incline to the exotic, Li: first Vaelren, and now this barbarian . . .'

There was a silence. Lors contemplated thin air. He had always been embarrassed by Lian's ill-placed love for the *kinder'el'ein*.

Alystra regarded Lian thoughtfully, but said, 'And, Thovalt, leaving aside the gossip, what have you learned?'

As Lors later observed, she should have known better.

The meeting ended in disarray. Thovalt's gift for sabotage was matchless. He flashed Lian a dazzling, conspirational smile as he swung through the hatch and out into the sunshine. The smile left Lian undeceived: it had not been mischief, but dead earnest. Thovalt would champion anyone, anything, against colony judgement, brilliantly, spiritedly, with the energy of rage. He had never forgiven the compulsory treatment order.

Alystra turned on Lors. 'Get him on to medication. We cannot have this mission put in jeopardy.'

Lors gave her a long, narrow look. 'Medication will not change Thovalt's character.'

Andra said, dryly, 'You never learn: you keep trying to win.' She unplugged a portable auxiliary from the station and flipped the strap over her shoulder. 'I'm going back to the Centre.'

'I'll come with you,' Alystra said. 'I want to see those paper records.'

The hatch closed behind them, taking away the air. Beyond the screen they walked away in silence, midday shadows crumpled at their heels. The bronze grass pitched and rippled dizzyingly.

'Lian,' Lors said. 'You've gone quite white. Sit down.'

'I should – see Thovalt. I need—' Lors sat him down. In the dimness around him, coloured lights flickered. A display glowed softly against Lors' fingers. Lors pushed him back and unfastened his jacket, cardigan and shirt. In Lian's mind, Alystra was already turning the crisp and flaking pages, already closing upon that one page with two lines in a small, cutting hand. Lian started to shiver. If Thovalt truly sympathized with the Burdanians, he should enlist Thovalt's help. But Thovalt was unpredictable, and deeply averse to ugliness. And what Daisainia had done, that was ugliness. Perhaps it was best that they know.

'Head back,' Lors said. He felt the sting of a pressure injector on the side of his neck. 'I'm sorry I did not do this before. I saw your telemetry.' He broke off. 'It must have been terrible for you, Li. Knowing we knew and had left you hurt.'

The dragging ache in ribs and shoulders abated. Lian stretched, covertly, pleased. Lors smiled. 'This will last about a day. Come back if you need more. But please, no more rashness . . . Lian,' this in a new tone. He was looking down at the instruments in his hands, 'Daisainia, the *isk'dar* – she is dangerous.' Lian stiffened. Lors did glance at him then, a diffident concern in his light brown eyes. The diffidence told Lian that what was coming was personal. Their friendship was marked by zones of reticence; Thovalt demanded it be so. He was jealous of the best attention of each of his friends. Lors took a deep breath. 'She is formidable, and admirable. But she is . . . like Thovalt. She had a kind of consuming, demanding personality. I am not saying that you are liable to suffer as I did, liable to be used up as I was. But, be careful.'

'Thank you, Lors,' Lian said, unbracing himself muscle by muscle. Beneath the warm luxury of the painkiller, he felt the throb of tears and bruises.

'I also . . . heard things,' Lors said. Abashed, he turned away, towards the scan station. And stopped, staring at one of the upper screens, which displayed rows of blue and violet symbols.

'What – is it?' Lian said.

He did not answer. He brushed the touchscreen with his fingertips, in quick, jerky motions. The display changed; a stretch of it became a bright lilac. 'It can't be.' The lower corner of the screen was crowded with small cryptic parameters and one very clear name: Tion D'Suran. 'It's a surgical virus. It's integrated into UV protective pathways.' The symbols on the panel shimmered slightly, adjusting to changing light as a cloud cast a flying shadow. Still staring at the screen, Lors said, 'Lian, they're to be used under the strictest containment. I've never seen anything like this. Where did it come from?'

'There was – a plague.'

'Of course,' said Lors, tight-throated. 'Tion told me.

Broken containment. Leakage into the surrounding soil. We'll have to locate and sterilize *all* those old labs—' Then, quite abruptly, he put his elbows on either side of the screen and his head in his hands. 'There's nothing I can do. I've got a small stock of surgicals, basic ones: wound and nerve repair and the like, but they're engineered for individuals, *us.* I haven't the expertise to modify . . .' He swung the chair round, and Lian drew his hand back. 'Sweet reason, Lian, what am I going to *tell* him? Hard enough to tell him that I cannot do anything for him, but this, this is one of our *instruments.*'

'You – *will* tell him,' Lian said, more sharply than was his wont.

Lors frowned, then sighed. 'You have the unhappy knack of anticipating my thoughts. But yes, I'll tell him.' He stared bleakly at the screen.

Daisainia herself was in *caur* D'Suran, seated, Tion down on one knee before her, winding the strapping round her ankle. The exposed skin was puffy, and muddy with bruising. Lors started forward, beginning to stoop. Tion settled back slightly, yielding his place. Daisainia lifted forbidding eyes. 'No need.'

'I could—'

'No,' said Daisainia. She turned her attention back to Tion, who went on with his work. His motions looked a little constrained, a little self-conscious. Gradually the discoloured skin was concealed by neatly overlapped bandage. Tion pinned it; Daisainia stood, balancing unobtrusively on her sound leg, and pivoted to face Lors and Lian.

'Was your meeting satisfactory?' she said.

'No,' Lors said, drily, but without elaboration.

'The D'Suran have been showing me what you can do.' She gestured towards the large round table, whereon Lors' equipment sat. It was the control apparatus for surgical micro-remotes, the seed-sized robots used for internal monitoring and surgery. Beside it sat a large earthenware pot of vegetable stew. Kylara glanced up at them, tucked back a strand of coppery hair, and returned her attention to the panel she was addressing. Her screen was several frames deep in impressions of fibrous pulp and disintegrating rind. 'Impressive,' said

Daisainia. 'But less valuable, I think, than fundamental knowledge. That was what we tried to derive from the relics, not their use; do you understand? The relics themselves were of limited use, being only fragments of a whole. We do not want fragments from you. This is not the Burdania you left. We know this Burdania as you do not. Knowledge is common; applications may differ. If you give us anything, you must give us everything.'

What was Lors hearing? Lian thought. Her message, or her autocratic possessiveness? He was afraid it was the latter: Lors looked at Daisainia much the way he looked sometimes at Lian, when his speech faltered more than usual. Lors looking compassionately upon the flawed, thinking how best to help.

'My knowledge is the product of years and ... must be augmented by databases. I cannot know everything I need to.'

'My medics must, and will, know what is important.' Daisainia said. With the same dark amusement as over the torches, she added, 'If it is a matter of years, then I should leave you to it.'

'I was going to come for you,' Tion said, another of his unobtrusive interventions. 'For Arkadin Nors. She has a degenerative neuromuscular condition, well advanced.'

'If you have a little time, first, I need to tell you what I learned ... about your eyesight.' Daisainia, her hand on the door, looked back. 'This will take some explanation. Because our sun is so strong in high light frequencies, not all of which are absorbed by our atmosphere, we have evolved protection against light damage: pigmentation, secretion of skin wax, scavenging of damaged proteins. In your eyes that protection has broken down. One of the genes involved in protection and repair has been ... disrupted. Your lens is being irradiated and damaged. The disruptive element is ... what we call a surgical virus. I can only guess it was released from one of ...' he nearly said, 'our'; Lian saw that. He did not want to. After a moment, he said, 'the old labs.'

'What is,' Kylara said, 'a surgical virus?'

'A virus is ... a parasite of cells. I explained the basis of genes to you. A virus carries its own genetic message – its own characteristics – into a cell, but uses the life-machinery of that cell to make more of itself. But we can . . . use viral properties to introduce other factors, messages, *instructions* . . . into cells.'

'I – was treated – with surgicals,' Lian said quietly.

Lors glanced at him, uncertain. 'Yes . . . Lian had a fall which caused severe brain damage. In early development, before and after birth, cells become . . . committed to various roles: hearing, speech, vision, cognition and so forth. One type of cells will connect to specific other types of cells and areas in the brain. They will send signals to . . . only those cells and areas. After a certain age the connections tend to be fixed; small lesions correct themselves, but large lesions show as deficits. In Lian's case, we could culture and graft to replace cells which had been killed, but to ensure they made the correct connections we . . . constructed surgical viruses which would help the connections regrow by sending them the signals they would have received in Lian's developing brain. Surgical viruses are ways of giving cells new instructions.'

'So,' Daisainia said, 'you will be able to correct the instructions to Tion D'Suran's eyes.'

'In principle, yes. In practice . . . I do not have the expertise,' Lors said, in a rush. 'I use transient infection routinely, to promote healing and repair, but chromosomal integration, *that* requires a specialist. Tion's is . . . a mild instance of what can happen with an uncontrolled virus.'

'Could that have been our plague?' Kylara said, tight-jawed. 'Our brother thought he brought it from buildings on the coast.'

'He died,' Fioral said, in a small, white voice. 'Many people died.'

'I . . . don't know,' Lors said. 'Surgical laboratories used . . . native viruses. The surgical which has affected Tion should not have produced the symptoms and . . . mortality which you described. But it may have come . . . from the same source.' There was a silence. His distress was visible, but after a hesitation, he said, steadily, 'I would say, yes. It did. But I would have to go there and make my own tests.'

Daisainia said, 'You cannot risk yourself so.' The concern startled her; the authority startled Lors. Covering herself, she said, sharply, 'There were many of these laboratories? Here? In Lltharran? How is it that we are not all dead?'

'Surgical viruses have many safeguards,' Lors said, stiffly. 'Physical containment is just the simplest. Most are too fragile to survive outside the laboratory. Tion's infection and . . . mutation is an extraordinary event.'

There was a silence. Daisainia said, 'You have a recommendation?'

'Only that you avoid the ruined laboratories. I can give you maps of where they were. Later we should be able to survey them.'

'But *can't* you fix his *eyes*?' Fioral appealed.

'Not now,' Lors said. 'Not here. On the colony or . . . in a few years. When we have reestablished the facilities.' He turned to Tion. 'There is no reason for them to deteriorate. If you protect them, wear eyeshields every time you are in sunlight, even under full spectrum lighting. We can make up a pair for you.'

Daisainia crunched the door open, swaying her weight sideways rather than bracing her leg. Undiffused sunlight fell across the bare floorboards. Tion looked down at the white-blond spray with visible wistfulness and ambivalence. Bright light had been an ally, tendering him normal vision. Now it was destructive.

Silhouetted in the doorway, Daisainia said, 'Bring me those maps. And,' she paused, 'if we may disinter further hazards from the past, advise me.' She swung the door closed behind her, and strode out of sight.

Arkadin Nors received them graciously. She was very much the power in *caur* Nors, treated with wry deference by her younger kin. She had been a masterweaver in her prime; the workroom, established for leatherwork, also housed a broadloom. Arkadin had seldom touched it: her hands were already failing when she came to Lltharran. But her work, and work produced by her kin and apprentices, hung across every door, and upon every wall, and lay over floors, beds, and chairs. It was a shambles of colour. Lors looked bewildered. To Lian it felt like home, except that green did not rule, except that it still had the chill, muddy, bright smell of the river.

Arkadin knew why they had come. Beneath the imperious-

309

ness, her eyes were wary, even, Lian thought, a little hurt. He looked at Lors through her eyes and saw a handsome, healthy man, of striking colouring. He looked at her through Lors' eyes and saw an infirm, ageing woman. And, perhaps, a hopeless case.

She lifted her pared face and looked Lors in the eye. 'No *might*, d'y'understand,' she said, almost explosively. 'Only if you can. Couldn't stand might. Yes, or no.'

Lors, taken aback, stumbled into honesty. 'It could only be might,' he said. 'I'm a field medic. I haven't the supplies.' He glanced at Tion, a mere flicker of the eyes. Perhaps Lors was even unaware of it. Lian was not: he thought, *good*, reliance goes both ways. 'If you will let me . . .'

'No mights.'

'I cannot tell anything simply by looking at you.'

She gave a tense, gusty laugh. 'Thought y'could. Tell you, then, I will. First th'weakness, in the hands, the legs. That two, three years ago. Spill food, drop work, falls. Broke m'leg coming off a *faun*. Set fine, but never worked right after. Then the swallowing went. Food goes down wrong, half time. Don't speak so clearly. Lately, the breathing. Body forgets *how*. Eyes good, heart good, mind good. No pain . . . No mights, remember.'

'I'll need some samples: blood and tissue. And a scan.' He began to unstrap his portable kit.

'This, too,' Arkadin said. There was the pressure of difficult decision behind the voice. 'Y'say you haven't supplies. Just one ship. 'M'an old woman. Had a good run. No regrets.' A small pause. 'Young ones come first, y'understand.'

'That's—' Lors began, in outrage.

'When there's not enough. That's the way.'

Lors was very pale. 'It's not our way.'

Arkadin's eyes did not move from him. 'Used t'happen when th'wintering was bad, when the currents stayed offshore and th'coast was cold, maybe icelocked, but th'seaweed and shellfish didn't grow. Then th'oldest would go into th'snows. Doesn't happen so much now: *cali* watch the shape of th'spring. *Cal* has t'say if th'spring's shaping wrong, whether this year there's to be few, or any children born. It's th'making

310

or breaking of a *cal*, if th'winter comes as they said.' She drew a deep breath, and looked at the pale Lors. 'But'm an old one, an'I r'member. I r'member when two walked out into th'snows so m'brothers and I would feed through th'winter.'

'I won't . . . *let* this happen.'

She reached up and tapped the hand that was clenched around his instrument. 'I'll make'y'. If there's no way otherwise. But find one, and be welcome.'

Lors' hands were trembling as he began his scan. Arkadin leaned back warily from the instrument, watching it as she would a stinging insect. It was Tion who said, 'Arkadin, be still. Lors has done it to me, and it does not hurt.'

She said to him, 'Too different. Can't believe'll all change so fast.' She said it with an authority which had taken the measure of the flow of change. Lian also heard resentment at the thought of a world going on without her. Lors drew a hair-capillary of blood, and sent a nanoremote into her spine and hands to sample atrophied cells. She held rigid, and shuddered uncontrollably when he withdrew the retrieval needle. 'No mights,' she barked at him. 'An'remember th'young ones.' Lors went to speak, lost the little colour that he had regained, and hastily left the room. They heard him stumble over one of the woven rugs.

Tion said, 'I should see if he's all right. Arkadin . . .' Into the name alone he packed fondness, chiding, and understanding. 'Behave yourself.'

As the door hanging dropped behind Tion, she turned a scowl on Lian. She was still shivering slightly, with the memory of that winter, perhaps, and what she felt obliged to offer. He scooped up a gaudy blanket and draped it around her shoulders. She pulled it snug with crossed hands.

He said, mildly, 'You were – hard on Lors.'

'None's easy on me,' she returned tartly.

He wanted to say to her, 'I think you were courageous.' But admiration would have been unkind; even understanding would have been offensive, unless she asked for his understanding. And, he acknowledged, he did not want to think that Lors would be forced to accede to her terms. To Burdania's terms.

311

He ran his fingertips along the smoothed frame of the loom. He knew better than to touch the strung warp. He heard a rattle of a crutch, and a grunt as she heaved herself to her feet. 'Teach you t'use that,' she said. He measured the need for truth against the need for distraction, and said, 'I – know how it – works. *Kinder'el'ein* looms are – like.'

'*Kinder'el'ein*? Ah, the other people.' He glanced up at her, startled that she already knew. She thumped over to join him, feet dragging. 'Y'r young Alystra's had words wi'me. Sh'sought out all th'ones at th'*caur'cali*; knew what'd been said to th'word. You "recorded", I s'pose. Lot of telling us they know better,' she said, somewhat irritably. 'Y'think I was hard on Lors, but they have t'*know*. It won't change for their asking. Works still got to be done: all the catching, planting, harvesting, weaving. Maybe *we* won't change for their asking. F'me, I'd sooner be riding than studying an'talking over every little living thing. Wouldn't like little box in m'pocket calling me back t'everyone's whim.'

'Nor do I,' Lian murmured. She was standing a little closer than necessary, close enough for him to feel the warmth of her brittle frame. He did not mind.

She balanced herself with a hand on his shoulder and pointed to the far wall. 'That's Kyarinn of the Islands.' The hanging almost filled the wall, in a rippling of shades of blue and violet, fanning and scissoring from scattered black. 'Sent him one of th'steppes in autumn. If he could do waves, I could do wind on th'grass.'

Lian saw the waves, then. She gestured to the hanging above the loom. 'That's me. Family portrait.' It was a pattern of tents around a campfire, with primitive flattening of perspective, and with all the tent doors pinned back to show the occupants. Lian was astonished that she could do so much with thread. The faces lacked fine detail, but she had characterized by task and posture. 'Took me three winters,' she said, ''n' more hides in trading than I ever c'nfessed.'

'All those dyes—' Lian said. 'Did you make—' He stopped. He had the sense, again, that he was on the verge of recognizing something vital.

'Not I,' she said. 'Some. Weavers and dyers, we trade. Many

from the south-seaweeds, fish – have dyesacs – some tropical *roh*, y'put mineral in the soil, grows coloured.'

He saw, then, as he had seen the waves. The pattern came to him whole. They had become like the *kinder'el'ein*. To replace technology, they had learned husbandry. He saw Burdanians living as *kinder'el'ein* lived, by an intimate knowledge of the natural products of their world. For a moment, it was truly possible, a union of the survival skills of the new world and the technology of the old, a union in which equality was possible.

And then he rememebred Alystra, Daisainia, and all the secrets.

'How – do you see it – going?'

'Restorers are in bliss. Computers, lights, airships, everything. Zharlinn . . . y'might have trouble yet with Ratha, over herself. You're more rival than he looked for.' She grinned wickedly at him. That was trouble she understood. 'Kylara'll suck your Lors dry. She's got a mind and a will, that one, t'match herself. Tion'll work t'th'death to learn . . . not believing he can. Vassar's standing aside. He'll stand aside at th'end of the world, taking notes. Be glad Illuan's laid low. Ionor'll give y'no trouble. Treat him fair and he'll make return. Herself . . .' She broke off, suddenly looking serious. 'Th'littlest D'Suran told me what she said t'you. What'll y'do to stop it going that way?'

'I – don't know.' Suddenly tired, he left her side, and sat down on her chair, resting his head in his hands. 'They do not – know about – Morian. Daisainia— You – do not know about us.'

He heard the thunk-scuff of her movements. A crutch jabbed his instep, not gently. He looked up to find her propped square on her crutches, scowling down at him. 'Never gave room, bed, or ear t'miseries an'I won't start now. If y'can do something, do it. If y'can't, be quiet about it. An'get up from my chair. I'm a sick old woman.'

'Just – when it suits you,' he said, flushed at her – too accurate – accusation of anguishing. He got up. She made him give her his arm to help her lower herself into the chair. She folded her pared hands primly upon her lap. 'Now,' she said.

'Now – indeed,' Lian murmured. 'Arkadin, it is not – only Daisainia's past which – concerns me. It is – ours.'

313

'This is bad,' she said, when he had done telling, and she, questioning. 'This is very bad.' Gone was the amiable lustiness; this was the woman who stood second to a *cal*, and spoke as bluntly to Illuan, Sidor, and Daisainia as to any of her young kin. Yet grim as she seemed, Lian knew he had not made a mistake telling her. She was capable of letting the past go.

She said, 'Y'must tell her. Y'must. I'd say bury it deep as y'can, but that Illuan knows. He *will* tell her; it is the surest way of turning her against. Dear life y'know that. Y'mark the plain, it's like y'mark her *skin*.'

'But – I – *cannot*,' Lian said. 'You have heard me – speak. In the colony I – am not thought – *adult* because I – could not pass the Trial. I cannot – persuade.'

'Who'd y'have do it? Illuan? Y'r young Alystra? Has't'be you. Alone. With her. Chance is she'll . . .' She stopped, shook her head. 'Y'll see the worst of her. But if y'can ride through th'storm, she might take from you what she'd take from nobody else. Weep if y'must. Plead if y'must. Remind her y'r Burdanian. Tell her th'past is *gone*, but don't expect her t'listen; *her* past is with her still. Remember, it's you, or worse.'

TWENTY-FOUR

TARIDWYN

'So,' said Alystra, 'let us hear what you propose.'

She sat, directly facing Thovalt across the circle of trampled grass. Thovalt had invited any who would come to the site of their discussions of a year ago, the seaside habitat. Lors, true to his ultimatum, had refused. As had Alandras, the psychologist. Andra had come. To Lian's mild surprise, Danas and Tarian had also: their daughter had been born only a month ago, seemingly an unequivocal commitment to the colony.

And, unexpectedly, Alystra had also come, dainty, impeccably groomed, and sceptical. More than anyone else except Thovalt, she still felt the first failure.

'Ah,' said Thovalt. 'First, you agree.' He swept glittering eyes round the circle. 'I am telling you nothing, nothing whatsoever, until you agree that you are with me. You may argue with me thereafter all you wish, but I am not offering myself up to doubters beforehand.'

Alystra drew a sharp breath, her mouth tense. Thovalt rocked forward on to his hands, and hissed, 'Not one single, little word.'

Lian was engaged in finger-talk with the baby, who was lying in a nest of grasses and blankets, snatching at air. He knew how the standoff would end: one or other would capitulate, Thovalt out of self-satisfaction, the others out of impatience. Meanwhile, he would do as he chose. He caught one tiny, flitting hand between his fingertips; the other folded around the side of his palm. 'Ah!' the baby announced, a small, sharp, triangular sound. Danas glanced aside at them indulgently: the children playing.

315

Andra said, 'I surmise that your new approach has something to do with the colony records you and Lian have been accessing of late.'

'*Colony* records,' Alystra said, with designing scepticism.

Thovalt leaned back on his hands, tilted his head back and regarded them all with half-shut eyes. 'About Burdania, is there anything more to say?'

Unexpectedly, Tarian D'Sal said, 'The *kinder'el'ein*.'

Alystra said, 'I will tell you now, you cannot found an argument on something you cannot prove.'

'We did,' Tarian said. 'The driveshock.' There was a silence. 'I am prepared to investigate the possibility that *kinder'el'ein* sensed life on Burdania.'

'Lors' hypothesis—' Andra said.

'Lors is a biomedical scientist, and a realist. I am neither. The question is whether there is a signal, or signature, of a living world which bypasses normal space – the *kinder'el'ein* were quite adamant that it was the present state of Burdania they sensed – and yet may be perceived by living organs. The bypassing of normal space is no obstacle: remember, if we could not do it, we would not be here. That is where I am best equipped to investigate: what signals, or signatures, might naturally travel through hyperspace, and might they interact with ordinary living matter, and therefore, be perceived.'

'You're not afraid to make a fool of yourself, are you,' Andra said, sourly.

The physicist looked coolly at her. 'The value of the potential gains, remote as they are, far outweigh the penalties of failure.' He shifted his tawny eyes to Thovalt. 'But given the potential for failure, I would not advise you to make this the foundation of your argument. Lors' hypothesis about the basis of *en'neen* may be correct, and their perception merely a compassionate delusion, inspired by Lian's durable concern for Burdania.' Tarian bowed where he sat, in Lian's direction, a respectful acknowledgement which left Lian mildly stunned.

'Ah, but,' Thovalt said, 'I am not.' He gave Lian a smile of pure wickedness and said, 'Tell them, Li.'

Lian's hand froze in the baby's grip. She tugged, found it

316

unyielding, and grumbled. Lian let her carry it to his mouth, and gave Thovalt an imploring look.

'Lian observed something interesting in the last minutes of the debate. When I had that "outburst" you cannot forgive me. Lian says that something changed in the hall, something changed in the atmosphere. That up until then, we had merely been treading old paths, "ritual", is what I believe Lian called it. And then I,' tiny emphasis on the word, 'spoke out. I shocked them.' He paused, provoking comment.

Tarian said, calmly, 'You were unwell.'

Thovalt rewarded him with a radiant smile. 'Most grievously. Of a malady shared by many of us. Guilt. Grief. Something left unfinished.'

'If you think,' Alystra said narrowly, 'we can make an argument from your neurosis . . .'

'No—' said Lian, the word jolted out of him by their expressions. The others looked at him. Thovalt glittered. Lian said, 'It has to – *change*. Not be – arguments of – knowledge. Simulation. Certainty. It has to be – argument of – heart.'

There was a silence. Tarian said, to Thovalt, 'How will you do that?'

Thovalt reached behind him, and brought forth a mobile projector, which had been hidden in the grass. He keyed it on. Beyond the fringe, suspended in mid air, Islain Nors appeared. He stood motionless, frozen in space, looking over them with his sad green eyes. Thovalt said, '*They* will give testimony. Our fathers and mothers; our grandfathers and grandmothers; our great-grandfathers and great-grandmothers. They will testify to what Burdania has been, meant, and *done* to us.'

Tarian said, 'So, what you propose to do is to . . . measure the cost to *ourselves* of our long ignorance, and persuade people that they, not Burdania, would be better if we returned, if we knew . . .' He looked down at his daughter, who was gnawing the tip of Lian's finger with sharp gums. Lian watched the thoughts pass behind his quiet face. The later ones he spoke. 'Is it better to know than to fear Burdania's destruction? If we find that Burdania and

317

Burdanians did not survive, we leave our children – and our parents and grandparents – with the unequivocal knowledge Burdania is gone. No room for hope . . .'

'I cannot countenance this,' Alystra said. 'It is antithetical to everything the hall stands for, everything the records stand for . . . even this . . .' she gestured towards the motionless, floating Islain, 'is a personal message meant for direct descendants of Islain Nors, and not for public view. As Andra will no doubt remind you, if indeed you were not already *aware* from your indoctrination in the ethics of systems maintenance, you do *not* extract personal records from context. It is a fundamental covenant that those who contribute to the Archives shall have the integrity of their presentation left intact. It is required for trust and candour. And what you propose to do in hall would not be an argument; it would be the rankest manipulation.'

'It is *all* manipulation,' Danas said, unexpectedly. 'Any argument involves organization of fact to make connections. You would excerpt factual records to support an argument. Our personal experiences are also facts.'

Thovalt leaned forward, long hands pressing down the grass in front of him. 'Tell me, Alystra,' he said softly, 'have you ever told anyone how you learned about Burdania? Have you ever told anyone what you felt, when you passed from innocence to helpless culpability, because you had taken on Burdania as part of your inheritance, as surely as any coding gene in your body?' Hazel eyes held dark blue ones; she blinked rapidly, but did not look away. 'Have you told anyone how the universe tilted slightly askew, and never came right again, or sang a single high note of anguish which you can still hear in the silences? Have you told your parents, your coparents, your first lover, any lover, your friends, your senior in the Archives, the man you might be thinking of having a child by: you know and are known by five hundred and fifty-eight men, women and children . . . is there a one amongst them who knows how you learned about Burdania?' He lowered his voice gradually. Unthinkingly, Alystra was drawn forward. So were they all. 'Is there a one amongst them who has told you how they learned about Burdania? Of course not. We do not talk about that part of Burdania, not amongst ourselves. We need not: we all know it

318

without speaking.' He placed a small, full silence between them; Lian, whose silences were mostly involuntary, admired the shape of it. Then Thovalt said, 'How did you learn about Burdania?'

She jerked upright, suddenly aware how she had been lured. Fine, pale nostrils flexed, not in amusement, but in anger. She said, striving for authority, 'This is not proper. This is not the way arguments are made.'

'*This* argument will be,' Thovalt said.

'Without my assistance,' Alystra said.

'Not even,' Andra said, drily, 'if he can win?'

'You think he can? That way?'

Thovalt leaned back on his hands, back arched, and smiled slyly at Alystra. She said, 'I will describe to the Advocate what you intend. They will rule.'

Thovalt said, 'Where is it written that the form of a debate must be approved?'

'Tradition—' Alystra began, stopped. She said, 'I will put your proposal to the Advocate.' She got to her feet, and brushed lightly at some clinging seed on her dark blue trousers. Looking down at Thovalt, she also said, 'I will have to tell them that it is *you* proposing it.'

Thovalt gave her his sweetest smile. 'Do,' he said.

Tarian was weaving a stalk of grass through his fingers. Lian watched with fascination: it seemed an oddly aimless diversion. As the inner door closed behind Alystra, he lifted tawny eyes and said, judiciously, to Thovalt, 'I am glad you let her salvage her pride; it could have been difficult if you had not.' Thovalt snorted. Tarian spread his fingers and let the stiff grass unravel, then plucked it from between his fingers. 'Yes,' he said. 'She does not like the approach, but she sees the power in it. As do I.' Something sombre lay beneath his tone; Lian wondered what it might be. He had heard it before. Reaching back in memory he found an unfinished sentence, 'No room for hope . . .'

Tarian looked sharply up at him, face oddly blank, caught between thoughts. Lian realized then he had spoken aloud. Lian watched the thoughts come, and reassemble themselves into a guarded watchfulness. But he did not speak to Lian; it was to Thovalt he said, 'There are worse things than ignorance, worse things than failure.' He glanced at his daughter, the same look he had sent before. 'If we went, and found Burdania gone, we would be better not to return.'

Andra ruffled slightly, sloughing off the suggestion with a shift of her shoulders. 'Yes,' she said, 'but first we must go. First we must win this debate. First, we must persuade them to let us present with Thovalt as Proponent. And first, *I* must be persuaded that this approach will succeed where others have failed. Tell me more as to what you propose.'

Lian told Vaelren about the meeting as they worked shoulder to shoulder on the balcony in the late afternoon. Vaelren was crushing a fungus which fed on fallen wood, whose enzymes were part of the digestive mix she worked with. Lian was staining sea-sand green, stirring a slurry of moist sand and chunks of intensely dark resinous dye.

'You Burdanians appall me,' Vaelren said.

Lian lifted his head from his work in dismay. He had not sensed her mood change, nor anticipated one so swift and harsh. He shrank within his skin at her condemnation.

She continued in her rough, silvery voice, '*You* would agree to die to protect *them* from learning about Burdania. Would you choose their peace of mind over your place in *vos'neen*? No *kinder'el'ein* would ask you to; no *kinder'el'ein* choose.'

'I am – not *kinder'el'ein*,' he said, in a whisper.

'I thought you had better sense than to fall into this—' she searched for words, found none but, 'Burdanianness.'

'I – did not say I—'

'You accepted that you might come to it. I sensed that in you.'

'But if – if Burdania—'

'We *sensed* Burdania. Do you disbelieve us because Burdanians cannot prove it? You give up too much to them. Your belief, your pride, and now you might give your life.'

There was a silence. Lian picked a chunk of dye from the surface of sand, holding back tears at the intensity of her love and anger for him. He said, 'I – had not thought.' Had not thought that it would matter so much to anyone but himself. He

320

said, 'Vaeli, Burdania might have – lived, but changed—'

'So Burdania is changed. Is that some wrong of yours? You will bring back the knowledge of Burdania's change. Is that a wrong? Is *knowing* and telling a wrong? Burdanians insist it is not so. You take too much upon yourself, and I dislike it in you. Be humble, and be at peace with yourself.'

He leaned against her, and tucked his face into the fabric-lined hollow between neck and shoulder. She smelled of the woodyards: of raw sap, moss, the salty-herbal smell of preservative seaweed. At times he felt she pulled at him, as Burdania pulled at him; and, caught between irreconcilable forces, he wondered why he endured such an impossible love. At others, as now, she brought him into balance, and he knew.

Then he felt her draw away. Heard her say, very quietly, 'Enough.' Unthinking, he tried to lean after her, lean into her, and nearly fell. Caught himself with a muted thud of his hand, clumsily trapping the edge of her robe against the mossy wood. He twisted his neck and saw close by the weave of her robe; and above it, her face, looking sideways down at him. She did not turn her head. He shuffled off the hem of her robe, and she drew it to her. She said, 'Lian, I am going away.' She turned her head then, to rest her beautiful aquamarine eyes coolly upon him, and lifted her hands. Her sign, like most of her movements, was deft and slightly clumsy. *I love you. But I cannot be near you now. So I am going away.*

She was talking about Burdania. He knew it; he had felt her withdrawal as he prepared for Trial. He had sensed her resentment of Thovalt's and Lors' visits. He felt her distance from him when he returned to the settlement in Burdanian garb of mind. The sum of his knowledge gave a terrible authority to her simple statement. He said, quickly, 'Vaeli, I'll – stop. Now.'

'I do not want you to be false to yourself.' Her voice was clear, silvery, detached.

'You do – not want *me*,' Lian said, baldly. He spoke rather than thought, for thought would bring feeling and feeling, offence. She folded her hands, and lowered her head, and did not answer.

'I was *recognized*.'

321

I know, she signed, with weary movements. *Lian, I am tired of not knowing where I end and you begin. I am tired of not knowing which are my wishes and which yours. You were recognized, yes. Now there is part of me which is part of you. Part of me which feels as you feel about Burdania, not because you feel it but because en'neen feels it. En'neen yearns towards Burdania, as you do. You stir that part of it. Sometimes I forget that I am* kinder'el'ein, *that I belong here, and not there.*

He stared at her, all self-consciousness or propriety abandoned. All he felt was shock and dismay for her. 'Vaeli!' He caught her sleeve, anticipating her motion. *Vaeli*, he signed, *I would not for the world have laid any of this on you.*

Her nostril slits flickered, weakly. *I know, Lian. That is what makes it nearly . . . tragic. We did not expect this; why should we: we have never taken anything alien into* en'neen.

Is everybody . . . all kinder'el'ein *. . . like you?*

Nobody else is so close to Burdanians, to Burdanians' cares and Burdanians' concerns. Except maybe Telien. And I am not Telien. I do not have kin prideful, stubborn spirit. I do not like to study myself outside vos'neen. *I love you; I feel your humiliations, your uncertainties, your worry about Burdania. And something in me, in* en'neen, *cries out. I am changed at my core, and I have never wanted to be anything more, or less, than* kinder'el'ein.

'Can – I – do *anything?*' he said, with difficulty.

'Think kindly of me, sometimes.'

Where will you go? How long will you be gone?

Away, she signed. And: *Until*.

Carefully, he got to his feet, using his hands to lever and balance himself before standing. He looked down on her upturned face from a height, upon the black, unreadable, planed face, the aquamarine eyes. He watched her breath moving in and out, causing infinitesimal shifts of her sinus cartilage. He felt as though his skull were filled with liquid grief, which, if he opened his mouth, or moved too quickly, would spill all over her, spatter her and the platform and the jungle below. He whispered, 'All the time – I will think of you.'

Then he turned very carefully on his toes and went through the curtain and along the corridor to the quiet room. The air conditioning was off; the air was close and stale. He lay face down on the bed, and let himself smother in darkness and grief.

TWENTY-FIVE

BURDANIA

To tell her, he thought. He. Himself. With his flawed language. Thovalt would be better, maybe. Except Thovalt would delight in unveiling her darkness, never seeing the consequences. Alystra would . . . he imagined Alystra telling her. Remembered the recorded conversation between Alystra and Daisainia, and thought of the cool, waxen aspect of the one and the hot core of the other. Andra, not Andra. Lors. Lors would refuse. Lors would say he had better things to do than take up the defence of people long dead, and undeserving. Lors would despise the distraction of the past from the urgencies of the present.

He thought, I will show her the records. I will let Islain Nors speak. She will see the marks their deed left upon them, upon us.

Alone in the shuttle, he was furtive and clumsy. The Archive seemed to resist him, its directory as impenetrable as one of Shaleen's mandalas, a silvery web linking symbols, spread across the touchplate. Nobody had thought to include the simpler directories accessible to children; nobody knew how much he relied upon them still. He thrashed in the web, tense and cold.

He found their debate, and used its pointers and cross-references to find Islain Nors' confessions, Thaorinn D'Halldt's debate, Thovalt's first debate. He looked for, and could not find, reference to the *en'vos'neen'el*. He had, in the end, to suspect omission, and found himself irked at Burdanian egotism. He had recalled his personal files, and found there his

324

fragmentary reflections on the *en'vos'neen'el* and on his last meeting with his father. Both seemed inadequate against the eloquent completeness of the other accounts. He assembled the records, and readied them for transfer. The snick of the shuttle outer door gave him barely enough warning to blank the last record from the screens, before Alystra came in, followed by Andra, Thovalt and finally Lors.

There was a moment's rough-textured silence.

'We were just about to page you,' Alystra said. Small muscles worked to hold her mouth neat. 'Lors said your monitor showed you were here.'

Lors stopped just within the hatch, gave Lian a single, searching look, and then gripped his arms across his body, and withdrew into himself. Andra displaced him from his seat without once looking at him. Thovalt hid his emotions behind a half-smile.

Andra unslung the portable archive from her shoulder and docked it beneath the console. She lifted her hair from her shoulders, shrugging it back, and took command of the system with swift, feathery touches. With a fingertip she uncovered what he had been doing, looked at it only enough to know what it was, and covered it again. Lian knew only because he was watching; Thovalt, aware he was missing something, frowned, thwarted and irked. Then the twelve screens filled with images of handwriting on paper: Krysanin's unpractised hand, Branduin's spiky scrawl, Morain's painted script, and Daisainia's own tight, cutting characters.

'I asked Andra to search for parameters which I could use for a simulation of likely outcomes of our involvement here,' Alystra said. 'Specifically, the methods of resolution of political conflict.'

The images flickered; years passed in the flickering. How, Lian thought, sickly, could he have imagined they would accord the records the respect of reading them, of treating them as they did their own personal records?

He watched the melting away of the painted script, until all that remained was two lines, in a small, cutting hand.

Alystra said, 'I hoped you might be more surprised.'

Lian said in a whisper, 'No.'

He heard Lors let out a breath. Alystra said, 'As you thought, Lors.' He looked up at her, not without difficulty. Her lips were thin, pressed white. Thovalt he still could not read, still found him hidden behind amused, glittering eyes, and a slight smile. He said, to Thovalt, 'You – do not know – why.'

Thovalt drew his lips back from his teeth. 'Do you?'

Alystra said, crisply, 'Morain D'Vandras initiated restoration efforts of the discarded knowledge. Daisainia Travassa's forebears suppressed that knowledge, by murder if necessary, and built a power base upon its ruins. *Anyone* who tried to use that knowledge was a threat to their power base. *Is* a threat to their power base.'

'Daisainia,' Lian said, tight-throated, 'is – better than that.'

'She committed murder, and has gone unpunished. In fact, she has been rewarded for it. She has removed a challenger and deterred others. There is no reason why she should not murder, or instigate murder again for as long as she might profit by it. You cannot deny the facts. Or their implications for us: *we* are a threat to Daisainia Travassa's power base, to her control over the old knowledge.'

For a moment all Lian could hear was the pulse in his ears. 'I – did not tell you – because. Because I knew. This would be. Your way. Give no chances. No hearing.'

'Then *yes*,' Alystra flashed back, colour high, 'we will give her a hearing. Let her reassure us that this world—' She checked. But Lian could complete the sentence for her, and did. 'That this world – is worthy.'

She had the grace to look abashed. Her hands flicked from hair, to collar, to cuffs, in a reflexive polish of her grooming. She brushed at invisible dust upon her jacket sleeves. Then, composed, she went on, 'These are our options, as I see them. One: stay in Lltharran, continue as we are, ignore what we have learned and do not challenge extant power structures. For many reasons, I believe that would be undesirable, if not impossible. Two: stay in Lltharran and attempt to effect change. That would put us, personally, at risk, and I fear the effects of a schism on the community. Three: withdraw from Lltharran and find a vital community removed from the influence of the *isk'dar* and her agents. Although she styles herself a power in Burdania, the poor communications weaken her influence; there are many thousands of people who only know of her by hearsay, and numerous communities largely independent of her. Any one of those could be the nucleus of an uncontaminated reconstruction. Four: withdraw from Burdania, return to the colony and present our findings to the hall, as our mandate, properly interpreted, dictates.'

Lors said, tersely, 'It is no more ethical for us to trade knowledge for influence than it is for Daisainia Travassa. The knowledge, the science, the skills which we have are their birthright also. *All* of their birthright. They have dealt with you in good faith, given you their records in good faith, knowing what was in them. Have we done likewise – no, I won't get into wrong for wrong. Colony records have always been completely open. Are we empowered to change that; I think not.'

'Oh, bravo,' Thovalt murmured.

'If you are worried about the abuse of knowledge,' Lors said, 'then the surest way to prevent it is to ensure that it is offered equally to everyone.'

'Which,' Thovalt said, smiling, 'is a noble sentiment which might have come from one Morian D'Vandras. Maybe you'd better aquaint us with the symptoms of *sonol* poisoning.' Lors did not answer. 'Lian's looking pale,' Thovalt remarked. 'Careless choice of dining companions, Li?'

Lian put a cold hand to his chilled face. Through it, he said, 'You – hate cruelty and – judgement – so, but can – be so cruel. I know and – accept – you. But I am not – invulnerable.' He dropped the hand. Thovalt's face was fixed between expressions, lips drawn back from his teeth. Thovalt relied upon Lian's understanding and endurance, relied upon Lian to be neither provoked nor hurt. Lian wondered, wearily, whether he had made a mistake in protesting before them all. 'Daisainia poisoned – Morain. *Sonol* is – a cruel death,' He saw Thovalt flinch. He should have chosen another word, but he could do no better. Thovalt would have to accept that. 'From the little – else I know, I have nothing – to defend her with. She – owns to what she did, says she has – no regret.' Lors put a hand on his shoulder. Did he seem so fragile? Lian thought. Probably. He steadied his voice. 'But that was – five years ago. I – see her

327

now. A fine person, a fine – leader. Alert to – everything about her – world. She will do what – must be done, though – she is afraid. I cannot – reconcile. But I must – trust what I see. Believe in – what I see. Daisainia – sustains her people.'

'And feeds on them, 'Alystra said, crisply. 'Let me cast a less flattering light. She perpetuates this nonviable community, because it is part of her power base. Her part in the restoration is opportunistic; as she could no longer suppress the knowledge, she elected to take control of it. I do not suggest that these were all deliberate strategies; I suspect that she acts not from conscious desire for power, but from psychological need. Which makes her all the more dangerous if threatened.'

'Withdraw,' Andra said.

'Stay,' said Lors. 'We accepted all risks coming back here. We accepted the responsibility for the effect of what we found on us and the colony. We *demanded* it.'

Thovalt relished his moment. He could choose with Alystra and Andra, and send them away. He could choose with Lors and Lian, and have them stay. He reached over Andra's shoulder to reset the displays to a tumbling series of images and words, images of Burdania, words from their records. He said, almost idly, 'Would I leave before the act is played to its close?'

Andra thrust his hands aside. The screens changed. On them, an ageing Islain Nors leaned forward in his chair; a young, fierce Thaorinn D'Halldt stood beneath the dome; Burdania flickered and dimmed. Alystra said, 'What's that?'

'What Lian was doing before we came in.'

Thovalt said, 'You were going to tell them.' There was awe in his voice. Alystra and Andra's look hardened his first impulsive reaction. He regarded Lian through slitted eyes, in appalled amusement. '*Lian.*'

'I – must. It is better me – than—'

Alystra did not let him finish. 'Given what we now know from these records – which you kept from us – you have placed us all in danger and put our mission at risk. Given now this further evidence of your – I do not know what to call it – I wish to put you on notice that I am considering invoking formal censure on you when we return.'

Lors closed to stand protectively behind Lian. 'That is unfair—'

'Lian is either a full member of this mission, or he is not. He is either capable of answering for his actions, or he is not, and if he is not, he is not entitled to either voice or action. He holds a privileged position, on account of our affection for him and our compassion for his handicaps, and he has abused it.'

Lors stepped forward; he now stood at Lian's shoulder. 'Then I will answer for him. You know he is not capable of presenting a formal argument; you would be offering him up to humiliation—'

'Then you agree with what he has done here? You will speak for him and take his censure on you.'

Lors took the final step forward, the one which Lian could not endure. '*Stop*,' Lian said. The anguish in his voice caused Lors to turn. He saw only concern and incomprehension on Lors' face. He said, 'I'll – answer. I *will* answer.'

He evaded Lors' touch. His fingers, looking for a hand, skittered over the touch panel. The hatch slid open, pitching him into the last horizonal daylight of the Burdanian sunset. Striking gravel, he ran.

Framed by the transparent door of *caur* D'Suran, he saw them. They were crowded around Lors' portable archive, Kylara, Rathla Zharlinn, Tion with Fioral tucked under one arm, and, squared before the console, Daisainia herself. There was a lamp upon the table, lighting up their faces and the little sprigs of green they held. Medics and botanist *isk'dar* were working on the analysis of the medicinal herbs. Fioral bounced on her toes to see better; Rathla Zharlinn reached over Daisainia's shoulder towards the panel, and she rapped his fingers. The flick of movement etched itself instantaneously on Lian's memory. Daisainia's face took longer; at ease, unmasked, her expression changed with her thoughts. He followed the shift of her attention between the plants offered her, the people around her, the console before her. He watched her transient perplexity and illumination as she deciphered the instructions. Her grasp of the detail of her world had seemed to him like *vos'neen*; but this was a deft, authoritative intelligence, in a rare moment of play.

And before they saw him, Lian walked away. He had no words for her. He stayed on the high side of the ridge, clear of fires and people. He followed the ridge to where the path rose like smoke through the *thail*. He stepped off the far side of the path and followed the escarpment round until the hill's curve was between himself and the shuttle, between himself and the settlement. Before him was nothing but flood and wasteland, all the way to the sea.

He let his legs soften and slid down the wall to a crouch, back against waxy stone. He should be glad she was accommodating, becoming involved. Daisainia was yielding; his four . . . his four would shy from any final decision. He examined his own bitterness like a rare mineral. They would talk, argue and accuse amongst themselves. It had taken sixty-six years for them to come back; let it take a portion of that for them to leave. They could not hide in the shuttle forever. Let what would happen to them happen. He could not prevent it. He laid his face in his hands.

It was not jealousy he felt, not the sight of Zharlinn beside her. Loving Vaelren had taught him that jealousy would gain him nothing and lose him even what he might have. He had learned a pleasure in love that did not depend upon reciprocity. He wished Daisainia joy of her choices, however they fell. She was valiant, proud and able. But, watching her work at the console, he had seen her in the context of the colony. He had recognized the dimensions and potential of her mind. She would have little difficulty securing a voice and vote in hall. She would be the peer of any. They all would. And he was not.

He lifted his head out of his hands and stared out over the darkening indigo plain. He had found a world of stone and plants, like the jungle of the *kinder'el'ein*. One which suited his own dimensions. But one inhabited by his own people. Including a woman who met him as a peer. And in finding it he had started it changing, started her changing, and leaving him behind.

The indigo darkened to near black; stars streamed overhead. He searched amongst them for Taridwyn's cluster and did not find it. He became aware that he was cold, and that time had gone by. So they must have decided to stay. If they had not, they would have tried to recall him. So it would go on.

He was so sunk in his own thoughts he did not hear the voices when they began. Thovalt's he knew as soon as he began to listen. The second voice, a woman's, he did not. He pulled himself up from his crouch and stood straining to hear. Thovalt's voice had a dangerous, defiant excitement to it. Hers was a wisp on the wind. Standing, Lian saw white moving below him. He saw Thovalt catch her and turn her in his hands, like a dancer. Spangles danced along his extended arms. Black hair hid her face. Lian leaned against the stone, and closed his eyes. Their voices lapped uphill, ebbing away. Lian looked down to see the last of them. He recognized the woman then: Shivaun D'Vandras. Thovalt held her close with one arm; her hands trailed. They went out of sight beneath the escarpment, towards the path.

Time passed. The path, when he reached it, was empty. He stood looking up and down the pale ribbon, telling himself that they could not have vanished so quickly. But he knew it had not been quickly. Down behind the dyke, in the dark, the bonfire had come into full bloom. Lian felt obscurely ashamed of himself. He should have done something, hearing that excitement in Thovalt's voice. He might have known Shivaun's shattered beauty would draw Thovalt. He might himself have paid attention to her. Instead, he had pushed aside all thought of her, rather than think on Daisainia's wrongdoing. And what to do now? Intervene? Present himself for another verbal mauling and humiliation? Or tell himself that even Thovalt would have no malice against someone so patently wounded and vulnerable. Tell himself that good might come of it yet. Something else which would just unfold as it would.

With dragging step, he started downhill.

Alystra and Andra were already at the fireside. He checked at the sight of them. Alystra was standing with Sidor and Ionor D'Alna. She was commonplace in slacks and jacket, her demeanour grave and respectful. As she moved, something twinkled on her shoulder: the faceted head of a recording pin, perched so it might take everything in. Later she would

331

deconvolve the overlapped sound and stabilize images against movement. It would not be difficult to learn everything which had been said.

Andra was arguing with Lara, Valancy and Vylan. She had her portable unit balanced on her hip and a pale light flickered upwards across her surly face. Lara was nearly stamping with frustration. Valancy's part was thwarted by her son, roaring and spiking through his blankets with tiny fists and feet. Vylan spoke briefly but thoughtfully. He glanced up at Lian across the fire, and waved.

Alystra caught sight of him, and raised a poised hand. Behind it, her gaze was cautioning, watchful. Whatever she saw in his demeanour must have satisfied her; she turned back to her conversation.

Daisainia was not there. Nor were Zharlinn, or the medics. They must still be up in caur D'Suran. Thovalt and Lors were also missing. Lian hoped Lors was up in the shuttle, resting; more likely, he would be downloading additional information. Thovalt: Lian pushed away the thought of Thovalt.

Arkadin Nors hailed him, across the fire, brandishing a crutch like a branch. He went to her reluctantly, remembering what she had sent him to do. She was perched on a flat boulder with a small, untidy fire snapping at her feet. He sat down heavily at her side. 'I – haven't,' he said.

She showed unexpected compassion, laying fingers as light as a fallen leaf on his knee. ' 'Tis hard. But y'must.'

'I – went to find – the records. But they— They know – about Daisainia. They will not – let me.' He put his head back, trying to cup the tears in his eyes. Knowing he was indulging himself and giving himself up to the indulgence. 'I thought – I was their peer. I – deceived myself. They would – not listen.'

'*Look at me*,' she said, distinctly, with an effort. 'I am old, *crippled*. I am useless. But n'body dismisses me. It's you lets them.'

'I am – under censure. For – acting outside – consensus. For wanting to – tell. Lors—' He could not continue, deeply shamed by Lors' defence of him, by his own inability to welcome it.

Her eyes were dark amber in the firelight. She said, 'This

332

isn't – where y'came from. Thought y'knew that.'

'D'Halldt,' Daisainia's voice said, from behind him.

The thin, flattened timbre of the voice chilled him. He twisted, and stared up at her, trying to penetrate the mask, and the hollows around the deep eyes. Focused on her, he did not see the others, ranked at her shoulders like the barbs of an arrowhead. Then, from behind her, Zharlinn spoke. 'We'd like you to come with us.' His field of vision widened; they moved from her side to half encircle him, Zharlinn and Kylara on his left, Tion and Fioral on his right. Arkadin Nors jammed a crutch into the ground and levered herself to standing with the other. 'What's this?' she said, imperiously.

'D'Halldt,' Daisainia rounded the rock with a stride, nearly scattering Arkadin's fire. She gripped his left arm, and started to pull him to his feet. Tion said sharply, 'Not his shoulders.' She transferred him to her right hand, seizing a fistful of his jacket above his heart, lifting it and him with it. Holding him, she said, 'I would rather not have this reckoning before all. D'Halldt, we *know* how your people left. Now will you come?'

He thought, of course. And: *no*. And: how?

He was too slow for her, she stepped sideways, pulling him offbalance and making him follow.

Arkadin heaved her left crutch across behind Daisainia's ankles. 'Take him w'out me, and I raise cry,' she said.

Isk'dar and Northerner stared at each other for several breaths, then Daisainia released Lian. The shock of disconnection jolted him like a shift of gravity. 'Aye,' the *isk'dar* said, stepping neatly over the crutch. 'Come.'

In *caur* D'Suran, Illuan D'Vandras was sitting at the circular table, examining one of Lors' programmed injectors. He handled it precisely, with his fingertips. He laid it down as Daisainia and Zharlinn put Lian first through the door. He was dressed in a coarse, heavy robe of rust and grey weave, with drawstrings on neck and sleeve. He balanced his head carefully on his neck, and turned it precisely, and there was a thin line of white round his mouth. The left side of his face was still distorted, a florid map of scabs and two-day bruises; the movement of his left eye shifted a sluggish lid.

He watched in silence as the room filled. Tion circled the

333

table and lifted a mug left beside him, glanced into it. D'Vandras said, 'In a while.' Tion sighed; D'Vandras glanced at him, moving only his eyes.

Daisainia said, 'Illuan. Tell him what you told us.'

D'Vandras' eyes shifted to Lian. He adjusted his head to follow. 'I think I already did,' he said. 'Though I cannot rightly remember. They,' he gestured, 'tell me I broke your communications device. I did not know I had done that. But I did tell you, didn't I, that the history which Linn and others nearly obliterated was kept by a few of the D'Vandras.'

'I am asking you,' Daisainia said, 'to confirm what D'Vandras says. The razing of Burdania was the doing of *your* people, not mine, not even Linn Travassa.'

'An accident,' Lian said, weakly. The room seemed darker. Or maybe it was simply that he was being pushed inside himself by the pressure of their emotion. 'And five – generations—'

'But this, too,' she said, grit in her voice, 'you would not tell me.'

He drew a deep breath. Made himself pay attention to its penetration of airways and airsacs. Made himself envision it lighting up the blood, illuminating the shabby chambers of his brain. Pity himself he might, as likely to be left behind while colonists and Burdanians went on together. But they had none of them set out yet. He was obliged to do whatever he could to make that possible. That was the obligation he had been evading, in his misery.

He said, 'Daisainia I – did not know how – to tell. But I am – I am glad you – know. I am glad – *I* do not have to – tell you.'

That checked her; she jerked her head minutely, and looked sharply at him. His momentary pleasure was overlain as he saw the full sight of him evoked associations. Whatever she thought of was personal, and caused pain. The fires the night before: her offer, her hopes. Unthinking, he said, 'Daisainia—'

And felt Zharlinn stiffen; felt him so strongly he nearly *heard* muscles rasp and joints click. 'I don't believe it!' Lian perceived that he did not so much disbelieve as *wish* to disbelieve. And that alongside the wish was an impulse to believe, and reject, and dismay at that impulse. Rathla Zharlinn had not had *kinder'el'ein* to teach him the futility of jealousy. 'I do not think it is possible,' Zharlinn said.

'It is – in our records. I can – show you.'

'No. You explain,' Daisainia said.

She was pitiless, blind to any appeal. He thought of the records he had compiled, to do the telling for him, and quailed. 'They were – chaos drives. They – interacted – shifted the – physical laws. Made things – random. Just for an instant—'

'No, *How*. In your well-ordered, cooperative, participative society.' She placed the words in quotes, and made her tone sting. He flushed slightly, but could not begrudge her that small revenge.

'A – failure,' Lian said. He told them about the testament of Islain Nors. About the debates, the one lost and the one won. He trudged through the telling, as though by endurance alone he might attain a different ending. Make black white, as Thovalt seemed able to do. Except for this one thing, which resisted inversion, even by the most skilled orators. But they all listened to him. Forced on by their silence, he grew fuller, if not more fluent, in the telling. He forgot his own incapacity, except as a fetter to be struggled against, and he tried to make them understand. Dragged deep within himself by the effort of retrieving and ordering words, he lost all sense of their reactions. It disorientated him.

When he stopped speaking, he found that Fioral was crying, making muffled snuffling sounds. Tion put his near arm around her shoulders, and stroked her hair with the other hand. She clung to him, whispering, 'All those poor people who'd never know it would be all right.' Her elders' eyes glanced uneasily off each other. Tion's sheltering arm tightened, but nobody spoke.

Daisainia had set both hands rigidly upon the table, and was resting her weight upon them, listening with lowered head. Nobody said anything. They left the first question to her. She seemed to take a very long time to realize it. Stiffly, she brought up a drawn face. 'Is that . . . all, at last, D'Halldt?'

'It does not matter,' Kylara D'Suran said. Lamplight glared from her copper ornaments. 'That was then, this is now, and we need their knowledge *now*.'

'They brought us to this,' Tor said.

'Does that change the need?' said Kylara.

Daisainia's dark, heavy eyes stayed on Lian. 'Yet for all those years, you did not come back. You did not come to see how we were.'

'We thought Burdania – was destroyed.'

'Burdania was,' Illuan said, hoarsely. 'The day you left. What you do today will not change the past.'

'I – know that.'

'But they, I fear, do not,' D'Vandras said. 'And theirs is the stronger voice.'

Zharlinn said to Daisainia, 'What do we do?'

Daisainia pushed herself upright. She looked balanced on a fine, fine edge, physically, emotionally. Her voice was flat. 'Your people destroyed Burdania, yet you accuse us of our losses. What kind of justice will we have from you?'

'Do – you need – justice?' Lian said, tentatively. 'You have – your own.'

'We need knowledge,' Kylara said. Her voice was raw with hunger. 'Illuan, you are a living example.'

'Yes,' D'Vandras said. 'Ironic,' he added, to Lian, 'that you and yours could spare me what they could not spare you.'

'If we do not have their help,' Kylara said, 'Tion could be blind in a year. Arkadin,' the older woman tilted her head, with the gesture ordering her to say it, 'will be dead. *You* might not survive childbirth – *if* you ever conceive.'

'Knowledge,' Illuan said. He tasted the word as Lian would have tasted an unfamiliar berry, with concentration and trepidation, poised to spit.

'Yes,' Kylara said. '*Knowledge*. Knowledge of medical techniques, of construction and architecture, knowledge of building materials. Knowledge which can keep us warm in winter, and safe across the plains and seas, knowledge which can let us speak to each other through the air.'

'And what else do we get with that knowledge?' D'Vandras said. Lian could see that he was suffering. And he had at hand the mug Tion had offered him, pressed juice and painkiller. But he resisted it, and mustered cogent argument through pain. His conviction was daunting. 'The potential for destruction.'

'History'd repeat itself?' Arkadin put in bluntly. 'Not this. This is a once one. Need only t'look outside to think better. We'll find other things t'get wrong. Them and us. Meddlers, they are. Be telling us where t'plant, and how t'breed *faun* and where t'set foundations. Advice we'll get, not knowledge, if we're not standin' fast.' She stopped, breathing heavily.

'Knowing,' Lian spoke slowly, straining after a glancing illumination. 'Knowing *how* – Burdania was damaged does not – mean you – could do or – *did* with them.'

Daisainia grasped his meaning, and clarified it brutally. 'D'you equate ignorance with purity, D'Vandras? D'you think knowing how Burdania fell will make us part?'

Lian winced for D'Vandras, so challenged and exposed in his irrationality. But D'Vandras was more than equal: he drew himself upright, bracketed by forearms braced on the table. His eyes were like ice-glazed obsidian. 'Let me tell you a parable, *isk'dar*. About knowledge, and about Morain D'Vandras.' The name assured their silence. Daisainia's face tightened; the mask threatened. 'I knew Morain D'Vandras. She was my first cousin, daughter to my father's brother. She was also the lover of my youth.'

Lian felt the sting of everyone's startlement. Daisainia looked at Illuan with indrawn sight. Illuan stared past them, at the door and the open darkness beyond. 'In every generation five knew about the past. Five are proof against accident. I was chosen. She was not.'

He paused, gathering thoughts of long gestation. 'The choice was our elders'. They decided. I was no besotted boy!' he said, with a kindling passion which gave the lie. 'But I thought she should have been chosen: she was passionate about the past. *I* told her.' His skin was damp with stress and fatigue. But his voice was resolute. 'My elders did not trust her, I see that, not only because I know now what I know now, but because I know now what I knew then.

'Morain left *tayn* D'Vandras. She asked me to come, but I did not want an exile's life. I had been chosen, she had not. She lived on the plains and in the Sor. She began to excavate and study the ruins. It occupied her energies and grew into a true vocation. One,' Illuan D'Vandras said, with grey amusement,

337

'even my elders respected. She began to gather people around her who thought as she did. She might have marked the world peacefully, despite herself. Had she *been* less, perhaps. But had she known less, certainly.

'Knowledge,' Illuan D'Vandras said, 'creates aspiration and greed. Morain wished knowledge. She wished mastery of its control and shaping. I see her in your people,' he said to Lian. 'I see her,' he said to Kylara, 'in you.' Suddenly, his hand jerked sideways to the mug; he got it to his lips and gulped its contents in a breath. Tor stepped in and took it from his hand before he dropped it. He slumped forward across the table, visibly fighting nausea. Confession had taken the strength that argument could not touch. He lifted his head and squinted at Daisainia who was directly across from him. 'They have the advantage of my weakness.'

'I . . . have had such thoughts too, Illuan,' she said.

'Trust them,' he said. 'For us all.'

She lifted a stiff hand and gestured to Tion and to Tor. Between them they helped Illuan to his feet and down the short corridor to his bed. Fioral padded after, with a backward glance at Lian. When Tor and Tion came back, she stayed behind.

'What will you do?' Tor said to Daisainia.

'What is there to do?' Daisainia said. 'It was sixty-six years ago that Burdania fell. I do not envy D'Halldt's people their memories. Kylara says we need knowledge. That is so; we do. Illuan says, and you, no doubt, that we do not need their knowledge. That it is a danger to us. The practical danger seems remote. The moral danger, an abstraction, compared to what faces us now.' She scuffed at a smudge of dried mud on her cuff. 'I would . . . like,' she said, with difficulty, 'to believe that we can survive alone. That knowing what is possible we can rescue ourselves by our own efforts. They *offend* me.' She turned, with a sudden flare of spirit, to face Lian. He braced himself, but the flare died. 'But *this* offends me too.' Her gesture took in Tion, Arkadin. 'Our *need* offends me, but I cannot deny it.'

'Don't fret on account'a me. 'M an old woman who's had a good run.'

'Then you are lying,' Daisainia said, harshly. 'You want your

338

life as much as I want mine. Yours is breath and walking and weaving and,' a glint of amusement, 'sex, and mine is holding back the river and replanting the plain and . . . Mine is seeing Lltharran become a *place* again. I am proud of what I have done, myself, with nobody's permission and only my people's help. I have made Lltharran, I. Given time I could remake Burdania. Is that to be shameful?'

Nobody answered her. Lian knew they were waiting for him. He said, 'No, *isk'dar*. Not – shameful.'

Lara said from the door, '*Isk'dar*. Lian. You'd better come.'

There was quiet around the fires. They need only follow the direction of turned heads to find its centre. At the edge of the firelight, Thovalt stood. The small mirrors on his overall sparked orange. He wore a tight, bold, glittering smile. Someone pulled back on his hand, hiding from the firelight and eyes in the shadow of his body. Lian glimpsed a pale shaving of a face.

A tiny tow-haired figure flitted and bubbled through the gathering, pulling on hands and hugging knees. Crystolan D'Vandras.

Daisainia's face in the firelight showed stark fury. Thovalt answered it with one of his silent snarls. Then, expression gentling, he stepped back and deftly moved the shrinking Shivaun in front of him. He held her firmly by one arm, and with the other gently felt for, and drew aside the trailing black hair from the woman's downcast face. Her eyes were half closed; she was shivering slightly. 'I'd like to introduce you to someone,' he said. 'This is Shivaun D'Vandras. And that's her daughter, Crystolan. They live just a little way up the hill. But for all that, they are hardly less strangers than ourselves.'

Daisainia had slammed a mask over her fury. 'That is her choice,' she said.

'Is it? Have you asked her lately whether she wants to live like a ghost in her own community?'

Daisainia took a breath which, plainly, hurt. She was very, very angry. But she would remember and consider Shivaun's fragility far longer than Thovalt would. Having made her cause his own, he would neglect her.

'He interferes,' she said to Lian, in a low growl. 'She is not ready for this.'

Nor, Lian thought, nerves shrivelling at the rage, are you. Her fury was quite disproportionate. Had Shivaun D'Vandras, Morain's daughter, been there at Morain's last meal? Had she witnessed the onset of symptoms, the realization, the futile purging . . . and listened to Daisainia's precise accounting of what she had done?

Perhaps in killing the mother, Daisainia had destroyed the daughter. And her protective rage was her only means of reparation.

Thovalt said to Shivaun, 'Come, you have every right to be here.' Shivaun looked at Daisainia; the *isk'dar* said, tightly, 'You do. If you wish it.'

Lian blessed Daisainia's protectiveness. She would not loose her fury with Shivaun there. For furious she was. It was her authority Thovalt challenged, her past and crimes he flaunted before them. If the peace would hold . . . If he could only get to her and explain. Explain that Thovalt mocked those half a galaxy away who had judged him, not they, for judging Shivaun. He mocked those in his own mind.

'Thovalt.' Lors' voice. For a moment Lian could not see the medic, then he saw the white hair in the shadows. Lors wove out of the crowd until he was close enough to address Thovalt unheard by any. He said several sentences in a low, adamant voice. And Lian, knowing Lors was the last person who should confront Thovalt now, in desperation caught Daisainia's sleeve. She jerked her arm free, unheeding; he did not think she knew who was there. He caught at her again. 'Daisainia – this does not – have to do – with you.'

She turned her head, her expression hard. He said, urgently, 'Thovalt – the colony medics – treated him. He felt – violated. He is – thinking of that – only. Not—'

Thovalt said, to Lors, 'Mad for the ease and convenience of others.'

Daisainia's head snapped round. 'Not you,' he said, to her profile. '*Us.* Lors was – his lover. Lors is a medic. Lors betrayed him. Nothing – to do—'

Across the firelight, Thovalt heard. Maybe not all, but

enough. His eyes locked with Lian, gone dark and bitter. Lian realized his mistake. He had thought too much of Daisainia, and not enough of Thovalt. He should not have told Daisainia what he had. He saw in Thovalt's face the gathering of retribution. A retribution which, though directed against Lian, would take in them all. Because Thovalt knew that Lian loved Daisainia.

Lian started forward. Thovalt moved to meet him, a shadow behind the fire. Leaving Shivaun, who shrank from Lors' touch.

He said, 'No, we are not so unalike, she and I. We have both been mad for the ease and convenience of others.'

'Thovalt,' Lors said, 'for pity's sake . . .'

Thovalt cast a glittering glance around the silent, gathered Burdanians. 'For the keeping of their secrets. For the bearing of their guilt. We thought you were the innocents. We thought you were the wounded ones. But you are not.'

Arkadin Nors said, 'Y'r illusions are y'r own matter, not ours.'

He ignored her. 'You have all wielded poison. You have fed Shivaun D'Vandras poison for years, the poison of your guilt. The poison of your act, and your collusion.'

Tion D'Suran said, tightly, 'Then you know nothing about it.'

'About what?' Thovalt demanded maliciously.

Tion's expression wavered in the firelight. He looked at the trembling Shivaun. Thovalt strode to him; the people between him and Thovalt fell away. Thovalt braced a hand beneath Tion's jaw, though Tion was already looking at him. 'Say it,' Thovalt advised.

Kylara said, 'Get your hands off him.'

Thovalt said, 'Then you say it.' Around the fingertips, Tion's skin whitened with pressure. The medic did not flinch.

Kylara swore at Thovalt. Thovalt snatched his hand away from Tion's jaw, as though he feared infestation. He paced the inner circle, demanding of them one by one, 'Say it.' Nobody obliged. Alystra caught at his arm; he swung away. When he stopped, he was facing Lian.

'Morain D'Vandras,' Thovalt said. He raised his voice.

'Morain D'Vandras. Morain D'Vandras. That is whom we are talking about, Morain D'Vandras.'

Shivaun D'Vandras screamed. A short, high cry, like one of pain. Then a longer, wilder ululation. She fisted her hands over her ears. Within the crowd, Crystolan stopped her flitting and looked back at her mother. Her merriment died; her vivid little face became expressionless. She stood stiffly and without moving, gripping Lara's trouser-leg in both small hands. Rathla Zharlinn bent and detached her, with difficulty, and lifted her. She did not soften against him; she resisted the hand on her head. She sat stiffly in his arms, watching Shivaun.

Shivaun's screams yielded to sobbing. There was a harsh, voluptuous quality to it, and it rose in volume and pitch when Tion tried to speak to her. Between them, Tion and Vylan guided her away. In Zharlinn's arms, Crystolan sagged against him. She pushed her fingers into her mouth and began to suck strongly. Zharlinn rubbed her back.

Then Daisainia spoke. 'We are not players in your dramas.' Lian looked round for her: she had moved into the clear space around Thovalt; she, Lian and Thovalt now stood at the points of a triangle. She stood with her feet set wide apart on the rugged ground, her hands thrust into her pockets. Firelight lapped up the side of her body, against her throat and her implacable face. She looked as she had looked when he first saw her, before he and his people had come to divide her against herself.

She said, 'Your forebears ruined Burdania. You say you have come back to make it right. You have not. You have come back to obliterate what they did. You cannot obliterate the past. You will not obliterate us.' She drew a deep breath. He felt her vibrate with the loosing of the anger she had contained so long. It came out in a muted roar, '*Get off my world.*'

'You cannot do this,' Alystra said. Lian saw her indecision as she measured the clear space around Daisainia. To respect or to defy; to trespass or not to trespass. She would define her stance, question or challenge, by that choice. He hoped that she would stay still.

Lors had a hard grip on Thovalt's arm, and was whispering to him in a voice harsh with threat. Lian wanted to go to them:

Lors never knew when to let be. Lian had seen Thovalt's brittle aggression shatter when Shivaun screamed. Thovalt saw Shivaun helpless in her madness; Lian saw, not helplessness, but the power to demand protection. His deeper sympathy went to those who did not demand protection, or could not elicit it. To Crystolan, Daisainia, even Thovalt himself. He caught Lors' eye at last, and handsigned, urgently, *Leave it be.* Thovalt saw the gesture, and gave him a pale, ironic smile.

Alystra moved. Lian saw decision, and wilfulness, set hard upon her oval face. Unlike Thovalt, Alystra would never say that she had not meant what she did, no matter what came of it. Pride made her claim even the unforeseen outcomes. She set her small, neat foot deliberately upon the clearing, and came forward to confront Daisainia. But it was to the Burdanians she spoke.

'We can do so many things to help you, but most of all, we can *free* you. We can offer you knowledge, and autonomy, true participation in decision-making. Amongst us, *everyone* has a say.'

Not I, Lian thought, seized unawares by bitterness. He had never been granted a say, never attained the standard of expression by which he would be judged adult, worthy. Silence was his only language, and anybody could overbear that. He had to offer up his insight to others. And nobody, not Thovalt, not Daisainia, not Lors, used his insights as he would himself have used them.

Alystra said, 'Amongst us, no one person decides. We debate, we vote. He have security against extremists.'

Daisainia snapped a mirthless laugh. Alystra flushed deeply. 'That was a mistake,' she said. 'A terrible, terrible mistake.' She pivoted to face the others. '*Has* she told you? No? You have a right to know the truth.' Lian saw in despair that she could turn even their secret-keeping against Daisainia. He could not match that agility; he could not see how Daisainia could. And if Daisainia, outmatched, turned to other strategies . . . 'It is *our* shame that our ancestors played a part in bringing you to this. It was the stardrives of their ships which damaged Burdania. By accident, by a terrible accident. Please, before you make any decisions – and the decisions *are* yours to make – view our files.

343

We have recordings of things as they happened, by automatic camera. They have not been edited to reflect any bias or viewpoint. They are as objective as records can be. Please, view our records, decide for yourselves as individuals whether you can accept our help.'

She held out her hands, in a beautifully stylized humility. Daisainia glanced once at them, and in silence, turned her back.

The one thing which Lian had not expected, that she would make silence as eloquent as words.

Alystra looked at the *isk'dar*'s narrow, tense back, and then around at the Burdanians. 'I know,' she said gently, 'we have shaken the foundations of your world. That some of you feel you owe the Travassan a debt for the unity they imposed upon you. I will not remind you of their history; you have lived that, and I am only an outsider. I am asking you to take what you already have, take your strengths, and go on from there. This is for the future, yours and ours.'

Stones crunched under Rathla Zharlinn's heel as he stepped forward. In his arms, Crystolan gave a startled squeak. '*Without* her, is that your condition?' Lara grabbed his arm. 'Don't talk to her!' she said, and swung him round against his will. 'Close your ears.'

'Nobody will be turned away,' Alystra said, and was checked by the grinding of gravel under bootheels. Around the rim of the clearing, in twos and threes, Burdanians turned their backs. There was Lara, holding Rathla Zharlinn against his impulse to shout back at Alystra. Tor D'Vandras, pulling around a hesitant Valancy. Alystra was silent for only a breath, only for long enough to see how many had not turned. But that was long enough to interrupt the spell of her voice. She began to speak again, urging them to view the records, the impartial records, to see how it might be possible to live. She spoke with growing passion, and that same innocent arrogance. And, one by one, they turned away. Their last looks were always for Daisainia, who stood unmoving and masked. One by one they turned, from Alystra, from Andra, from Thovalt and Lors, and those nearest him from Lian himself. Lian was appalled at how he was reduced by the sight of those turned backs. There was

344

something brutal about it. He found himself wanting to catch them and plead with them that he was different, to deny his friends and his origins.

A few, a very few, did not turn: Kylara stood facing inwards, her fists clenched in silent fury. Zharlinn tried to make her; she slammed the edge of her hand on to his wrist. Vylan D'Caul squared shoulders and stance, and nodded once towards Lian. Arkadin Nors jammed a crutch into the ground. 'Stupidity,' she growled. 'Rank, stinking stupidity.'

Alystra's manicured hands hung limply at her sides. Daisainia pivoted abruptly. '*Go* now,' she said. 'Go back to your ship. Go back to your colony. There is no place for you here.'

TWENTY-SIX

TARIDWYN

In the golden hall, Thovalt said: 'I am going to tell you a story.'

Lian heard small, unsettled movements, suspended breathing. He was hardly breathing himself, for listening, sensing. Thovalt, on the dais, smiled. He wore the same black-starred suit he had worn then; he opened with the same words. He did not hide in shame from the memory of that last debate: he announced it. It was their chosen theme.

Thovalt clasped his hands behind his back, standing square in the middle of the dais. Behind him, centred on a frozen screen, was Burdania, a small white world on black. White ice, white clouds, pale, reflective seas. Thovalt told the story, as he had told it before. As he of the fifth generation might tell it to his son or daughter, of the sixth. His wording had changed: there was less bewilderment, more brittle knowledge.

Then he went on, 'Two years ago I debated Burdania. We lost. I will not go through our arguments again. I no longer believe them. We do not know. We cannot know. We cannot know whether Burdania lived or died. Maybe there were nodes; maybe there were survivors; maybe those adapted, and if not prospered, endured. But we do not know. What, in the absence of knowledge, do we do? How do we choose?

'Lian D'Halldt believes we do know, through the *kinder'el'ein*. But he is in a fortunate minority, those who understand, or think they understand, or believe or accept *kinder'el'ein* abilities. Lian D'Halldt says yes, we should go back.' He gave Lian a glittering smile. 'Or he would, if asked. His accounts of *en'vos'neen'el*, and Lorscar and Tarian D'Sal's investigations into the possibilities of *kinder'el'ein en'neen*; those are amongst the records. If you are amongst those who believe, then I envy you. Because I do not believe, and I will not believe until I see.

'Do you remember what I said last?' Thovalt said. His voice swung briefly higher. 'Do you?' Lian focused eyes and will on him, willing him to calm. Thovalt said, with strident challenge in his voice, 'We are not going to talk about Burdania. We know nothing about Burdania, about the lives they lead, the legacy they carry. We know nothing about whether Burdanians live or die. We are going to talk about this colony, about ourselves. We are going to talk about the lives we lead, the legacy we carry; we are going to talk about whether we ourselves will live or die. Listen now.' He stepped lightly to the edge of the dais and dropped down. His feet swung gently as he spoke, heels bouncing on the dais. He told them the history of the colony. The debate as to whether to go on. The debate as to whether to make landfall, and the landfall itself. He described the strange, hot, red-lit world they found, and the char-skinned beings who came out of the jungle to meet them. He quoted the message left by one of the three captains, on the night of his suicide. He quoted Islain Nors. He described the raising of the hangar, and the entombment of the third ship. He spoke the recorded words of the parents of the first child born to exile.

He called no records; he needed none. He *was* the record. Timbre, face and form were unmistakably those of Thovalt Aslinn. Yet the words, inflections and gestures were those of five generations of exiles, united within him, and speaking through him. Lian shivered. How nearly they had missed creating this. He might not have insisted upon his wordless insight; Thovalt might not have listened. Alystra might not have capitulated over excerpting the records. They might not have stumbled upon this ultimate simplicity of presentation, and the true gift of their unpredictable Proponent. Thovalt was made for art, not argument.

Lian tried to resist enchantment; he tried to attend to the texture of silence in the hall, watch quarter-profiles and lie of hands, posture of backs. He could not. During the recess when Thovalt asked, he had to say, shamefaced, 'I – listened to you.'

347

Even Thovalt's skin seemed lit, flushed with blood and energy. He smiled magnanimously; 'I suppose that is an answer.' He set his hands on Lian's shoulder and turned him to look up the curve of seating. 'Now, tell me what *you* see.'

Self-consciousness momentarily unfocused Lian's senses. People, that was what he saw, the Burdanians of the colony, in their formal hall attire. Temperament was effaced by the occasion: even the ones who favoured bright colours and self-adornment had dressed subduedly. He knew them all, by name and something of their nature. He looked from one to another, wondering what there was to see. They were speaking to each other, albeit quietly. Some were stroking touchplates, accessing data. He heard Alystra say, 'Thovalt—' and Thovalt, 'Hush! Lian's going to tell me how I'm doing.' He heard the little puff of breath through Alystra's nostrils: she did not believe in Lian's insight. But at that moment, he saw. His hand lifted unthinkingly to clutch at Thovalt's long fingers. 'Yes,' Thovalt whispered close to his ear. He felt the heat of Thovalt's flushed face against his hair.

They were talking, yes; they were not stricken silent, as they had been in the last debate. But they were not talking to colleagues, about facts, arguments and probabilities. They were talking to the parents who might have told them about Burdania, or the children they might have told. They were talking to the lovers and friends who might know how they felt, when the world tilted askew and never came right again.

The Burdanians left the hall in silence. They filed past Thovalt sitting on the edge of the dais like an abandoned puppet, spent, blank-faced. Filed past him without gesture or congratulation. Above the dais, the screen simply read: three hundred and forty-five.

No one had asked for the other figure. Lian thought someone should. It was unjust that the others' thoughts, their feelings, should be simply cancelled out. He saw those feelings in their faces as they passed Thovalt. Most did not look at him. They had been chosen for, and yet would be obliged to share what would be done. Thovalt would no doubt say that all those

348

who, through the years, had wished to return had been chosen for. He believed in that kind of equation.

For himself, Lian hoped no one would ever have cause to pass by him as they were passing by Thovalt. Even those who must have voted with Thovalt had faces immobile with shock; or hard, doubting respect; or contained betrayal and aversion. He hoped Thovalt was too insensitive to be aware of them, or would misinterpret it flatteringly; then he saw Varidian, his own grandfather, break step with Iryssan and turn to Thovalt, and say something. Thovalt's eyes widened; Lian saw the stilled points of light, like pins. Varidian turned away, and took Iryssan's arm, leaning a little upon her. Thovalt pulled himself upright and looked from one to another of the people passing him, rousing himself into bewilderment.

Lian had not intended to leave his place until they were all gone. This second dispensation for his attendance had been more grudging than the last; he did not want to draw attention to himself. But when Varidian paused, he stood, and when Thovalt began to look around, he started along the row to the chairs.

Lors was there before him. When Lian reached the floor, Lors was squared before Thovalt, forcing the sombre recession to detour around him. Thovalt's wide eyes were fixed on him. Lors offered him no opening. He said, 'I owe you an apology. I did not believe you could do this.'

Thovalt tried to glitter at him, but the glitter was dull. Alystra walked along the edge of the dais to stand at Thovalt's side, balancing neatly with one foot parallel to the edge. She had been watching him throughout, but had not chosen to approach before. She looked down at Thovalt's glossy head. 'It may not be over. There will almost certainly be a counter-proposal.'

Thovalt said, to Lors, 'He said, "What have you done to us?"'

Lors said, 'It was a true vote.'

Alystra said, 'The presentation was manipulative.'

'Anything else,' Lors said, 'would have been a lie to our experience.'

'There will be a challenge,' Alystra said.

349

'I think not,' said Tarian, who had come up behind Lors, hand on Danas' shoulder. 'I think that it will, quite simply, hurt too much to discuss Burdania in these terms, in this *language* again . . . and none other will ever again suffice.' He said, 'Lors, the mission will still need your speciality.'

With his noiseless jungle step, Lian backed and left them. Thovalt was watching Alystra's carefully placed foot with newborn mischief. Danas saw Lian withdraw; she half raised a hand, drew breath, and then lowered the hand, released the breath, with a wistful, dismissive smile. She wished it were otherwise, but she concurred with his understanding: he had no place.

He decided he would sit for a while in the bay beneath the lagoon. He felt as though he were staring through the canopy at the midday sun: his mind was all scattered bright points and moving shadows. The glory of what they had done. The script they had created; the accomplishment of the player. The moment of *seeing* people turning to their intimates. And the fear. He had heard the snap of time uncoupling, future disconnecting from past. He had not been alone. He had seen healthy, able people moving as *he* used to move, so as not to disturb a precarious balance. They were coming to know what they had chosen. He was frightened for them. He was frightened for himself. Without proof, without reason, he believed that there was life on Burdania, but what life; would they think what they found *worth* what they had done? Such thoughts made him no fit company for *kinder'el'ein*. He wanted to sit with the moving shadows of the fish mottling lap and floor, and listen for the tiny rasp of small mouths on glass. When he could hear that, he would be peaceful again.

But someone was there before him. He did not immediately recognize the sound, not with his mind. His skin knew it. A contraction shivered up his spine and over his scalp; he felt his temples tighten. Between recognition by skin and mind, he had drawn level with the mouth of the bay. Two people sat on the bench. He could see only legs, feet and hands. Four hands twined and knotted in each other, two with dark skin, two fair. He stooped, and realized only belatedly what had prompted him to such familiarity: he knew those colours. But his

350

grandparents did not see him. Above their locked hands, their heads were bent together, foreheads pressing against each other. Varidian was the one who had made the sound, the sob; his face was contorted with the effort to contain others. Iryssan's tears ran silently down her silvery, immobile face. Blue fish-shadows glided unseen across their hair, their hands, the floor around their feet.

Telien found him at dusk, sitting on a rotting log, feet trailing in mud. He had let his feet take him where they would, and they had taken him downriver, past the settlement, to where the river turned briefly to swamp and shallow pools. He watched the shiftings and squirmings of the mud; the little mud-skimmers and mud-jumpers; the bright-winged beetles and moths settling upon the surface. Insects lifted and settled in clouds, in ribbons. Beetles bumbled stoically along the edges of his overalls. He liked their creeping trust, their indifference to his alienness and his thoughts.

Telien lowered *kin* bulk carefully on to the mossy, crumbling trunk of the log, and sketched a caress on his temples. 'We know,' *kin* said.

He wanted to ask whether what he had seen, what he perceived, was true. He wanted to ask if they had, after all, done the right thing. The first question would be an imposition; the second, unanswerable. He said, 'It does not – feel – as I thought – it would.'

'What will happen now?'

Lian thought the wording odd. To a *kindereen* everything had essence of life, and having essence of life, intent. Even the winds had personality, the rain spirit. Nothing happened without an agency. The passive voice was not part of *kinder'el'ein* grammar.

He said, 'They must – adapt the ship. Only – a few – people will go.'

'And you?' Telien said; and Lian understood the wording. Telien had offered him a blankness, to fill in as he would. He said, apologetically, 'They will need – specialists.'

'They will need courage, *i'vad'neer.*'

Dark hands intertwined with light; tears tracking down

translucent skin. 'I – know,' Lian said, on a dying breath, and let himself slump forward.

'There is life on Burdania. Whether it will suit Burdanians,' Telien said, with a hint of ordinary tartness, 'is another matter.'

'But – Burdanians. Like us.'

Telien's minimal facial muscles shifted minutely in a frown. 'They burn warmer,' *kin* said, after long thought. 'Your people are a white fire; theirs is redder. Fire, light; it does not translate.' But Lian had a sudden, indistinct vision of Burdanians lit by the clear, red sunset of the coast. 'People,' he said. 'Burdanians. Like us.' He did not know he had feared otherwise until that moment.

'Strangers,' Telien said, unsettlingly. 'Unlike you.' Lian twisted to look at *kin* more squarely. Telien regarded him steadily, unblinkingly, with *kin* great, slitted eyes. 'Strangers,' *kin* repeated. 'Like us. You are good with strangers. They are not.'

'You think – I should ask to go.' He gripped his hands, one in the other. 'Teli, I would – if I thought – but I am not – adult. I am not – skilled. I am only – me.'

There was a silence. Then Telien let out a slow breath. Lian felt fleetingly betrayed, but Telien, though loving, was always truthful. 'I am glad they will take the ship. That metal . . . sings of death and grief.'

'But you never said!'

'No; but we will be braver now.' *Kin* stroked his face with a firm, warm thumb.

'Staying – will not seem – so bad. I have – work. Making it easier between – Burdanians and *kinder'el'ein*.'

And maybe, maybe now, Vaelren would come back.

'When will the ship leave?'

Another unexpected question. Telien, like most of *kin* long-lived race, was usually sparing of 'when'.

'Three or – four years yet. The little ship must be – built, the voyage – planned. Being very careful with the drive. More – mathematics needs – doing.'

'Will you visit Thaorinn, now?'

Taken again by surprise, Lian caught at Telien's sleeve, but remembered himself in time and let the coarse fabric slide between his fingertips. He suspected that Telien was arranging to spare him the Burdanian's immediate enthusiasm, ambivalence and turmoil. He baulked at the thought: he had had a part, unmeasured but true. He had a responsibility, more because he seemed able to see what the others did not. Suppose there were a counterproposal, suppose Thovalt's iridescent euphoria proved too fragile, suppose he panicked at what he had brought about . . . Then Lian remembered Danas' hand lifting and lowering, and her small, accepting smile at his departure. Thovalt had the others around him; they knew what he was, and what he could do. They were his, and he theirs, and Lian they had let go without notice or question. That was a hurt to equal the interview beside the stone pool. He thought of the *meer* drawing back fastidiously from his emotion, his father drawing back, ambivalently, from his disability, his failure. But he had *not* failed; *en'neen* had recognized him, and though him, Burdanians. Admittedly, he had gained very little understanding, as Thaorinn defined understanding. But he had gained something *he* valued: inclusion, and a precarious love.

He said, testing, 'I – would like – Thaorinn to – think better of me.'

'He does,' Telien said.

Lian parted the moss between them with his fingers, watching grubs and insects wriggle into the light. He did not look at Telien. Telien would know his pleasure. It was himself he thought to distract. The hope seemed too great and brittle. 'Will you – look after Thovalt? If – anything happens. If – they counterpropose. If – anything changes—' He stopped, unable to say what he thought, or feared. He did not want to recognize his importunity. He did not want to coerce himself into staying. If the Burdanians could make even this precarious peace with the memory of Burdania, perhaps he could make peace with Thaorinn, with the memory of his accident.

'Go,' said Telien, for him.

TWENTY-SEVEN

BURDANIA

The interior lights of the shuttle were acidic to Lian's eye. He stood with his back against the door. Lors, uncharacteristically, paced the length of it. Thovalt watched him with a bright, sulky eye, but did not quite dare to speak. Alystra had pulled down a chair and sat square and prim in it, wrestling with self-justification. Only Andra seemed relaxed. She said, 'I've sent a message to the parentship.' They looked at her. She returned the look, with narrowed eyes, daring them to choose the hostile night.

Alystra said, in a stifled, guilty voice, 'I cannot believe they would choose oppression.' Her fingertips flicked at collars, cuffs, hair, seeking reassurance of perfection.

'You tried to dictate terms,' Lors said.

'I *will not* accept I am wrong to champion the right of individuals to decide.'

'You *were* wrong,' Lors said, starkly. 'You put your idea of political purity above all other considerations. Government is not an objective in itself. It exists to provide a framework for other things. You are as arrogant and autocratic as Travassa herself. And she at least has a mitigating sense of the concrete.'

'She committed—'

'And how many deaths have you caused by setting yourself against her? How many do you think will die for lack of our teaching?' He sliced air with his hand. 'No. I will not indulge you. I am going down to my medical bay. I am going to *try* and decide what I can leave them that may prevent—'

'You have no—' Alystra said.

Lors overbore her. 'When were my person and art ever subordinated to yours? Ethics *demand* that I do this.'

'Your private conscience . . .'

Lors turned his back on her.

'Andra,' said Alystra. 'Stop him.'

Lors swung on Andra, grasping that, of them all, she *could*. She knew the ship's systems and databanks as no other did; certainly enough to lock his databases and equipment control files beyond his reach.

'You have no hold over my memory,' Lors rasped.

'You know that much?' Thovalt said.

Lian looked from one to another of them. Lors was breathing heavily, his skin mottled with anger. Then, quite suddenly, his colour drained away. His breathing quietened. 'All right,' he said. 'Do what you will. But I will still do what I can.' He stepped into the lift to the lower deck; the clear shell closed around him. Light welled up from beneath him. Shoulders deep in the floor, he turned at last to look up at them all, his underlit face a stranger's, his yellow eyes fathomless. Lors, who could never detach himself, had done so now. To commit himself elsewhere.

Lian saw a tremor pass through Thovalt. His fingers tightened on his chair.

'Andra,' Alystra said, sharply.

'What?' said the Archivist, hands folded before her. 'You know, what he said is right. There is very little to choose between you. Except that we are accustomed to the autocracy of hall protocol.'

Alystra looked as though she had been slapped. Andra said, 'So, no, I am not going to stop Lors. We can give them knowledge; it costs us nothing, and it is nothing to us whether they use it well, or abuse it. I, for one, never want to see this blighted world again.'

Even Alystra would not go that far. 'There is no reason we should not try again, elsewhere,' she said, with a note of pleading. 'Communications limit Travassa's influence, and the Islands are full of independent communities. We could be well established, well accepted, before we need have any contact with Lltharran. We do not need the equipment in the Centre.

355

Lors could spread his medical knowledge; he will have more students than he can manage, whatever he does. This need not be the end.' She turned a look of bright appeal on Thovalt, on Andra, and, belatedly, on Lian. Whatever she saw, or perhaps merely their silence, encouraged her to go on. 'We will have to do it soon. If we went and came back, word of us could have spread; we would be suspect. And the restorers are already working on radio, and optical fibres, and if in no other way than by showing it is possible, we will have helped them. If they see maps of the old networks . . . It will spread Travassa's influence well beyond Lltharran, and it could be a generation or more before we can reestablish . . .'

Lian saw that they were being persuaded. Out of compassion, or guilt, or an aversion to failure. Lors might see it as a solution, too. Lian rested his hand against the door behind him. It was finely balanced; it moved with only a gentle pressure. He remembered doing this on the first morning in Lltharran, when he had gone to persuade Lors to talk to the others about hiding from the settlers. Alystra was describing independence of the Islanders, the way they had held aloof from Lltharran and preserved the old knowledge longest. Lian slid his arm round the door and overrode the forecabin lights. Then he opened the door to the width of his shoulders, and stepped backwards into the shadows. Andra was saying something disdainful about a fish diet as Lian delicately closed the door.

She was there, in *caur* D'Suran. As were Tion, Rathla Zharlinn and Kylara. Kylara and the taller Zharlinn stood face to face. He jabbed a hand at her, blunting the blow on air. She, with an animal gesture, arched her back, flexed her neck, presenting breast and throat. Defying, goading. Tion stood behind them, Daisainia sat at the table. Her face was well lit by Tion's lamp; she watched extinguished and unstirred.

Quietly, Lian slid aside the door. Only Tion saw him come in. He made to step forward, made, perhaps, to give a warning. Then sighed, half smiled, and with a tiny hand movement, invited him in.

Kylara said, 'I *want* what they have. I will not be denied it. I

356

do not care who opposes me, or with what, because if you oppose me, you are criminal, and I despise you. You are *evil*.' She stopped, panting slightly.

Zharlinn said, '*Evil*. What *they* did is evil. What they are doing is evil—' Daisainia suddenly became aware of Lian, and turned her head. For an instant, before the mask slammed down, she showed him anger, grief, hopelessness, regret. She had taken full measure of what she had done in rejecting them. But that instant gave him hope, both in what he saw, and that he had seen it. Daisainia would never have granted Lors or Thovalt that insight. Whatever he had been party to, he still had a portion of her trust.

Zharlinn said, 'What are you doing here?'

Lian fervently wished him elsewhere. He was the worst audience to have, someone to whom Lian's intimate knowledge of Daisainia would be a personal offence. An offence, and cruel.

He said, quietly, 'Will you – let it – end this way?'

Her eyes flicked to Zharlinn. From that, he understood that she understood personal as well as political meaning. And that she would not forgive him for speaking of it. Her definition of cruelty was even more stringent than his, where Rathla Zharlinn was concerned.

'It is not I,' she said, tightly.

'There has – been wrong on – both sides.'

'That,' Zharlinn said, 'has been abundantly demonstrated.'

'Thovalt – should not have – spoken as he did.'

'Should he not?' Daisainia said. 'Perhaps 'tis best to have it said.'

'Is – it?' Lian said. He thought, then took the risk. 'I – begin to understand – Linn Travassa.' He saw her appreciate that, both his meaning and the allusion to her ancestry. 'Will you – let past – be past?'

'Past be past.' Zharlinn gestured towards the darkness beyond the door. 'You essentially accused us all of murdering Morain and driving Shivaun insane.'

Daisainia said, quietly, head lowered, 'Your people left this world, left it damaged and in great need, and stayed away for sixty-six years because you lacked the *courage* to look on what

357

you had done. You are outraged because we have put you out of our minds, and you are offended because we do not follow your forms, and you are condescending because we have done so *little. We have survived.* You have not survived with us.'

There was a throbbing silence. She continued in the same unyielding voice, 'Your ships destroyed us. What you did not understand, and what *I* did not understand until now, is that your ships also destroyed you in us. You are dead to us, D'Halldt. You are as dead to us as the ruins on the plain.'

Kylara said, 'You cannot do this!'

Daisainia reared from her seat to confront the Medics' Guildleader. Lian saw the fright in Tion's face. 'Can I not? I am *isk'dar*. I need no leave from you or from them to be that.'

'Dai—' Lian began. She half shouted, 'No!' Rejecting the name, and any intimacy implied.

'You have – *no right* to choose – for your people.'

'They chose for themselves.'

'I,' Kylara said, 'did not.' Lian hardly heard her.

'You could have – received us. You could have – made us welcome.'

'Planet killers and cowards, D'Halldt?' she said, with a dangerous, clear inflection.

The blood suddenly roared in his ears. He thought for a moment he was ill. Then he knew he was only angry. Was this what it felt like, such energy, such invulnerability? On the table was one of Tion's fine, barbarous instruments. He lifted it and dug the tip into the back of his hand. The skin parted with startling ease and little pain. Dark, coppery blood welled between its lips. He heard Tion gasp and murmur, 'Oh, Lian.' Daisainia was staring at him as though he had shapechanged before her eyes. He brandished his bleeding hand before her. 'We are not – aliens. We are – Burdanian. Burdania is – *home*. I am not – dead. I am living. This is – living blood in me. Burdanian blood.'

He could see shock in her eyes, shock and offence. For someone so adept at self-inflicted pain, his small cut outraged her. He saw that he had lost her. His hand itched and bled over his cuff. He did not have the conviction for grand gesture, or the stamina for righteous rage. Thovalt might have carried this off, but he was a lame-minded, ridiculous man. He shook the scalpel out of his hand and plastered his fingers over the cut and pleaded, with love and tattered hope: 'Do you think this would end it – you and I? The *caur'cali*, the mission. We will have – children. They will want – to know. What will you do – to your children? What will you do to your – memories? Will you tell yourself – we were evil when we were no more—Daisainia, we are no more than Burdanians.' His words washed across her like the sea over a stone. Like the stone, her aspect did not change. Unlike the sea, he did not have epochs to change it. Her eyes no longer drew him in; either she had withdrawn, or he had. His fingers were stuck together with blood, and he was beginning to feel nauseated.

But he had one last thing to say. His final condemnation in terms he knew she understood. 'When I – came I did not know – *isk'dar*. I had to learn its meaning. You – taught it to me.' He paused, and said, distinctly, 'I cannot call you *isk'dar* now.'

Outside, he stood bewildered and sick in the backwash of anger. When the anger abated, he felt only the cold of the wind from across the floodwaters. In barely a day, it had all turned to disaster and conflict. Daisainia against the colonists. Zharlinn against the colonists, and himself. Kylara D'Suran, Guild-leader and *cal*, against Daisainia. Himself, against Daisainia, learning to be afraid of someone he loved. Learning to be knowingly, calculatedly cruel to someone he loved. He held one hand in the other, not looking at the bloody smears on skin and cuff. Lors would be appalled.

If he had not delayed, if his courage had not failed him, and he had told Daisainia about the Leaving, and the colonists about Morain . . .

Would it have made any difference?

He could appreciate that Daisainia had chosen crushing guilt over the awareness of her own powerlessness. He had not understood why or how, until now. He could better bear to think that if *he* could have done better they would not have come to this. Better that than to think that it was the only way it could be. He could not believe that colony and Burdanians would be alien and enemies forever. But, despite what he had said to Daisainia, he did not at this moment care about children or grandchildren. He cared only for the people of here and now, the people he knew and loved, and was responsible to. Their enmity was tragedy too much for him.

He had to own that probably what he had done or not done had very little part in what had happened. Except to himself. He knew he had not done what he could, or might have done. He would have to do better hereafter. He had something to work for. He remembered a pattern of blue and green waves, a pattern of potential glimpsed. Arkadin.

He looked down towards the fire. He could not see it, but the light of it wove between the buildings, reflecting upon walls and half-falls. He could hear voices, subdued, determined voices. A drummer tried out rhythms and fragments of rhythm, trying to catch, or create, a mood. The changeable beat told Lian how unsettled they still were. He remembered all those turned backs. He could not, he realized. He simply could not go back amongst them.

He could go to *caur* Nors and wait in the workroom for Arkadin, if she were not there already. He would look at the weavings, and think about their kind of husbandry. If he could show Alystra and Andra how to view their competence . . . but he knew neither woman appreciated the practical accomplishments. They had always had their physical needs tended to, merely by asking the monitor. They did not see mastery in the practical, merely degeneration. They needed time, Lian despaired, time to learn . . .

He was halfway down the grassy slope above *caur* Nors when his transceiver shrilled in his pocket. He reached for it by reflex, but stopped, muscles locked, just as he touched it. If this was a demand that he come back, for a finalized decision . . .

Above the single section of dyke, a stand of three lanterns was trembling. A figure clung to the stand, reaching up to unhook one of the lanterns. Balancing precariously, it turned towards the ridge, and began to swing it in wide, shaky arcs. From the fire, the drumbeat checked briefly and became a fast, urgent roll, the drummer summoning all the sound possible from the light dance instrument. A moment later, from higher on the ridge, a larger, deeper drum took up the alarm.

The com shrilled again. The lantern flew out of its arc and the figure scrambled sideways along the dyke, four-footed and clumsy. Upon its heels, Lian saw the rough edge of the dyke melt away in a heave of black and silver. He saw the figure fall forward, extending in the air, and merge with the shadow of one of Illuan's crossdykes. An instant later, Lian heard the roar, and the cry. Appalled, he took a step towards the dyke. And stopped, transfixed at the sight of the black and silver watermass churning uphill to meet him.

The surge slammed against his legs. More by instinct than reason, he dropped into a half-crouch, and froze there, hands outspread and grasping at air. Water swirled around his shins. White foam streamed between his legs. Bright points of panic and vertigo danced in his vision. *Things* nudged and grabbed his legs. *Hands*, he thought: and thought his heart would implode in panic.

There was fresh blood in his mouth; he had bitten his inner lip.

He had never experienced anything so cold as to kill all sensation. He felt nothing from his feet but for a massive, bone-bred ache rising outwards and up. Unsteadily, he took a step forward. And stayed upright. He felt his terror begin to abate, and he was able to see and hear what was around him. Everything was transformed. Restless, dark water filled the cleft in the dyke. But where Lian stood the water was already becoming still, beginning to shine under the starlight. He could hardly grasp the speed of the change, from land to water, from surge to stillness. Already it was as though the water had always been there.

On the crossdyke, a mound, a boulder, lifted itself, and limb by limb became a stooping man. He began to creep along the dyke, away from the collapse, a slow, unsteady progress.

Beside the bridge, a pall of smoke lingered from a scattered and vanished fire. The water had reached as far as the second row of buildings; the first stood in water as deep as Lian himself was standing in, except . . . He looked for *caur* Nors, below him in its field behind the wall. He did not know it at first. It was shrunken. Its walls ended in water just below the windows, nearly waist height. For a moment he thought, he hoped, and then he saw that the hide shutters were faintly, motionlessly, backlit.

He looked back at the settlement, seeing lanterns winking between the buildings, and circling above and below. Hearing voices and the distant splashes of people wading in water. They seemed yet preoccupied with each other. He could not see anyone well enough to hail, and he could not trust his voice to carry . . . and if he went for help himself, by the time he came back . . .

The water fought his desperation. The faster he tried to move, the more it hampered him. When it reached his thighs, he pushed it back with his hands. His heart thundered in his ears. He fell once, but landed on his knees, up to his throat in water like an age of glaciers. It crushed the breath out of him, and his vision blackened. Something clawed at his face, and he beat it off in panic, and struggled to his feet. By the time his vision cleared, it was gone.

For the first time it entered his conscious mind that he could die, alone, unsteady on his feet, shocked by cold. He looked towards the main settlement, hardly a great distance. From here he could hear their voices, though not their words, and even a faint, surprisingly musical sound, the splashings they made as they moved through the water. They were clustering around the doorways of the flooded buildings, passing lanterns in, and furniture and possessions out. He could nearly see their faces. But between them lay a stretch of shivering darkness, and he had no light. If he called to them out of the night, if they heard, how could they see him?

Above the settlement, on the slope of the knoll, he saw a lantern descending like a slow star.

He knew it could not be she: she was in *caur* D'Suran, where he had left her with his accusation. With his curse and his cruelty. Nevertheless, the cry rose from his viscera.

'*Daisainia!*'

The nearest lights flickered. Then three lights peeled off, and moved towards him. Somebody shouted to him. He strained to catch their words, to offer them what they needed to know to find him.

Instead, from behind him he heard a bubbling sob.

As he had cried out, so, without conscious decision, he floundered towards that sound. When he met the wall of *caur* Nors, he used it to hold himself up and pull himself along, forcing his stiffened hands to hook into clefts in the stone. A tree lay across the door; he took the shivering to be twigs and clinging leaves breaking the water's surface, but its rhythm was wrong, the currents swirled slowly now, yet the shivering came in starts and flurries. And then from the midst of the shivering came a choking gasp. Lian hauled himself along the wall, floating as much as wading on sensationless feet. He saw small fingers breaking the water, clutching at air and bark. He saw the hump of a forehead, a cheek, a mouth unable to turn clear of the water. In the starlight, he saw the the face was a child's and the hair an orange which even the mud could not veil.

He dragged himself along the trunk, reaching for Fioral's hands. They caught and gripped, with such desperate strength she nearly pulled him off his feet and over the trunk. But even so she could not bring her face clear. Her forehead and cheek were like part of the water themselves as weakly they humped and sank; below the surface, all was opaque in the darkness. He realized that the trunk had her pinned; he freed his hands to drag upon it, his feet sliding, but could not move it. Fioral caught his sleeves. He looked through the doorway into a shadowed hall, deep in water. A light from one of the inner rooms laid an oblique and unseeing light across the waters, sufficient only to show their colour, and the way they filled in the volume. 'Arkadin!' Lian said, but his voice was little above a whisper.

Fioral let go his sleeves to claw at air. Her mouth came half clear; she sucked air and water, choked and sank, thrashing. Lian leaned over the trunk and found her head, and then deeper, feeling down neck and shoulders. One of her hands tangled in his hair. Already offbalance, he fell against the trunk. His face went under. His nose and sinuses and staring eyes seemed to flood with water. He saw a faint, brown murk. He thought ... I am drowning. Then his heel caught upon something and gave him the leverage to heave back, against her, pulling on her armpit and neck, heedless of any injury he might do.

It was not enough. She must have been able to keep her face clear for a time, to have struggled so long. But cold and terror had drawn her so taut that Lian simply could not raise her. He felt her breathe water under his hands. He felt a fleeting warmth pass his wrists as she choked it out again. Her fingertips scored his skin. He held her as her struggles weakened, and then ceased. He kept holding her, immobile with disbelief.

He did not hear the voices, nor see the lamplight splash around the corner. He turned his head mutely towards it as it fell on him. Somebody said, 'Lian—' and somebody else, 'Ah, no.' He looked down at Fioral in the water. Under the relic light the water was no longer opaque. The light showed her sunken profile, blurred with drifting brown, one eye open. Her hair, dark auburn, drifted across her cheek and curled around his wrist. One small hand in a green sleeve nudged his arm. Copper beads twinkled, dully.

A fourth person came around the corner, lantern held up. Her face, somehow, Lian could see. Daisainia. She said, in a low voice, 'All this darkness. I thought it was *you*.'

That made no sense. Lian whispered, 'Why weren't you sooner?'

Rathla Zharlinn waded forward, wiping at his face with muddy hands. 'Let's get her free.'

Lian said, to him, 'Why weren't you sooner?'

Vylan, who was holding the relic light, came round to his side, not looking at the drowned child. 'You can . . . let her go, Lian.'

'Why weren't you sooner?' Lian said. He raised his hand, the cut hand, but what he wanted to show was the marks Fioral had left, to show how hard she had fought for life.

Daisainia understood at once. She plunged her hand into the water beside his, felt Fioral's pulse, and then broke his grip, shouldering him back. 'Take the lights. Zharlinn, D'Alna, there must be stones holding this . . . D'Halldt, *stay clear*.' She pulled off her jacket and left it to drift or sink. Before anyone could object, she had taken a deep breath and disappeared beneath the cold, brown waters. Lian felt something strike his numbed feet in passing. Zharlinn had half shed his own jacket when Vylan laid a hand on his arm. 'One's enough.'

364

The crown of the tree had been shattered, leaving a jagged spar on the near end, a shadow beneath the water. Roots jutted out of the water at the far end, a filthy, ropy mass.

Daisainia's head broke water beside the roots. She hauled herself up by them, and stood breathing in great shudders for a moment before she pushed her hair back and started towards them. Beneath the mud her skin was translucent, bluish. 'Stones . . .' she gasped. 'This end. Other free. We must . . . push on the other . . . as a lever.'

'Her legs . . .' Zharlinn said.

'Lame perhaps; drowned surely,' Daisainia said. She forced her way back through the water. Her loose shirt made a ghostly, floating mantle around her waist. Lara was already pulling herself behind the trunk, tucking to brace her feet against it. With a glance at Fioral, Daisainia swung herself over, folding her small height into the narrowest space. She said, 'D'Halldt, stay clear,' and swept one arm sideways in his direction. Lian stumbled towards the corner, as Vylan and Zharlinn took their places, Vylan beside Lara and the taller Zharlinn taking a grip of the spar. Daisainia said, in a harsh, desperate voice, 'Get to the corner and wave that lantern, and hope we do not need help, for it will come too late . . . Ready, *now!*'

Lian watched her face as she dug both booted feet into the sunken trunk and strained, her expression ferocious, nearly possessed. The effort turned the translucent pallor of her skin a dark bronze. Lara and Vylan both gasped and released their load before either she or Zharlinn. He watched her eyes shift to Zharlinn and lock with his, each defying the other to break.

Lara gasped, 'Lian, the light. *We need help,*' before she sucked a breath and renewed her effort.

Lian groped his way along the side of the house, and, balancing himself against the wall, lifted the lamp in a dripping hand and . . . heard an incoherent shout, and the sound of slow, drowned movement. He swung the lamp round and in the wheeling light saw the trunk moving away, saw Rathla Zharlinn lose his balance and fall sidelong into the murky water, and Lara and Vylan slide into the widening gap between trunk and wall, and right themselves. Unyielding, Daisainia forced the opening wider, head braced back against the wall. A little blood

365

trailed from her nose. For a moment the Burdanians stared at her, and then Vylan said, '*Isk'dar*, enough.'

She looked at him as from a very great distance. Then she stepped down into the water, turned, and brought Fioral to the surface. Vylan made a soft, anguished sound as the child's face broke the water. Her eyes were fixed, shocked wide. Lara reached around to help Daisainia with the dead weight. Daisainia said, quietly, 'Quickly now, if there is to be any hope.'

Lian leaned his face against the cold stone of *caur* Nors. He heard them start towards him. Zharlinn said suddenly, 'Arkadin.'

Daisainia said, 'I *told* her . . .' and stopped herself, in futile anguish. 'Do,' she said. 'But carefully.' Lian clung silently to the stone. Lara and Vylan's passage lapped gently at him, but he did not turn round. He knew what they carried.

Daisainia's hard hands pulled his from the stone. She took the lamp from his hands, said, 'Rathla . . .' The garish light arced away from him as she threw it to Zharlinn. Lian saw Zharlinn pluck the lamp out of the air, wave and disappear through the flooded doorway. Lian thought of the light falling upon Arkadin's face. He whispered, 'Arkadin. I should . . .' Daisainia applied her shoulder to his back, and started him walking around the corner and uphill, in the wake of Lara and Vylan. 'You have done enough,' she said.

He heard multiple meanings in that, and nearly wept. She said, as though in confirmation of his interpretation, 'I have been in dread all this night. I thought it was you and your people and what they had brought. I did not see *this*. I did not.'

'Daisainia—'

'I do not want your kindness,' she said harshly. She put an arm around his waist and dragged him along with her, so that he was silenced by the effort of keeping his balance.

On the wet grass just above the water, the Islanders had laid Fioral down and were forcing brown water from her lungs. As Daisainia pulled Lian through ankle-deep water, they rolled her over, and began to apply resuscitation, Vylan compressing her heart, Lara breathing into her lungs. Her open eyes were muddy, and full of wet strands of hair. She stared through them, innocent, betrayed. Daisainia stood a moment then said,

366

'Zharlinn should not work alone,' and turned and waded back into the water, lanternless. Lian alone saw her go.

He heard running footsteps and looked up at lanterns and several people. Foremost amongst the arrivals was Tion, who carried a relic light in a net bag. He fumbled up the intensity, and in the fierce illumination looked into the streaked, staring eyes of his little sister. He made no sound. Kylara stepped from behind him and let out a high scream of anguish, and anger. Tion dropped to his knees beside Fioral's head. Lara looked up. Tion said, 'Don't stop.'

Kylara said, in a high voice, 'Look at her eyes.'

'Don't stop.'

Vylan said, very gently, 'It's too late.'

'Not for me.'

The voice was Lors', but one Lian had never heard Lors use. There was something absolute in it, unarguable. The Burdanians looked up at him, Kylara with an angry threat in her eyes, Tion imploringly, Lara with scepticism and Vylan with concern. None of it moved Lors. He said to Vylan, 'Keep on; I need circulation,' and to Tion, 'Hold her head.' He placed an injector precisely over Fioral's fine neck artery, and injected the contents in a sustained stream. Whatever it was, it was a massive dose. That done, Lors pulled out a scanner, and touched it to the probe points. He said to Vylan, 'You can stop now . . .'

'Stop,' protested Tion, hands tangling in his sister's soaked hair.

'. . . and we must take her to the shuttle,' Lors said, getting up as though Tion had not spoken. The Burdanians did not move. Lors said, impatiently, 'I've managed to interrupt all the major destructive sequelae to oxygen deprivation, uncontrolled ion leakage, neurotransmitter release . . . I have essentially imposed a pause in her dying, but I have also, in effect, finished killing her, because all those processes are involved in life.' There was a murmur amongst the listeners. Lors said, with authority, 'What I must do now, and I need the equipment in the shuttle to do it, is to restore her metabolism and brain function by reaerating her, and then neutralizing the substances I injected.' Vylan slid his hands beneath Fioral and

367

lifted her. Jerkily, Tion reached up and closed the green, staring eyes.

Kylara said, grimly, 'What do we do to help?'

'Nothing,' Lors said.

'There must be—'

'There is nothing.' Lors started uphill. Vylan followed him, Fioral's limp, dripping hand swaying against his thigh. Lors said, 'I will need to monitor her second by second; the outputs are extremely complicated; I will need Andra's help and I cannot take the time to explain . . .'

'Lors!' Tion said.

Lors turned. At that moment Lian heard the sound of wading feet. Rathla Zharlinn with Daisainia at his side, trudging out of the water. Over Zharlinn's shoulder, he carried . . .

Lors' face registered the same anguish and fury as Kylara's had, at the brutality and injustice and unarguability of it all. He said, 'I can't . . . I can't. Not both.' Rathla stretched Arkadin out on the grass. Daisainia set the lantern down at her head. Lian saw the flickering light on thin, closed eyelids before Daisainia gripped her jaw, and bent to set her mouth to the other woman's. Her exhalations were steady as a machine's, while Zharlinn's breathing was broken with weeping. But he straddled Arkadin and began the heart compression. Tion and Kylara both watched Lors, who stared at the drowned woman and her rescuers in open torment. Kylara snatched at his arm; Tion caught her. 'We have no right,' he whispered, in a raw voice.

Lors said, 'I've never had to choose. Help me, Lian.'

Me? Lian thought. He looked down at Arkadin. He felt Fioral's hands clutching his. He saw Arkadin leaning against her loom, Fioral dancing at the gather, white flowers in her hair. He knew what Lors had started to do with Fioral; he knew it had been done on him after his fall. Knew that it was an intricate, demanding procedure. And Lors had to do it alone, with only Andra and field equipment.

Tion held Kylara. 'Let's go to the Guildhouse and get the equipment we borrowed. He may need it.'

She gave Lors one last unforgiving, imploring look and ran

along the shallows, splashing silvery water behind her. Tion started after her, and then turned back to watch.

Lors crouched beside Arkadin and touched the scanner to her temples, pushed Daisainia's head aside and turned Arkadin's head to scan its back. Lian said, so quietly he was not sure Lors would hear him, and not sure if he should, 'She – spoke to you – of this. It would be – her choice.' Slowly, heavily, Lors stood. Daisainia and Zharlinn looked up. Read his face. 'She was under too long,' Lors said. 'And she was already ill. If I were not alone, if . . .'

Daisainia stood up, in one powerful motion, although she looked as chilled and shocked and nearly drowned as Arkadin. 'No ifs, D'Sal. This is Burdania.' She reached across Arkadin's body and physically turned him uphill, taking the choice upon herself. 'Your work is with Fioral. *Go*. D'Halldt, D'Suran, take him.' She looked down at the woman lying at her feet. 'She is ours and we will see to her.'

Lors broke away from them and walked quickly towards the shuttle, not looking back. Zharlinn watched him out of sight, and then laid his head on Arkadin's unmoving chest and sobbed. Daisainia knelt, and began, with her fingers, to smooth Arkadin's face. Her fingertips left narrow smears of mud.

Tion said, quietly, 'Lian, let me look at your hand.' Fioral's fingers had reopened the cut; it was bleeding thickly through the wash of mud. Tion brought the lantern up to inspect it, spreading it lightly with his fingers. Fresh blood welled, nearly gold. 'This should be stitched.'

Daisainia suddenly pitched forward on both hands. She rocked, head swaying from side to side, making no sound. Tion put the lantern in Lian's hand, and crouched down beside her. '*Isk'dar*,' he said, 'there *was* nothing else you could have done.'

'I could have foreseen,' she said, in a sick voice. 'I should have foreseen.'

Tion pulled a cloth from his pocket and wiped the mud from Arkadin's face. Lian could see that he was trying to hold his composure. Eventually, he said, 'Is seeing it *once* not enough for anyone?'

Daisainia stayed huddled a moment longer, and then slowly, excruciatingly, got to her feet. She trudged towards the settlement without a backward glance at any of them. She moved as though her filthy, sodden clothing burdened her to collapse. She passed a group of people, led by Vylan and the seaman Ionor D'Alna, and carrying a great fold of canvas between them. She did not acknowledge them; she did not even see them. Tion drew Lian back as they spread the canvas beside Arkadin, drew him into the shallows, although neither of them noticed. They stood and watched as the Islanders and Zharlinn lifted her on to it and carried her away.

Tayn D'Suran was crowded with the soaked, shocked and injured. Kylara D'Suran was giving orders and instructions in a high, hard-edged voice. Toring was trying vainly to fade into the walls. Kylara said, 'Ah, Tion.' Tion ignored her. He sat Lian down at the table, collected a fibre-wrapped bundle from the understair store, and sat down beside Lian. He said, only, 'This will hurt, at first. Please stay still,' and laid about Lian's hand with a swab soaked in what felt like glacial acid, but which began, slowly, to numb the skin. There was a glassy intensity in Tion's gaze; Lian doubted he knew whom he was working on. Tion was in shock. Kylara reached the same conclusion; dismayed, she reached to stay Tion's hand as he lifted a small, viciously hooked needle. But her hand quivered, and Tion's was steady as stone. She snatched hers back. Someone behind her demanded why Lian should be treated first.

As Kylara started to reply, Illuan D'Vandras appeared in the mouth of the corridor. He had authority, even barefoot, stripped to the waist, and unsteady on his feet. He set a shoulder to the wall and issued orders in a cold, slurred voice. Kylara, he set to deciding who needed treatment. The shocked, and merely panicky, he dismissed. Toring, he sent to find Daisainia. Watching D'Vandras, Lian did not see Tion ready the needle over his hand. He felt it, though, like a spike driven through; jerked his hand back; yelped. Tion let go the needle in time to save him from torn skin. 'Hold *still*.' Illuan D'Vandras made his way to the table, lowered himself into the chair on Lian's other side, and pinned Lian's wrist to the table with his hard hand. Lian endured as Tion closed the cut with three tiny, meticulous stitches, reanointed it with numbing solution, and applied a bandage. Without looking at Lian, he said, 'Get out of these wet clothes, and find someone to take you in for the night.' He gathered together his instruments, got up, and went to look at a young man who was nursing a nauseatingly distorted wrist.

Illuan D'Vandras watched him go assessingly. Then he put Tion out of his mind, and turned to Lian. 'You were out there. How much of it went?' Lian merely looked at him. Illuan struck the table with the flat of his hand, and winced at the jolt. 'Dear life, man, we can't leave it fallen like that. The river's still rising.'

Falteringly, Lian described how the dyke had collapsed. He needed prompting, falling silent as the images rose before him. The figure, creeping along the dyke; the wedge of grey water churning uphill towards him. Illuan's questions were exigent: depth of water, width of the breach. Lian kept seeing Fioral's open green eyes, and the burdened sail with the water dripping through it.

He heard D'Vandras say, 'If you are not to lose Lltharran, you will have to close that breach.' He looked up at Daisainia, a Daisainia grey and defeated, as he had never seen her. Mud streaked her face; her hair was coated in it. She had pulled on a dry jacket over her soaked and muddied shirt. She sat down, in silence, and said to him, 'How?'

Illuan pulled a sheet of paper towards him and began to sketch. 'We bridge the dykes at either end of the breach with wooden platforms. Use them as mounts for our pulleys. Fill in from both ends. Even better, we use flotsam to make a framework. Enough trees and the like are coming down.'

'No,' said Daisainia. 'We evacuate. We take the bridge and boats across the river, to the high land. I will risk – no more.'

Illuan regarded with mingled irritation and unwilling pity. Before he could speak, the door opened with a cool draught of dawn, the paper fluttered, and an oversupple hand reached down to pluck it from beneath his fingers. Illuan jerked round, face twisting with the pain of the unreadied movement. Thovalt stood over him, bright hazel eyes scanning the sketch. He looked rested and clean, and to Lian's tired eyes, shimmering with energy. Illuan tried to retrieve the paper; Thovalt flicked it just out of reach. 'Ah, don't be like that. I'm told you're the resident expert, so, one pilot and general robotics operator, reporting for orders.' He slid lithely into a chair and spread both long hands on the table, paper between them. His fingertips plucked the edges as he spoke. 'Along with one shuttle, and sundry all-purpose repair rigs, adapted to free fall and gravity, and, as a bonus, water-sealed, though we'll have to retune the transmitter to take account of water and mud; a mere recreation; even Li could do it. And please,' Thovalt said, 'none of this tedious "We don't need you" and all that. I'm better at rational argument than any of you,' he inclined his head towards Illuan, 'except maybe you. And I'm better at irrational obstinacy than any of you,' he bowed towards Daisainia, 'except you. And neither of you is presently up to spec, and I assure you, *I* am. And, if nobody tells me what to do, I'll improvise. I'll do it my way.'

Something clattered on the table, falling from Daisainia's clenched hands. They looked at it: it was the blue metal ring. She said, to it: 'Linn Travassa made an *isk'dar*, because he desired – certain things. I can unmake one, because I have – because I— Because my—' Her voice dragged to silence. She sat unmoving, staring at the ring in mute pain. Her fingertips turned white on the edge of the table, holding fast to renunciation. Tion left his patient to come to her side. Kylara stood up where she was. Lian drew breath to remonstrate, but her next words silenced them. 'I cannot endure this darkness any more. I will not be the one to—' She pushed herself to her feet, and reached out blindly for the door. It took all her strength to open it. Lian heard her catch her breath like a sob; he snatched up the ring, and started to stand . . . and Illuan caught his wrist and bent it, forcing elbow, shoulder and body painfully back down. He pinned Lian until Daisainia was gone. Kylara closed the door behind her.

Thovalt moved to release Lian. Illuan anticipated him, lifting his hand from Lian's arm and holding out the hand, palm up. Lian stared stupidly at it. 'Give me the ring.' Lian hesitated, briefly, then laid the ring carefully in Illuan's hand, his senses coming to a single focus. Illuan knew it. 'I demanded that she be stoned,' he said, so quietly that perhaps only Lian heard. He looked up at Lian, facing him straight on, to let him know: 'I want to enjoy this.'

There was nothing of pleasure or satisfaction in his expression. Only the bitter knowledge that, whatever the punishment meted out to the living, the dead were gone forever. *Cal*, lawgiver, he added for himself the equation of justice and found, not a balance, but a summation of wrongs. Even for himself, Morain and Daisainia Travassa.

After a long moment of watching, Lian lifted the ring from Illuan's palm, not touching the skin. D'Vandras did not stop him. The warmth of her hand, the surprising warmth, was gone.

Lian thought: there is no one left to blame. No one to punish. No one to make suffer. Except ourselves, and each other.

He closed his hand on Daisainia's ring, and got up from the table.

TWENTY-EIGHT

TARIDWYN

Two Taridwyni years after he had left, Lian returned to the *kinder'vos*. He went the slow way, down the river, though Thovalt had offered to fly him, impatient with the time he would be gone. But Lian could not see that Thovalt or any of them needed him now. They were immersed in the design of the ship and the planning for the voyage.

His own lone journey took twenty-seven days, by raft, riverboat and jungle paths. It was exhausting travelling; he had never gone so far alone, and in the past two years had never gone far from the colony.

In the last days, he fell in with three adult *kinder'el'ein*, accompanying their widower *kindereen* parent to the *kinder-'vos*. They had never met a Burdanian in the flesh before, but they were courteous. He took his turn at the raft poles and steerage, and scouted for their foraging. The gathering itself he left to them.

On sunset of the twenty-seventh day, they reached the *kinder'vos*.

Sara waited just inside the main alley. Sara in robes of silver-grey, not much smaller than he remembered her, because he was not much taller. But she looked at him as though she did not recognize him; then she came forward and her smile was thin and weary. 'Lian,' she said, sombrely, and laid her head on his shoulder. He looked beyond her, but the corridor remained empty. He saw that the leaves lay heavy on it. His throat locked on the question.

Sara eased herself upright. She saw his face. 'You did not

know,' she said. She lifted the back of her small, cool hand to his face. 'I thought they might have told you, and that is why you are here. He did so want to see you.' He could say nothing. Her words had a falling tone, like a knell. The empty corridor.

Before, she would have tried to tease words out of him, or waited for a question; now, she paid no attention to his silence. She spoke according to her need, not his. 'He's had a series of infections, infestations. Mainly his lungs, and his intestines. He's lived out here so long, in the heat and the moisture; his immune system no longer reacts to alien parasites.' She gave him a tiny, kinked smile. 'He's flattered. Jahde and I treat him as best we can, but every one just weakens him for the next. He's not able to digest; he has difficulty breathing . . . One of these times, soon, or later, he's not going to be strong enough . . . to live, Lian.'

Telien knew, Lian thought. That is why *kin* sent me now.

'I won't try to make you understand as he has made me understand. Make him explain to you, his son.' He heard her hope, heard her say, make him explain, make him fail, make him change his mind.

He had never been in Thaorinn's cell, even as a small child. Sara's he knew, Thaorinn's was always curtained, a handsome, dark blue curtain, glinting with the silvery mesh of psi-shield. Sara said, 'Thaorinn, Lian's come.'

Thaorinn had always been gaunt, his skin always snug to the long bones of his face. Now it was taut over them, thin and transparent as an insect's wing, throwing nose and brows into fine definition. He was fully dressed and cauled, his wasted body hidden. The sleeping shelf was padded and cushioned with treated moss, stitched on to a backing of fabric; even the pillows at his back were so covered. That indulgence, more than the gauntness, marked his father's extremity.

He lifted his head, looked at Lian out of great, dark eyes. The breath he drew sucked and crackled in his chest. But he rolled his legs over the side of the platform, pushing down the robe as it rode up from fleshless ankles, and, with another crackling breath, stood. His hands moved in greeting like a dying sapling in the wind.

Lian stepped forward, touched his father's wrists with his

375

fingertips, slid them up his arms and around the bony shoulders. Thaorinn was still taller than he was. Ear against his father's shoulder, he heard the breath whistling in the infected lungs. He held the fragile husk as lightly as he could.

'So,' he heard Thaorinn murmur.

Lian felt himself begin to tremble. He drew back, with an irrational fear that he would cause his father to crumble away. Thaorinn lowered himself down on the platform.

'Water,' he said, to Lian, and gestured towards the stone basin. Sara's robes rustled. Thaorinn said, to Lian, 'Sara – would have me drink boiled – water. Revolting.'

His speech was hesitant and full of effort. Like, Lian noted remotely, Lian's own.

Sara said, 'I simply do not see why you should add more parasites to your system while you are yet so weak.'

'It is a – matter of how I choose to live,' Thaorinn said.

'More a matter of how you choose to die, you impossible man,' Sara said. From behind him Lian heard the slosh of a scoop in water, the rising tone of a cup filling. Sara swished past him to thrust an earthenware cup at Thaorinn. Thaorinn looked up at her, flecks of light swimming in his eyes. He held her hand against the base of the cup as he drank. 'Much better.' She set the cup down, and helped him to lie back. His closed eyes stood out like water-rounded pebbles. Sara stroked his face, watching it as though she was trying to memorize it. The sight evoked a multilayered pain: for them, and what they were losing; for himself, and what he was losing.

'So,' Thaorinn said, 'Burdania.'

'You – know.'

'*Kindereen* told me.' His tone was courteous, but disinterested. Lian's throat ached. He wanted to say, 'If you would wait, if you would live . . .' He knew it was not enough.

Thaorinn's eyes opened. 'Sara, would you leave us for a little while.'

With a last, light kiss, and a featherweight touch to Lian's arm, Sara did. The curtain shingled closed behind her.

'When you went away,' Thaorinn said, straightaway, 'I expected – nothing of you.'

Lian remembered that parting, Thaorinn walking away from

376

him and disappearing beneath the arch in the rain. He bent forward slightly, thinking he could not bear it if this final farewell were no different.

Thaorinn said, 'I was wrong. You have given me – something I never expected, something beyond price. You have given me a – place in *en'vos'neen'el*. When I die I shall be – gathered in amongst the *kindereen* and *kinder'el'ein*. I shall not be conscious, but I will – be present in their consciousness. That was – your accomplishment. Your gift. Lian, I – thank you for it.'

The knowledge that his father valued what he valued, the inclusion, was overborne by utter dismay. 'Do you – want to die?' he said like a child. 'Because you'll go to – *en'vos'neen'el*? Is that what I *have done*?'

Thaorinn eased himself up on one elbow. The effort made him cough, mucus thick in his throat; he spat yellow into a cloth and wiped his mouth. 'Come closer,' he said, hoarsely. 'Sit down.' When Lian sat, he let himself roll back. With small, tremulous motions he signed, *Of course I would like to live, because of you and because of Sara, and because there are still things I would like to learn and experience. But the jungle is taking this alien body into itself, as* en'vos'neen'el *will take this alien spirit. I have* lived, *and living is the essence of it, in this jungle for longer than you have been alive. I belong here. I want to stay here. And, Lian, it matters more to me that I stay in the jungle than I live on. For me, now, the colony would be a living death.*

'*Lors* would come – come here—'

Thaorinn looked pained. 'Lian,' he said, 'I let you leave. Now let me leave.'

'You let me leave with – your anger.'

Thaorinn folded his hands on his stomach and simply watched him, acknowledging that this was so. But as he had had no power to prevent Lian from leaving, so, his quiet look said, so Lian had no power to prevent him leaving.

He said, instead, 'I am glad you have come. There is much I have wanted to ask you.'

The Burdanians let Lian be for nearly seventy days. Then the shuttle came. Before the mist had settled, before the grasses

377

had stopped twitching, Lian was down on the flats. He recognized Thovalt, as the Burdanian swung down from the cockpit. White hair shone yellow as Lors slowly followed. Lian stood, breathing hard, feeling the last warm vapour settle on his skin, trying to find a welcome in himself for his friends. Three days before, they had carried Thaorinn D'Halldt into the jungle for the last time.

Thovalt would never notice a lack of welcome. 'Found you, at last.'

Lors, more perceptive, said quietly, 'Hello, Lian. We were worried that something had happened to you.'

'Something *has*,' Thovalt said. 'He's been repossessed.' He swept a supple hand the length of Lian, indicating heavy, stone-coloured robes, headdress, jungle pallor and folded hands. 'I thought you were Thaorinn himself, come to scold me. I suppose that's a delight I can anticipate.'

'No,' Lian said.

Both heard his tone. Thovalt reared back in mock offence. Lors said, uncertainly, 'We expected you back – days ago.'

'Thaorinn has died,' Lian said. He found, without having thought about it, that he had turned his back on them. That surprised him, the sense that they did not belong here, with his grief. He looked up the slope to the curved mossy walls of the *kinder'vos*. He heard them behind him, shifting; he did not want to listen to their voices. He said, to forestall them, 'We – gave him to – jungle three days ago.'

Lors said, 'Gave him to—'

Lian walked away across the sand. In his mind, he saw that haunted place in the jungle. The *kinder'el'ein* gave it no name, seldom spoke of it. There was no need to speak of the flesh and bone of those who had entered *en'neen'el*. The place was a morning's walk inland, away from the watercourse, a clearing in the jungle, planted with a lush, strangling moss which kept pods and seeds from rooting. Upon the moss, cleaned bones lay scattered, some grey, some faintly mossy, some stained teak with groundwater or old blood. There were a few high-domed *kinder'el'ein* skulls. Before they laid the newly dead out, the *kinder'el'ein* gathered and wrapped the old bones and bone fragments. They would be scattered anew when next they came, but still they did so, moving silently upon the moss. Sara went with them, a frail, tiny figure sheltered by their height and bulk, lifting long limb bones with trembling hands and bent head. Lian noticed she did not touch the skulls, or the scattered ribs. There was something terribly personal about those shapes. Lian could not; he tried to step forward, he tried to bend and reach, but he found suddenly that he did not trust his legs, or his hands. Although he had been with his father for most of either of their waking hours, when Thaorinn died, Lian had been dozing, leaning awkwardly against the curved stone wall. Thaorinn had gone away without Lian's noticing. Some part of Lian's mind still expected that they would simply carry their burden back and nurse him to wakefulness. Until he looked at the grey and brown bones, and knew that this was Thaorinn's true destination. He could not help to gather bones because at that moment, for him, his father died.

He walked obliquely shorewards, not wanting to lead them towards the *kinder'vos*. He found he had passed the *kinder'vos*, and was facing the long receding curve of the jungle, a smoky cliff in the midday sun. He let his eyes unfocus until all he saw was dark green below light green.

Lors said, behind him, 'I am . . . terribly sorry.'

'*Kinder'el'ein* tradition.' Lian said. 'Thaorinn chose.'

There was a silence. He turned slowly to face them, feeling the movement of the sandgrains underfoot. Thovalt was standing where he had left them, at the end of a long track of footprints. He looked irked and acutely uneasy. Lors was almost oppressively near and sympathetic.

Lian sought something appropriate to say. 'Come – when I can.'

Thovalt caught his words, and shouted back with sudden exuberance, 'Make it soon. We have a mission to prepare.'

Lors said, 'The hall has selected the nine who will go back to Burdania. Thovalt and I are going. So are you.' Lian stared at him in deep bewilderment. Through the past seventy days, Burdania had been mentioned only once, when he first arrived. From that moment on, he had been immersed in Thaorinn's needs and concerns. He had forgotten that he had another allegiance. He did not remember well enough even now to wonder why *he* should be chosen. Lors, plainly, thought that was what he was wondering. He said, 'You were selected because of your ... personal qualities. Your emotional stability. Your adaptability. And your liaison work with the *kinder'el'ein*. But what made us consider you – you were, I will admit, not an immediate choice – was the *kinder'el'ein* themselves. Eighteen or twenty adult *kinder'el'ein* came to the colony ... there's been nothing like it since landfall. Did you know they were going to do that?' Nothing in Lian's face would give him any answer; Lian was only just beginning to understand. 'They want you to go ... to come ... as *their* representative. And after we started to think about you, to think what you had managed to do towards our debate, and what you *were* ...' The wet-wood eyes searched Lian's face. Lors said, uncertainly, 'Lian, you *will* come ... ?'

TWENTY-NINE

BURDANIA

He found outside a land redefined. They were an island now, an island in an indigo ocean, under an indigo sky. The ocean's edge, ragged with grass and stones, was but a few steps from the Guildhouse garden wall. The shadows were textured with fine eddies, moving water snagged by the sunken land. Where the wind glanced upon it, the water streamed and burred. In the alleys between walls, it was lightly polished, nearly still. In the nearmost, a hanging lantern lit walls and water, yellow smudge of reflection gently rocking.

The buildings, the *caurim* and Guildhouses, rose fore-shortened and black before him. They evoked, in negative, the broken white walls of the ruins.

He could see people trudging between the buildings, dark except where they passed through pools of dangling light. They were still trying to salvage what they could, item by item. They worked in near silence, the only sound that of legs dragging through water, of murmuring voices. Even the river was quieter, sated.

He glimpsed droplets twinkling as they fell from a wrapped bundle a man carried from the water into a pool of relic light. He watched the man kneel at the water's edge and unfold a length of fine weaving; the lamplight showed blue and violet run together and fouled. The man stood, pulling the sodden cloth taut between himself and the lamp, casting a dense shadow over the lower half of his face.

The man was Kashar Nors, Arkadin's nephew. The sight

381

became another strut in the delicate architecture of Lian's resolve.

None of them looked askance at him when he asked them if they had seen Daisainia. Perhaps they did not recognize him. He was wearing Tion's drab clothes, which were broad for him, though he was slightly taller than the medic; his face was grimy, his hair cloyed and drying, and his hand was bandaged. And he heard the difference in his own voice. It had the sound of Burdania in it, something absolute.

They did not know where Daisainia had gone; so he took his leave, and walked on along the new waterline, asking whomever he met. Some recognized him, some did not; nobody challenged him. They had other things to think about. Presently, he found someone who had seen her go up to *caur'isk'dari*.

Caur'isk'dari felt hollowed of life. Lian leaned against the grey-painted railing, shaking, trying to recover his breath. The climb had been punishing for him in his chilled, exhausted state. He remembered the stillness in the Explorer's shrine. The stillness which came just before the ghosts crowded in, whispering their memories. Even when the hammering of his heart abated, and his breath no longer sucked in his throat, he could not hear anyone.

So he searched, making his quiet, listening way through the corridors. The spooky, irregular lighting tracked him, making shadows shiver in corners. He found a child's toy, a tangle of cords and spars, lying in a corner. One room he passed without looking: her shrine, the closed room of her grief. He did not want to find her there. If he had to, let him look there last.

He found her, to his relief, in her conservatory, rummaging beneath the trestle tables for trays and equipment. When she heard him, she spoke without looking up: 'The medicinal plants in *caur* D'Suran. They must be taken in, before the roots rot.'

Then she straightened, and saw him. It was as though not merely blood and energy but life itself drained out of her face. She stood with trowel dangling, looking at him with hollow eyes.

'Get out,' she said.

Shivaun D'Vandras crept in the door at his side, with a tense, fearful set to her lips. Daisainia gathered herself, saying, 'I can settle with him.' Shivaun hesitated, shrinking but not yielding. Daisainia said, firmly, 'Go down to *caur* D'Suran and start to dig out the medicinals planted in sand: the desert soil ones.' Her fragile cousin faced her a moment; Lian wished he could see her face. Daisainia's was firm, but not masked. 'Go down, Shivaun.'

Lian stood aside as Shivaun gathered trowels and trays and slipped past him. The inspiration he needed had come. He said, 'You are – very protective of her. Would you – even take on – her guilt?' Daisainia reared up, staring at him. 'If Shivaun gave – Morain – *sonol*, not you . . .'

She looked at him, for so long he thought his strategy had failed. For so long that he thought he might even be right. Then, in a colourless voice she said, 'No, D'Halldt. It was I.'

'And Shivaun – was there?' He checked himself. But, having begun, he was committed, for his own people and hers. 'Was it the shock, Daisainia? That broke her—'

He could not have said what about her expression told him how wrong he was. It reminded him somehow of Illuan D'Vandras. Only Illuan D'Vandras had once loved Morain.

Loved her and yet seen her clearly. Seen, even as a young man in love, what in Morain had made her elders refuse to entrust her with their knowledge.

He remembered the thick volume which harboured Morain's account of her tenure. He had suppressed his doubts, impressed by the intellect and assurance of the mind driving that painted hand. But now he knew what had disturbed him. Morain's record was empty of the names that crowded Daisainia's accounts. Other people were as much effaced from Morain's records as Daisainia effaced herself from her own. And then there was Shivaun, Morain's daughter, broken in spirit, and yet trusting Daisainia. As though it had not been Daisainia who did the breaking.

He said, quietly, 'Morain D'Vandras had the *caur'cali* judge you unfit.'

Her face was masked. 'I was not fit.'

'They thought it was because of the deaths of your parents.'

383

Her pupils constricted and a pulse leaped in her throat.

Lian said, 'My – people think Morain – challenged you, as – *isk'dar*. So you – killed her. I am – not sure.'

'D'Halldt—'

'I – think Morain – was destructive. I think – she harmed Shivaun. I think she harmed – you.'

Daisainia lurched back against the trestle table. Then twisted away, hand to mouth, making no sound.

He touched her shoulder. When she did not react, he left his hand there and put the other on her forehead and pulled her head back against his own shoulder. Her skin was cool and damp. She clutched at his wrist, but her hand did not close. It fell away.

Her breathing quietened gradually. He felt her begin to resist him. Then she lifted her hand to his and pushed it aside. Quite deliberately, she stepped away, squaring herself a moment before turning to face him. She looked haggard and dazed. 'Are you satisfied now, D'Halldt?'

That was no answer. He did not risk the question again, immediately. 'When I read – her records I was – impressed,' he owed her truth, even though her eyes darkened at it, 'and – I was troubled. I did – not know why then. But I see that – nobody else – existed for Morain.' Daisainia closed her eyes. She stayed steady on her feet, so he quelled the impulse to reach out to her. 'I had not – met that before. I did not recognize it. I did you a great wrong.'

She opened her eyes. The violet stare was knifelike. 'You do me no wrong. I did what they say. I did what she—' She snapped the phrase off, and watched him, so tense she shuddered with each breath.

He said, softly, 'Do I – pretend not – to hear—'

A complex, hunted expression rippled across her face. He regretted his last words at the sight of it. Whatever had prompted that unfinished sentence, she did not need him flaunting his insights.

'Why,' she said, 'do you pursue this? I killed Morain D'Vandras. I killed her out of hatred, because while I was – while I did not have the strength to resist she—' She stopped, gathered herself. 'The *cali* wanted strength,' she said, in a low voice. 'I had no strength.'

384

'You were – a child. Orphaned. Grieving.'

He glimpsed sheer horror in her face.

That stopped him. Morain had come to Lltharran after Ky Travassa and Branduin Vassar's deaths. Daisainia had broken down after those deaths. The deaths had been by drowning and the river was an obsession with her. He drew together all the connections he had, and added the horror he had just seen.

'So – it was – about their deaths.'

She started past him, forcing him aside. He caught her clumsily, one hand gripping her shoulder, one tangling in the fabric of her sleeve. He used his weight to turn her to face him, as she had used hers in the dancing. For an instant he thought she might hit him to get free. He said quickly, 'What – was it?'

She broke. He felt it through her bones and his, as though her joints and muscles disconnected. The blank agony on her face made him dizzy. He pulled her down with him on to the dirty floor, though she might have been able to remain standing alone. But he could not let go of her, not now. He had stripped away the barriers she had raised within herself, ignorant of what was confined. She had worn the same look while he had first tried to talk to her abut Morain and she had been obsessed with falling dykes and *shikarl*.

Shikarl.

Of course, he thought. How very simple. She could not accept helplessness even if the alternative was an annihilating guilt. 'You think you – knew beforehand,' Lian said. 'You think – you foresaw it.' He stroked her hair back with both hands, bending her head so that she looked at him. She was so pliable. Her eyes did not focus.

'Could you – not warn them?'

Her voice was barely recognizable. 'I did not try.'

'Why not? Did you think it was – a dream?'

She shuddered. He said, as gently as he could, 'Did it say – "They will die tonight"? Did you know – that certainly? Everyone dreads – losing people dear to them. I – had that dream myself. It is – part of living, caring. Nobody – told me it was prescience.'

'Did it happen?' she demanded starkly. 'When you dreamed it?'

385

He said nothing.

'It happened to me. They drowned. They burned. I saw them before, and after—' She doubled forward. Lian caught her and pulled her into his arms. She did not resist. He had time to wonder at that while he held her, fingers tangled in her hair, one hand across her back. Her arms were pinned between them, he felt her clenched fists like stones against his upper ribs.

He saw it as clearly as if he had been there. She had needed comfort, and drawing down from her lonely citadel of guilty power. Instead, there had been Morain, ambitious and greedy for the knowledge to which Daisainia was heir. Morain who had helped Daisainia erect her tower of delusion and stood by as she was crushed beneath it.

'Morain knew,' Lian said. For a moment he hesitated, but it seemed selfish, at such a moment, to insist upon his own viewpoint. He put it in her words. 'Morain knew you – had foreseen. Tell me, Daisainia. Tell me – the rest.'

She was rigid in his arms.

'Tell me,' Lian said quietly.

She did not seem to be breathing. He thought he could not bear the silence, the waiting. But he had to.

'She would not let me be,' Daisainia said, at last. 'She must know what I knew, what I foresaw.' She released, and drew in, a strangling breath. '*I could not bear it.* Every day the same question, what did I know, what could I sense.'

The cruelty was greater than he had imagined. His arms tightened around her, his hands closing on her shoulders and ribs. She seemed unwitting. She said, 'I could not bear it. But I was *isk'dar*, D'Halldt, I had to go on with their work,' and from her tone, the 'they' could only be Ky and Branduin. 'I had to finish what they had begun. It was the only way I could *live* . . .'

What he heard her say was, it was the only way I could deserve to live. He murmured her name into her hair, unheard.

'And they would take it from me,' she said, in a raw voice. 'She. The *caur'cali*. They would take everything from me.'

Lian said, 'Why could you not – ask for help?'

'I asked,' she said, and he flinched at the tone. 'As *isk'dar*, Ky's daughter, Faul's grandchild, I asked for help. I asked my

386

people to stand behind me, and they did. They stood behind me when I went to treat with her, and they fought for me when she tried to take me.'

'Daisainia,' he whispered. It was her tone which made it so unbearable. The words were nothing, spare as they were. He knew most of what she said already. He felt her stiffen and square her shoulders slightly at his protest. She would not let him argue with her self-loathing. She drove the next words through his heart.

'And I asked for *sonol*, and Zharlinn brought it me.'

Lian closed his eyes. In the darkness, he heard her say, 'She said to me, "It's proven." That I was mad. That the *caur'cali* would rule for her once more. We were waiting, she and I, for them to return. She was at ease: she would sleep, and eat, and show it. I could do none of these things.' Her voice had taken on that exquisite, detached clarity. 'You might have seen *sonol*, amongst the medicinals. It is much like a common edible plant in the North. There are small differences, in the shaft of the veins, in the leaves. Morain did not care much for living things. She never learned or observed the difference. And so she fed of it from *caur'isk'dari* stores.'

There was a small silence.

In a distant voice she said, 'Is that what you wished to know, D'Halldt?'

He could not speak. She freed herself from his arms with a forceful twist, and rolled to a crouch, looking at him with bitter eyes. In his silence, his stricken aspect, she read condemnation. He struggled to find an argument, holding her eyes. Thoughts of Morain made him flinch, inwardly; he set her aside for the moment.

'Ky. Branduin. Why were – they on – the riverbank?'

She blinked, for the moment left unguarded by the shift of subject. Lian pressed his point.

'They were – checking, as you – check. Checking the dykes.'

He could see the upwelling of the old pain, the old guilt. The guilt which Morain had used to destroy her. 'Daisainia, if I said – to you tonight – or some such night – do not go because I – fear danger.'

'You do not believe,' she said, and averted her face.

'If I said to – you. Or if Rathla – said to you. Or Lara. Or – anyone – do not go. Because I am – we are – afraid for you—'

She said nothing. He reached out, with a cold hand, and slid it under her jaw. Her jaw tightened. He gave her a moment to accept the touch and then he lifted her face so that she had to look at him. He had never been so glad that his own face hid nothing.

'You – would go. Whatever I said. Whatever – anyone said. *You would go.*' She was looking directly at him now, her gaze drawing on his. It did not matter; he knew what he was saying. He took her face in both hands. 'That – is – your way of – caring. Your conscience. Your way of – righting what Linn Travassa – did. It is your way because – they taught it you. It was their way. Death mattered less. Than they betray their care. Daisainia, had you – warned them, they *would yet have gone.*'

She did not accept that. He let his hand slide away, let her go. He had given what he could, and she would take what she could.

'Ach, D'Halldt.' She drew a breath, and gathered herself, got slowly to her feet and stood poised a moment, testing her own balance. He started to do likewise, shaky with fatigue; she looked down at him, and then put out a hand. He took it, and let her pull him up. He thought that he should have trusted her throughout, for that readiness to offer her hand, that solid, giving grip. She stood watching him, waiting.

Morain, he thought. But he was the one now unable to talk about Morain. Experience had taught him subtlety of insight and imagination. But he had not believed in evil. He believed in accident: accident had scarred Burdania and himself. Individual flaws, carelessness, arrogance, preoccupation, in collision, created disaster. He believed everyone capable of the best will, if lacking the ability to realize it.

The light lay differently on the walls. In time, if he applied himself, he might come to understand Morain, to appreciate why she saw the people of this world as shadows for her shaping. But the thought repelled him. He did not want to understand her. He had only one thought: I would have poisoned her myself, for what she did to you. And that could not be voiced, not to Daisainia, who would take it as his corruption. Which it would be.

He had come to persuade Daisainia to rescind her abdication, and to defend what she had done. For the sake of the meeting of peoples, and the future. He had come prepared to do whatever he had to, whatever he could, to make her.

Bereft of words, he brought the ring out, and offered it to her. She hissed out a breath, and stepped back, fetching up against a trestle so hard it set leaves to rustling.

Lian said, in dismay, 'Why – Daisainia?'

She said, with face averted, 'It must be me, or you. I and your people, we cannot coexist. I felt – the darkness. The madness. It was all happening again.'

'You would not,' he said. He went up to her, and tried to draw her face around, feeling the hard line of muscle as she resisted. He did not force her. He did not let go, either. He said, with an effort at lightness. '*I* know the – difference between *sonol* and – the other. I *care* for living things.' She did not respond. 'Daisainia – you would not have – warned me – so often. If you had meant.'

She turned her head so swiftly he stepped back, jolted by the force of those violet eyes. 'If I cease to be *isk'dar* it is because I choose to cease to be *isk'dar*, because it is my last act as myself. I have seen your records, not many, but enough. I know the world will change, and there will be no place in it for me. But to the end I will be *isk'dar*, and *you will not take it from me*, and *you will not give it back to me*. Do you understand, D'Halldt?'

'Yes, Daisainia,' he whispered. 'I understand.' He stood for a moment, hearing the wind in the hollow places outside. 'But, if you – cease to be *isk'dar* and Burdania – ceases to be Burdania, there will – be no place for me. I – never belonged to – there as I – belong here. Even now, caught – between your people and mine. I never loved any woman in – the colony because loving is – seeing yourself in someone else's eyes, and to them I was – always Lian, who had fallen – who could not think quickly, who could not – talk. I loved – outside the colony, but she was – *kinder'el'ein*, and it had to end. Here, nobody knew – what I might have been. Here I could do – things as well as anyone else. Here I learned – I had courage and I could – be a peer amongst my own kind. Although I know, I already see, that that must – change.' He blinked, but the tears he meant to keep back spilled instead. 'I love this world, Daisainia. As it is. I love you – I do love you. As you are. I fear I – will be lost again if I leave—' She put out her hand and covered his lips with her fingers. She had moved without thought, for he saw her glance at her own hand, and be surprised. Then, deliberately, she shifted the hand from his lips to the track of his tears. He felt the coolness her fingers left behind as they passed through it, slid down on to his neck, and settled on his shoulder. All the time her expression was intense, concentrating on that moving hand. Each moment of her touch was a balanced decision. He shivered. She lifted her eyes.

'Afraid, Lian?' she said in a transparent voice. 'When you can do to me what you have just done?'

I did it to myself as well, Lian thought.

'Stay,' she said, in that same, transparent voice. 'With us. With me.'

He caught her hand in both of his, and pressed their clasped hands to his forehead. She tensed, but did not pull away.

He had never known a temptation so strong. To stay here, with her, amongst people on his own scale. He was familiar with stone, grass, earth, water; he could master the finer manual skills, the ones which did not require strength. He could cultivate, extract and prepare medicinals, teach a little, keep records. He could sort components, as Vylan did. They could have the child, the children, they both wanted. The Burdanians would have his knowledge, for what it was worth; and any records they could persuade the others to leave. They would have the hope that in time, in a year, or a generation, the colonists would come back. And if he and Daisainia did their work well and prepared their welcome, this time they would come to stay. But he and Daisainia would still have time, a little while or a lifetime, before they lost their world to change.

But set that against the benefits and necessities of that change. This world of stone, grass, earth and water was a cruel world. He thought of Thaorinn, dying in his cell. His father's choice; his father's joy, even. Set that against Arkadin, drowning in the dark. He thought of Valancy, bearing her son

390

in pain. Even if he accepted that for Daisainia, even if their children survived all the dangers of this world – as, he thought, they *should*, bequeathed her stamina and protection – there would always be the others, like Arkadin, or Tion; like Illuan, or Fioral. Suppose the colonists never came back. Suppose, half the galaxy away, they remained unreconciled, believing Burdania gone to ruin and barbarism. The one great hope betrayed.

'Oh, Daisainia,' he whispered, 'I understand you now.'

No wonder she had been bleak and raging by turns, trapped between self and conscience. No wonder she had threatened and baited at being brought to choose between herself and her people. For Daisainia, being *isk'dar* was not merely a responsibility, it was an identity. And the one demanded that the other be renounced.

For him, it was simpler. He would continue as himself. He would do what he could: even censure would serve his purpose, for if censured, he would have to speak in hall. He would be able to tell his part. He could do that, even if he could not do it well. But they deserved better than to have him do it badly.

What would it matter if he stayed?

She was holding his head against her shoulder; he felt her hard, calloused fingers on his neck. He let go her hand, and slid both hands across her back. The coarse material rasped his fingertips. She felt brittle, narrow and angular against him, harsh woven fabric over skin, muscle and bone. His jaw fitted above her ear, her steady breath warmed his throat.

He said, 'We – need you, Daisainia. The future. Burdania. I – myself.'

From his pocket, the transceiver gave an electronic shriek. Alystra's voice overlapped the alarm signal, shrill with panic. 'Lian, they've taken Thovalt. Lors is— Don't – Lors! Lian, *get back here.*'

Daisainia grasped the import before he did. She pulled away, catching him hard by the upper arms. 'D'Halldt, no!'

He looked at her in bewilderment; she was objecting to an intent yet unformed. She thrust him back against the trestle. 'I will go down. *Wait for me here.*'

'Lian!' Alystra's voice again. 'Lian, respond. Where are you?'

391

Lian tried to move against Daisainia's hands. She had her weight set against his, keeping him offbalance. 'Daisainia, these are – *my* people. I – must – go down.'

He felt the shift in her weight, felt an inner collapse which drained all animation from her face. He had just illustrated his own argument about Ky and Branduin. She *could* not have kept them from doing what they had to. She started to turn away, bringing a hand up to her face, whether to shield her from seeing or being seen. He caught her wrist, knowing the comfort he had to offer her. 'Daisainia – love. This time – you shall be – there.'

THIRTY

TARIDWYN

Sixty-six years (Burdanian)
after departure from Burdania

The chamber where the ship had been stood open to the sky. The roof had gone; the doors had been removed. The transparent walls remained, enclosing the vast, unowned space. Jungle had already begun to fill it; the white floor was matted by fallen leaves, flowers and vines, and streaked green and brown. Through the wall, Lian watched his mother scatter leaves over Danas' and Tarian's younger daughter. The toddler shrieked and hurled her wad at Sara's feet. Sara lept in the air, tucking both feet high beneath her, arms thrown wide. She seemed to linger in the air longer than anyone should, a creature of air and sunlight herself. The elder daughter was held entranced with her double handful of leaves at shoulder height ready to throw.

Danas said, '*Look* at her. She might be their age.'

Lian thought wistfully that they were the kind of children merry Sara should have had. After the years of silence, Sara wanted talk, song, laughter; after Thaorinn's austerity, Sara wanted play. Her merriment marked the depths of her grief. She had to have everything different from the way it had been. Lian was too inarticulate and fragile to divert her. All his connections with her were wordless ones, the blood bond, the common loss, the common experience of *kinder'vos* and *kinder'el'ein*.

Danas said, 'She is the only adult who goes in there. Even most of the children . . . How does she *do* it, Li? She is the only person who is not frightened of what you are going to bring back.' She ended on a gasp, breathless with the thick noon air.

393

He checked her with a glance; she avoided his eyes. Waiting for his response.

'Sara – thinks – like me – that the – *kinder'el'ein* sensed – truly. They have again – at *en'vos'neen'el* – when Sara – and I went. We – believe that – Burdania is – living.'

'Tarian keeps trying to make the mathematics resolve. But he would have gone, wanted to find out. It was I.' She broke off, then repeated, 'Only I.'

'I know,' Lian said.

She looked at him, startled. Then half laughed. 'I should have known.

'Lian, I was so afraid of being thought a coward. And I was. And am. I am afraid of knowing what has happened to Burdania. I'm being a coward again, in talking to you.'

'You – cannot make me – regret going,' Lian said. 'Any more than I – can make you – not be afraid.'

A high burble, muffled by the walls, caused them to turn. Sara came wading towards them, swinging the delighted young child by the ankles. The other reeled with laughter at her side. Danas said, 'How can she, in this heat?' The inverted child waved frantically with both hands. Danas knelt, to bring her face to her daughter's level. She matched her hands against the little splayed hands on the far side of the wall. Above her smile, Sara's bright, sharp eyes observed Lian. She said something to the elder girl, who straightened, composed herself, and with great care handsigned, *Sara says to look behind*.

He heard the rustle of robes behind him as he turned. More than one: Telien, with Vaelren behind *kin*, sheltering behind *kin* parent's shoulder. He had not seen Vaelren for four years; he held his breath, not daring to think, to feel. Telien deliberately stepped aside without a greeting, leaving them to face each other.

He did not expect her to have changed, but he thought he might see her differently. It did not seem so at first. He felt a great surge of feeling gather and go out to her, the last lingering breath of the dark quiet room of four years ago. She endured it with only a flicker of white in the eye. And after that feeling was gone, he had to look at her again to recognize her. He saw that she had grown taller and heavier, into full adult stature. Her skin might have darkened fractionally. Her eyes were the same deep cobalt; he tried not to look at them directly, lest they deceive him. In her face he discovered stillness, detachment; a more gentle detachment than Shaleen's, but nevertheless there. And probably, certainly, always there. Although he loved her, he had seldom looked at her.

He felt a bouyant sense of confidence. He loved her still, but temperately. He knew exactly what he could give her, and what she would take.

He offered his hands. 'Vaeli.'

She slid her huge hands beneath his, palm to palm. The touch of the warm, moist skin made his confidence waver. His importunate passion was not so quiet after all. He said, 'You came – to see me – away.'

Sara came through the gaping door, the child straddling her hip, eyes watering and face flushed. The elder daughter ran to Danas, to be lifted. Sara put her free hand around Telien's waist and settled her shoulder against Telien's ribs. 'You are a meddler,' she scolded *kin*. She waved to Lian, and the five straggled away across the landing field.

'Did Telien—?'

Vaelren drew her hands back and turned to lay them on the transparent wall. 'It feels different here, Lian.'

'The ship – gone.'

'Quieter. A waiting peace. There is fear, of course.'

'And – the Burdania in *en'neen'el*.'

'Waiting, too. We *do* know you will find life.'

How odd, he thought. We talk to each other like strangers, saying things we would never have thought to say before. And yet we talk like intimates, trusting and not needing to explain.

'I think – I would be very – frightened if I did not – know that.'

Vaelren did not answer. They watched a leaf tumble from the canopy heights.

Vaelren said, 'I made a promise to Telien, too.'

He did not understand. Sensing this, she said, 'As Shaleen did. But I can keep that promise.'

He knew then. Shaleen had promised to return to the settlement when *kin* felt the need to make the life-bond. He,

395

and she, were shocked at the upwelling of emotion in him: renewed loss, jealousy towards her yet unchosen mates. She stepped back. 'Don't, Lian. *Please.*'

'It is not – voluntary.' He concentrated on another falling leaf, putting his mind up there with its loops and turns. Except imagination gave him vertigo. With the detachment of vertigo he said, 'So it was – not me.'

'It *was* you. I wanted to wish you well. I have never . . . had to say goodbye.'

He remembered that day on the platform, the day which had ended in him drowning in grief. She might never have had to say goodbye, might have left him and still been able to touch him through *vos'neen* without his knowledge and his imposition. But he had felt the full and brutal parting. He turned to her, with pride, resentment and compassion and signed, *We talked about it. But Tarian and Danas, who wanted it that way, chose not to come. All of us who are going* will *come back.*

THIRTY-ONE

BURDANIA

From high on the slope, they saw smoke enfolding the shuttle and towering in the cold air. At its base the smoke glowed orange; at its height it was dull grey. Fire lights and hues shifted on the shuttles flanks. Torches circled and eddied around it.

The sky was pale mauve with dawn, the floodwaters, the grass, Daisainia's grim face all washed with a weak, colourless light.

Beneath the lowest of the escarpments, she left the path and started down the open slope towards the ridge and the shuttle. She cut a matt track of downtrodden grass and churned up dew. The grass twined around Lian's feet, tough and slippery. He was holding her back; he could see it by the way she moved, as though strung between cords, head pulling towards the sight below her.

Lian took in the scene in quick glances as he stumbled and slid. The crowd had the faces of ordinary people, people Lian knew. What they were doing seemed quite ordinary: they were throwing flotsam on to a pyre and passing torches. Even their expressions, of determination, rage, hatred, were ones Lian had seen before, as they fought the river.

But these flames twined and licked the struts of the shuttle, and flowered on its underside. The hatch was sealed; shields blinded the high viewport. From the speaker in Lian's hand, Alystra said, voice drained of panic, 'Lian, it's too late for you to try and come through. Wait. We have to free Thovalt and Lors. Stay clear. Don't put yourself at risk.'

As bodies moved, he saw Thovalt, held at the fireside. He

was slumped forward, being held on his feet. Lors, in the centre of the tight-locked cluster, ws struggling against somebody's arm across his throat, shirt and jacket in disarray and face contorted. Lian's feet slid from beneath him; he thudded on to his side in wet grass.

The cord between himself and Daisainia snapped. She flung one unreadable glance over her shoulder and broke from the border of the grass, sprinting across the broken ground.

Lian got to his feet. He had lost sight of Thovalt and Lors; they had been reabsorbed. There was an inner core which was tight and turbulent, and a wide broken circle of people standing still, in ones and threes. People were joining the circle, thickening it. Words were hurled, like stones, between circle and core. Somebody broke from the circle, and ran into the centre. The words dissolved into a roar.

Beneath the shuttle, Lara D'Alna was trying to pull a burning torch from Zharlinn's hands. Each had a two-handed grip on it, and each was trying to lever it loose from the other's. Their feet ground and scuffled on the gravel. Lara's heel clipped the fire, spilling smouldering twigs and leaves. The flame flailed arcs between their faces, dangerously closely. Then Zharlinn deliberately turned it towards Lara's eyes, and she let go with a scream of fright and anger, and fell, writhing away from the fire. The far side of the circle jerked and collapsed inwards, as people started towards him. And Daisainia burst into the centre of them, threw out her hands and bellowed with all the power in her small frame, 'Enough!'

Lian skidded the remaining few yards of grassy slope and started across the open ground. Alystra's voice checked him: 'Stay there, Lian. If you come any closer, you'll be affected by the gas.' He made a disbelieving, inarticulate sound which she took for question and accusation both. 'We had to think of it, when it looked like we'd have to retrieve you. It's quite harmless, but it will immobilize them. So stay back.'

High on the curve of the shuttle, a panel glinted dully as it moved aside.

Daisainia had opened up a silence. She gave them no time for recovery; she rounded on Rathla Zharlinn. Or would have, but for the sight of his face. Lian had never read so many emotions so clearly. Anger, accusation resentment, anguish, shame. Utter bewilderment, and cruel awareness. He might not know how he had come to this, but he knew for whom. His face was streaked with soot, and with tears.

The only sounds were the crackling of the fires, and the crunch of her feet on the stones as she walked up to him. Zharlinn did not move. She set both fists solidly against his chest, and said, 'I will not permit you to do this for me again.'

A second panel glinted and slid away from darkness. Lian whispered, in disbelief, 'You – cannot—'

Alystra muttered, 'If Thovalt and Lors were just a little further from the fire . . .'

Lian pulled the transceiver from his pocket and closed his hand upon it, muffling her protests as he started towards the crowd and the shuttle.

Zharlinn looked down at Daisainia's bare fingers, and said, in a shaky, wondering voice, 'Illuan said – you had given up. To them.'

Daisainia turned her head, and found, seemingly without seeking, the tall, cold-eyed man standing at the edge of the inner circle. From his approach, Lian could see only his unmarred profile.

Daisainia said, 'That was unworthy of you, Illuan.'

'It was necessary,' he said.

Zharlinn jerked in realization at the use to which he had been turned, and would have started for Illuan, but Daisainia's hard hand stayed him.

She flicked a glance over her shoulder, to the people holding Thovalt and Lors, Tor D'Vandras amongst them. 'Let them go.' She did not look to see that it had been done, but returned her attention to D'Vandras. Lors jerked his arms free, and turned to Thovalt. Tor, and his two companions, followed close his every move. Lors utterly ignored them, refusing to be provoked, and started to examine the bruise forming on Thovalt's jaw. Thovalt, eyelids flickering, tried to roll his head away. Lors said, audibly, 'Hold still.'

Alystra said, in a low voice, 'Lian, try and get them away from the fire.'

Lian slid through the crowd, head down, trying not to

obtrude. Smoke wound round his face. Sparks drifted past his eyes. He risked a glance at faces and saw them watching, waiting. He eased unseen into the clear space beside Illuan D'Vandras. Tion was examining Lara's hand and arm, while the young woman set her teeth, eyes bright with tears. He saw Lian, murmured something to Lara, and ran to meet him, stones flying from beneath his feet. 'Let me talk to them,' he said, urgently. 'Fioral and Kylara are still in there.'

Illuan glanced at them both. His face seemed composed part of bone, part of rotting fruit. He had pulled a cloak on over his bare torso, and held the fastenings closed with one hand. To Daisainia, he said, 'You told me, as I wish. The occasion presented itself; so I did as I wish.'

'But you are – justice – *just*,' Lian cried.

'Much good it has ever done me,' D'Vandras said, not to him, but to Daisainia.

He seized Lian's wrist and bent it back so he could take the transceiver. Into it, he said, 'I surmise you can see me. Return Fioral and Kylara D'Suran, and we will return—' he held up Lian's hand, 'yours. Then you may leave. You have desecrated Burdania enough. I do not want any relics of you. Least of all your blood, and bone.'

'They saved your life,' Zharlinn shouted at him, from behind Daisainia's shoulder.

Without switching it off, D'Vandras replaced the transceiver in Lian's hand and let him go. To Lian, he said, 'You have our curses, our opprobrium, the marks of our fire in your hull and our fists in your skin. What more will it take to drive you away?'

'I never wanted,' Zharlinn said, heavily, 'to drive them away. Although I did not know it, I have been waiting for them,' he glanced over his shoulder, at the shuttle, 'all my life. But if it comes to a choice, between them and,' he looked down at Daisainia, and suddenly was speaking only to her, 'you, then I choose you.'

'We agree,' Alystra's voice said thinly, but audibly, from the speaker. 'Lian, tell them we agree. Give Lors and Thovalt back their equipment; let them and Lian come aboard unobstructed. Let Tion D'Suran come aboard to help move Fioral.'

'And then,' Illuan said, distinctly, 'you will leave.'

400

'No,' said Lian.

Daisainia released Zharlinn, setting him carefully in place, and walked up to stand on Lian's far side. Wordlessly, she held out her hand. Wordlessly, he put the ring into it, his fingertips brushing her skin and tracing cold on warmth.

Alystra said, tersely, 'Lian, even if you have no regard for your own safety, have some regard for ours.'

'Look,' D'Vandras said, 'what you have brought us to.' His gesture took in the fires licking and sucking on the landing array, took in the quietly distraught Tion, the devastated Zharlinn, stunned Thovalt and hot-eyed Lors. Took in Daisainia herself.

Daisainia turned away from him. Her voice lashed across the open space. 'Stand away from them. Quench those fires.'

There was a moment's hesitation, a moment's considera-tion, before people moved to do as she said. Perhaps it was no longer than it might have been, hitherto. But it seemed unnervingly long; he could tell by the stiffening of her back that she felt it, and he could see that D'Vandras was pleased.

Then the ring of people around Lors and Thovalt swelled and broke like a soap bubble. Thovalt was standing unassisted. Lors stooped to gather his scattered equipment, examining each piece individually, using the time to regain his composure. Lara and Vylan led a handful of people in breaking apart the fires, stamping out individual sticks and embers. Smoke blotted the lightning sky. Sunlight lit upon a few fine clouds overhead, then upon *caur'isk'dari* on its knoll. But it was too soon for relief. The fire-breakers were still few, going methodically about their slow task, and ignoring all others. People gathered in shifting little groups, which knotted and circled, and slid past each other. The shuttle squatted over them, sombre against the violet sky, dying firelight and rising daylight shining weakly on its hull. Lian sensed, distinct as the smoke, the grievance in the air. These were exhausted, overtaxed people; they had endured too much. They were ready to abandon reason, abandon fairness, and condemn those who had abandoned them. The fires were still laid and tinder-dry, and Illuan knew where to set the taper. He had known where to set the taper to Rathla Zharlinn.

'*Cal* D'Vandras,' Lian said. 'Do – not *do* this. I – beg you.'

Illuan tilted his head slightly, but did not turn it.

'You stayed your – hand. Against Daisainia. You knew – what Morain – was. You gave Daisainia – fair – consideration. All these years. Give us – consideration.'

Pain cross Illuan's face. Lian could not tell whether it was physical or emotional. Lian said, 'It was – Burdanian against – Burdanian. As here. Is any – part better? To your eyes?'

Illuan pressed long fingers to his bruised forehead.

As he drew breath, Alystra's voice said suddenly, 'I'm sorry, Lian.'

Illuan's head came up; he stared at Lian, demanding an answer which Lian did not have to give. Then a whisper reached him; he looked up at the shuttle, where a faint mist was forming and slipping down the flanks. The gas condensed slightly in the chill, catching the fine early light. Lian cried out.

Daisainia swung, turning a glare on Illuan. Lian pointed, left-handed. 'Gas. Get – away.'

'Lian,' shouted Alystra from the speaker.

D'Vandras swooped, snatching the transceiver out of Lian's hand. 'What have you done?'

Daisainia shouted orders, cutting outwards. The Burdanians scattered, scrambling away from the shuttle, dropping torches and sticks. All but two, who started towards Lors and Thovalt. To be checked as a hurled stone cracked off the shuttle's underside before their faces. Face brilliant with fury, second stone in hand, Daisainia roared, 'Leave them be.' Zharlinn reinforced her stone with a threatening move of his own. The two backed away.

From between Illuan's clenched hands Alystra's voice was saying, '. . . harmless . . . necessary . . . forced intervention . . .'

Illuan closed the circuit, silencing her. For a moment he looked as though he would dash the instrument to the ground, grind it into the gravel. But then, quite civilly, he handed it back to Lian.

'So it ends,' he said, quietly.

The Burdanians were circling, gathering at their back, keeping himself, Daisainia and Illuan between themselves and the shuttle. There were no clusters, no knots, only a tight, dark unity. Lian felt ill.

Daisainia said, face masked, 'How far away must we be?'

Lian looked at the shuttle. The mist had cleared, the released interrupted. He said. 'Here. Fine here.'

Daisainia said, 'If you go now, D'Halldt, none will stop you.'

'They were – frightened,' he said, to her.

'There are few worse things than fear. And few worse things than those things caused by fear.' She stepped back, and a little to one side, extending an arm as though clearing his way.

He looked at the strong, masked face, trying to grasp her intent. Did she mean him to go; or was she merely refusing to insist upon his staying. Stepping aside from his choice. Refusing to take part in it. But no, Daisainia would not do that. If she thought he should leave, she would have given him no choice. He felt, suddenly, the beginnings of a smile. She was giving him a choice, and trusting him to make the right one.

The hatch opened, a distraction. Lors and Thovalt moved from their shelter beneath the landing array, the new sun striking Lors' white hair. Lian thought of the morning of their arrival. As they reached the hatch, Kylara D'Suran appeared in it, carrying in her arms a small, blanket-wrapped figure. Lors and Thovalt, between them, helped her down. Lors paused, smoothing a fold of the blanket. A small hand lifted to cling to his. Tion pushed free of the Burdanians and ran across the open ground. Kylara spoke to Lors, Lors to Kylara, and then the young woman started back towards them. Her hair and copper ornaments sparkled in the sun. Thovalt disappeared through the hatch. Lors pulled himself up, looked back, to where Tion had met Kylara, had stopped her, had put his arms around them both. Lors looked at them, and over their heads, straight at Lian. Lian could not interpret what he thought, or felt, or meant to convey. Alystra caught his arm, and, against his resistance, pulled him into the shuttle, and resealed the hatch. In Lian's hand the contact-requested light flashed stubbornly.

Kylara made to skirt the crowd between herself and *caur* D'Suran. Tion put a firm hand on her shoulder and steered them towards its centre. The Burdanians opened a clear corridor for them, but the ranks behind the corridor pressed close, watching Fioral's mud-streaked face and shifting, half-open eyes.

The bitter chill left Illuan D'Vandras' face, briefly.

Lian keyed the transmission-only switch, and turned the flashing light into his palm. He felt he had never stood so solidly on any part of any world. When Daisainia turned back to him, he strung the words smoothly on a breath, 'I am not going. The past is not my fault. It is not yours. I want to start. To start again. Here.'

Daisainia gave him a look of blazing triumph and swung round to face the gathering. 'Listen. Listen to him now. He is Burdanian; he will not leave.' There was a swell of sound from the Burdanians. Daisainia thrust forward through them and climbed upon the broken wall at the rear of *caur'isk'dari*, which raised her head and shoulders above the tallest of them. Lian could hear the strain and resolution in her voice, yellowing its rich timbre. '*Yes*, they come of the people who left Burdanian, destroying it and us. *Yes*, they kept from us the knowledge of how and why they left. *Yes*, they accuse me of unjudicial murder; they say I am unsuitable to be what I am to you. I am an insult to them, to the Burdania that they cherished. *Yes*, they are frightened by us, and have behaved offensively to us. *But they are Burdanian*. They are *our* people.'

'No,' said Illuan. He stood out of the crowd, clear on the high slope. The marks on his face were gaudy in the sun; he squinted with pain; and his black hair was matted to his head. But there was chilling lucidity in his voice. 'They have been away too long. They are strangers to us, and we to them. Consider their actions, deception, division, and, lately, threat.' Daisainia drew breath. Illuan said, 'I acknowledge the good they have done,' touching his bruised forehead lightly, almost in salute. 'The reason which informs this argument is their gift, is surely as is Fioral D'Suran's precious young life. But the good they have done only condemns them, for it reveals their powerlessness.' He transferred his dark regard to Lian. 'Sixty-six years ago, Burdanians were divided. One segment of the society withdrew to pursue its own preferred ends. That withdrawal, that estrangement, led inevitably to conflict. Neither side intended ill; both wished the best for their world, for their people. But between them, they brought disaster down on themselves, and on us.' He waved his hand, including shuttle and gathering both. 'D'Halldt, you and your people might intend no ill, but you are powerless to avert it. You are as much strangers to us as your ancestors. Now, go as they went, before you do further harm.'

'I never wanted this,' Zharlinn said, in a low voice, from behind Lian. 'Please believe me. Tell – the others. I don't want any more harm coming to you. Go back to your ship, Lian. Maybe some future time—'

'No!' Lara, white-faced and cradling her burned arm. 'Lian, we *want* you to stay. You have so much to teach us. What happened here was our fault, too. I know that's the twisted point he's making, but surely as we come to know each other . . . *Isk'dar*—' She appealed to Daisainia.

'The decision,' D'Vandras said, 'is not hers.' To Daisainia he said, 'What you have relinquished, you cannot have back.'

Lian heard a ripple of voices, growing to a row. Daisainia, standing on her wall, scanned them with an intent face, the same face she turned towards the rising flood. The noise was like a flood; it was going to drown him. Lian caught hold of Daisainia's sleeve and scrambled up on to the wall; with an effort, she kept her balance and turned to lift him. He swayed beside her, his feet slipping. 'It isn't—' He saw angry faces; people shouting. The noise was sweeping him off the dyke. Lian shouted, 'It isn't—' Daisainia threw her hand into the air; with the other she steadied him. 'You don't *know* us!' Lian shouted, against the battering. Unexpectedly, the flood ebbed. The drowning sensation abated. He managed to find his balance, and felt Daisainia's hand carefully place him, and withdraw. He said, 'You – do not know us. We – do not know – you. It has all been – the past. Working in us. All the blame and – bitterness of the past. Even this – is like something – happened – before. With Morain.' Out of the corner of his eye he saw Daisainia lift her head. It made him hesitate, lose his next words. All he could find to say was, 'There is no one left. No one to blame. No one to make suffer. Except ourselves. And each other.' Dizzy with the force he had put behind his voice, he lost his balance and slid down the side of the wall. Tion and Lara caught him between them.

He heard Daisainia say, 'What D'Vandras said is true: I did

relinquish my care. I did relinquish you. Because of the season, because of my shadows, because of this . . . past which I feared to live again. But I ask to finish this. *I claim it as my right*, because of my ancestry, because of my,' her voice changed slightly; he knew she was looking down at him, 'past, which shackles me still. I am descended of Linn Travassa, who stole our past from us. So I give you my word: I will find the strength to do well by you. But in return, you must do well by me. These people will go, or stay, as we, and they, choose. "There is no one left. No one to blame. No one to make suffer. Except ourselves. And each other." And there has been enough suffering. D'Halldt,' Lian lifted his head, and met that breathtaking gaze, 'ask them to come out.' She lifted her head, looked out over the gathering with a challenging face. 'Anyone who threatens them will contend with me.'

They won't, he thought. They are too afraid.

That was not an answer he could offer her. Neither, he realized, was it one he could accept himself. He felt his voice rasp in his throat. 'I'll – have to go in. Speak to them.' Without looking at her, he held up the transceiver, and felt her take it.

Alystra pulled him aboard so forcibly he nearly fell. She had the hatch closed and sealed before he righted himself. Tension and hostility was like a stench in the closed cabin. Thovalt was in the pilot's seat, gloved and helmeted, the screen before him streaming with symbols. Andra barely glanced up from the auxiliary station. Lors started up from the rear chair. He looked like he had been thrown into it. His eyes were hot, a furious yellow.

He said, 'Lian, curse you, why did you come in?'

Alystra said, 'Lian, sit down. Thovalt, *go*.'

Lian felt the deck lift slightly. He moved without thought, dropped on to the pilot's gantry, slamming against the screen, and half fell across Thovalt's gloved hand. The shuttle jolted violently and grounded. Andra shouted something. Lian lurched back against the screen and slid down its smooth curve to sit at Thovalt's feet.

Thovalt, hand immobile, stared at him through the flickering interior display of the helmet. His expression, Lian noted peripherally, was shocked. For the first, and likely last, time in their lives, he, Lian, had shocked Thovalt.

'Launch aborted,' said Andra. There was a pause. 'No damage reported.'

Alystra appeared above Thovalt's head, looking down in anger and utter disbelief.

Thovalt smiled dazzlingly, pushed back the helmet, and leaned forward, offering Lian his ungloved hand. Lian took it, and Thovalt, without rising, levered him to a crouch. He got his feet under him, and slid up to a standing position, shoulders against the screen. Thovalt offered him up to Alystra with a sweep of a supple hand.

The energy of desperation had not yet left him. Tides of heat and cold raced across his skin. He looked up at Alystra and said, fiercely, 'I am – sorry. But we – will *not* leave. This way.'

Alystra glanced aside at Lors, who had come up to her shoulder. 'Lors,' she said tightly, 'will you take care of him?'

Lian started forward. He stumbled against Thovalt's chair, and caught himself, one hand on the platform, one enmeshed in the armoury of the glove, looking up at her above him. 'Do not – dismiss me!'

'You have just shown we cannot afford to.'

'You do,' Lian said. 'You – always have. Because of my speech. They—' He threw out an arm, bruising his wrist against the screen. 'Burdanians – do not. She lets me – speak. For them. For Burdania.'

Lors said, 'Lian—'

'No!' Lors flinched. Lian straightened against the screen, taking command of himself. He had forgiven Lors his protectivness all these years; he could not do less now. 'No,' he said, more quietly. 'I need – attention. Not – sympathy. Did you – agree?'

Lors blinked. 'The danger—'

'We – chose danger!' Lian said. 'Coming here was – danger – dangerous.'

'Our own danger,' Alystra said. 'We have not done as you have, and placed others at risk.'

'We *have*. We *chose* – for everyone. We *act*. For everyone. In – the colony.' Lian remembered Varidian and Iryssan, weeping

407

together beneath the glass sea. 'We did not know – what we would find. Burdania – gone. Or lifeless. That was – the danger. We chose for them too. Their danger too.'

'And look what we will bring back to them,' Andra said bitterly.

'We do – not have to take – this back.' He looked from Thovalt, who was lounging in his chair, feigning languor, to Alystra, to Lors. 'This is not even – a beginning.' Their faces were shuttered. Thovalt keyed something with his non-dominant hand, and Lian tensed. But all that happened was the light changed, the colour of his head changed from white-streaked grey to clear violet. Involuntarily, he looked to his right, towards her. With the curvature, she was a blur amongst other blurs. But beside his feet he saw the ochre dawn shadows of tufts of grass and ridges of stone. Two metres fall away. The tides of heat and cold became a single surge of cold. If he moved his head, he would plunge headfirst into bright infinity. He would not fall, he would not faint, and he would not accuse. Even that faint smile on Thovalt's face. He closed his eyes, and extended his hand back into space until it touched wall. Then he leaned deliberately back upon that wall. Framed by Burdania, he looked up at them all.

Andra joined Alystra. 'You are surely not going to suggest we go out there. Zharlinn assaulted Thovalt.'

'He had provocation,' Lors said, nearly dispassionately. But his gaze glanced off Lian. That, Alystra's thoughtful look, and Thovalt's expression told Lian everything he needed to know about the nature of the provocation: Lian's having gone after Daisainia.

He glared wordless anger at Thovalt.

Thovalt's eyes glittered. '*I* have never fed anyone poison, have I?'

'I know – the truth of that, now.' He looked Thovalt steadily in the face. 'Will you – hear it?'

'That does not pertain to—' Alystra began.

'It *does*,' Lian returned. 'You *made* it do. So listen! Morain broke – Daisainia's mind – with guilt.' Andra drew breath. '*Put* it to – your analysis then. Put – their records to analysis. Their characters are there! See – other people in Morain's. None.

She – appropriates! Other people in Daisainia's – everyone. You might – believe – analysis if you do – not believe me.'

'Lian,' Alystra said, 'even if that were so, what we have experienced today would—'

The word leapt to his tongue. 'Justify. Leaving. *As they left*. The ships. Our people. Afraid. Unthinking.'

'There is no parallel,' Andra said, stingingly.

'None?' Lian returned. 'Afraid. Threatened. Running. Away.'

'You've made—' Alystra's voice snapped high, and broke, a sound they had never heard before. She fisted her hands rigidly at her sides, and said, very low, 'You've made your point.'

Lian swung on Thovalt, 'You – said – *evil*. That first debate.' In his peripheral vision, he saw Lors take a step forward, and said urgently, 'About feeling – evil. For what – they did. Thovalt. I – *beg* you. Do not make more evil. Do not – take us – away.'

Lors crouched, and closed his hand punishingly hard on Lian's wrist. Thovalt's eyes were suddenly brilliant with tears; he rested his head back, closed his eyes, and the tears ran freely down his face. Lian thought: I have done a terribly thing. Thovalt danced along the edge of an abyss. Terror compelled his carelessness: he dared not connect his actions to their consequences. He dared not be responsible. And Lian had just pushed him to the edge. He was demanding responsibility of him.

Thovalt's eyelids shivered. Lian felt deep pity for him. He reached over and took Thovalt's free hand. 'Open – your eyes.'

Thovalt did so, staring up at Lian with a dark, unwavering stare.

'Look – at – that. Properly. Burdania, Thovalt. Not – habitat six. Not a – holoimage. True Burdania. You – *brought* us here.' Thovalt's eyes shifted to the screen, at the rising burnished sweep of the hill and the violet sky beyond. For a long moment, he simply looked. Lian could tell nothing from his profile. Then without warning, Thovalt bent and bit Lian's hand.

Lian jerked free with a stifled cry of pain. Thovalt swivelled the chair, crowding him, and smiling his old glittering smile. 'I need never feel overawed by your virtue again; you have a peerless capacity for nastiness. What need we fear from the barbarians with you as our ally?' He swung to face the front again, and began to key open the fastenings on the exoskeleton glove.

Alystra said, 'Thovalt!' and stepped off the platform on to the gantry, landing neatly. She closed on Lian, who stood between herself and Thovalt.

'Yes, *isk'dar*,' Thovalt said.

Alystra winced. What she had started to say went briefly unsaid, and in that moment, when she was as silenced as himself, Lian perceived her.

Alystra's spine was ambition, directed by the strict hierarchy of the Advocate. She was exquisitely suited, having shaped herself to be so. She had challenged nothing, transformed nothing, outside herself. But here was Daisainia, who was unconstrainted by protocol, unstrictured by hierarchy. Who had formed a political structure around her personality and powerful conviction. Alystra's outrage was more than an aesthetic offence at the challenge to the structures she revered. Daisainia was as much a threat to her identity as she was to Daisainia's.

Alystra said, with harsh calm, 'Thovalt, if it is doing harm you fear, think on what has happened, between them and us, and amongst them and amongst,' with a gesture she presented Lian as an illustration, 'us. We risk less by leaving now and by giving ourselves a chance to assimilate what we know and consider what to do next. We *need* the perspective offered by hall; we are too few and too – strongly involved – for any rational or wise consensus.' She spoke with a simple, level humility such as Lian had seldom heard her use, and never to Thovalt. Thovalt heard it too – not consciously, or he would have goaded Alystra with her surrender – but Lian saw him look between Lian and Alystra as though he found an argument to weight. And he saw the small shift of Thovalt's left hand as it moved to close a clasp he had just opened.

He had never truly known defeat until this moment. All his failures were minor and, in some respect, chosen, because he had never before committed everything he had. He turned to look at the vista on the screen. Vertigo came and passed.

He said, simply, 'If you will – not listen – then *leave me.*'

Thovalt snapped a laugh. There was gravel in it. Alystra said, 'Out of the question.' Andra said, 'You cannot be serious.'

'I am – serious. Let me – stay.'

Lors said quietly, 'Remember that Lian is the preferred liaison between Burdanians and the *kinder'el'ein*, who are far less like us than those people out there.'

Relief came closer to undoing Lian than all their previous assaults. He held on to the edge of the platform, and stared up at Lors in abject gratitude.

'It is out of the question,' Alystra said, hollow-voiced, 'to leave anyone behind.'

Lors had heeded the earlier lesson; he ceded the floor to Lian with a glance. Lian summoned his resources with a great effort, and spoke to the Advocate. 'We need – new forms. Debates – consensus – *work* without – crises. When – the ships left they – failed us. We stayed on – Taridwyn so long. Another failure. But here – here on Burdania – someone must decide. Must lead through crises. The *cali*. The *isk'dar*. Daisainia. But that – led to wrong. No one could – protect – Daisainia. She killed – Morain D'Vandras died – because no-one was there to protect her – from Morain, Morain – from her. It cannot be—' he dredged the words up from his heart, 'either way. Theirs, or ours – any more. It does not – work. But together – we could – they could – she could – you could – make something *new.*' In Alystra's face distrust struggled with illumination. 'Something to – fit Burdania. And us. Together.' Instinct told him to be quiet. He was offering temptation of the basest kind to one who strove to be the exemplar of the Advocacy. If she even glimpsed his design, guessed he had such a design, he was lost.

He watched her without anticipation as she climbed the pilot's ladder and sat down at the scan console. She recalled images of Daisainia, Daisainia on the dykes, Daisainia at the fireside, Daisainia setting both fists on Zharlinn's chest. He had no idea they had recorded so much. She cleared the screens and stood, offering the chair to Andra. 'Can you set up a simulation: likely outcome if we negotiate for mutual accommodation. Include all data regarding Daisainia Travassa, with additional weight on our direct interactions with her, recorded and reported. Include reliability weighting on reported accounts.'

'No,' Andra said, 'I will not.'

Alystra turned on her. 'This world needs *changing*, these people need freeing, and we *cannot* do that from Taridwyn. And if this—' she gestured towards one shimmering image of flame snaking up towards the camera, 'is the best we have to show, then think how long it would be before we might be allowed to come back.'

'And so it should be,' Andra said, pushing back black hair. 'They are a separate people, with a right to settle their own destiny. We can leave them the materials they need to re-educate themselves. Beyond that, their future is up to them. I have no interest in saving them from themselves.'

Alystra looked from Thovalt to Lors, to Lian, with a slightly desperate eye. 'If we ask Daisainia Travassa to come aboard—'

'No,' said Andra and Lian together.

Andra's objection was expected; Lian's startled them, and it was to Lian they all turned.

Having spoken, Lian had time to realize his objections, and to realize his dismay. Could he come so close, only to lose now by asking too much of them?'

He said, pleadingly, 'You – *cannot* ask her. You – we – *must* go out.'

'After that scene—' Alystra said, and checked herself to ask him, 'What do you mean, Lian?'

'After – the gas. Illuan said: so it ends. He knows. Betrayal. Aversion. It will take – *this* of you – not to end it. Daisainia knows. She asks. This most difficult thing. Stay. Go out. Trust.'

Alystra walked across the deck and sank down into Lian's chair.

'Not without unanimous agreement,' she said, heavily. 'We are risking our lives doing this.'

'We risked our lives from the very start,' Lors said. 'Our lives, our sanity, our spirits. I say, with Lian, yes. Thovalt?'

Thovalt glittered up at him, one hand poised over the release, or the fastening, of the glove. Lors glanced back at Lian, and then crouched down on the edge of the gantry. He said, simply, 'Thovalt, this is our chance to be *better* than they were.' He pushed himself to his feet, and went back and sat beside Alystra, opened his instrument case, and hid behind it. Lian and Alystra watched Thovalt, watched the long, over-supple hand hover, and hesitate . . . and reach down and snap open the fastenings in a rapid staccato, ending with a flourish. Alystra sighed. Thovalt stood, and stretched against the violet sky.

Lian said, quietly, 'Thank you, Lors, Thovalt.'

Alystra said, to him, 'Do you believe we will be safe? Do you believe that the *isk'dar* can keep us safe? Will keep her word?'

'Yes.'

Lors said, tersely, 'Does it matter? We have to do it. Or leave, leave as our ancestors left.'

Alystra breathed out slowly. 'No, I suppose it does not matter.' She looked at Lian, and with that look, capitulated.

Andra turned her back on them all. With a sweep of her hand she erased the images of Burdania as it was; with a flicker of her fingers she conjured pictures of Burdania as it had been. White buildings shining in the sun. Sails bending on the river. The plain stretching away, gold, pale green, in parts tinged with blue. The hill beneath *caur'isk'dari*, the Centre, was dressed in flowers. To Lian they were only pictures, slightly artificial, entirely unreal. Burdania was beside him, on the screens. Burdarnia was outside, waiting for him. And they, in here, waited for him. To speak for Burdania.

He gathered himself one last time, and went over to stand beside Andra. Alystra and Lors came quietly after; Thovalt vaulted noiselessly up on to the platform. They stood watching the hands in the stained white cuffs plucking at the web of the directory. Plucking with all their hopeless skill. Lian felt Andra's mourning. He felt all their different strains of mourning.

He said, quietly, 'It – will be a – long time before – it is – like that again.'

Her fingers moved again. The images changed almost too quickly for him to recognize them, but he knew she, and the others, was seeing them, in full.

413

'But if – we leave now—' Lian said, 'it might – *never* be – like – again—'

Outside was all a singing dazzle, the way he had felt it when he first pushed his head around the blind at *caur'ynani*. Light filled his eyes and ears. He had no words left him. He needed one hand on the lintel of the hatch to steady him. And then, carefully, he took the long step down into the brightness.

GLOSSARY

BURDANIA

Burdanian Homeworld

isk'dar	The direct descendants of Linn Travassa. Individual status has been determined by personality and circumstance. Linn was dictator of Lltharran, and through his agents sabotaged salvage attempts throughout Burdania for over thirty years, while he conducted and controlled his own policy through the Guilds. His influence waned only as the Islanders withdrew from contact with the North, and especially with Lltharran. By the fifth decade, Ky Travassa (Linn's great-grandson) and Branduin Vassar were trying to encourage the gathering of knowledge, using the vestiges of Linn's Guilds, and their own contacts and personal charisma. This work is being continued by their daughter Daisainia.
Guilds	Skills Guilds. Established by Linn to preserve essential disciplines (medicine, botany, communications amongst them) under his control. After Linn's death they added to the deterioration by their rigidity and overexclusivity. Ky Travassa challenged the ossified Guilds with new knowledge from the regions, managing to restructure or dismantle all but the powerful Medics' and Runners' (Communications) Guilds. The Medics' Guild yielded to takeover by the D'Suran (with

Daisainia Travassa's backing), and the Runners' Guild is under threat by Restorers' Guild innovations.

tayn Any self-supporting community, ranging in size from a few to several hundred families, who are not necessarily blood-related. *Tayni* originated in the banding together of survivors in the aftermath of the Leaving. Their names may be derived from geographical area (D'Alna), or from the names of a dominant family (Vassar, D'Vandras). *Tayni* in the tropical or temperate islands, or in the subtropical mainland (Vassar, Zharlinn) tend to be permanent, based on fishing and agriculture. Above the temperate latitudes *tayni* are nomadic throughout the summer, but overwinter in permanent settlements on the coast (D'Suran, Nors). Children are elected to whichever of the parents' *tayni* is best able to provide for parents and child while the child is dependent.

cal An authority in the *tayn*, whose role and influence varies. A Northerner *cal* may decide the timing of migrations, an Islander the despatch of ships, the *cal* Vassar the planting of crops. The *cal* may be called upon to resolve internal disputes, and arbitrate upon membership (as for a newborn, or a newly independent young adult); the *cal* sees that records are kept, and if need be acts as *tayn* representative (as when Ky Travassa instituted the *caur'cali*). *Cali* usually appoint their own successors, but the choice is formally and informally ratified by the membership of the *tayn*, and an unsatisfactory *cal* – one whose decisions are unpopular, or detrimental to the *tayn* – may be replaced at any time.

caur'cali Twice-yearly meeting between *isk'dar* and *cali*, instituted by Ky Travassa. The declared objective was the exchange of information and the easing of the alienation of the regions. It is completely open, but in practice most who attend have some sympathy for the Travassan.

caur' (name) In the Islands, a single-family croft. In Lltharran and *tayni* large enough to have numbers of visitors, a common-house for visitors from other regions. *Caur'ynani*, for example, is a 'household of the Islands'. In Lltharran, members of a common-house may share point of origin, interest or skill (Guild membership).

caurim Three to six people (usually including both or one parent, but sometimes not) committed to the care of a young child. In the mobile, technological societies of pre-Leaving Burdanians and colonists it was a formal arrangement. Homeworld Burdanians are more casual, since households are more stable, and the *tayn* as a whole has responsibility for the children named to it.

chronicler A large *tayn* may have several, their function being to keep records of events, decisions, anything and everything affecting the *tayn*.

tarwyn An exile or an outcast, usually as punishment for a capital or violent crime. This can be tantamount to a death sentence in times of privation, since only one's *tayn* of name has the obligation to provide for one.

shikarl Amongst Islanders *shikarl* is the ability to predict, reliably, the weather and currents, and particularly any danger which may arise from weather and currents. The rarer, Northerner meaning of the word has spread to the Islands: amongst Northerners, *shikarl* is prescience.

417

kindereen	The 'third sex' amongst *kinder'el'ein*, distinguished by their longevity and heightened sensitivity to *en'neen*. *Kindereen* can be either male or female, physically, but are infertile; however, their presence is essential for gestation and birth: the rare posthumous child is inevitably stillborn. They are the spiritual parents of their offspring, and the spiritual guardians of their species.
aneel	*Kinder'el'ein* in the first thirty (Taridwyni) years of life, sexually neuter and empathically immature. Children are born with both *vos'neen* and *en'neen* active, but immediately after birth *en'neen* becomes latent.
maeren	*Kinder'el'ein* in the second thirty years of life. Sexual characteristics develop, *vos'neen* increases in sensitivity, and *en'neen* gradually reawakens.
tris'neen	The three-way life partnership bond which develops between newly adult *kinder'el'ein*. Choice in partners – and infidelity and dissolution of partnerships – are alien concepts to *kinder'el'ein*. The bond forms without conscious decision (although it may be influenced by proximity and familiarity), and is for life. Conception only occurs within *tris'neen*, but infertility is uncommon. The *tris'neen'el* will have three to six children, of whom one or two will be *kindereen*. By tradition, it is the young *kinder'el'ein* and *kin* mates who remain in the family dwelling.
kinder'vos	Retreat for widower *kindereen*.
vos'neen	The *kinder'el'ein* sense of living things, vegetable, animal and sentient, usually encompassing the whole fecund planet.
vos'neen'el	The commonality of living things.
an'neen	The common mind, mostly used in a history

sense, since *kinder'el'ein* do not tend to distinguish the *kinder'el'ein* presence in *vos'neen* from the whole.

en'neen The *kinder'el'ein* sense, or awareness of the dead.

en'neen'el The commonality of the dead; also known as the Hundred Thousand Generations, very approximately the number of generations since *en'neen* developed.

aer'en The dead of any living things who lack *en'neen*, and are lost to death – animals, ancient *kinder'el'ein*, or Burdanians.

en'vos'neen'el The mystic ceremony of the meeting of living and dead, in which the *kindereen*, acting in concert, catalyse a heightened awareness of *vos'neen'el* and *en'neen'el* in their less sensitive fellows. It occurs irregularly, according to conjunctions of Taridwyn's three moons.

i'vad'neer A term of endearment for a child.

All Orion/Phoenix titles are available at your local bookshop or from the following address:

Littlehampton Book Services
Cash Sales Department L
14 Eldon Way, Lineside Industrial Estate
Littlehampton
West Sussex BN17 7HE
telephone 01903 721596, *facsimile* 01903 730914

Payment can either be made by credit card (Visa and Mastercard accepted) or by sending a cheque or postal order made payable to *Littlehampton Book Services*.
DO NOT SEND CASH OR CURRENCY.

Please add the following to cover postage and packing

UK and BFPO:
£1.50 for the first book, and 50P for each additional book to a maximum of £3.50

Overseas and Eire:
£2.50 for the first book plus £1.00 for the second book and 50p for each additional book ordered

----

BLOCK CAPITALS PLEASE

name of cardholder ....   *delivery address*
....   *(if different from cardholder)*
address of cardholder ....
....
....
....
postcode ....   *postcode* ....

☐ I enclose my remittance for £ ....

☐ please debit my Mastercard/Visa (delete as appropriate)

card number | | | | | | | | | | | | | | | | | |

expiry date | | | |

signature ....

prices and availability are subject to change without notice